The
Perfect
VICTIM

The
Perfect
VICTIM

Linda Castillo

JOVE BOOKS, NEW YORK

THE PERFECT VICTIM

A Jove Book / published by arrangement with
the author

Copyright © 2002 by Linda Castillo
Cover art by Franco Accornero
Book design by Julie Rogers

ISBN: 0-7394-2806-3

A JOVE BOOK®
Jove Books are published by The Berkley Publishing Group,
a division of Penguin Putnam Inc.,
375 Hudson Street, New York, New York 10014.
JOVE and the "J" design
are trademarks belonging to Penguin Putnam Inc.

PRINTED IN THE UNITED STATES OF AMERICA

prologue

"Let us return to the magic hour of our birth for which we mourn."
— KOFI AWOONOR

SHE HAD DREAMED OF HIM. DARK, DISTURBING DREAMS filled with blood and violence and a vague sense of terror. Dreams that choked her with the familiar sting of shame and dredged up memories of a past she'd spent her entire life trying to forget.

Huddled in the threadbare recliner, Agnes Beckett watched the hands of the clock sweep to midnight, knowing sleep would not come again. It was the kind of night that evoked demons. The kind of night that made her wonder why her subconscious had waited until now to torment her. She'd always believed she'd come to terms with her past. It was somehow disappointing, and strangely ironic, to realize after all these years those demons still frightened her.

A faint rasping, like the frenzied gnawing of a cold rodent, sounded just outside the front door. Hauling herself to her feet, she made her way to the kitchen, the thought of rats bringing a curse to her lips.

At the door, she flipped on the porch light and spread the

homemade curtains. Beyond, a thin veil of snow whispered across the plowed field, gathering at the frozen peaks of earth, stark and white against black.

She leaned close to the glass, straining to see the maple tree that grew alongside the mobile home. Spindly fingers of ice clung like transparent talons to the branches and grated against the siding. A sigh of relief slid from her lips. It wasn't rats. Just the wind.

An instant later the door burst inward, striking her in the chest hard enough to knock the breath from her. Shock flashed through her, followed by a fleeting sense of realization, and an instant of disbelief.

A man entered her kitchen. Terror snaked through her as she took in the sight of him—long black coat, shiny leather gloves, face concealed behind a ski mask.

"Who are you?" she cried.

Reptilian eyes stared at her through the slits of the knit mask. "Destiny," he whispered.

Not much frightened Agnes Beckett these days. She'd led a hard life filled with the kinds of experiences that destroyed the weak and made the strong stronger. But as she watched the intruder close the door behind him, a fear she'd never experienced in her youth wrapped around her and squeezed, like a snake crushing the life from its prey.

It was the stare, she realized, inhuman in its intensity, the eyes dispassionate and resolute, filled with unspeakable purpose.

Spinning, she propelled herself into a dead run for the bedroom. She was aware of him moving behind her, but she didn't stop. She ran blindly, arms outstretched, tripping over the cheap throw rug, righting herself just as she flung herself forward into the narrow hall. She sensed his closeness as she ran, heard the sound of his boots on the carpet, his breathing above her own labored gasps.

A sliver of panic pierced the last of her control and worked its way into her like a shard of glass into flesh. Lunging at the night table, she snatched up the phone and punched zero.

But the line was as silent and cold as the terror exploding in her brain.

Breaths rushing between clenched teeth, she spun on her attacker. The sight of the knife sent a scream pouring from her throat. In that instant, she knew she was going to die. A vile bitterness welled up inside her that her life would be wiped out this way. So suddenly and with so much violence.

He leaped forward, tiny eyes fixed on hers, as cold and emotionless as a taxidermist's glass. She raised her hands in defense. The blade came down, slicing into the flesh between her fingers, rising again, then cutting deep. The scream that followed was hoarse and weak. Her own. And the blood. So much blood . . .

A split second of flittering light and the knife plunged again. There was no real pain, but the knowledge that she'd been badly injured flowed into her as surely as the blood coursed between her breasts.

She lashed out with her fists, but she was too weak to fight. As she sank to her knees in the narrow hall, she knew, after all these years, he'd finally come for her. Master of her fate. Her past. And, now, her destiny. The realization came with a rush of pain, of unfulfillment, of hatred. She'd been living on borrowed time. His time. Bastard.

The knife slashed upward. She felt the pressure of the blade as it bit into her throat. She tried to scream, but her voice was gone. Her vision blurred. Panic fluttered away. Her senses dimmed as if a switch inside her head had been suddenly and viciously turned off.

She heard gurgling, an undignified sound that had come from somewhere deep inside her. Light ebbed into darkness. Thoughts fragmented, memories tumbled away into oblivion, lost forever, as though they had never existed. She slid to the floor, her blood-soaked flannel shirt catching on the nails in the cheap paneling.

Outside the front door, the maple danced with the wind.

chapter
1

ADDISON FOX HEAVED THE LAST BOX ONTO THE DAP-
pled marble counter and stepped back to catch her breath. "I
am *not* going to panic." Tossing her coat onto the bar stool
next to her, she shot a glance at the clock above the massive
brass espresso maker. The clock glared back, daring her to
take the time to make a pot of coffee.

It was already past six A.M., which gave her less than an
hour to prepare for the morning rush. "Great," she murmured, blowing a breath of frustration through her bangs.

It was the day after Thanksgiving, and the holiday season
had fallen over the city of Denver with all the vivacity of a
first snowfall. She'd had every intention of being prepared,
but it was going to take much more than good intentions to
get three boxes of Christmas decorations up in forty-five
minutes.

Hands on her hips, she studied the boxes, trying to decide
which decorations to put up now and which ones would have
to wait until later. She opened the first box and wrinkled her
nose at the rise of dust and the sight of the thrice-used coil

of garland. Shoving the box aside for an expeditious return to the attic, she reached for the second and pried it open.

As always, she wanted everything to be perfect in the gourmet coffee shop she owned and operated. Located in the historical district of downtown, the Coffee Cup was the center of her life. She went to impossible lengths to keep the Kona fresh-brewed hourly, the apricot scones warm and soft, and the porcelain teapots arranged just so. It was that kind of perfectionism, according to the *Rocky Mountain News*, that had earned her the reputation of having the best coffee in town.

Addison spent countless hours blending unusual combinations of beans, experimenting with temperatures and grinds, striving for a more perfect cup of coffee. It was a career she cherished in a town she loved passionately. She adored her customers, with their quirky demands and tastes, and knew it was her attention to detail that had them coming back again and again.

After sinking her life savings into buying the previous owner's failing coffee shop, she'd spent two months redesigning the interior herself, combining antiques with the avant-garde, and old-world tradition with modern-day high-tech. The old-fashioned soda fountain inspired an aura of yesteryear while the scientific brewing techniques maintained the sophisticated tastes her customers demanded.

"They also expect you to open on time," she said aloud, shoving the box aside and attacking the next.

The bell mounted on the rear door jingled merrily. Addison looked up to see Gretchen Wentworth lugging a cardboard box onto the bar. "Don't ask," the woman said crossly, taking her bifocals from the tip of her nose to wipe away the condensation.

Addison lowered her eyes to hide the smile lurking behind them, knowing Gretchen didn't have a cross bone in her body. "I'll forgive you for being late if you make coffee, Gretch."

"You're easy when you're desperate." The older woman

shoved the glasses back onto her nose and scowled at the clock.

"Would you make it Sumatra?" Addison added. "I need the extra caffeine this morning."

"It's going to take more than a little caffeine to get all these decorations up before the rush." Gretchen pulled off her coat and picked up Addison's, taking both to the small storage room at the rear of the store. "It's been twenty years since I overslept," she grumbled, sliding behind the counter.

"I didn't ask," Addison said, unconcerned. She opened the box her friend had hauled in, pulled out a string of tiny, colorful lights, and felt a flutter of childlike excitement. "Do they blink?"

Gretchen scooped coffee beans from the glass display case and poured them into the grinder. Neither woman spoke as the grinder worked its magic. "Yes, they blink," she said when the grinding was finished. "At least they did last year."

Addison succumbed to a smile as she pulled the bundle of tangled lights from the box and carried them to the window at the front of the store. "Perfect," she said and went to work.

Two hours later, she stood behind the bar, watching the lights at the front window blink in an electrical rainbow of color that had her smiling again. Christmas was her favorite holiday, one she went all out to enjoy. She knew, however, this year would be different. It was her second Christmas at the Coffee Cup; her first without her parents.

The thought sent a familiar pang of sadness slicing through her as it had so many times in the last nine months. She still found herself disbelieving that fate could be so cruel, that at the age of twenty-six she had been faced with the deaths of two people who had given her unconditional love her entire life.

Patty and Larry Fox had adopted her at birth, loved her as a child, and spoiled her as a teenager. They'd put her through four years of college, then given her a hand in purchasing the upscale coffee shop. She couldn't have asked for better parents, and she couldn't have loved them more. She'd been devastated when they'd perished in a car accident near their home in Breckenridge.

Until recently, she wouldn't have believed it was possible not to feel that gut-wrenching, life-altering hurt. But with the passage of time the pain had eased and, finally, Addison knew she was beginning to heal.

"Looks like we survived another caffeine rush." Gretchen's voice jerked Addison from her melancholy thoughts. Thoughts she had no right to be thinking on such a busy morning.

Shaking off the reverie, Addison produced a smile and flipped the switch on the espresso maker. "Speaking of caffeine, do you want an espresso?" she asked, hoping her friend didn't notice the lack of zeal in her smile.

The older woman's eyes caught hers and held them. "You look like you've been up all night again."

Addison laughed, an automatic response designed to conceal, something she did far too often these days. "Best-selling mystery novels and sleep don't mix, Gretch," she said, hating that she'd fallen to telling little white lies. Pulling two demitasse cups from beneath the bar, she poured espresso.

"You're not a very good fibber, Addison. I suspect you were still researching."

"You make it sound as if I've been designing weapons of mass destruction."

"The only thing you're going to destroy is yourself. I know how hard you push."

"I dabble in my spare time, Gretch. Nothing wrong with that."

"Honey, you don't *have* any spare time."

Addison didn't expect Gretchen to understand the urgency that had driven her to spend the last nine months searching for her birth parents. Gretchen had three children and four grandchildren to fill her life, while Addison had no relatives she knew of. How could she stop searching for her birth parents, knowing that somewhere she had family?

"I'm closer to finding them than I've ever been, Gretch. This search is the most important thing in my life right now. Until I've exhausted every possible lead, I can't stop."

"I'm not asking you to stop. I just want you to realize that there may come a day when it will be time to put this to rest and get on with your life."

Addison took a deep breath, grappling for patience that had worn thin over the months. "I *need* to know where I came from. I need to know who they are. What they're like—"

"Why they gave you up?"

The question hit a nerve; it always did. But Addison didn't let herself react. It was silly to let that bother her. After all, she was a well-adjusted twenty-six-year-old woman with a successful business that kept her too busy to sneeze most days. "I'm sure they had very good reasons for giving me up."

"Have you considered the possibility that they may want to remain anonymous? That they may not want their privacy invaded?"

"I'm prepared for that." Even as she said the words, Addison wondered just how prepared she really was.

"Honey, I'm proud of what you've accomplished so far. I just don't want you to drive yourself so hard." Gretchen's voice firmed. "I don't want you to get obsessed with something that may never pan out."

Addison had always admired Gretchen's straightforward manner. There was no second-guessing her opinionated friend, and Addison loved her dearly for it. Gretchen was the closest thing to a grandmother she'd ever had, and Addison cherished their relationship. "I'm not obsessed."

"You put in sixty hours a week here, then spend what little time you have left writing letters and making calls. You're twenty-six years old, Addison. You should be going to parties and out on dates."

"You wouldn't be saying that if you knew how badly my last date turned out."

"That strapping young stockbroker?"

"The strapping young stockbroker who was old enough to be my father and failed to tell me he had a wife and four kids in Peoria."

Gretchen managed to look appalled. "One bad apple doesn't mean you should give up on the entire male population."

Addison knew her friend was right. She didn't socialize much. She didn't go out on dates or get invited to parties. With a business that demanded her attention seven days a week, who had the time? Finding a man simply wasn't on her list of priorities.

"I haven't given up. I'm just . . . prioritizing." Hoping to return the conversation to the matter at hand, Addison came up behind Gretchen and kissed her cheek, taking in the subtle scent of Chanel. "If I don't get a break or uncover some new information soon, I'll ease up for a while. I promise."

Turning to her, Gretchen placed a gentle hand on her shoulder. "I just want you to be happy."

"I *am* happy. I'm doing exactly what I want." A wistful sigh escaped her lips. "I just wish I'd had the chance to tell Mom and Dad. I'd started searching before . . . the accident. I wanted their blessing."

"Your parents would have encouraged you, Addison."

Emotion swept through her, and for a moment she had to blink back unexpected tears. God, she missed them. "I know," she said quietly. "Thanks for reminding me."

Gretchen busied herself wiping the counter with the ever-present towel she kept tucked into the pocket of her apron. "Well, are you going to keep me in the dark or tell me what you've been working on?"

Excitement rippled through Addison. It felt good to talk about her search and everything she'd accomplished in the last nine months. "I found a new Web site on the Internet last night."

"Be careful out in cyberspace, honey. You know what happened to Sandra Bullock in that movie."

Addison pursed her lips to keep from smiling. "I drove up to the cabin last weekend."

Gretchen stopped wiping and looked at her. "I wish you'd told me. I would have gone with you."

"I needed to do it on my own. I should have gone through their things months ago, Gretch. I couldn't put it off any longer. Anyway, when I was looking through Dad's desk I found some old papers."

"On the adoption?"

Addison nodded, remembering her shock upon discovering the tattered file in the bottom drawer of her father's desk. The documents inside were the only clues her parents had left behind.

"I was born in Dayton, Ohio. My birth mother relinquished me when I was three days old. According to one of the documents, my original name was Colleen Glass."

"Odd to think of you as anybody besides Addison Fox."

"It's a strange feeling to know my name and identity, my very fate changed in the span of a single day."

"At least you have a name to go on."

"I've contacted every Glass in and around Dayton with no luck." Addison sighed, remembering with painful clarity the frustration and heartache each time she came up empty-handed.

"You're the only person I know who considers the City Directory quality reading."

Thankful she had Gretchen to keep her sane, Addison laughed. "I've taken the search about as far as I can."

"What about that ambulance chaser you hired?"

She bit back the need to defend. "Jim Bernstein's only charging me for expenses, since he and Dad were friends." Knowing the information she was about to relay wouldn't be well received, Addison braced. "I have an appointment to speak with a private detective this morning."

Gretchen cut her a sharp look. "Someone reputable, I hope."

Smiling at a customer who'd brought a set of musical

Christmas mugs to the counter, Addison started for the cash register. "Jim recommended him."

Gretchen rolled her eyes and followed. "That's supposed to make me feel better?" she muttered in a low tone. "Lawyers. You can't trust them as far as you can throw them."

"I trust Jim."

"As long as you're not expecting Tom Selleck in a Hawaiian shirt."

"Hawaiian shirt or not, a private investigator may be able to cut through some of the red tape I haven't been able to unravel." Addison counted out change and handed it to the customer.

"Cut through your checkbook, more likely."

"Give me a little credit, Gretch. I'm a businesswoman. I can handle this." Glancing at her watch, Addison frowned. "I've got to get going."

"Don't sign anything," Gretchen warned.

Hoping for a quick escape, Addison snagged her purse and headed for the alley door. "Can you get by without me for an hour or so? I'll be back before the lunch rush."

"If you're not back by noon, I'm calling the cops."

From the door, Addison shot Gretchen a wry smile. "Better make it the S.W.A.T. team. I hear Jack Talbot's as crazy as he is good."

He remembered the chill, the kind that seeped through the skin to permeate muscle and bone and sent the body into involuntary shivers. The moment he left the chopper, he smelled the fire, that horrible stench he'd inhaled too many times to ever forget. Around him the air was heavy, cold, and wet. The jagged horizon above the trees was barely visible, and full darkness would soon fall, a black cloak trapping him with the dead.

Emanating from the darkness beyond, a symphony of chain saws worked in unison to clear the trees so the emergency vehicles could pass. He'd never felt more alone as he walked toward the wreckage of Allegiance Air flight 335. It was as though he was traveling through a vacuum, devoid of sound and light, his senses assaulted instead by unspeakable stimuli. Silently, he repeated the only line he could recall from a psalm he'd memorized as a boy. Yea, though I walk through the valley of the shadow of death ...

The area resembled a war zone. He stopped twenty yards from the fuming crater where the main portion of the fuselage had slammed into the earth. Rescue workers dressed in yellow slickers glowed like beacons against the spotlights. Smoke blended with fog and curled upward into the cold, still air.

"This guy went straight down," he heard himself say in a voice devoid of the panic and horror thrashing inside him. "No survivors." The voice came again, his own, sounding strange among the surreal flashing of lights and the screaming of chain saws. Somewhere in the distance the rise and fall of a bulldozer's engine added another degree of bedlam.

Then he was standing at the brink of the jaggedly cut cavity. Around him, teams of rescue workers moved in slow motion, in and out of the crater, lugging stretchers, plastic buckets, or body bags. Nearby, an ambulance stuck in the mud rocked back and forth, its bumper hammering against the trunk of a walnut tree. Back and forth. Hammering ...

Pounding dragged him from the nightmare.

Randall Talbot opened his eyes. The need to cry out clenched at him. His heart pummeled his ribs. The putrid taste of horror pooled at the back of his throat like vomit. He jerked upright, flinching as a cramp shot across the back of his neck. Cursing, he rubbed the sore muscles and tried to remember where he was, and how he'd gotten there. The scenario was all too familiar these days.

Christ, not even the booze can keep the nightmare at bay, he thought bitterly and lowered his head back onto the desk.

The pounding persisted.

Muttering an oath, he rose. The room swayed. He blinked, realizing belatedly that he was still drunk—which suited him fine. Somehow, the alcohol made it all easier to take. At least for now, he thought grimly.

Gray light slanted through the single window of the office, and he realized with some surprise it was well past dawn. As he staggered to the door, he plucked his flannel shirt off the back of the chair and pulled it on, not bothering with the buttons. Fighting a spell of dizziness, he leaned against the door, relishing the feel of the cool wood against his forehead. At least until the frame rattled under someone's persistent knocking.

"Yeah, dammit, hold on a minute," he croaked, sickened by the taste of whiskey at the back of his throat. Vaguely, he remembered breaking the seal as he'd waited for his two A.M. appointment. A topless dancer who worked at the Cheetah Lounge, he recalled. A woman who owed his brother, Jack, a fee for some surveillance work. She hadn't shown and, of course, Randall had ended up getting comatose drunk. Just like a woman to show up late and expect a man to wait, he thought sourly. Considering she owed Jack four hundred dollars, he was surprised she'd shown at all.

Spotting the bottle of whiskey on his desk, he strode to it and thumbed off the cap. It wouldn't do to waste the expensive stuff. Tipping the bottle, he drank deeply, swished, then spat in the wastebasket. The bottle followed with a *clank!*

Despite the headache raging behind his eyes, Randall smiled as he started for the door. It was a smile that had little to do with good humor—and everything to do with the fact that he was ripe for a fight. Any woman who took advantage of a man confined to a wheelchair—especially his brother—deserved a good verbal trouncing. The way he felt this morning, he might even enjoy it.

Steadying himself against the wall, he unlocked the door and swung it open. "You're late."

A young woman with dark, almond-shaped eyes and skin as flawless as new snow stood staring at him. Her mouth was full, heart-shaped, and painted an interesting hue of red. It was the kind of mouth that made a man think about the finer elements of a woman—and the even finer elements of sex. Her cheekbones were delicate and high, the flesh there blushed with cold. Soft bangs brushed past delicately arched brows. An unruly mass of brown hair tumbled onto her shoulders like strands of raw silk.

She didn't look like a topless dancer. Too soft, he thought, not to mention the fact that he couldn't make out much of her beneath the thick, fuzzy sweater. She wore a skirt that could have been her grandmother's and lace-up boots that would have looked more appropriate on a construction worker.

Her eyes flicked over his bare chest. "I must have the wrong address." She stepped back.

If he hadn't known better, Randall would have sworn he saw her blush. "Not so fast." Reaching for her hand, he pulled her inside.

She yelped and tried to jerk away, but he was prepared and hauled her into the office like a recalcitrant child. Her hand was small and cool in his. He caught a whiff of her perfume and ignored the flutter of pleasure that wafted through him.

"You have thirty seconds to cough up the cash," he said, resisting the urge to hold his head to keep the room from spinning.

Gasping, she tried to twist away. "What are you doing? Let go of me!" Her eyes narrowed. "What cash?"

She was small and vulnerable-looking, like somebody's little sister, he mused. Her body was fluid and graceful, all subtle curves and sly lines with a dangerous air of understated sexuality. It was a lethal combination for a woman who made a living off men willing to shell out their hard-earned cash for a peek at her goods.

Kicking the door closed with his foot, Randall forced her over to the shabby vinyl chair in front of the desk and thrust her into it. Placing his hands on the armrests, he leaned close to her, enjoying the way her eyes widened. "Fifteen seconds," he said quietly.

Indignation heated her gaze. "I have no idea what you're talking about. You obviously have me confused with somebody else."

She was breathing hard, and Randall could see that she was shaking. Temper, he thought, and warned himself that women turned unpredictable when they were angry. They tended to lose control. He wondered if she was a screamer or a hitter.

She pressed herself into the chair as if she were trying to put some space between them, but he went with her, refusing to give her a respite. "The money, Felicia. Four hundred bucks. Then you can go."

"*Felicia?* My name is Add—"

Randall snatched the purse from her shoulder. "Time's up." Without waiting for a response, he dumped the contents on the desk. A gold-encased tube of lipstick rolled over the edge and hit the floor.

She came out of the chair like a spring-loaded jack-in-the-box. "You can't treat me like this! Who do you think you are?"

Ignoring her, Randall found the wallet, an overstuffed piece of goatskin jammed full of crinkled receipts and coupons. Christ, he hoped he didn't find drugs. The last thing he wanted to do was cart a screaming topless dancer down to the police station.

He rifled through the cash pocket, pulling out a ten-dollar bill. "Is this all?" He waved the bill. "Where did you stash your tips?"

She blinked and stepped away from him. "Is this a robbery?"

Anger rippled through him that she would try to use that innocent facade to weasel out of paying a man who sorely needed the money. "Where the hell's your sense of decency?" he growled. "The man's in a wheelchair, for chrissake."

"I don't know what you're talking about. I have an appointment. . . ."

Randall hated liars. Especially good ones with big brown eyes and a body that could give a man wet dreams for a week. A man was never quite safe around a woman with such formidable weaponry.

Even a man like him.

Intent on teaching her a lesson she wouldn't soon forget, he gave her a blatant once-over. "Maybe we could take it out in trade." He tried not to notice when her tongue flicked nervously over those ripe lips. This was a hell of a time for him to realize he'd gone too long without sex.

She looked like a prim little housecat that had just stepped into the ring with a snarling junkyard dog. "Touch me and you'll be singing soprano with the Vienna Boys' Choir," she warned in a voice that was refreshingly tough.

Captivated, and oddly pleased, he leaned forward and hit her with a look that had brought more than one tough guy to his knees. "Why don't you show me?"

chapter

2

ADDISON HAD KNOWN SHE WAS IN TROUBLE THE MO-
ment she set eyes on him. Now, as she took in the mussed
black hair, the unforgiving eyes, and the cruel mouth, she
could only wonder how she was going to get out of it.

Dressed in a pair of faded jeans and a red plaid shirt, he
had the haunted eyes of a prisoner on death row and the
rough-hewn face of a gangster. He towered over her like a
giant sequoia, without the beauty, all brawn and muscle and
temper. The way he moved reminded her of a big predatory
cat, a hungry one that enjoyed the kill as much as the feast.

Under different circumstances, the image might have been
appealing in a physical, fundamental way. Too bad he had
the intellect of an ice cube and a mean streak that had her
shaking in her shoes. Her throat constricted when she considered the possibility that he might actually try to hurt her.
But she reminded herself that he was a private detective—
and that she was merely a victim of mistaken identity. Surely
they could handle this like mature adults.

He stuffed the ten-dollar bill into the front pocket of jeans that stretched snugly across lean hips. For an insane instant she found her eyes drawn to a part of his anatomy she didn't want to think about. Squaring her shoulders, she raised her chin and gazed at him squarely. "My name isn't Felicia. My name is Addison Fox, and I had a nine A.M. appointment with Jack Talbot."

His eyes glittered menacingly. "My name is Randall, and I'm Jack's brother from hell. He asked me to fill in."

"You're making a huge mistake . . . Randall."

"Ah, now that we're on a first-name basis, I should tell you I'm not as nice as Jack. I'm certainly not above frisking you."

Indignation punched through her. "How dare you speak to me like that."

"How dare *you* take advantage of a man in a wheelchair."

"I've never met your brother. I don't even know him."

"Ten bucks isn't much of a down payment." His eyes raked over her. "Maybe we could work something out."

Realizing he seriously had the wrong impression about her, Addison snatched her bag off the desk and began throwing the contents back inside. "I'm not going to take this." She refused to tolerate brutality, verbal or otherwise. As far as she could tell, this man was stark, raving insane. She started for the door.

Heavy footsteps thudded against the floor behind her. Even with her back to him, Addison knew he was coming after her.

"You're not going anywhere," he said in a rough baritone.

Not trusting her back to him, she spun and walked backward. "Don't come any closer." She raised her hands, knowing they wouldn't stop him. Her bottom connected with the door. Her hand shot to the knob. She tugged, but the door didn't budge. Locked, she thought, and realized what it must feel like to be a rabbit caught in the sights of a rifle.

"On the other hand a little striptease is hardly worth four hundred dollars." He peeled the purse from her shoulder and tossed it onto the desk behind him without looking at it.

Her legs went weak. "You're out of line."

One side of his mouth curled. A smile or a snarl, she couldn't tell which. "Stealing is out of line." He braced an arm on either side of her, effectively pinning her against the door. "I don't have much tolerance for thieves."

Addison told herself it was outrage that had her pulse hammering. But when his shirt parted, her eyes took on a life of their own and swept down the front of him. His chest was wide and rippled with muscle. A sheath of thick black hair tapered to a stomach that was hard and flat. The sight of such blatant maleness sent an uncomfortable awareness surging through her.

Incredulous that her hormones were about to betray her, she raised her head and found herself looking at a harsh, unshaven face. Prominent cheekbones and a nose that looked as though it had been broken and never properly set dominated his features. His mouth was sculpted and distinctly brutal. But it was his eyes that commanded her attention. They were haunted eyes. The kind that looked through people and saw all the way to their souls.

"So what's it going to be, Felicia?" He assessed her boldly. "You going to pay my brother what you owe him? Or are we going to have to find another way for you to make good on your debt?"

She could feel the heat of his gaze as surely as if he had touched her. The thought made her shiver. "There is no debt," she said. "And you're a thug."

"Yeah, well, at least I'm honest about it. I don't march around claiming to be something I'm not."

He was so close she could smell the musky male scent of him and the smoky tang of whiskey on his breath. A tremor of fear barreled through her when she realized he'd been drinking. "I'm going to scream," she warned between clenched teeth.

A cruel smile curved his mouth. "Why don't you just hand over the cash like a good little girl and we'll be done with this?"

Scant inches separated his mouth from hers. For a single, wild instant she half expected him to close the distance between them, lean close, and kiss her. She wondered if he would use his tongue, if the kiss would be ruthless or gentle. . . .

Thoroughly unnerved by the bizarre turn her thoughts had taken, Addison gave herself a hard mental shake and forced her gaze to his. "Unlock the door."

"We're not finished."

"Yes, we are."

"I'm not going to let you rip off my brother."

"Get out of my way."

When he made no effort to move, she braced against the door and pushed him with both hands. The sudden contact stunned her. His muscles were like warm steel beneath her palms. He stumbled back, catching his balance on the desk. She stared at him, trembling, every nerve in her body on edge.

Humiliation washed over her when tears stung her eyes. She wasn't prone to displays of emotion, but the outrage burgeoning inside her—and the fact that this man seemed to be enjoying every second of this—was too much.

She knew it the instant he realized his mistake. He went perfectly still. The intensity drained from his eyes, and he just stood there staring at her as if she had suddenly transformed into a rare and endangered species. It was her tears, she realized, that had finally convinced him she was telling the truth.

"I want my purse." Her voice shook, but she didn't care. God, she hoped he didn't try to apologize. An apology now would only make her angrier, and she didn't want to go another round with this dim-witted Neanderthal. "I'm leaving."

Lowering his head, he closed his eyes and pinched the bridge of his nose between thumb and forefinger. "I don't believe this," he muttered.

Addison choked out a humorless laugh. "We'll see how

overcome with disbelief you are after my lawyer gets finished with you." It took all her concentration not to sway as
she started for the desk to retrieve her purse. The last thing
she wanted this man to know was that he'd shaken her down
to the tips of her toes—and then some.

He regarded her through dark, somber eyes. "I thought you
were . . . somebody else."

Addison gathered more of her things and dropped them
into her purse. "It must have been a dead giveaway when I
shouted out my name." She felt sane, almost normal now
that he was a safe distance away. With a little luck she might
even be able to convince herself nothing had happened between them.

He stooped to pick up the gold tube of lipstick and handed
it to her. "I guess that means you're not open for an apology."

Addison studied his face and looked deep for something
redeeming, something that would explain her reaction to him,
but she came up short. "Not on your life." She snatched the
tube from him, vowing to call the Better Business Bureau as
soon as she got back to the shop. "I ought to have you arrested." She shoved the lipstick into her purse and pulled the
drawstrings tight.

"Since when is arousing a woman a crime?"

Her cheeks flamed. It appalled her that she *had* reacted to
him in some base, animal way. "You're having dangerous
illusions." She fled for the door.

"Am I?" He didn't follow.

"I guess it would take an illusion to keep that ego of yours
so inflated." She reached the door, remembered belatedly that
it was locked, and slammed her palm against it. "Open it!"

He strode to the door, gave it a good yank, and held it
open for her. "Sorry. It sticks."

Feeling like a fool, Addison sent him a final, scathing look
over her shoulder and bolted. She tried valiantly to avoid
the man in the wheelchair, but she was moving too fast. The
collision stopped her cold. His glasses flew into his lap. The

armrest rammed painfully into her thigh. She cursed.

"Are you all right?" The man steadied her with one hand and grappled for his glasses with the other.

The smell of cigarettes and budget aftershave drifted to her as she extracted herself from the wheelchair. She looked at him, noticing immediately that his features were disturbingly similar to those of the man inside. Hard, direct eyes that weren't quite friendly. Jack Talbot, Addison thought. Her heart sank when she realized the hem of her skirt had somehow become ensnared in the chair's wheel.

"I'm just peachy," she snapped and yanked at the material.

"Let me help you." Awkwardly, he grasped the fabric of her skirt and tried to untangle it from the locking mechanism.

Addison looked up to see Randall Talbot leaning against the door frame, taking in the entire scene as if it had been choreographed for the sole purpose of his entertainment. "Need some help?" he asked affably.

Grinding her teeth in anger, she took matters into her own hands. With an ungraceful yank, she jerked the material free, tearing her skirt. "Go to hell," she said and limped toward the safety of the sidewalk.

"AH, ANOTHER HAPPY CUSTOMER," JACK SAID AS HE rolled the wheelchair into the office.

Despite the headache and the lingering effects of Addison Fox, Randall managed to smile. "Morning, Jack." He wondered if he should tell his brother how badly he'd screwed up his nine o'clock appointment.

Jack wheeled past him. "Did Felicia show?"

Randall winced, deciding it would be best not to complicate an already complicated situation. Things were tense at best between him and his brother. No reason to make matters worse. "No," he said.

"Or were you too drunk to answer the door?"

Not in the mood for a lecture, Randall started for the coffeemaker.

"You could have drunk yourself to death in Washington," Jack said. "Why the hell did you bother coming back here to do it?"

"I couldn't cut the mustard back in D.C., remember?" Randall didn't like the bitterness in his voice. He hadn't wanted to be bitter about walking out on his career. He hadn't intended to disappoint himself. To his dismay, he'd managed to accomplish both.

Expertly maneuvering the chair, Jack closed the door behind him and headed for the thermostat. "I suppose any man who enjoys tramping over dead bodies is one sick son of a bitch anyway."

Randall shoved his hands into the pockets of his jeans. He'd never imagined himself as a candidate for posttraumatic stress disorder. He hated it that the illness had taken him down so hard and fast without so much as a warning. He hated even more the vulnerability he felt knowing he might not ever be able to resume a career he'd invested twelve years of his life in.

Shoving the feelings aside, he watched his brother struggle to reach the thermostat. "You got anything for a headache?" he asked, feeling as though days had passed since he'd picked up that bottle of whiskey.

"You'd be surprised how far a little self-discipline goes."

Randall frowned, relieved when Jack succeeded in adjusting the room temperature. He didn't like watching his brother struggle to accomplish the little things most people took for granted. But having lived with him for the past four months, he knew better than to offer assistance.

It was Randall who had needed his brother after the crumbling of his career at the National Transportation Safety Board. For the first time in his life he'd needed family, someone to fall back on, someone he could count on.

Four months earlier, he'd gotten his walking papers. He'd been officially diagnosed with post-traumatic stress disorder—which meant a mandatory six-month leave of absence. Shaken and angry, uncertain about his future and the state of his health, he'd sublet his town house in D.C., packed all of his worldly possessions into his Bronco, and headed back to the only home he'd ever known.

"It's not like we've got clients to spare. What the hell did you do to her?" Jack demanded.

Randall wished he hadn't come down so hard on the lady. He'd awakened feeling mean and itching for a fight. She'd merely been in the wrong place at the wrong time. What the hell had gotten into him? Jack couldn't afford to have him scaring off clients.

"I guess my customer service is a little rusty." It galled the hell out of him that he could still feel the hard knot of arousal in his groin.

"You always were a charmer." Shaking his head, Jack rolled the chair over to his desk and reached for his cigarettes.

"I thought the doctor told you to stop smoking," Randall said.

"A man in a wheelchair's got to have some vice. I sure as hell can't womanize anymore."

There was bitterness there, too, and Randall moved to quickly stanch it. "You've always had an infatuation with your dick."

Jack laughed heartily and, for a moment, looked much like the man he'd been before the motorcycle accident that had severed his spinal cord five years earlier. "Don't we all, little brother."

Randall spooned coffee into the filter basket and flipped the switch. "What's on the agenda for today?"

"I was hoping you'd start that ramp you promised me four months ago."

In an effort to earn his keep, Randall had offered to build a wheelchair ramp off the rear deck of Jack's home. He'd bought the lumber and power tools six weeks ago. But time had gotten away from him, and he had yet to haul the supplies out of his Bronco. So much for good intentions.

"I'll start this morning," he said.

Jack only shook his head. "Don't worry, little brother, I won't hold you to it." He wheeled over to the computer. "I'm going to work on the Allen divorce case. I've got to hack into the wife's bank account to check the balances. See if she's holding out on her old man."

"Doesn't the IRS do that?"

"Not in the Cayman Islands."

Randall nodded, never ceasing to be impressed by his brother's computer-related talents. A programmer before the accident, Jack had spent much of the last five years playing computer games. When he became bored with playing, he immersed himself in writing them. When he'd conquered both, he began hacking. At first, it had been a way to pass the time and alleviate the boredom and depression that had come with the wheelchair. Today, he was a master and put his uncanny abilities to use in the private investigation firm he'd founded two years earlier.

Jack switched on the computer. "I'll make a deal with you, Randall. I'll cut out the cigarettes if you cut out the liquid diet."

Rather than make a promise he probably wouldn't keep, Randall remained silent, hoping his brother would let it pass. As far as he was concerned, his jaunt down the superhighway of self-destruction was his business. He'd get his shit together when he was ready.

After pouring two cups of coffee, Randall set one on the desk in front of Jack and watched as he played the keyboard like a finely tuned musical instrument.

"When are you going back to D.C.?" Jack asked, skimming deft fingers over the keys.

Because he hadn't been sure how long he would be staying in Denver, because he hadn't been too sure about anything at the time, Randall had moved in with Jack, but soon found that a roommate was the last thing his independent-minded older brother wanted. Self-reliance was too important to Jack, especially since he'd been confined to the wheelchair. He made no bones about giving Randall a six-month limit on his tenancy.

"My leave is up in a few weeks. I'll be going back to work then." *If I'm deemed competent,* a little voice chimed in.

Jack spoke without looking away from the monitor. "You're welcome to stay on here a little longer if you want. You became a resident. Got your P.I. license. If you weren't sleeping with your bottle every night, I might have offered you a partnership."

"Next time I need a lecture, I'll let you know," Randall said tightly, wishing his brother would stop treating him as if he were some kind of alcoholic. Admittedly, he drank too much, but he didn't think he was in over his head. At least not yet.

Setting the cup on his desk, Randall noticed the manila folder. He reached for it, flipped it open, and found himself looking at a copy of a birth certificate, letters from a local attorney, and handwritten notes. The name Addison Fox drew his gaze, and an uncomfortable sense of guilt settled over him.

She'd caught him off guard. Not hard to do after a bottle of whiskey and three hours of sleep, he thought sourly. Not that his general frame of mind was a plus these days. He'd acted like a loser, and she'd treated him accordingly.

Randall wasn't proud of what he'd become, and he felt the loss of his personal integrity like a stake through his heart. A man had hit bottom when he started making mistakes like the one he'd made this morning. He'd cost his brother a client and, in the process, his own self-respect had slipped another notch.

A business card with the depiction of a steaming cup of coffee was clipped to the front of the folder. Frowning, he plucked it off and realized she owned the upscale coffee shop on the corner a few blocks down. He wondered why she needed a private detective.

He stared at the card, taking in the faint scent of her perfume, trying in vain to ignore the tug of shame that drifted over him. Something about her had him thinking about the sorry state of his life. She'd looked young and wholesome and undamaged by the same world that had nearly destroyed him.

He considered stopping in at the Coffee Cup but doubted she would be receptive to an apology so soon. Might be best to let her cool off a couple of days. As he walked out the door, Randall realized he was looking forward to seeing her again. Next time, under different circumstances.

ADDISON WANTED TO BREAK SOMETHING, PREFERABLY Randall Talbot's skull. She was still furious when she arrived back at the shop. Not even the brisk walk or the sight of the falling snow had cooled her anger. Talbot was a crude, unethical man who had the nerve to call himself a professional, then prey on unsuspecting people in need.

It only disgusted her further that her body hadn't noticed.

As much as she didn't want to admit it, she couldn't remember ever being so physically aware of a man. She'd never been one to ogle biceps or tight jeans or other such superficial attributes. It grated against her sense of propriety that her hormones had gone into overdrive for a crass, mean-spirited jerk like Talbot.

Gretchen was right. There were shady private investigation firms out there just waiting for the unsuspecting client to happen by. The thought made her feel gullible, and she hated it. Next time, she'd be more cautious.

It took every ounce of control she possessed not to slam the door behind her when she entered the shop through the alley. She stood in the storage room for a full minute, shaking, trying to get her pulse rate down so she could face Gretchen. It wouldn't do her a bit of good to bite her friend's head off, then face her lunch customers when she couldn't even muster a smile.

A moment later, the door swung open and Gretchen approached her with a tray containing a cup of coffee, a pow-dered scone, and the cordless telephone. "I thought I heard the bell." She set the tray atop a small stool. "How did your meeting go?"

Addison reached for the scone and coffee simultaneously, ignoring the phone. "Let's just say he wasn't Tom Selleck in a Hawaiian shirt."

"That bad, huh?"

She bit into the scone. "Unscrupulous doesn't begin to cover it."

"Oh, my." Frowning, Gretchen looked down at the phone. "You can tell me all about it *after* you take this call."

The scone stopped in midair. "Who is it?" Addison asked suspiciously. If it was Talbot, she would simply excuse her-self, step out into the alley, and let loose with the long string of expletives she'd thought up during her walk back to the shop.

"It's Jim Bernstein."

Addison's stomach tightened. Her attorney never called unless it was important. Unwittingly, she'd stepped back on the emotional roller coaster, she realized. She told herself it was probably nothing. It was her way of mentally bracing. If she didn't get her hopes up, she couldn't be disappointed.

She reached for the phone. "Hello, Jim."

"Are you sitting down?" he asked.

Her heart stuttered. "Have you found something?"

"You might say that. I've located your birth mother."

chapter

3

JIM BERNSTEIN'S OFFICE WAS A SHORT DISTANCE FROM the shop in an affluent section of lower downtown, nestled among upscale cafés, trendy shops, and tastefully refurbished warehouses. Needing the time to gather her thoughts, Addison decided to walk.

After nine months of searching, she would finally know the identity of her birth mother. For the first time since she began her search, she found herself facing questions she hadn't yet considered. How would she approach this woman who was little more than a stranger? Would her birth mother welcome her with open arms? Or would she turn Addison away at the door?

She ruminated the questions as she walked. By the time she entered the reception area of the law office, she was trembling. She'd looked forward to this moment for so long, she hadn't paused to think about what would transpire after this climax. With the end of her search finally in sight, she could only wonder what kind of relationship she would share with the woman who'd given birth to her.

Jim Bernstein strode into the reception area and welcomed her into one of his uncomfortably tight bear hugs. "Addie, you're lovelier every time I see you."

His warmth eased her nervousness. "Thank you for seeing me."

He was a large man with a voice like a foghorn and the personality of a bull terrier. "Did you see Jack Talbot this morning?"

Addison thought of her disastrous meeting with Randall Talbot and wondered how Jim had managed to hook up with such a loser. "You should keep better company, Jim."

His brows furrowed. "Jack Talbot's top shelf."

"I saw his brother, actually." She hoped Jim didn't notice the hot blush she felt on her cheeks.

"I didn't know Jack had a brother."

"He probably wishes he didn't," she said wryly.

"I'm sorry if I put you in an uncomfortable position."

"It's okay. I didn't hire him."

With a shrug, he said, "Well, now that I've found your birth mother, we won't need them, will we?" Smiling reassuringly, he motioned toward the hall from which he'd emerged. "Shall we go into my office?"

Addison followed him to the small office and settled into a wingback chair opposite his desk. She held her breath as Jim seated himself and opened a manila folder. Inside her chest, her heart did a little dance, stopping, then speeding up, rising into her throat and then plummeting.

"Her name is Agnes Beckett," he began.

The name struck her, then swirled in her head like a leaf caught in a gale. Nine months of hope and need and anticipation tangled up inside her until she felt she might burst.

"She lives in Siloam Springs in west central Ohio. Forty-three years old." He paused, grimaced. "Her last known profession—barmaid."

Addison winced. A combination of disappointment and shame passed quickly through her. She knew it was a snobbish reaction, but she couldn't help herself. Somehow she'd expected more from her birth mother.

"So young," she said. At forty-three years of age, Agnes Beckett would have been only seventeen when she gave birth to Addison.

His expression grew concerned as he stared at her over the top of his glasses. "Are you all right? You're pale."

"I'm fine," she said quickly. "I'm overwhelmed, excited . . . afraid." The words were close, but didn't completely convey everything she was feeling. She wondered if she could even begin to describe the emotions banging around inside her.

Jim continued. "The name on your birth certificate, Glass, was also the name given to her at birth—before she was adopted."

The news jolted her, not because it mattered now that the search was over, but simply because such a coincidence was so unusual. "Are you saying my birth mother was also adopted?"

"At birth."

"Which means her records were sealed just like mine."

"That's why you were having such a difficult time finding her."

"How did you find her?"

Leaning back in his chair, Jim smiled. "I called the doctor who delivered you. The name of the hospital appeared on your amended birth certificate."

Addison had seen the document, yet she still didn't understand how Jim had managed the impossible. "But how did you get his name and address?"

"By writing to the Medical Quality Assurance Board."

She shook her head, feeling as though it had been something she shouldn't have overlooked. "So simple. . . ."

"Not simple," he corrected. "It took some doing."

Her heart seemed to stop when he handed her a single sheet of paper. Quickly, she scanned the contents, knowing she was about to lose the battle with her emotions. Antici-

pation clashed with uncertainty. The pain of losing her adoptive parents surfaced briefly, and Addison felt her eyes grow
hot with unshed tears.

"Make the initial contact over the telephone, Addie."

Addison started at the sound of his voice and realized
she'd been staring at the print, reading the name over and
over.

He looked at her thoughtfully. "When you're ready, of
course. And don't expect too much."

Tears blurred her vision. "Now I'm going to embarrass
myself," she said, digging in her purse for a tissue.

He handed her a monogrammed handkerchief. "Your biological father was not named on your amended birth certificate."

"Perhaps Agnes Beckett will be able to shed some light
on the identity of my birth father."

He shrugged noncommittally. "Perhaps." Shoving the file
into the glossy wood cabinet behind him, he checked his
watch.

That was her cue to leave. She rose on unsteady legs. "I
don't know how to thank you, Jim."

Smiling, he reached for her hand and squeezed. "I hope
this works out exactly the way you want it to, Addie."

She gripped his hand tightly. "I'll let you know."

THREE WEEKS LATER ADDISON STRODE THROUGH THE
revolving glass doors of the Dayton International Airport
with an overnight bag slung over her shoulder, the keys to
a rental car clutched in her hand, and the resolve to meet
Agnes Beckett set firmly in her mind.

After leaving Jim's office, she'd spent the remainder of
the morning trying to decide how to approach her birth
mother. Later that afternoon, she'd dialed information, finally
summoning enough courage to make the call that evening.
To her surprise and utter dismay, the number had been disconnected. The following day had been a marathon of tele-

phone calls—all to no avail. Physically and emotionally spent, Addison had poured her heart into a letter and mailed it the next morning.

The letter had been returned unopened two days ago.

She'd known beforehand there was a possibility of failure, that she may never actually meet her birth mother. She just hadn't expected the reality of it to hit her so hard—or hurt so badly. A small part of her still harbored the weary hope that by some stroke of luck Agnes Beckett was still in Siloam Springs. Unable to put it aside, Addison left the shop in Gretchen's capable hands while she made the trip she'd dreamed of for nearly ten months now.

As she pulled onto the interstate, she wondered how her birth mother would react to a face-to-face meeting. Would she welcome Addison's sudden appearance? Or would she refuse to see her? Would she be overjoyed? And why had the letter been returned unopened? Had she taken ill? Or had she simply moved away?

Addison considered herself mentally prepared for whatever might accost her in the hours to come. Good or bad; disappointment or fulfillment. She could handle it, she assured herself.

Even so, her heart did a little jig beneath her breast when she spotted the sign for her exit. She slowed the rental car to the speed limit upon entering the town limits, taking in the neat rows of houses with large front porches, the manicured shrubbery, and the tall, bare trees that lined either side of the street. Cheesy Christmas decorations adorned the streetlights, red candlesticks and weather-beaten garland brought to life by blinking lights. A typical small town, Addison mused, endearing and quaint, without the traffic and crime and stress of the city. She wondered what kind of a life her birth mother led here. Absently, she glanced over at the map spread out on the seat beside her. Inside her chest, her heart drummed steadily against her breast.

At the intersection of Route 40, she passed the Red Rooster Motor Lodge, wincing at the sight of the Truckers

Welcome sign and the murky swimming pool. Instead of turning in, she continued north. She drove past a boarded-up gas station and an antiquated apartment building with peeling white paint. A Beer on Tap sign blinked in the front window of a shoddy bar called McNinch's. In the distance, a tall, stark-looking grain elevator rose out of the earth like a giant gray pillar, pale and smooth against the slate sky.

She slowed for a double set of railroad tracks, noticing for the first time that the houses weren't quite as large or well kept, the yards not so manicured on this side of town. Addison began to watch for the address.

The reality of what she was about to do hit her when she saw the street sign. She stopped the car and stared at the rusty sign as it fluttered in the brisk wind. Her mouth went dry when she turned onto the street. Potholes marred the asphalt. Modest clapboard homes with rutted driveways and threadbare yards lined the north side of the street. Opposite, bare-branched trees clawed at the horizon as if trying to save themselves from the impending cold, the apparent poverty. Addison took it all in as the rental car idled down the street. At the end of the cul-de-sac, a small mobile home park with a dozen or so trailer homes lay spread out like a grouping of tin boxes.

She knew she should have checked into the motel before coming here. She should have taken a deep breath and counted to ten before rushing in to confront a woman who may very well want to be left alone. But it was emotion driving her now, not logic, and she wouldn't stop until she was at the front door introducing herself to Agnes Beckett.

A cluster of mailboxes punctuated the entrance to the mobile home park. She stopped the car. A flutter of trepidation shot through her when she saw the name. She hadn't realized Agnes Beckett lived in a mobile home.

Addison parked curbside and stared at the rusty blue and white trailer. *This is it,* she told herself. Right or wrong, she was going to meet Agnes Beckett.

Taking a deep breath, she opened the car door and stepped

into the brutal wind. Though it was barely noon, the sky was dark and the temperature had begun a bone-numbing descent. Thankful for her full-length coat, she wrapped it more tightly around her and started for the mobile home.

The lot was well kept and landscaped with evergreen shrubs. A giant bare-branched maple stood next to the trailer like a soldier standing guard at a point of passage. Inside her kidskin gloves, her hands were icy. She climbed the stairs and knocked quietly, unable to keep herself from peering through the modest curtains. A built-in bar separated the kitchen from the living room. She saw fake wood cabinets. Cheap paneling. A rusty yellow stove that had probably been around since her kindergarten days. She knocked again, shivering as the wind penetrated her coat.

"Are you the new owner?"

Addison spun, the words *new owner* ringing uncomfortably in her ears. An elderly woman wrapped in a crocheted shawl stood at the foot of the stairs looking up at her. "I'm looking for Agnes Beckett."

The woman cocked her head. "Who are you?"

"I'm Addison Fox." Stepping down, she extended her hand.

"I'm Jewel Harshbarger. You a relative?"

The question caught her off guard, and Addison didn't know exactly how to reply at first. She hadn't actually considered herself related to Agnes Beckett. Realizing a little white lie was in order, if only to protect her birth mother's privacy, she said, "I'm a friend of the family. Does she still live here?"

"Honey, it's cold as a well digger's butt out here." She looked across the plowed field and pulled the shawl more tightly about her shoulders. "Would you like to come next door and have a cup of tea?"

Puzzled by the woman's reluctance to answer her question, Addison nodded. The wind had grown downright nasty, and she didn't want this elderly woman out in the cold. She followed her to the adjacent lot.

Inside, the mobile home was hot and smelled of mothballs, old carpet, and Ben-Gay. "You were telling me about Agnes Beckett," Addison began.

Jewel shuffled to an old gas stove, poured water into a copper kettle, then set it over the flame. "Why don't you make yourself at home in the living room, child," she said, pulling a tin of shortbread from the cupboard. "I'll be right there."

Staving off irritation, Addison wandered into the next room, noticing the hand-crocheted afghans draped over the sofa and easy chair. The TV was on with the volume low and a little silver Christmas tree blinked merrily in the front window. Grateful to be out of the cold, she pulled off her gloves and coat and draped them over the arm of the sofa.

A moment later, Jewel returned with a tray bearing two cups and a plate of shortbread squares. "Here we are."

Addison reached for one of the cups, the warmth easing away the iciness in her fingers. "I understand Agnes Beckett used to live next door. I've been trying to reach her, but she hasn't answered my letters."

The woman's expression turned grave. "I hate to be the bearer of such terrible news, child, but Agnes Beckett was murdered three weeks ago."

chapter
4

THE FLOOR SHIFTED BENEATH ADDISON'S FEET. IT WAS as if the wind tearing around the mobile home had finally succeeded in uprooting it. The cup slipped from her fingers and fell to the floor. She looked down to see the hot liquid spew onto the carpet and the leather of her boots.

An odd quiet descended. "I'm sorry," she heard herself say in a voice that didn't sound at all like her own. She watched the dark stain spread on the carpet. Disbelief swirled in her head, like butterflies caught in a blizzard. Agnes Beckett. Her birth mother. Murdered.

"No, child. I'm sorry. I didn't mean to upset you." Jewel struggled out of her chair and hobbled to the kitchen, returning a moment later with a worn dishcloth.

"Please, let me do that." Still reeling, Addison usurped the cloth, then stooped to soak up the spilled tea, using the time to regain her composure.

"I didn't know Agnes Beckett had anyone who cared for her," the older woman said.

The thought that her birth mother had been alone and unloved cut Addison to the quick. "I cared for her very much."

After pouring another cup of tea, Jewel settled into a comfortable-looking chair. "We were neighbors for nearly ten years. Last few years she kept to herself. Spent most of her time alone."

Setting the damp towel on the tray, Addison reclaimed her seat on the sofa. "Did she have any family? Any close friends I could contact?"

"No family that I know of. Don't know about friends. She was a loner, that one. Didn't have many visitors the last few years. Whole town was in shock when she turned up dead."

"How did it happen?" Addison's voice was hoarse with emotion. She wasn't quite sure what it was she was feeling, but it was powerful. Loss. A stark sense of disappointment. The fact that something she'd desperately wanted would never be. Never was forever, and she knew firsthand the finality of death.

"Stabbed to death in her own home."

The words crawled up Addison's spine like icy claws. "Jesus."

"I was home the night it happened, but didn't hear a thing. Mailman saw the blood the next morning. I never heard a man scream like that. Ran like a screaming banshee over here to call the sheriff. Threw up on my rosebush. Sheriff McEvoy said the place was a mess. Blood everywhere. Poor woman was butchered like a cow."

A shiver swept through Addison. "Was the killer caught?"

"Cops never found him. I'll tell you this: Folks around here lock their doors at night. And they will for a long, long time."

"Does the sheriff know why she was murdered? Was it random?"

"I was never friendly with the woman, but I can tell you she had a reputation."

The need to defend rose up inside her, but Addison held it at bay. "What kind of reputation?" she asked, knowing fully what the word meant and how it was usually applied.

"Some speculate it was one of her men who killed her. Believe me, child, she had a lot of them over the years."

Addison lowered her cup and leaned back into the sofa. She felt sick inside. She wanted to be alone so she could sort all this out. But she wasn't, so she simply acknowledged the information. "I see."

"Child, I don't want to be the one to tell you all this. Siloam Springs is a small town. Talk is cheap and vicious in small towns. Agnes Beckett received her share over the years."

She nodded her acceptance of that.

"If you're looking for information on the murder, I've got the last three editions of the weekly newspaper in my recycle pile."

Addison brightened somewhat at the idea of having some solid information at her fingertips. Information that wasn't hearsay or rumor. "I'd appreciate that very much."

Jewel took the last bite of shortbread. "I hope you're not too terribly upset with all this. Did you know her well?"

"No, not well."

"I guess that's a blessing under the circumstances." The older woman rose and disappeared into the rear of the trailer.

Addison let out a breath. She looked down at her hands, found them shaking. She hadn't known Agnes Beckett. But she did know one thing for certain. The day Agnes Beckett had given up her three-day-old baby, she'd saved Addison from what probably would have been a very hard life.

Jewel returned with a small stack of newspapers. "It made quite a stir here when it happened. First murder in over fifteen years. And so brutal."

Addison winced, not wanting to imagine the brutality of a stabbing. It was incomprehensible what human beings could do to each other. It was incomprehensible that it had happened to her birth mother just three weeks earlier.

"Thank you." Rising, she slipped into her coat.

"The stories in there will be more objective than the ones you'll hear from anyone in this town, including me."

"Where is she buried?" The question sprang free before she'd realized she was going to ask it.

"Twin Oaks, I imagine. Down the road a ways, past the bridge on the left. Only cemetery in town."

It was sleeting when Addison walked back to the car. Tiny particles of ice mixed with rain pelted her as she stood on the broken asphalt staring at the mobile home where her birth mother had lived—and died—just three weeks earlier. She wondered what had become of her belongings. If she'd had a decent burial. If anyone had mourned her passing.

Feeling more alone than she'd ever felt in her life, she slid behind the wheel and headed for the motel.

AN HOUR LATER, ADDISON SAT CROSS-LEGGED ON THE queen-sized bed in her room at the Red Rooster Motor Lodge, using her manicure scissors to cut articles from the newspapers Jewel Harshbarger had given her. On the bed next to her lay a half-eaten club sandwich, a bag of soggy french fries, and the soda she'd picked up at the motel restaurant.

She'd read each story twice, forcing the words into a brain not ready to absorb, each time their significance cutting a little deeper. The Preble County coroner had ruled Agnes Beckett's death a homicide. The sheriff's department concluded later that the murder was the result of a robbery. Judging from the marks on her neck and left wrist, what little jewelry she'd been wearing was yanked off and taken, as well as her purse, which was found a few days later minus the wallet.

What Addison found most disturbing was the fact that in the three weeks since the murder, a suspect hadn't been mentioned. The thought sent a powerful sense of outrage rolling through her. Was it because of Agnes Beckett's lack of social status that the police weren't pushing for an arrest? Would the murder of a more affluent person have generated a greater degree of public outrage? Would the woman who had lived in that tiny mobile home be forgotten? Her murder left un-solved?

The questions troubled her deeply, and Addison knew she couldn't let it end this way. It seemed incredibly unjust that she had lost her family not once, but twice. First the only parents she'd ever known, then the woman who'd given her life.

There was a lack of closure in the way her search had ended. She had come here to this strange little town to meet her birth mother. Three weeks ago, someone had taken that dream away from her forever. She would never meet Agnes Beckett. After all the effort and the hope, fate had intervened in the cruelest way, leaving her with nothing but a solitary trip to the cemetery.

The reality of that hit her hard, striking her in a place that was raw and exposed. She sipped the soda to ease the tight-ness in her throat and read the articles again, focusing this time on the status of the case. She put them in chronological order by date, realizing only then that the stories became smaller as the news grew older. Even in small towns people grew tired of news quickly, she mused.

Even brutal, unsolved murders.

But there were positive steps she could take to make sure her trip hadn't been in vain. She could visit the sheriff and make sure the case was being investigated in a professional manner. It was a painful thought, but she could go back to the mobile home and go through her mother's belongings. It might give her some insight into the kind of woman Agnes Beckett had been. It might give her some closure.

With a renewed sense of purpose, Addison rose from the bed and pulled on her coat, deciding her first stop would be the sheriff's office.

"YOU WANNA KNOW *WHAT*?"

Addison resisted the urge to sink into the vinyl chair op-posite Sheriff Delbert McEvoy's desk. She was bone tired, but somehow felt she'd have the upper hand if she stood. "I'd like to know how the investigation into the murder of Agnes Beckett is progressing."

McEvoy eyed her suspiciously. "You some kind of a reporter or something?"

"I'm a relative." She'd gone over the conversation they would be having during the drive to his office. She had foreseen the questions, and she was prepared.

"The newspaper has been carrying the story," he said.

She took a deep breath and grappled for patience, wondering why he seemed indisposed to helping her. "I've read the articles and have yet to see anything that tells me how the case is progressing."

He sat up straighter, his belly shifting to expose a large silver belt buckle. "Miss . . ."

"Addison Fox," she said, extending her hand. She hadn't realized it until now, but she'd accepted the responsibility of making sure her birth mother wasn't forgotten. Certainly not before her murder was solved.

Taking her hand, he shook it gently. "Just how are . . . were you related to Agnes Beckett?"

That was the question she'd pondered most. Had her biological mother been alive, Addison would have kept her relationship to Agnes Beckett confidential. Now that the woman was dead, she supposed it really didn't matter. "I'm her daughter." Her voice seemed unnaturally loud in the silence. The words sounded strange, and she realized it was the first time she'd spoken them aloud.

"You're pullin' my leg." His face split into a lopsided grin as if one side of him believed her; the other, that she was somehow trying to dupe him.

Irritation sparked inside her, and she did her best to squelch a nasty retort. "No," she said coolly. "I'm not kidding."

As if realizing his rudeness, he lost his smile. "That's a mite surprising, is all I'm saying."

"That she had family?"

"Well . . . yes."

"Why is that surprising? She was capable of reproducing, wasn't she?"

Crimson crept into his cheeks. "That's not what I meant."

"What exactly *did* you mean?"

"I had no idea she had kin. No one in town knew it," he said.

No longer feeling the need to stand, she sank into the chair, letting a long, tired sigh slide between her lips. "Well, she does, and I'd appreciate a little cooperation."

He leaned back in his chair and slid the wad of chewing tobacco from one side of his mouth to the other. "I reckon Pete Lyons down at the funeral home will want to talk to you."

"She left a debt?"

"The trailer is foreordained for auction to pay for the funeral expenses. Ladies Club paid for the marker."

"I'll take care of the debt," Addison said quickly. "And I'd like to go through her things." Both sentences were out before she realized her thoughts had taken that route. Odd what shock and stress did to one's mindset, she thought dully.

"I'm afraid that won't be possible until the estate goes through probate." His chest swelled with newfound authority.

"In that case, I'll have my attorney contact you." She felt a moment of satisfaction when he stiffened. "For now I'd just like to know if you've got any leads or if you're any closer to making an arrest."

Glowering, he sauntered to a vertical file cabinet. He reminded Addison of a big, fat turkey that had had its feathers ruffled by an unassuming hen.

"Her credit cards haven't been used." He paged through the file. "No checks have turned up."

She nodded, feeling minutely better now that he was cooperating. "Do you have any suspects?"

"Not yet." He pulled a file from the drawer and walked back to the desk, dropping it in front of her. "Excuse me while I get a cup of coffee." Snatching a Cincinnati Reds mug off the desk, he stalked out of the office.

Jerk, she thought with disgust, wondering how, in the span of just a few hours, this promising day had transformed into the afternoon from hell.

Her gaze dropped to the file. She stared at it, not sure if he'd meant for her to look at it or if she was supposed to wait for him to return. It took her all of two seconds to open it.

The police report was on top. She scanned it first, making a mental note that there were no witnesses or suspects listed. She skimmed the particulars of the crime scene, the condition of the body, and the description of the weapon. She tried in vain not to allow the gristly details to affect her, but her hands began to shake despite her efforts.

Next, she found the autopsy report. The cause of death was listed as massive blood loss due to the severance of the carotid artery. Other injuries listed were blunt force trauma to the skull along with an array of superficial knife wounds. The autopsy report had been signed by Dr. Stephen Westfall just over two weeks ago.

Addison closed the file. Spotting a copier across the room, she rose, hoping to get the police and autopsy reports copied before the sheriff returned. She'd just reached the copier when a half dozen photographs slipped from the file and fell to the floor. Looking quickly over her shoulder, she bent to retrieve them. When she turned back and looked down at the photo in her hand, the sight that accosted her nearly sent her to her knees.

The photograph was of the crime scene, in horrible, vivid color. She saw blood. A shock of dark hair. Pasty flesh. Addison stared helplessly for what seemed like an eternity, unable to breathe, unable to move or tear her eyes away from the horrific sight. There were no inscriptions on the photo, but she knew with utter certainty that the twisted, butchered heap was her mother.

She straightened, felt the room around her begin to spin.

The file slipped from her hands and hit the floor with a resonant thud, scattering the papers it held. Addison fought back a crushing wave of nausea. She closed her eyes, trying to erase a sight that would forever be etched into her brain.

Knowing there would be no more conversation with Sheriff McEvoy, she staggered to the desk and pulled her coat from the back of the chair. Still not sure if her lunch was going to stay down, she left the file on the floor and rushed out of the office, nearly running into the sheriff as he passed through the door with a cup of coffee in hand. He called out to her as she pushed open the front door, but she didn't stop. He didn't bother to come after her.

Once outside, Addison stopped and stood vacillating for a moment before grasping the rail with both hands and taking a deep breath. She took another and another until the nausea passed. Slowly, she became aware of her surroundings, the hiss of tires on wet pavement, the sound of sleet hitting the sidewalk.

But it was the cold that brought her back. The wind slithered through her coat and wrapped around her, sending involuntary shivers through her until she was shaking uncontrollably. Grappling in her bag for the car keys, she started for her car.

She sat behind the wheel another five minutes with the heater running full blast, waiting for the chattering of her teeth to subside. Agnes Beckett had met a terrible end. Violent. Senseless. Addison knew she must deal with that. But even as she struggled to accept, she couldn't help but wonder how much her mother had suffered in the minutes before death had taken her; whether or not she'd given any thought to the tiny daughter she had relinquished twenty-six years earlier.

They were questions that would never be answered now that her birth mother was dead. Addison would have to accept this twist of fate and go on, knowing this final chapter would put an end to her search forever.

When the shaking subsided, Addison put the car in gear

and pulled into the street. Though she wasn't sure at first exactly where she was going, she found herself heading west toward the cemetery. The only one in town, Jewel Harshbarger had told her, past the bridge on the left.

Twin Oaks Cemetery was located several miles out of town, nestled between a clapboard Methodist church and a cornfield. The grounds were well kept, surrounded by a wrought-iron fence and manicured shrubbery. The skeletons of maples and oaks and a variety of evergreens dotted the property within.

The gate stood open. Addison turned the car onto the smooth asphalt drive and passed through the entrance. Even if she didn't find Agnes Beckett's grave, this trip to the cemetery was something she needed to do. It was a step she needed to take, one that would help her grieve, to accept, and to go on. Though she hadn't known, or had the chance to love Agnes Beckett, she had over the last months of searching for her developed a sort of bond with her. She knew there was a part of herself that was mourning.

To her surprise, among the dozens of graves she had no trouble spotting the mound of freshly turned earth. Her throat constricted at the sight of it, and Addison knew that in a town the size of Siloam Springs, burials were probably infrequent.

Leaving the warmth of the car, she slowly made her way toward the plot. Around her the wind had calmed, but the air possessed a sharpness that cut to the bone. Sleet continued to fall, mostly snow now, filling the silence with the high-pitched tinkle of ice particles striking the frozen earth.

A single spray of plastic flowers lay against a small granite headstone. Addison faced the monument, wondering who had left the flowers. As she read the simple inscription, a sense of loss pierced her. The familiar sadness began to flow. Before she realized it, before she could make herself stop, she felt tears on her cheeks.

She cried for the birth mother she had lost. She cried for the parents fate had stolen from her earlier in the year. For the first time in months, she allowed the sadness to completely overwhelm her, to take her to a place she didn't often go, and she let her emotions run free. She dropped to her knees and cried openly, her sobs lost among the graves of strangers, the naked trees, and the dry, brittle corn.

chapter

5

RANDALL PARKED IN FRONT OF THE COFFEE CUP AND sat there for five minutes trying to get his courage up. For the life of him he couldn't figure out why the hell he felt so damn compelled to go inside and apologize. Apologizing wasn't his usual modus operandi, particularly when it came to women. But in light of the fact that he'd made a complete ass of himself, he was going to bite the bullet and make amends. It didn't matter that she'd lodged a formal complaint with the Better Business Bureau against Talbot Investigations. It didn't matter that his brother's professional reputation was on the line and that Jack had, in no uncertain terms, threatened to put him out on the street if he didn't make things right.

It didn't matter that for the better part of the past month, Randall hadn't been able to get Addison Fox off his mind.

An array of colorful Christmas lights flashed in the front window as he approached, reminding him that it was the holiday season. A fact he could just as well live without since he couldn't remember the last time he'd bothered celebrating.

The first couple of years he'd lived in D.C. he'd socialized with his coworkers at the NTSB. Back before the darkness of his profession had sent him crashing and burning.

Shaking off thoughts of the past, Randall opened the front door and stepped inside. The robust smell of coffee and the more delicate aromas of fresh-baked pastries and chocolate flowed over him, filling him with the vaguely pleasant memories of a childhood he hadn't remembered in years. Soft yellow light rained down from overhead tulip lamps, casting circular shadows onto a long, marble-topped bar. A row of old-fashioned stools ran the length of the bar. Several bistro tables were scattered near the front window. Tony Bennett's smooth-as-silk voice filled the shop with music from a simpler era.

The Coffee Cup was upscale and small, like many of the businesses, restaurants, and microbreweries that were revitalizing Denver's lower downtown.

It was closing time and the place was nearly empty. A man in a trench coat sat at the bar sipping coffee and browsing through the morning edition of the *Rocky Mountain News*. A young couple shared a cappuccino at a corner bistro table.

Randall spotted Addison behind the bar and felt his mouth go dry. It was an odd reaction for a man who hadn't felt much of anything in the last six months. The company shrink had slapped a technical name on his emotional isolation, but Randall didn't put much weight in doctors, especially the nonmedical type.

He knew it wasn't wise for him to be there. He didn't like the responses this woman evoked. It had been a long time since he'd cared what somebody thought of him. He wondered how she would react if she knew he was a mental case. Of course, she probably already thought he was one.

Randall was thankful her back was to him since he wasn't sure how she was going to respond to his being there. He approached the bar slowly, watching her, wondering how he could have ever mistaken her for a topless dancer. Not that she didn't have the body for it. She most definitely did. But he could tell by her body language that she wasn't the type of woman who enjoyed being the center of attention.

She was vigorously scrubbing a stainless steel sink, oblivious of his approach. Her shoulders were slender with a rigid set. The black turtleneck she wore hugged a body that was willowy and nicely shaped. Because of the height of the bar, he couldn't see the rest of her and, frankly, he was glad for it. It wouldn't do him any good to waste his time thinking about how she filled out her jeans or wondering just how long those legs of hers were.

She was at least ten years his junior. Probably shallow-minded and immature to boot. Definitely not his type. Not that he was interested, he quickly reminded himself. A quick apology, a cup of coffee, and he was out of there.

Randall slid onto a stool and set the manila folder on the bar in front of him. He watched her work, mesmerized, amazed that a woman could look so damn sexy cleaning a sink. Her hair was mink brown and fell to her shoulders in unruly waves. From where he sat, he recognized the citrus and musk scent of her perfume from that day in his office. The warm, exotic scent he'd dreamed about on more than one occasion in the last three weeks.

As if she possessed some kind of sixth sense and had been alerted to the route his mind had taken, she straightened, then slowly turned. Clutching a pink sponge in one hand and a container of industrial-strength scouring powder in the other, she stared at him through brown, doelike eyes. For an instant, the corners of her mouth turned up in a smile that would have been dazzling—had she not ultimately recognized him.

He knew it the instant she did. Her smile faded. Her eyes cooled. She set down the scouring powder with a resonant thud. "I'm getting ready to close."

"The sign says you don't close for another ten minutes," he said.

Wordlessly, she turned away and left her place behind the bar. At the front door, she turned the sign to the closed position. As if on cue, the couple finished their cappuccino and started for the door. Calling them by their first names, Addison bid them good night. The man at the bar folded his newspaper and followed. Randall noticed he left a five-dollar tip, and he wondered if Addison Fox affected all men the way she did him.

She made a show of fumbling with the tie of her apron as she slipped back behind the bar. "There's a beer joint two doors down. Please tell me that in your drunken stupor you've wandered into the wrong place."

He had to hand it to her, she definitely knew where to hit a guy. But because he had it coming, he let the comment pass. "I guess you're not going to make this easy on me."

A delicately arched eyebrow went up. "How perceptive of you."

He had the sinking feeling that she was just getting warmed up. Even if the conversation they were about to have wasn't going to be pleasant, it would definitely be interesting. "In case you're wondering, I take my coffee black," he said easily.

"To be perfectly honest with you, Mr. Talbot, the way you take your coffee is the furthest thing from my mind, unless, of course, you take it in your lap. What I'm really wondering is what the hell you're doing in my shop with that stupid grin on your face when I'm about to close."

Randall stared at her, not sure if he was insulted, amused, or embarrassed. He did find himself a bit relieved that there was no one else around to witness the verbal trouncing he was taking from this woman. "Better make it decaf," he said.

Frowning, she snagged a cup from beneath the bar and moved to the coffee brewer. He watched as she poured, noticing the jerky movements, the rigid set of her shoulders, and the stubborn set of her chin. Unfortunately, he also noticed that she was one of those women who only looked sexier when they were angry.

"Here you go." She set the cup in front of him and looked at her watch. "Decaf. Black. You have five minutes."

Unable to keep himself from it, Randall smiled. "You might want to work on that customer service routine, Ace."

She crossed her arms in front of her, inadvertently plumping her breasts. Randall kept his eyes on hers. The last thing he needed to know about Addison Fox was that her breasts were full and upswept. That kind of knowledge was dangerous business for a man who couldn't even remember the last time he'd had a date.

"I'm sure I couldn't begin to compete with your unparalleled customer service," she said. "In fact, I don't believe I've ever manhandled any of my customers for stealing sugar packets. Nor have I searched purses for tips when they forgot to leave one. I've certainly never threatened to frisk them."

"Yeah, well, the Better Business Bureau is hassling my brother for something I did. But I don't suppose you'd know anything about that, would you?"

"You're lucky I didn't have you arrested."

"I'm sure that would have been interesting." His gaze skimmed her mouth. "But I don't think either of us would have enjoyed it."

"Why are you here?" she asked.

Deciding it wouldn't be wise of him to answer the question truthfully, Randall took a deep breath and plunged. "I came here to offer a truce."

A frown tugged at the corners of her mouth as she studied him. "You came here to ask me to call off the BBB dogs."

"That, too."

Her eyes narrowed, and he realized with some dismay that she was enjoying this more than he was. "Surely you can do better than that," she said.

"All right." He added *tough* to the growing list of traits he liked about Addison Fox. She knew better than to trust a man like him. He couldn't blame her. Gazing at her steadily, he folded his hands on the bar in front of him. "I came here to apologize."

Something resembling sympathy sparked behind her eyes. "That didn't hurt so bad, did it?"

"No worse than the time I broke my leg skiing."

"You do have an ego, don't you?"

"Groveling isn't my style, but whatever works."

She regarded him coolly.

He was starting to wonder if she was going to let him off the hook. "Look, the day you came into my office was an innocent case of mistaken identity—"

"There was nothing even remotely innocent about what happened in your office."

Even as she said the words, her cheeks bloomed with color, a fact that told him more about how she felt about that fateful day than anything she might have said. *Bingo,* he thought, and realized with a sense of relief he wasn't the only one who'd been aware that *something* had gone on between them.

Pleased by this new morsel of information, he offered his hand. "Apology accepted?"

She ignored the hand. "I'd like my ten dollars back."

He'd forgotten about the money. Sending her a look he hoped relayed that he was only going to let her push him so far, he withdrew his wallet and dug out a ten-dollar bill. "Do you want interest, too?"

She reached for the bill. "No."

Taking him completely by surprise, she offered her hand. His fingers closed around hers. A pleasant jolt of awareness ran the length of his body on contact. Her hand was warm and small encased within his. The palm was slightly damp, but her grip was substantial. His gaze drifted from her eyes to her mouth. Her lips were full and red, and he couldn't help but remember how close he'd come to kissing her that morning in his office.

She released his hand, and the spell broke. Momentarily stunned by his reaction, Randall raised the cup to his lips and sipped, wondering if she had any idea how profoundly she'd just affected him.

Lowering his gaze, he spotted the manila folder he'd brought with him, and decided this might be a good time to see if his intellect still functioned. "You left this in my office."

Her eyes flicked to the folder. He didn't miss the spark of recognition. Nor did he miss the quick flash of another emotion he couldn't readily identify. He wondered what secrets she had buried behind those pretty eyes.

"Thank you for returning it," she said, pulling the file to her, but not opening it.

"If you're interested, that is, if you haven't already hired another firm, Jack and I are willing to take a look at your case." He hadn't planned on saying it; he hadn't even discussed it with his brother, but there it was. Admittedly, he was more interested in getting to know her than he was in her case, but given the circumstances—mainly the way that turtleneck swept over her body—he wasn't holding himself responsible for anything he said.

"How much of the file did you read?" she asked.

"All of it." Three times to be exact, but he thought it best if he didn't mention it. He didn't want her to get the wrong idea.

Picking up the folder, she strode to the end of the bar and dropped it in the trash. "You couldn't have known, Mr. Talbot, but I've since found who I was looking for."

When she turned back to him her eyes were huge and filled with a kind of defiance that contrasted sharply with the vulnerability he discerned just below the surface. He was no judge of people, even less of character, but he knew there was more going on than she wanted him to see.

From the notes in the file, he'd been able to deduce that she was searching for her birth parents. Belatedly, he realized the subject could be an emotional one for her. It was an area as foreign to him as the moon. "You were looking for your birth parents," he said.

"My birth mother, actually." Her eyes darkened. "I . . . located her just a few days ago."

Whoever she'd found, she wasn't happy about it. Randall

let the thought pass. If she needed his help, she'd ask. "I'm glad things worked out for you," he said.

Casting a glance at the front door, she crossed her arms in front of her. "I'm sorry, but I really need to close the shop."

Rudeness had always come naturally to him. It pleased him that she had to put forth so much effort to manage it. Charmed, he winked. "I can take a hint." Pulling out his wallet, he laid a five-dollar bill on the bar.

ADDISON KNEW SHE SHOULDN'T HAVE LET HIM OFF THE hook so easily. Randall Talbot might wear that boy-next-door charm like a comfortable pair of old jeans, but she knew something darker lay just beneath that steady gaze and crooked smile. Still, it was difficult to stay angry when he was so clearly sincere. After all, he *had* apologized, she told herself. God only knew what that had done to his ego.

At first, she'd had no intention of accepting the apology or listening to whatever frail rationalizations he'd conjured up. She'd enjoyed watching him struggle with that giant-sized ego he wielded so artfully. Perhaps even a small, cruel part of her had just wanted to see him cut down a notch or two. But he'd been determined to make amends, and Addison hadn't had the heart to snub him. Even if it had taken him three weeks to work up the courage.

His offer to take her case had thrown her. The jolt of pain that followed was surprisingly sharp. It had been three days since her ill-fated trip to Siloam Springs, and she was still trying to accept that Agnes Beckett was dead. As much as she didn't like to think about it, a small part of her had died that day in the cemetery. She'd lost one of her dreams. Now, she couldn't help but wonder if things might have turned out differently if she'd hired this man early on.

Studying him across the bar, Addison realized he looked like a different man than the scoundrel she'd met that day in his office. Gone was the heavy five o'clock shadow, the bloodshot eyes, and the nasty disposition. The transformation was complete and not at all unpleasant. There was still an inherent ruggedness about him, but the harshness and the vague sense of violence she'd sensed before had vanished.

He was taller than she remembered, well over six feet. He looked fit and relaxed in well-worn jeans, hiking boots, and a blue parka. His eyes were dark brown and a little too intense for comfort. He was a stickler for eye contact, she noticed, and at times she found his gaze unsettling.

She was about to offer him a refill in a "to go" cup when the bell on the alley door jingled. Her gaze snapped to the door leading to the back room. Mild puzzlement skittered through her. She and Gretchen were the only people who used the alley door. Besides, she'd locked it. Hadn't she?

She looked at Randall only to find his eyes already on her. "Expecting company?" he asked quietly.

"Not through the back door."

"You keep it locked?" he asked.

"Always." Slipping her apron over her head, she started for the back room. "I'll be right back."

Reaching over the bar, Randall stopped her with a light touch on her arm. "Let me check it out. You stay put."

Something in his eyes kept her from arguing. Closing the cash drawer, Addison placed the money bag on the shelf beneath the register, out of sight.

"Give me that," he said.

She hesitated an instant before passing the bag to him over the counter. The thought hit her that she didn't know him from Adam, but she quickly reminded herself that he was a licensed private investigator.

"Where's your phone?" he asked.

"I left it in the back room. It's a portable."

Another muffled sound emerged from the back room. The alley door closing, she thought, and felt the first real jab of alarm. Soundlessly, she came around the bar and approached Randall.

"Go stand at the end of the bar," he said and started for the back room.

In the two years she'd owned the shop, Addison had never been afraid. Not of her customers or the hours she kept. She'd never considered the possibility of a robbery. Yet tonight, as she listened to an intruder slink through the rear door, an uncomfortable layer of fear settled over her like cold fog.

The knob squeaked. Randall stopped, took a step back. An instant later the door swung open and slammed against the wall. Shock crashed through Addison when a man stepped into the doorway. In an instant, she took in the full-length coat, black leather gloves, and knit ski mask. A tiny chrome pistol glinted like a cheap trinket in his hand.

In her peripheral vision she saw Randall scramble back. The intruder glanced toward the front door. Addison stood frozen at the end of the bar. Her heart rocked hard against her ribs when he raised the gun and leveled it at her.

Then she was being shoved violently to the floor. A gunshot snapped through the air. She fell flat on her back hard enough to take her breath. Randall came down on top of her. Before she could move, he sprang to a crouch, cursing as he worked an ugly pistol from beneath his parka. To her utter amazement, he took aim and fired.

The blast deafened her. She sat up, pressing her hands to her ears. Her brain screamed for her to run. Before she could move, Randall gripped her arm. "Stay down!"

Addison watched helplessly as he tossed the bank bag toward the rear door. "What are you doing?" she cried.

"Saving your life. Stay the hell down!"

As if in slow motion, the man in black loomed into view from behind the end of the bar. Legs apart, he aimed the pistol at Addison.

She screamed. A bullet pinged against the bar stool next to her. Randall fired four shots in quick succession. The intruder's pistol flashed in response. Addison ducked. Bullets zinged past her. Bits of wood and plastic pelted her.

Then, as suddenly as the chaos began, an eerie silence fell over the shop. Traffic hissed beyond the shattered front door. Cold air streamed in, enveloping her with icy hands.

Vaguely, she was aware of Randall rising. Broken glass crunched beneath his boots as he jogged to the rear door. She wanted to rise, ordered herself to move, but she was trembling so badly, she didn't trust her legs to support her.

For a full minute, she crouched next to the bullet-damaged stool, grappling for control, trying in vain to stop shaking. She didn't hear the footsteps behind her. She cried out when a pair of strong hands closed around her shoulders.

"Easy." Randall's voice broke through the haze of shock. "He's gone. It's only me."

Addison's ears rang from the gun blasts. She shivered, feeling disoriented and dazed. Thoughts rushed at her in senseless order.

"Oh, my god," she heard herself say. Gripping the bar, she somehow managed to get her legs under her.

Randall looked at her through narrowed eyes, then cast a glance toward the back room. "Stay here. I'm going to call the cops."

She stared blankly after him as he strode to the back room. She listened, stunned, as he dialed then relayed to the police what had happened. It hit her with sudden incredulity that he was talking about her shop. *Her* shop. *Her* refuge. Outrage jolted through her at the thought of such a violation.

A moment later, Randall reappeared. Setting the phone on the bar, he strode toward her, assessing her the way an emergency room doctor might assess a trauma patient. "Are you hurt?"

Despite the fact that her senses were still reeling, Addison shook her head. "No. I'm not hurt." She thought about it a moment. "I'm scared. And I'm really pissed off."

"That's good, Ace. I'll take pissed off over hysterical any day."

She blinked at him, the sudden realization of what had

almost happened slamming into her like a lead weight. "Jesus, he was going to kill us."

"Yeah." Randall raked an unsteady hand through his hair and blew out a curse.

Blood glistened on his cheek. Vaguely, she remembered the flying shards of plastic and glass, and realized he'd been cut. He looked dangerous standing there, a wicked-looking pistol in his hand, a streak of blood sliding down the side of his face.

"You're bleeding." Surprising herself, she pulled a napkin from the counter and pressed it against his cheek.

"Piece of glass caught me."

Because of his height, Addison had to step close to see the cut. "Hurt?" she asked.

"Not much."

She forced a laugh. It was either that or cry. "You'd say that if you were gushing buckets, wouldn't you?"

"No, I hate pain. I'm a weenie from the word go." Clasping her wrist, he lowered her hand from his cheek. "You're shaking."

"Call me weird, but flying bullets and masked gunmen scare the hell out of me."

He regarded her through shuttered eyes. "You're pale, too. Maybe you ought to sit down."

"No. I'm okay. I want to stand. Jesus, I'm alive. I'm pretty happy about that."

"Just don't faint, all right?" He didn't look pleased by the possibility.

"I don't plan to." She struggled to absorb the full impact of what had happened, realizing belatedly that she probably *did* need to sit down. "If you hadn't been here, I'd be dead right now."

"And to think you wanted to throw me out."

"You saved my life."

"Just doing what any self-respecting P.I. would do."

Addison stared at him. He stared back, his face as inscrutable as stone. There were a hundred things that needed to be said, but at the moment she didn't trust her voice to say any of them, let alone to this man whose actions had just turned her opinion of him on its ear.

The police arrived ten minutes later. Addison stood next to the bar, watching helplessly as a swarm of cops in blue uniforms tramped over what was left of her coffee shop. She felt as if she'd stepped onto the set of a horror movie. A set complete with a down-and-out private detective and a villain in black that had nearly sent her to an early grave.

"Ma'am?"

Addison started at the sound of the voice and turned to face the man who'd approached her. He wore a nicely cut suit, and she knew immediately he was a police detective. She guessed him to be in his midforties. He had the beginnings of a paunch and short brown hair that was thinning at the top, graying on the sides. His hands were small and pudgy, fast-moving because he was excited. Bright blue eyes were red-rimmed as if he were prone to allergies. He was staring at her, his expression an odd combination of type A impatience and shabbily concealed male appreciation.

"I'm Detective Adam Van-Dyne." He offered a handshake.

Uttering her name, she raised her hand to his. "Are you in charge?" she asked.

"I'm the primary." Grimacing, he looked toward the damaged bar. "You own this place?"

"What's left of it."

"You look like you could use a chair and something to drink."

She nodded and allowed him to guide her to a nearby bistro table. He pulled out a chair and she sank into it, aware that a bullet had taken a chunk of wood out of the backrest.

"What happened?" he asked.

Leaning forward, she closed her eyes and rubbed her temples with her fingertips. "Jesus, it doesn't seem real. It happened so fast."

"That's the way it goes sometimes. Takes a while for something like this to sink in."

Addison recounted the shooting in a low, raspy voice that didn't sound at all like her own. By the time she finished, her hands were shaking so badly she could barely grip the cup of water a uniformed policeman had brought her.

Van-Dyne leaned back in his chair and flipped through the pad where he'd jotted notes. "The convenience store two streets over got hit last week," he said. "Thug got about a hundred bucks and change."

"Was anyone hurt?" she asked.

"No, but he shot up the place." The detective looked around her shop. "Similar M.O."

"You think it's the same guy?"

"Probably." He toyed with the napkin holder on the table between them. "A witness reported seeing a chrome pistol. Suspect wore a black coat. Ski mask."

"That's him."

"This guy's good at what he does. Doesn't leave anything behind."

"You mean like fingerprints?"

"Or anything else."

"Hell of a way to make a living." Spotting the shattered Italian bowl at her feet, Addison leaned forward, picked up the biggest piece, and put it on the table between them. "You hear about crimes every day on TV, people being hurt, lives ruined, but it's different when it happens to you."

The detective looked at the broken piece of ceramic. "You're lucky, Miss Fox. This could have turned out much worse."

"There was less than eight hundred dollars in that bank bag, Detective. I like to think my life is worth more than eight hundred dollars." She knew there had been more horrible crimes committed for less, but it frightened her to know how little value criminals placed on human life.

"If it's any consolation, he didn't get the money," he said.

Her gaze snapped to his. Something inside her stirred, a

foreboding that had her gripping the mug with white-knuckled hands. She distinctly remembered Randall tossing the bag over the counter. "Are you sure?"

"The money bag was on the floor in front of the bar." He shot an annoyed look over his shoulder where Randall sat at a bistro table talking to another detective. "Guess the lone ranger over there scared him off before he could take the bag."

Van-Dyne pulled his business card out of his wallet and put it on the table between them. "If you think of anything else, give me a call. If I'm not at the station, you can leave a voice message."

After the detective left her, Addison sat alone at the table, watching the chaos, wishing she wasn't the one right in the center of it. A sick sense of dread twisted through her as she assessed the damage. Bullet holes peppered the front of the bar. A hole the size of a dime marred the facade of the antique cash register. Atop the counter, two glass canisters filled with some of the rarest coffees in the world had been shattered. Dark beans were spilled onto the floor like loose gravel.

Suddenly tired, she lowered her face into her hands and closed her eyes. Her refuge had been invaded. A place where she'd always felt safe. A place she'd built with her own two hands. A place that defined who she was, and where she fit into an increasingly complex world.

She struggled to put what was left of her control into play. The last thing she wanted to do was break down. She refused to play the role of helpless victim. It was her anger that saved her from it. A deep, burgeoning fury that kept her mind working when it wanted to shut down, her eyes dry when she wanted to cry.

"Christ, it looks like Bonnie and Clyde happened by."

She started at the sound of the newly familiar voice. Raising her head, she found Randall Talbot taking in the scene around him with the nonchalance of a cop. He looked right at home among the bedlam as if getting shot at was a routine part of his day. A fact that irked her despite the reality that he'd saved her life.

"You okay?" he asked, taking the chair across from her.

"No," she snarled. "Dammit, I'm not okay."

"I guess I'm not the only one who takes it personally when people start shooting at me. At least you're not in shock. That's good."

"I didn't mean to snap at you," she said. "I just feel so . . . violated. This is my shop. *Mine.*" She rapped her fist against her chest. "I deserve to feel safe here. He had no right to take that away from me."

"No, he didn't."

"The worst part about this is that he'll probably get away with it."

"Maybe, but he won't soon forget. He just about got his ass shot off."

She tried to smile, failed miserably, and ended up staring at the tabletop between them. "You saved my life."

"I saved my own ass. You just happened to be there."

Her gaze flew to his. "No. I saw the way you put yourself between me and that gun. If you hadn't been here, he would have—"

"Take my advice and don't play the what-if game. It sucks, and you lose every time."

"Maybe. But I just want you to know. What you did. It matters to me." A breath shuddered out of her when she realized she meant it.

He didn't look happy at the prospect of her gratitude and cut her a hard look. "I'm no hero, Ace. You'd be wise to remember that."

chapter
6

RANDALL STOOD AT THE BAR AND WATCHED DENVER'S finest walk through the shattered front door, leaving Addison to worry about securing what was left of her shop. Just like a cop, he thought sourly. They see too much, too often, and they become immune.

Just like you, a bitter voice added.

He looked at the woman behind the bar and felt his chest tighten. She was clutching a yellow mug as if it were her last link to the world. Two hours had passed since the shooting, but her face was still the color of bleached flour. She looked shaky at best, close to shock if he wanted to be truthful about it. He figured the least he could do was patch the broken pane of glass in that front door before he left.

"I've got some plywood and power tools in my truck," he said.

Her eyes traveled to the door. Cold air and the sound of traffic crept in where the glass had been blasted out by gunfire. Broken glass sparkled like diamonds on the floor. "I don't remember the glass breaking."

"Ricochet probably."

She ran a trembling hand through hair that looked incredibly soft beneath the yellow light of the tulip lamp overhead. Annoyed that he'd noticed something so irrelevant, Randall strode to the door and went outside. Standing curbside, next to his Bronco, he wrapped his carpenter's belt around his hips and pulled a single sheet of plywood from the bed. Good thing for Addison he was still carrying around the materials he'd bought for Jack's ramp. In the back of his mind he wondered how long his brother's patience would hold.

Something about the shooting nagged him as he contemplated how best to patch the large oval pane. There was a detail that unsettled him, but he wasn't sure if he should share it with her. He didn't want to upset her any more than she already had been tonight, but the implications of not telling her seemed much more disturbing. Holding that thought, he lugged the plywood to the door.

A few minutes later, Addison joined him.

He stopped working. "Any idea who might have been shooting at you?" he asked. "Ex-boyfriend, overzealous customer, anything like that going on?"

She looked appalled by the notion. "Van-Dyne seemed to think it was an attempted robbery. What makes you think it wasn't?"

Her voice was shaking again, and he didn't like the way she was trembling beneath that coat. But knowing her safety was at stake, he tamped down on the urge to back off.

"Don't you find it odd that this so-called robber didn't take the bank bag?" he asked.

"You mean the one you just about hit him with? How ungrateful of him."

Randall stared at her, unable to shake the feeling that there was more going on than either of them had considered. "Why did you need a private detective?"

"I told you. I was searching for my birth parents."

"You found them?"

A minute jerk of her shoulders told him he'd hit a nerve.

Her gaze dropped to the sidewalk. "My attorney, Jim Bernstein, located my birth mother in Ohio. A few days ago I
flew up and . . ." She crossed her arms protectively in front
of her. "When I got there I found out she was dead. She'd
been . . . murdered."

Uneasiness rippled through him. "Murdered," he repeated,
trying in vain to ignore the nagging little internal voice
chanting *I told you so* like a mantra. He was suspicious by
nature and didn't care for coincidence any more than he
cared for someone taking potshots at him.

"How long ago was she murdered?" he asked.

"A little over three weeks."

He wondered what this rather benign woman had managed
to get herself into. "Maybe you should start at the beginning
and tell me everything."

"You think what happened tonight is somehow related
to—"

"I don't think anything at this point. I just want to hear
the story."

"Okay." She sucked in a deep, shaky breath and began to
speak. Randall listened intently as she relayed to him the
details of her search for her birth parents and her recent trip
to Ohio.

Using a circular saw, he cut the plywood in half, carried
the larger piece to the Bronco, and shoved it into the rear
bed. At the front door, he fitted the remaining piece over the
broken pane and pulled a nail from his carpenter's belt.

"Do you know of any reason why someone might want to
hurt you? Any arguments over money? Angry boyfriends?
A stalker?" Even as he said the words, he felt his protective
instinct kicking in. Resisting it, he drove the nail through the
plywood with three even strokes of the hammer.

"You're purposefully trying to frighten me," she said.

"I'm asking questions that need to be asked."

"I lead a boring life, Talbot. I don't have any enemies. No
deep, dark secrets. And I've never been part of the KGB or
Colombian cartel, in case you're wondering. Satisfied?"

"What about family? Work? The shop here? Anyone been hitting on you recently? You piss anyone off?"

"Look, just because the robber didn't take the money doesn't mean I'm on some kind of a hit list. If you're that desperate for customers maybe you ought to put an ad in the Yellow Pages."

He drove another nail through the wood. How the hell could he tell her, without scaring her half to death, that he believed someone had tried to kill her tonight? Hit her with the truth, he supposed. She was too damn stubborn to be affected by something watered down.

Hooking the hammer over his belt, Randall turned to her and took a step closer. "The shooter was carrying a Walther TPH .22 pistol. Designed for close range, very expensive, and deadly as hell. The coat he was wearing cost more than you make in a month. He didn't so much as look at the cash register. He didn't ask for money. Not once did he point the pistol in my direction despite the fact that I was about to blow him to kingdom come." Frustrated by the whole damn scenario, Randall gave her a harsh look. "How do you explain that?"

She paled all the way down to her lips. "Maybe he was high on drugs. Maybe he changed his mind at the last minute—"

"Maybe he tried to blow your damn head off." With the plywood securely nailed to the door, he strode to his truck and tossed the carpenter's belt into the rear.

She held her ground at the door.

Her reluctance to listen to him was beginning to annoy him. No skin off his back. He didn't owe her a damn thing. If he was smart, he'd get in his truck, drive away, and never look back.

"Do you have someone to look after you tonight?" he asked.

She stared at him defiantly. "I don't need anyone—"

"You wake up screaming and you're not going to want to be alone." He hadn't meant for the words to come out so harshly, but they had. He was irritated with himself, annoyed with her, and downright pissed off by the turn of events that had him in a position he didn't want to be in. Dammit, he didn't want to be responsible for her tonight.

"I hate to ruin your image of me, tough guy, but I don't fall into the hysterical female category." She opened the door, casting him a frigid look over her shoulder. "Send me a bill for the door."

Before she could close it, he planted his booted foot in the jamb. "We're not finished."

"Yes, we are." She glared at him through the gap. An angry cat protecting her den from a prowling tom.

He bit back a nasty comeback. He wasn't sure why, but he wanted inside. With her. Right now. "You shouldn't be alone tonight."

"I do alone really well, Talbot. You should try it some-time. Builds character." She shoved at the door, squeezing his toes together uncomfortably. "You need it."

"Did you tell Van-Dyne about your birth mother's mur-der?" he growled.

Uncertainty climbed into her eyes. "I didn't think it was pertinent." Her gaze narrowed. "What's your point? It's two o'clock in the morning. I'm cold and tired, and I want to go home."

Randall studied her soft features and decided she really didn't have a choice but to listen to him. He wasn't leaving. For reasons beyond his good judgment, he was feeling pro-tective of her. "You were going to hire me to find your birth mother, weren't you?"

"*Were* being the operative word. You know, past tense. As in, it's not going to happen."

"I'm a P.I. I could look into this for you."

"You're a bully. I'll take my chances with the guy in the ski mask."

He squashed down his temper. "You're not the only one who got shot at tonight, for chrissake."

That stopped her. She relaxed her grip on the door. "You're serious about this, aren't you?"

"I'm not standing out here in the cold because I like your smart mouth. And if I merely wanted to jump your bones I'd find a different approach." He almost smiled when her cheeks colored. At least she wasn't pale anymore.

"I'm glad you're at least smart enough to know that would be a waste of time for both of us." She moved away from the door, giving him room to pass. "You're wrong about this."

"I hope so." He stepped inside, the victor in a tiny war, but one of great importance. "Lock up and I'll take you home."

ADDISON HELD A MATCH TO THE GAS LOGS AND watched the flame erupt. She was chilled, inside and out, and couldn't seem to warm herself despite the thick sweater she'd pulled over her shoulders.

Randall Talbot sat at the dining room table, a large mass of male looking inordinately out of place in her tidy apartment. A lock of dark hair fell onto his forehead as he scrutinized one of the documents in the file she'd compiled during her search for her birth parents.

She couldn't remember the last time she'd had a man in her apartment. Perhaps her disastrous date with the stockbroker she'd met at her shop last year. He'd been old enough to be her father and possessed the I.Q. of a teenager and the manners of an oversexed gorilla in heat. A single, rather unforgettable date, and she'd sworn off men indefinitely. That had been over a year ago, and she'd yet to miss them.

Tossing the spent match into the fire, she turned and contemplated her guest. He was not handsome in the conventional sense. There was a roughness in his appearance, an uncouthness in his manner, a vague restlessness in the way he moved. He was baseline male with a mouth that was too harsh and a nose as crooked as his smile. But his eyes, she decided, took command of a face that was less than perfect. They were striking, expressive pools of onyx that saw too much and divulged too little. Dangerous eyes that could slash as effortlessly as they caressed.

Remembering her initial response to him that day in his office, she felt a ripple of heat and immediately attributed it to the fire. She wasn't a sexual creature by nature. Surely it was trauma and fatigue that had her thinking of intimate caresses on such a terrible night. Randall Talbot was the last man on earth she'd ever have any interest in. Unless, of course, it was to fix her washing machine or change the oil in her car.

Addison made her way into the galley-style kitchen. It was nearly three A.M. and she was fading fast. Her hands trembled as she spooned coffee into the filter. She tried not to think about the shooting or the damage that had been done to her shop, but the images came at her out of the shadows like graphic film clips. She closed her eyes, trying to shut them out, but they continued to burst forth in her mind's eye. Brilliant images. Cold, colorless terror. The knowledge that death had all but whispered her name. She heard the sickening, tinny thud of the bullets as they penetrated the front of the bar. She saw clearly the gunman's eyes, the way he'd stared at her through the ski mask as he'd aimed the gun and fired. She'd seen murder in those eyes.

"Does this lawyer friend of yours have any more documents in his possession?"

Addison started when Randall came through the saloon doors. "Don't sneak up on me like that," she said irritably.

"Sorry." He raised the papers. "Are these all the documents you have?"

Frowning, she shoved a cup of coffee toward him. Her heart was still in her throat, and it took a moment before she could speak. "I don't know. Jim might have more information at his office, but he told me I had everything I needed."

He accepted the cup and sipped. "You got anything stronger than coffee?"

Addison stared at him, the memory of his drunkenness on the day they'd met flashing quickly through her mind. "If you're going to be working for me, I'd prefer if you didn't drink."

He choked out a laugh. "Oh, for chrissake."

"I'm serious."

"What's the matter, Ace? Worried I'll lose control and ravage your body?"

Despite the cool intensity of his gaze, she didn't look away.

"I'll let you know if I get the urge," he said.

"I don't appreciate the innuendo."

"I don't appreciate the insinuation."

"I merely asked you not to drink while you're on the job. That's not an unreasonable request, is it?"

His jaw flexed. "You think I have a drinking problem, and that pisses me off."

"I didn't say that."

"You were thinking it."

"I was thinking about how you acted that day in your office. Frankly, I'm not up to another round."

One side of his mouth curved into a humorless smile. "Don't worry, I'm not going to pull a Jekyll and Hyde on you. What you see is what you get."

That was what worried her. "I have the right to know who I'm dealing with."

"I'm the man who saved your ass tonight." His eyes flashed darkly. "That's all you need to know."

Intuition told her to back off. She stared at him a moment longer, then turned away and walked into the dining room.

Randall met her there a moment later. "Look, I'm sorry." Not meeting her gaze, he reached for his parka draped over the back of the chair. "This isn't working out—"

"You're leaving?" To her utter dismay, and for the first time in her adult life, she was afraid to be alone.

"No hard feelings. I was out of line just now. Bad habit

of mine. If you still want someone to look into this for you, I'll have Jack call—"

"I don't want Jack."

"Don't let the wheelchair fool you—"

"The wheelchair doesn't matter."

"He's good at what he does."

"I want you," she blurted.

The words hung between them like a thunderhead. His fingers closed around the parka, but he didn't pick it up. Addison saw his inner struggle clearly, but she didn't understand it.

Scowling, he cut her a hard look. "Why?"

She met his gaze levelly. "You saved my life."

"Don't discount your instincts about me," he said darkly. "They're probably not far off the mark."

"Right now my instincts are reminding me you nearly took a bullet for me."

Surprise flashed in his eyes before he could shutter it. "Don't make something out of this that isn't there. I was in the right place at the right time—"

"And I'd be dead right now if you hadn't been."

His harsh expression faltered, and for a moment he looked uncomfortable. She wondered why it was so hard for him to accept her gratitude.

"If you're looking for a hero, you've got the wrong man," he growled.

"Look," she began, "I'd like to hire you. I want you to look into my birth mother's murder." Starkly aware of his nearness, the faint scent of his aftershave, Addison pulled out a chair and sat down at the dining room table. "I want you to make sure the local sheriff is doing his job."

Never taking his eyes from her, he took the chair opposite her. "You don't know anything about me."

"All right. Then I'll just ask you a few questions." Trapped beneath his gaze, she felt a moment of awkwardness, not quite sure how to proceed with an impromptu interview. "How long have you been a private detective?"

"Now you're going to *interview* me?" he asked incredulously.

"I thought since I'm going to hire you I should get some background information." When he merely stared at her, she added, "That's usually how it's done, isn't it?"

"What's it going to be, Ace. Do you want me or not?"

"I already said I did." She swallowed. "How long have you been a P.I.?"

He rolled his eyes. "Oh, for crying out loud."

"How long?"

"All right, dammit." He shifted in the chair. "About five years."

"How long have you been with Talbot Investigations?"

"Five years."

"Do you solve most of your cases?"

"Most of them aren't a matter of being solved, but merely gathering information."

"I see."

"It pays the bills. Well, most of them, anyway. Do you mind if we get down to business now?"

"I'm ready when you are."

He looked down at the file and opened it. "How long had you been searching for your birth parents?"

She sighed, relieved that they were back on business. "A little over nine months."

"Did you know them at all?"

"I was adopted at birth."

"Anything in particular prompt your search?"

"I dabbled at first." Aware that he was watching her, she reminded herself that the pain wasn't as acute as it used to be. "Then my parents were killed in a car accident. After their deaths, finding my birth parents became a lot more important to me, and I started searching in earnest."

He leaned back in his chair, studying her. "So, your lawyer helped you find your biological mother way up in Siloam Springs, Ohio. When you get up there, you find out she's been murdered."

She nodded.

"When you get back here, some crazed robber in black shoots up your shop, tries to kill you, then forgets to take the bank bag."

An eerie sense of foreboding snaked through her. She shivered with a sudden chill. "Yes."

"Do you know who your biological father is?"

"I ran into a dead end searching for my birth father. He wasn't named on my amended birth certificate. The court documents were sealed at the time of my adoption."

"Is that typical?"

"The only way Jim—my lawyer—was able to find my mother was through birth records." The image of Agnes Beckett's tiny mobile home flashed in her mind's eye. "She was . . . poor. Her standing in the community wasn't the best. I want to make sure her case gets the attention it deserves."

"You want someone to light a fire under the local cops' asses."

"Well, yes."

He closed the file, then gazed at her steadily. "I'll do it."

Addison returned his gaze, relief and a newfound sense of rightness settling over her. "Thank you."

"I'll need the rest of the documents from your lawyer."

"I'll pick them up tomorrow."

"You can pay the advance tomorrow, too. Six hundred dollars. I'll bill you for expenses."

Disappointment drifted through her when she realized he was thinking of money rather than her safety. For a moment, she'd almost fooled herself into thinking he was actually concerned about her well-being. Stupid thought. Business was business. Men were men.

He rose and walked to the French door that led to her rear patio. He checked the lock, then turned to her. "Keep this locked. Keep your phone handy. Don't let anyone in unless you personally know them."

"Of course. I'll be careful."

Snagging his coat off the back of the chair, he started for

the front door. She followed, hating that she suddenly felt uneasy about being alone.

Before opening the door, he withdrew his wallet and handed her his business card. "My pager number's written on the back if you need it."

His fingers brushed against hers when she reached for the card. His eyes skimmed down the front of her. A renegade jolt of pleasure barreled through her.

"I'll call Van-Dyne first thing in the morning and fill him in." He opened the door, checked the hall, then looked at her.

She raised her eyes to his, strangely disconcerted by the dark intensity of his gaze. God, he was one of the most unsettling men she'd ever met.

"I'll hang around the building for a while." But he didn't move. His eyes flicked to her mouth.

Addison's pulse jumped in response. She told herself it was because she didn't quite trust him, but she was in tune with herself enough to know it was because she wasn't the only one who'd just felt the arc of electricity.

Feeling uncharacteristically awkward, she stepped back, thankful her intellect had kicked in before she did something stupid. The last thing she needed in her life right now was a man, especially a volatile, unpredictable man like Randall Talbot.

"Thanks for the coffee." He tapped the bolt lock with his finger. "Don't forget to lock it."

"I won't."

His gaze lingered on hers an instant longer, then he turned and walked away without so much as a backward glance.

Addison closed the door, then leaned against it. The elevator down the hall chimed. She had the crazy urge to call him back, but of course she didn't. Instead, she leaned against the door, trying to turn off her thoughts, trying not to be afraid. But her sense of security had been shattered. She felt as if she were riding in a car that was careening out of control, and she could do nothing but hang on for dear life.

The tears came with surprising force. Body-wracking sobs that shook her all the way down to her toes. It was as if all the emotions she'd suppressed in the last hours had finally been unleashed. The memory of the shooting rushed at her like tiny spears. The terror, the helplessness, the knowledge that death had come so perilously near.

And with a stark sense of dismay, she realized that even locked away in her own apartment, she no longer felt safe.

chapter
7

BEYOND THE GLASS WALL OF HIS FOURTH-FLOOR OF-
fice, rain fell in sheets, bringing a rise of fog to the street
below. He watched the people on the sidewalk with a mixture
of disinterest and disgust as they went about their daily rou-
tines like mindless herd animals.

He should have been celebratory, sitting where he was,
looking down at the rest of the world from his exalted position. He should have felt superior perched above the scam-
pering rats beyond the glass. He should have felt in control
and relaxed. But he didn't feel any of those things.

The demons of his past had finally come home. Tasks he'd
left unfinished as a careless and irresponsible young man
were tumbling back into his life to haunt him, like a persistent ghost that had become as dangerous as it was frightening.

He'd dreaded this moment his entire life. Not because he
was afraid. Fear never entered into his decisions. Nor was
the dread he felt induced by the thought of violence. Vio-

lence was merely a part of doing business, many times necessary, invariably effective.

It was the lack of control that troubled him most. There were too many people in too many places asking too many questions. There were too many loose ends. Predictably, it was the loose ends most men failed to deal with. Loose ends that eventually destroyed them.

Swiveling in the black leather executive chair, he faced the man who'd entered his office. He considered the nondescript features made important not by the European suit or Gucci loafers, but by the knowledge stored beneath the scrupulous facade. He paid his employees well. As a result, they did his bidding for him without objection and without question.

His eyes traveled to the fully stocked wet bar. He watched with a rich sense of satisfaction as the other man walked to the bar, poured two fingers of Rémy Martin cognac into a crystal snifter, then returned and set it on the desk in front of him.

"Our little problem in Denver is no longer a little problem," he said, leaning back into the plush leather.

"I take full responsibility for the error." The other man fingered the Hermes tie at his throat as if the hideous colors were choking him.

"Of course you do." From the top drawer of the desk, he removed an emery board and filed the tip of a short, perfectly manicured nail. In a world where perceptions were everything, it wouldn't do to overreact. Even if control of the situation had slipped beyond his grasp, at least he could maintain the illusion. "This young woman seems to be quite resourceful. How much does she know?"

"She found out about the Beckett woman. Of course, her trip to Ohio wasn't fruitful."

"She seems to be very determined."

"We have some options."

The other man's naïveté irritated him. "Such as?"

"We could pay her off—"

"Don't be an idiot." He smiled inwardly when the man wearing the Hermes tie winced. He'd always enjoyed inflicting humiliation. He'd always enjoyed possessing that kind of power.

"I assumed that since she's—"

"Buy-offs are temporary and dangerous. You should know more about human nature by now." He considered himself an expert on human nature, particularly the dark side. "I'm interested only in permanent solutions."

The man's eyes darted to the window and the rain beyond. "I understand."

"I don't want any more questions raised. I don't want any more people involved. And I don't want any loose ends. Make certain your solutions are definitive."

Their eyes met. An explicit understanding passed between them. One of them would act. The other would pay an exorbitant fee.

"Consider it done."

"Make sure the remaining records are destroyed."

"I'm working on it."

His perfectly manicured hand tightened around the snifter. He didn't like vague answers. "Do it quickly." His voice lowered ominously. "You've got all my resources at your disposal. I don't have to remind you what's at stake."

The other man rose. "I know precisely what's at stake. I'll take care of it."

"LORD CHRIST ALMIGHTY!" GRETCHEN WENTWORTH took one look at the front door and came through it like a Peterbilt skidding around a hairpin turn.

Having gone most of the night without sleep, Addison winced at the other woman's worried-grandmother tone, wishing she'd taken the time to swallow some aspirin before driving in to the shop to assess the damage and fill in her overprotective employee.

"Hi, Gretch."

Gretchen looked at Addison as if she wasn't quite sure whether to hit her or embrace her. "I ought to throttle you for not calling me last night!" The older woman pulled her close, hugged her tightly, then shoved her to arm's length. "Good God, honey, what in the bejeebers happened?"

"I told you. There was an attempted robbery."

Purse flying, Gretchen swung a wiry arm toward the bullet-riddled bar. "You didn't mention *that* when you called me this morning!" Her mouth flew open at the sight of the hole in the cash register. "Or *that!* Good Lord, I got more details from my TV!"

Addison had called her friend at five A.M. and explained that there had been an attempted robbery and that the shop would be closed for a few days. She hadn't gone into detail—and hadn't expected Gretchen to show up before lunch. Now she had some explaining to do. "Sorry, Gretch, but I just didn't want to go into it over the telephone. I didn't want to worry you."

"Oh, honey, I'm as sorry as I am mad at you. You didn't have to go through this alone."

The fact that she hadn't actually been alone made her think of Randall—for the dozenth time that morning. She told herself she wasn't preoccupied with him. That her thoughts had wandered to him repeatedly only because he'd saved her life and they'd spent a few intense hours together the night before. Just because she'd hired him didn't mean she was going to start thinking about his dark eyes or that crooked smile of his. Clearly, he wasn't her type. Not that she *had* a type, she reminded herself.

"I'm not a puff, you know." Gretchen raised her hand and touched Addison's cheek with the backs of her fingers.

"You've got enough on your mind with Brittany about to give birth," Addison said.

"There's enough mother in me to take care of my three daughters *and* you, honey. You know that."

Forcing a smile to head off the emotion that tightened her throat, Addison covered Gretchen's hand with her own and squeezed. "You never let me forget how lucky I am to have you as a friend."

"Friend?" Gretchen huffed. "Family, more like. I consider you one of my own."

"Keep this up and I'm going to cry, Gretch."

"We can't have that." The older woman smiled. "Sit down and tell me what the heck happened."

Leaving out some of the darker details, Addison relayed the incident from beginning to end. She kept her voice even and controlled. When her hands began to shake, when the images rushed at her—the gun, the ski mask—she rose from the bistro table and busied herself making a pot of New Guinea dark roast. She'd been operating on coffee most of the night. She supposed one more cup wouldn't hurt.

"Thank God that private detective showed up when he did." Gretchen followed her behind the counter, angrily digesting the information. "God forbid, Addison, you could have been killed."

On a day when the reality of her own mortality hovered so near, Addison had little to say on the subject of death. She filled two mugs with coffee and passed one to Gretchen.

"You should have called me. You had no business spending the night alone after such an awful ordeal." The older woman looked at her chidingly. "You should have at least called me to take you home."

Addison raised her cup to her lips. "Actually, Randall Talbot took me home." An unexpected flutter of pleasure wafted through her at the mention of his name. God, what was it about that man that had her acting like a schoolgirl?

Gretchen's eyebrows rose and she peeked at her from over the rim of her glasses. "Nice of him in light of the fact that you lodged that complaint with the Better Business Bureau."

Realizing her business arrangement with Talbot might need some explaining, Addison tried to clarify. "He came into the shop to apologize."

"He must be a real charmer."

"I assure you, charm had nothing to do with it." It was

just a little white lie. She didn't want Gretchen to think she was a pushover, especially after she'd spent so many weeks casting insults about the man. "He offered to look into Agnes Beckett's murder."

"You *hired* him?"

"I just want him to follow up and make sure her case is being investigated the way it should be."

Sympathy flashed across the older woman's face. "Oh, honey, Agnes Beckett is gone. I know that's painful for you. I know how much it hurts. But you've got to let go and move on."

"I don't want her forgotten, Gretch."

"What in the world do you expect him to find?"

Justice. Closure. The words flitted through her brain, but she didn't voice them, wasn't sure she could explain any of them. "I just want some answers."

Addison had decided not to mention Randall's theory that the robbery hadn't been a robbery at all, but an attempt on her life. There was no proof, and she didn't want to worry her friend needlessly. She wasn't even sure if she believed it herself. Masked gunmen just didn't fit into her safe, wonderfully dull life.

Standing in her coffee shop with the sunshine streaming through the windows and the smell of fresh-brewed coffee in the air, the terror of the night before seemed light-years away.

"I want you to have those answers you need so desperately, honey. But even more, I want you to get on with your life."

"Before I can do that, I've got to get this out of the way once and for all. To do that, I need closure, Gretch. That's what this is all about."

Reaching out, Gretchen sighed and tucked a stray lock of hair behind Addison's ear. "At least you'll have someone looking out for you, I suppose."

"I wouldn't exactly say he's looking out for me."

Gretchen's lips twitched. "There was a picture of him in

the newspaper this morning. Strapping young man."

Addison rolled her eyes. "Strapping or not, I'm paying him for his time, Gretch. It's not like he's doing this out of the goodness of his heart."

"I'm sure the man needs to make a living."

Ignoring her friend's tone, Addison stepped behind the counter and ran her hand over the espresso machine, pausing at the hole left by a bullet that had been meant for her.

She hated seeing her shop damaged. She'd poured too much of herself into the place to let someone walk in and destroy it in a senseless, random act of violence.

Reminding herself that damaged equipment could be replaced, she glanced at the clock above the espresso machine and gasped. "I was supposed to be at the police station half an hour ago to talk with Detective Van-Dyne." She caught her friend's eyes and held them. "Will you be all right here?"

"In broad daylight?" Gretchen huffed as she picked up a push broom and swept the scatter of coffee beans into a neat pile. "Back in Missouri, we shoot back."

Addison forced a laugh, telling herself it was silly to worry about the robber returning. She didn't keep much cash at the shop. Only an idiot would hit the same place twice.

"The insurance adjuster is supposed to come by late this afternoon," Addison said as she started for the alley door. "If he gets here before I get back, be nice to him."

THE TRIP TO THE POLICE STATION WAS EVERYTHING Addison had imagined it would be, only worse. She waited nearly an hour before seeing Detective Van-Dyne. When he finally took her into his office, he spent most of the time on the telephone and the rest ogling her legs.

He was in his element at the station, and she was light-years out of hers. They both knew it, and it seemed he did everything in his power to impress that fact upon her. She figured out why when he suggested they finish the report over lunch. A true whiz at getting out of unpleasant engagements—especially with men—she quickly mentioned that she had a date with her lawyer. He spent the remainder of the interview acting like a spoiled twelve-year-old.

In the end, a report that should have taken forty-five minutes took nearly two hours. Addison was never quite so glad to leave a place in her entire life. A quick stop at Jim Bernstein's office to pick up the remainder of the records, and on to Talbot Investigations to pay the advance. Then she could go back to the Coffee Cup and figure out which equipment she would need to replace before reopening the shop. Hopefully, the insurance adjuster had left good news with Gretchen.

She was thinking about Agnes Beckett when she parked her Mustang in front of Jim's office. Her search had, indeed, come to an end. At least she could quit with the knowledge that she'd done her best. That her birth mother wouldn't be forgotten. Hopefully, with Randall's help, Sheriff McEvoy would find the killer, and Addison would have the closure she needed to move on.

Shivering with cold, she stepped into the elevator and rode alone up to Jim's office on the fifth floor. She was hungry and had decided to ask him to have a sandwich with her at the lobby deli if he wasn't too busy. He worked long hours and, like most workaholics, never took the time for a decent meal.

Her mind was already jumping ahead to corned beef on rye as she pushed open the door to his office. To her surprise, his paralegal was nowhere in sight. The telephone beeped incessantly. Resisting the urge to pick it up and take a message for him, Addison left the reception area and made her way down the hall. She peered into the small, doorless storage room as she passed and found it empty.

"Jim?" Her voice came sharply in the dense silence. Inexplicably, the hairs at the back of her neck tingled. She moved down the hall, silently cursing when the first thin ribbon of unease skittered through her.

"Get a grip," she mumbled, telling herself he'd probably

taken his overworked paralegal out for a late lunch.

But it was odd that he hadn't left anyone in the office to cover the phones. Even in this day of voice mail and e-mail, no lawyer would leave his telephones unmanned. Not even Jim Bernstein, with his relaxed atmosphere and anything-goes dress code.

She reached his office a moment later and found it empty as well. Puzzled, trying in vain to ignore a growing sense of alarm, she stood in the doorway, taking in the heaps of paper and files and briefs stacked on his desk. Deciding to leave him a note, Addison walked to the desk and picked up his Mont Blanc.

She was looking for a piece of scratch paper when she realized the pen was sticky. Puzzled, she looked closely at the bright red stain on her palm. At first glance she thought it was ink, then her heart began to pound.

Blood.

Revulsion vibrated through her. The pen fell to the desk, leaving a grotesque red stain on the blotter. Addison stared, horrified, and heard herself whisper his name.

She wanted to run. Out of the room. Out of the building. But the part of her that knew and cared for Jim Bernstein wouldn't let her walk away, no matter how scared she was. Heart hammering, she leaned forward and peered over the desk.

Behind the chair, Jim lay on his back, legs apart, arms sprawled. His head was turned severely to one side. His eyes were open and staring. His mouth was stretched taut, as if frozen in a scream. Red-black blood coagulated on his lips.

Horror and disbelief ripped through her. She stood motionless for an instant, unable to tear her eyes away from the red stain that stood out starkly on his white shirt. It spread from collar to belt, encompassing the tie and spilling onto the carpet in a perfect arc.

Adrenaline burned like fire in her gut. She backed from the room, her heart pummeling her breast. The smell of death hovered. Blood clung to her hand. Gasping, she wiped it against her coat, horrified by the smear it left.

Her back hit the wall. The impact jarred her back to reality. A mass of jumbled thoughts raced through her mind. She staggered to the reception area.

Jim was dead.

Disbelief tumbled through her. She looked down at her hands, shocked once again by the sight of blood. Fresh terror streaked up her spine.

"Oh, God. Oh, *God!*" Staving off a crushing wave of panic, she ran to the receptionist's desk and snatched up the phone.

chapter

8

"LOOKS LIKE YOU SHOULD HAVE TAKEN ME UP ON THAT offer for lunch." Detective Adam Van-Dyne crossed to the window, hooked his finger under a miniblind slat, and peered outside.

Addison barely heard him as she watched two men from the medical examiner's office bring a gurney through the front door. A wave of disbelief rolled over her as she realized they would be taking Jim's body to the morgue.

Unsure of her balance or the strength in her legs, she lowered herself into the receptionist's chair and watched the men maneuver the gurney down the hall toward Jim's office.

Van-Dyne dropped the slat, crossed the room to her, and perched his hip on the desk in front of her. "What were you doing here today, Miss Fox?"

The small office teemed with police officers, paramedics, and firefighters. In the hall, Channel 7 had arrived with their cameras and lights, swarming like sharks in the throes of a feeding frenzy. In the midst of it all, Addison huddled in the receptionist's chair, arms wrapped tightly around her, vaguely aware that Van-Dyne was speaking to her as if she'd been a mischievous child.

When she didn't respond, he leaned forward, placed his hands on the arms of her chair, and swung her around to face him. "There was no appointment listed for you. Why were you here?"

His face was inches from hers and Addison could smell garlic on his breath. "Is he dead?" she asked.

"I'm afraid so."

"Oh, God." Nausea roiled in her stomach. "I can't believe it."

Resting his hand on her forearm, he spoke over his shoulder to a uniformed officer. "Get me a glass of water here." He turned back to Addison. "Did you know him? Were you friends?"

"He's . . . my lawyer. I've known him for years. He was a family friend."

"Was there anyone else in the office when you arrived?"

"No."

"Did Bernstein know you were coming today?"

"No. I just . . . stopped by to pick up some records."

"What kind of records?"

She stammered, feeling too disoriented to explain something as complicated as her search for her birth parents. "Records on my biological parents."

His brow creased. "Biological parents?"

Irritation sparked through her. "Yes. I'm adopted. Jim helped me locate my birth mother."

"He was working for you?"

"No." She sighed. "I mean, yes. But he was doing it as a favor, in his spare time. He wasn't billing me. He was a friend of my father's." It was the third time she'd answered that question, and she could tell by the way the detective was watching her that he wasn't quite sure what to make of her answers.

Van-Dyne accepted the paper cup the officer brought him and handed it to Addison. "Here, drink this. It'll help."

She accepted the water and sipped carefully, not quite trusting her stomach. "Thanks."

Digging into his pocket, the detective removed a white handkerchief and handed it to her. "It's not often I see someone like you in the middle of something like this twice in two days," he said.

Addison reached for the handkerchief and wiped the drying blood from her right hand. "Seems like I've been in the wrong place at the wrong time a lot lately."

"Did you touch the body, Miss Fox?"

"No. I—I couldn't. . . ."

He held out his hand for the handkerchief. She passed it to him, then watched with a feeling of sick dread as he removed a small plastic bag from his coat pocket. He dropped the handkerchief into it. "How did you get blood on your hands?"

"I . . . I picked up the pen, the Mont Blanc. I was going to leave him a note. Jesus, you can't possibly think I had anything to do with . . ."

He raised his hands in a gesture that did little to reassure her. "I'm just trying to get a picture of what happened. But I must admit I'm curious as to why you've been in the vicinity of two shootings in two days."

They stared at each other, his expression hard and unsympathetic, hers aghast at what he might be thinking.

"Why the show with the evidence bag?" The voice was imperious, challenging, and vaguely familiar.

Addison looked up to see Jack Talbot rolling his wheelchair toward her. Relief flooded her. "Jack."

He wasn't a conventional-looking private detective. Clad in black leather and denim, he more closely resembled a revolutionary from the 1970s. His black hair was pulled into a tight ponytail that reached halfway down his back. Two days of stubble darkened his jaw. A gold hoop glinted at his left earlobe.

Without speaking, he removed his identification from his wallet and flashed it at the detective, all the while eyeing

Addison as if trying to gauge her state of mind.

"Are you all right?" he asked.

She nodded, vaguely remembering the call she'd made to his office after dialing 911. "I'm okay. Thanks for coming."

Jack shot the detective a hard look. "What's the problem, Van-Dyne, did you run out of junkies to hassle?"

"Just doing my job, Jack. How's the back these days?"

"Can't complain."

Addison risked a look at the detective. "I've told you everything I know. I'd like to go now."

The detective glared at her. "You can leave when I say you can."

"I didn't do anything wrong."

"Nobody said you did."

Jack made a rude sound and very quietly suggested Van-Dyne do something anatomically impossible. "Come on, Adam, you've had her for nearly two hours. What the hell else do you want?"

The detective's glare swept from Jack to Addison. "Don't leave town."

She jerked her head once.

Wheeling his chair around, Jack started for the door. "There's a car without a permit parked in the handicapped zone, Detective. You might want to grab your ticket book and check it out." He winked at Addison. "Your place or mine?"

Wondering what she was getting herself into, Addison rose, relieved when the floor felt solid under her feet. She started for the door.

"Miss Fox?"

Van-Dyne's voice stopped her dead in her tracks. Jack continued rolling toward the door. She turned to the detective, aware that Jack had reached the door.

"I expect you to make yourself available to the police for questioning for the next few weeks," the detective said.

"Of course," she replied, then turned and followed Jack.

*   *   *

IT AMAZED ADDISON TO WATCH A MAN WHO COULDN'T walk slide his body from wheelchair to driver's seat, then quickly fold the chair and toss it onto the backseat of his antiquated Corvette like a lightweight piece of luggage. He'd even paused to open the passenger door for her first. A gentleman to boot, she thought. Too bad good manners didn't run in the family.

He was an older version of his brother, shorter of frame and heavier in the upper body. Both men shared the same penetrating eyes, but Jack's face was deeply lined with the years of what had probably been a hard life.

Neither of them spoke as he drove her to her apartment. Though Addison felt the need to help as he lifted the wheelchair from the backseat, she quickly realized he was much more adept than she. In less than two minutes, he was back in the chair and they were riding the elevator up to her second-level apartment.

Once inside, she made a beeline for the bathroom, where she scrubbed the blood from her hands, holding them under the hot water until her skin turned pink. Then, needing to move, to embroil herself in normalcy, she went to the kitchen and made a pot of coffee.

She was still shaking, but the worst of the tremors had ceased during the drive to her apartment. Physically, she was functioning. But that didn't say much for her frame of mind. She'd known Jim Bernstein since she was a child. She couldn't believe he was dead, much less by an act of violence. Shock waves rippled through her every time she closed her eyes and saw him lying on the floor in a pool of blood.

Van-Dyne's attitude toward her hadn't helped matters. She hadn't made a very good impression on the detective. But she couldn't bring herself to believe he considered her a suspect. Maybe he was just angry because she'd turned down his invitation to lunch. She wasn't sure how she would have managed if Jack hadn't shown up when he did.

After pouring two cups of coffee, she met Jack at the dining room table and slid one of the cups in front of him. "You and your brother really have this timing thing down to a fine art," she said. "Thanks for rescuing me."

"Randall told me what happened last night at your shop. You were lucky."

"He saved my life."

Jack cut her a sharp look. "He didn't mention that."

She didn't miss the flash of surprise on his face. "He's got this annoying habit of being modest."

"He's got quite a few annoying habits."

Addison didn't comment on that one. Lowering her head, she rubbed her aching temples with her fingertips. "Jesus. I still can't believe any of this is real."

"What happened back there at the lawyer's office? The message you left was hard to follow. You were hysterical."

She swallowed, an involuntary action that made her realize she'd wanted to put off that part of the conversation a while longer. Raising her head, she took a fortifying breath. "I went to Jim's office to pick up some records. When I got there, the place was deserted. I walked into his office, and . . . found him on the floor behind his desk. There was blood. . . ." Bile rose in her throat when the scene flickered in her mind's eye. "I panicked, called 911, then your office."

"You see anyone else there?"

"No."

Pulling a pack of cigarettes from his jacket, he stuck one between his lips and flamed the tip. Addison usually didn't allow smoking in her apartment, but she didn't have the energy to stop him. In light of everything that had happened in the last twenty-four hours, a little cigarette smoke didn't seem very important.

"I guess the question now is whether all this is somehow related," he said, exhaling a silver ribbon of smoke.

The implications of the statement punched her with brutal force. Numbly, she leaned back in the chair, an icy realization settling over her like a cold, penetrating rain. She'd considered the possibility that the events of the last week were somehow connected, but there had always been a small part of her that didn't believe it, didn't want to believe that something sinister was in the works.

"That's the same thing Randall said," she replied.

He shrugged. "It's the logical assumption."

"The idea of some kind of conspiracy seems . . . far-fetched."

"Not a conspiracy. Just somehow linked."

"It just doesn't jibe with my lifestyle."

"How so?"

"Well, I work a lot. I don't go out much. I don't have any enemies. I don't even have that many friends. Just Gretchen and her daughters and grandchildren."

"Any odd customers in the shop? Ex-boyfriends?"

"No. Randall already asked that, and there's no one."

"Okay. Is there any reason someone might not want you to know who your biological parents are?"

Somewhere in the back of her mind, she'd considered the possibility, but never imagined it would come to this. Not in a thousand years. "I don't know. I can't imagine why."

"Have you told the police about your search?"

"I met with Van-Dyne earlier today. I told him about Agnes Beckett, but he didn't seem very receptive to the idea that her death had anything to do with the attempted robbery at the Coffee Cup last night. He made me feel like I was being paranoid."

He pushed away from the table. "Where's your phone?"

"In the kitchen." She rose. "Who are you going to call?"

"I'm going to leave a message for Van-Dyne."

Addison followed him to the kitchen and listened intently as he left a message for the detective. He wheeled his chair back to the table. She refilled their cups.

"Was he hitting on you?" he asked.

The question jerked her head up in surprise. "Earlier today, when I went in to give my statement, but he was pretty subtle about it." She studied the faint lipstick mark she'd left on her cup. "You're pretty perceptive."

Laughter rumbled in his throat. "Van-Dyne's a son of a bitch. I've gone a couple of rounds with him in the last two years, since I started Talbot Investigations."

"So you started your company two years ago?" She distinctly remembered Randall telling her he'd been with Talbot Investigations for five years. Interesting.

He nodded. "Beats the hell out of staring at the walls."

"How long has Randall been with you?"

"About five months."

She filed the information away, deciding to confront Randall with it later. "What did he do before he started working with you?"

"He worked for the NTSB out of D.C."

"What did he do for the NTSB?"

His gaze sharpened, letting her know in no uncertain terms that she was prying. "Maybe you ought to ask him that."

"I will." She admired his loyalty despite the fact that she didn't like being lied to. Especially when she didn't know why. "What about Van-Dyne? Is he a good detective?"

"He's a decent enough cop. But he's overworked, underpaid, has too many cases and not enough time. He can be a prick to deal with."

"What about you?"

The eyebrows shot up. "Am I a prick?"

She laughed, realizing he'd purposefully taken her mind off the shooting. There was a quiet strength and solid character behind that tough-guy facade. To her surprise, she found herself liking him. "I was referring to your detective skills."

"Oh." He grinned. "I'm the brains behind the operation. Randall does most of the legwork." He looked down at his chair. "No pun intended."

She remembered the angry, reckless energy that seemed to surround Randall. Despite the wheelchair, Jack seemed more content. The contrasts between the two brothers intrigued her. "You seem happier than your brother."

"Probably because I've accepted my limitations."

She didn't miss the shadow of pain that flashed in his eyes. "How did it happen?" she asked, hoping she hadn't trespassed into an area that was too painful for him.

"Motorcycle accident. Rode too fast too many times. My luck finally ran out."

"I'm sorry."

"It was a tough hand, but I've dealt with it. I've come to terms, moved beyond it. Acceptance is the key."

"And what limitations hasn't your brother accepted?"

He dropped the cigarette into the last bit of coffee and watched it sizzle out. "Let's just say he's in the process of realizing what they are."

A knock on the door sent Addison out of her chair. Jack motioned her back, put a finger to his lips to silence her. She watched in amazement as he pulled a revolver from beneath his coat. God, did everybody carry a gun? Cocking it, he rolled his chair toward the front door, and gave her a nod.

"Who is it?" she asked.

"It's Randall. What the hell's going on?"

Relief flitted through her at the sound of his voice.

Jack opened the door.

Randall stood in the doorway, his dark eyes concerned and more than a little angry. He looked like an overprotective father about to confront his daughter's suspicious-looking date. "What the hell kind of a message was that you left on my voice mail?"

Jack looked at Addison and laughed. "He's talking about the message you left when you called from Bernstein's office."

She blinked, barely remembering the phone call she'd made after discovering Jim's body.

Not waiting for an answer, Randall stalked past them into the apartment. He wore faded jeans, hiking boots, and a parka. "Is someone going to tell me what the hell is going on? What happened to Bernstein?"

The way he was acting made her wonder if he'd been worried about her, but she quickly shoved the notion aside. Men like Randall Talbot didn't worry about other people. They spent too much time worrying about themselves.

"Jim Bernstein was murdered," she said.

He stared at her with astonishment. "Your *lawyer*? When?"

"Earlier today," Jack said. "He took a slug in the chest." His eyes shifted to Addison. "She found him."

Randall swung around to face her, his expression incredulous. "You found him? Dead? In his office?"

She nodded.

Scrubbing his hand over his five o'clock shadow, he shot a canny look at Jack. "Feel up to sweet-talking that computer of yours tonight?"

Cool excitement flickered in Jack's eyes. "She's a bitch, but I can usually persuade her to cooperate." He pulled a notepad and pen from his jacket. "Shoot."

"I want information on Agnes Irene Beckett."

Addison's heart stuttered at the mention of her birth mother—and the possibility that Randall had new information.

He continued. "I want to know everything about her. Arrest record, past marriages, hospitalizations, births, anything you can find. Check Ohio and Indiana state records along with the Ohio counties of Preble, Darke, and Montgomery."

Jack scribbled on the pad, smiling the way a boy smiles in the minutes before a forbidden, but very fun game. "I hope you're not going to ask me for anything difficult."

"Have you ever tapped into adoption records?"

"No, but that doesn't mean it can't be done."

"That's what I thought. I left everything I've got on your desk."

Addison listened to the exchange, aware of her heart beating wildly in her chest. "What have you found out?" she asked Randall.

Jack already had his coat on and was wheeling toward the door. "Give me a few hours."

Addison reached out and squeezed his shoulder. "Thank you."

He reached the door and backed up to open it, nearly running over her in his haste. Before he could escape, she leaned forward and kissed his cheek.

Grinning, Jack wheeled into the hall.

She turned, anxious to talk to Randall. He stopped her with a single look from those perpetually angry eyes.

"What?" she asked cautiously.

"Don't tease him like that," he said with dangerous ease.

Addison stared at him, speechless. "I hope you're not insinuating what I think——"

"He's in a wheelchair, for chrissake."

The anger came with such vehemence she nearly choked on it. "It was an innocent peck on the cheek!"

"He doesn't need you laying kisses on him, making him want something he can't ever have."

"How dare you accuse me of something so sick!" Had there been something within arm's reach, she would have thrown it at him. Since there wasn't, she used the next best thing: her voice. "You son of a bitch."

"Don't——"

"I can't deal with you. I won't."

"Addison——"

"I'll deal with Jack. I want you to leave. Now, damn you." The words tangled in her throat. "In fact, you're . . . fired. I'll send your check to your office."

"It hurts him," he said levelly. "He's been through enough."

The look in his eyes deflated her temper so quickly, she could only stand there and stare stupidly at him. "I would never hurt——"

"I didn't say you meant to. I just asked you not to do it again."

"I don't appreciate the insinuation."

"There was no insinuation."

Feeling misunderstood and angry, she shoved past him into the living room, not exactly sure what to do next.

"Look," he said from behind her. "I didn't mean for that to come out the way it did. I didn't mean for it to hit you the wrong way. But I know Jack."

She turned to face him. "He's a human being. Human beings need to be touched. To—"

"He's a man, Addison, with too much pride."

"You're overprotective."

"I'm his brother. I know him."

She studied his harsh features, realizing belatedly that he was sincere—and not nearly as angry as she was. It irked her that he could make her so damn irate, so damn quickly. Jack was easy to be with. Addison liked him. But the moment he'd left, and she was alone with Randall, something had shifted. A keen awareness that changed everything despite her efforts not to let it.

"Why did you lie to me about how long you've been working with Jack?" she asked.

An emotion she couldn't name flashed in his eyes. "Jack gave you an earful, did he?"

"No. He said to ask you."

"He's always had more integrity than me."

"Why did you lie to me, Randall?"

His eyes met hers and held them unflinchingly. "What do you want to know?"

"The truth, if you can manage it."

"All right. I'm on leave from another job. I came here to spend some time with Jack. End of story. That's the extent of my dirty little secret. Disappointed?"

Addison didn't believe it was that simple. "Your job at the NTSB?"

He blinked. It was the first time she'd surprised him, and she found herself oddly pleased when he looked down at his boots. "You want to hear about that, too?"

"I'm just curious why you lied to me. Maybe it's not important. Maybe it is. I was hoping you'd tell me."

A shadow darkened his features. He raked a hand through his hair. "I'm a crash site investigator, Ace. A field investigator. I'm the guy who gets there first when a plane drops out of the sky." He smiled unpleasantly. "I get to see it all. If you're morbidly curious like most other people I've met, we could spend a few hours together and I'll give you all the juicy details."

Not sure whether to be annoyed or sympathetic, she merely stared back at him. He wasn't the kind of man who invoked sympathy. "I still don't understand why you lied to me."

"I've got my reasons," he said after a lengthy silence. "I'd appreciate it if you'd respect my privacy." He shifted his weight from one foot to the other, inadvertently opening his parka so that lean, male hips loomed into view.

Addison cursed herself for allowing her eyes to drop, appalled by the unwelcome awareness that rushed through her at the sight of his long, muscular thighs. What was it about this man that had her thinking of everything except what she should be thinking about?

"I don't like being lied to," she said.

He stared at her with such intensity that she wanted to look away. "I won't lie to you again."

She held his gaze a moment longer, wondering what secrets he kept and why, wondering if those secrets had anything to do with the haunted look in his eyes. Needing to get out from under his discerning gaze, she let out a long, pent-up breath and headed for the fireplace.

"I was hoping you'd be more interested in my trip to Siloam Springs than a one-on-one interrogation," he said.

She halted, her heart kicking in her chest. How was it that he managed to knock her off balance every time he opened his mouth? Slowly, she turned to face him. "I didn't know you'd gone."

"I took a red-eye. Spent the morning with your buddy Sheriff McEvoy. The afternoon at a little bar called Mc-

Ninch's with a woman who'd worked with Agnes Beckett.
I got back about an hour ago."

"What did you find out?"

Curiosity had her pulse racing as she went to the kitchen
and poured two cups of coffee. She returned to the living
room to find Randall lighting the gas logs. She set his cup
on the coffee table, then took the armchair opposite the sofa.
"I want to know everything."

He sat across from her. "McEvoy wasn't the most coop-
erative public servant I've had the misfortune of working
with, but I managed to get a look at the file. The police report
states Agnes Beckett was murdered in the commission of a
robbery. I don't buy it."

"Why?" Addison leaned forward, anticipation warring
with dread. A small part of her didn't want to hear what he
had to say next. The stronger, more logical side of her knew
she must if she wanted to get to the bottom of this.

"Whoever killed her was smart enough to make it look
like a robbery," he began. "The sheriff's department took an
inventory of her place and found some items no petty thief
would leave behind."

"Like what?"

"They left a twelve-inch color television in the bedroom.
TVs sell like hot cakes at just about any pawn shop. They
also found a few pieces of gold jewelry and a mason jar with
just under two hundred dollars in it. The jar was out of sight,
but not hidden well enough to keep a robber from finding
it."

"What *did* the thief take?"

"Her purse and what little jewelry she was wearing."

"Whatever was convenient." Visions of the murder scene
flashed in the back of her mind. Steeling herself against the
images, she forced her thoughts back to the matter at hand.
"If the motive wasn't robbery, then what?"

"Whoever went in there that night didn't go in to steal.
They went in to kill. A vagrant or local thief isn't going to
go to the trouble of cutting the phone line. Not for twenty

bucks and a cheap gold necklace. The bolt lock on the front door was either left unlocked or picked by someone who knew what they were doing."

"My god."

He sipped his coffee, watching Addison over the top of the glass. "Her place had been ransacked, yet the intruder left most of the valuables. The entire scenario makes me suspicious as hell."

Addison felt as though she'd stepped out of the safety of her own life, and into someone else's—someone she didn't necessarily know or trust. "But why? Why would someone kill Agnes Beckett? She lived in a mobile home in a small town. She didn't have any valuables."

"From what I've been able to find out about Beckett, she was the kind of woman who kept her door locked."

"What's that supposed to mean?"

He grimaced. "You're not going to like it."

Her heart began to pound. "Don't hold out on me just because I might not like what you've got to say."

"I went to the bar where she worked."

"McNinch's." She remembered passing the bar the day she'd driven through town. High, brown grass. Torn canopy. The kind of place she would never venture.

"Agnes Beckett worked there as a waitress and barmaid. I spoke with one of the waitresses she worked with. A woman by the name of Dixie McGriff claimed to have known her pretty well."

Addison braced. "What did she tell you?"

"Up until a few years ago, Agnes Beckett was a prostitute."

chapter
9

RANDALL WATCHED THE BLOOD DRAIN FROM HER FACE. Her eyes filled with denial and shock. She sat quietly, her mouth partially open, staring at him as if she were waiting for him to admit the words were all part of a cruel joke. For her sake he wished he could.

"My god." She stood abruptly. "Jesus."

He'd expected the news to shock her, but hadn't foreseen how badly. It had been a long time since he'd cared enough about someone else to worry about what they might be feeling. "Hey, Addison . . ."

Crossing her arms protectively at her chest, she turned away from him. "Are you sure?"

"There's no mistake." He'd never been good at cushioning the truth, he realized, except perhaps for himself.

"A prostitute. Oh, God."

Before he could stop himself, Randall was on his feet. He reached for her and made her face him. "It doesn't mean anything." It was suddenly very important to him to make her believe the news didn't change who she was—or lessen his respect for her in any way.

She raised dark, shimmering eyes to his. "Where did I come from? Who am I?"

"You're the same person you've always been. Those two people who raised you are the ones who shaped your life and made you who you are." Though he believed the words, he realized he had ventured into an area where even the doctors disagreed on whether traits were inherited or learned. "Nothing that happens today or tomorrow can change who you are, who you've always been."

Realizing he was gripping her wrists, he released her. The sudden loss of contact made him acutely aware of how warm her skin was, how badly he'd wanted to touch her. She was standing so close he could smell her hair, that exotic mix of citrus and musk that made him dizzy every time he was near her. It was a crazy thought, but he suddenly wanted to bury his hands in that dark, wild hair, draw her to him, and kiss away the pain in her eyes.

Unaware of the war raging inside him, Addison swept a trembling hand across her forehead and let out a shaky breath. "Where does this leave us, for God's sake? How does this tie in with what happened to her? With what happened to Jim?"

"Jim—this lawyer—do you know if he handled your adoption?" he asked.

"I don't know. There was no mention of an attorney on any of the documents I've seen."

"If he did, then his murder ties in with your adoption."

"But why would he keep something like that from me when he knew I was looking?"

"I think the answer to that question is locked away in a file sealed by adoption and confidentiality laws. A file someone doesn't want you to find." Randall studied her face, liking what he saw, wanting badly to touch her, but knowing it would only lead to disaster. "A file that contains information someone is willing to go to great lengths to keep from coming to light."

"Information worth killing two innocent people for?" she asked.

"Maybe. It looks that way."

"Who?"

He shrugged. "That's what we need to find out."

She pressed her hand against her stomach. "My biological father?"

"That was my initial reaction. We have to take the possibility seriously." The thought of someone wanting to hurt her sent a quiver through his gut. For the first time, he wondered just how wise it was for her to continue this search. She was a decent person who still believed people were basically good. He didn't want to see that belief tarnished. He didn't want to see her hurt. He sure as hell didn't want anything to do with the lofty task of keeping her safe.

The notion that he was starting to care about what happened to her made him want to pull back and recoup. Even as he felt himself spiraling toward her, drawn by the most fundamental of needs, another side of him struggled for distance. Caring for a woman in Denver was dangerous business when he would be moving back to D.C. in a few short weeks. Especially when her eyes knocked him for a loop every time she looked at him.

Randall had always prided himself on his ability to keep his male instincts in check. So what if he was attracted to her? He could handle his hormones. He wasn't the kind of man a woman like Addison Fox would consider a relationship with, anyway. He didn't have relationships. He didn't get emotionally involved. Certainly not with a woman who did most of her thinking with her heart.

Unless, of course, it was just sex.

"Sit down," he said. "We need to talk."

Her eyes swept to his, and she studied him from beneath long lashes. "Look, Talbot, if you're trying to bow out gracefully, now is the time. I don't need you to finish this."

He guided her to the loveseat. "I hate to undermine that unscrupulous image you've drawn of me, but I'm not going anywhere until this is finished."

Lowering herself to the cushion, she drew her legs beneath her and curled like a cat. "I can't afford you indefinitely."

"I'll work for expenses." The words tumbled out before he could stop them. Damaging words his brother would probably kill him for later. But it didn't take a rocket scientist to figure out that money had absolutely nothing to do with his reasons for wanting to help her.

"Can you find the person responsible for this?" she asked.

"I can try. But I'll need your cooperation. Do you think you can handle that?"

"Coming from you, I'm sure that's a trick question."

"You'll have to agree to my terms."

"What terms?"

Randall liked the stubborn set of her mouth and the way she raised her chin every time he pissed her off. He wondered if she could kiss as well as she argued.

Forcing his mind back to the business at hand, he said, "Look, Addison, I'm not sure what you've stumbled into, but it's serious and apparently dangerous. Not only for you, but for the people around you and anyone involved in your adoption. I want you to understand that fully before we delve any more deeply into this."

She seemed to sink more deeply into the cushions. Reaching for a pillow, she hugged it against her. "What terms, Talbot?"

He studied the shadows of fatigue marring the porcelain skin beneath her eyes. She didn't look as though she'd slept much in the last couple of days. He wondered how well she would hold up if things got really rough. "Until I figure out what's going on, I don't want you to be alone. I don't want you staying here alone."

"You're serious?"

He'd expected an argument, and he was prepared. "You can stay with somebody until this is over."

"Just in case you need a reminder, I'm missing some vital parts of the family structure. No siblings. No parents."

"What about friends?" Discomfort flickered in her eyes, and for the first time he realized how very alone she was—and how much that disturbed her.

"My best friend is sixty-two years old with a daughter about to give birth to twins," she said. "Albeit she keeps a double-barrel shotgun next to her bed, I can't ask her to baby-sit me."

"A shotgun?" Had the situation not been so dire, he would have laughed.

"She's from Missouri," she added, as if every grandmother from Missouri wielded enough lead and gunpowder to blast a man in half. "Besides, I plan on taking an active role in this investigation."

"Active role, huh?" His hackles rose. "We're not talking about a purse snatching. We're talking about murder. An active role might just get you killed."

She met his glare in kind. "You're working for me, re-member?"

"I guess that settles it."

"I guess it does."

"You'll have to stay with me."

Indignation flashed in her eyes. "You're pretty sure of yourself, aren't you?"

"You have no idea." He admired her tenacity. It didn't help matters that she was so damn good to look at. He wondered if she had any idea what she was up against or how drastically this could change her life. "Jack and I can take rotating shifts. Those are my terms."

Ignoring the protest in her eyes, he looked around, taking in the room. The apartment possessed the bold character of the fifties modernized by clean, contemporary lines and a touch of feminine clutter. The red plaid loveseat and sofa were separated by an antique chest that served as a coffee table. Above the fireplace, a Matisse abstract flared in red and black and hues of gray. A slightly worn wool rug softened the hardwood floors and gave the entire room a sense of warmth and comfort.

The apartment spoke volumes about her. From the galley-style kitchen with its incessant aromas of coffee and spices to the bathroom with its pink heart soaps and frilly hand towels. It was her home. Her refuge from the world.

A place where she was no longer safe.

"I don't want you at the coffee shop, either." He wondered how in the hell he was going to work the case and keep his eye on her at the same time. He and Jack would just have to work it out.

"I've got a business to run," she said levelly. "I can't just close the shop. I need to be at the shop."

"You'll be closed for the next couple of days, anyway."

"Look, I'm not going to put my life on hold for a suspicion that's unfounded at this point," she tossed back. "We don't even know for sure if this is all connected, much less that he's coming after me."

"He's already come after you at the shop. Beckett is dead. Bernstein is dead. Come on, Ace. You're smart enough to know when you're out of your league."

Her chin went up, but he knew she was about to concede. "I hate this."

"So do I. We've got to deal with it."

"Dammit." She released a frustrated breath. "I'll keep the shop closed for a few days."

"Good girl—"

"But only until my equipment is replaced."

Randall shook his head. He wasn't sure if the reality of her situation—or the inherent dangers of it—had penetrated that stubborn brain of hers yet, but he knew it would. He wanted to make sure he was there for her when it did.

OVER TAKE-OUT FRIED RICE AND EGG ROLLS, ADDISON and Randall sat at her dining room table and pored over the file of papers she'd accumulated while searching for her birth parents. There were legal adoption papers. A copy of her amended birth certificate. Correspondence from Jim Bernstein.

"If Bernstein had additional documents in his office, we'll need to get copies." Randall stretched, revealing his shoulder holster and pistol.

It was as if the gun was an extension of the man, Addison thought. Hard. Dangerous. Studying him, she realized she wasn't quite sure if she was relieved or dismayed that he'd decided to stick around. True, she needed his help. But on the other hand, she didn't like him telling her what to do. She didn't want him stepping into her life and telling her how to run it.

She'd called Gretchen and relayed the news of Jim Bernstein's death. Her efforts not to alarm her friend were in vain. Had it not been for Gretchen's baby-waiting assignment, combined with the fact that her son-in-law was out of town, she would have rushed over like a retired guard dog thrust back into the line of duty. The thought made Addison smile.

"How long will it be before Jack can tell us something?" she asked, shoving her plate aside.

Randall smiled, as if the thought of his brother tapping away on the keyboard amused him. "Computer crimes take time." A dimple appeared on his right cheek when his smile deepened. "He'll be at it all night."

Refusing to let herself be charmed, she rose and collected their plates. Now wasn't the time to start noticing dimples, for God's sake. It was bad enough that she was starting to like his smile.

He followed her to the kitchen, pausing at the door. "Addison."

She looked up from the sink. He was leaning against the doorjamb with his arms crossed at his chest, watching her. Finishing the plate, she faced him, thankful she had the towel to keep her hands busy. What was it about Randall Talbot that had her acting like a nervous cat?

"You mentioned earlier that your parents were killed in a car accident," he said.

Apprehension danced in her chest. "That's right. It happened about ten months ago."

"Did your father or mother know who your biological parents were?"

The implication sliced her like a blade. The thought that followed was unfathomable. She leaned against the counter. "You don't think . . ."

He approached her, placing his hands gently on her upper arms. "We need to talk about that. I need to ask you some questions."

"About the accident?"

He nodded. "How much do you know?"

"Enough." The old pain transformed into something much more terrible. Vaguely, she was aware of the heat of his fingers coming through her sweater. So strong and reassuring. How easy it would be to step forward and fall into his embrace. . . .

"How did it happen?" he asked.

She stared at him, realizing with some discomfort that his dark eyes had seen things she couldn't imagine even in her nightmares. She studied his face, hating it that he was so shuttered, that she couldn't even begin to read him.

She allowed him to guide her into the living room, needing that instant of contact before she uttered the words that curdled like old milk in her stomach. "Their car slid out of control on an icy patch in the road and went down a ravine. They were killed instantly."

"Had you been looking for your birth parents prior to the accident?"

"Not seriously. I dabbled mostly. I was always afraid I would hurt them. . . ." Her chest ached with the thought. "I never wanted them to think it mattered."

He looked uncomfortable for a moment. "I need to look into the accident."

"You don't think it was an accident, do you?" She sank onto the sofa.

"That's what I need to find out."

In all the months since their deaths, Addison had never considered any other scenario. She refused to believe her parents had been murdered. Not until it was proven to her. The consequences were much too painful.

Taking the loveseat opposite her, he gave her a sage look. "I'll drive up tomorrow."

"I'll go with you."

"You'll only slow me down," he said. "Besides, Jack could use some help with the computer. He'll need social security numbers. Birth dates."

Anger snapped through her like a whip. "Don't you dare try to shut me out of this."

"You'll be safer with Jack."

"This is important to me. I need to do this."

"You need to stay alive."

"You work for me. This is my call. My decision. Dammit, I go with you." She hadn't meant for the words to come out so angrily. But she refused to be shut out of something so important, even for the sake of her own safety.

"We had an agreement," he said. "You agreed to abide by my terms."

"I agreed before you told me what you knew. That wasn't fair. I won't abide by that."

"I'm not taking you with me."

"My parents were killed in that ravine, not yours. I'll be damned if I'll let you go up there without me. I deserve to know what happened."

Rising abruptly, Randall started for the door.

Addison watched him, apprehension pumping through her. "Where are you going?" she asked, appalled by the alarm in her voice.

At the kitchen door, he turned to her, hitting her with the full force of his stare. "I'm going to call Jack and ask him to find out what he can about the accident." His lips curled into a dark smile. "You didn't think I was leaving, did you?"

That was exactly what she'd thought, but she'd rather have her fingernails pulled out than admit it.

Punching in the number, he raked her with a blatant once-over that made her want to squirm. "I'll sleep on the sofa tonight."

The image of that long, hard body stretched out on her sofa flashed in her mind. As much as she didn't want to admit it, the image intrigued her. He was such a difficult man, so uncompromising, that she found it hard to imagine him vulnerable in sleep.

Telling herself she was crazy to let her imagination—or her hormones—run amok, Addison turned on her heel and headed for the linen closet. The past week had taken its toll on her emotions and obviously affected her ability to handle stress. Funny how it had affected her libido, she thought, disgusted. She was crazy to be thinking about a man like Randall Talbot in the physical sense. They were about as compatible as water and oil. "More like fire and gasoline," she mumbled as she opened the closet door.

He was standing in front of the fire, looking into the flames, when she returned to the living room lugging a comforter and sheet. She'd purposefully chosen pink, knowing it would grate against that macho facade he wore so well. Without sparing him a glance, she draped the sheet over the sofa and proceeded to tuck the edges into the cushions.

Satisfied with her work, she brushed her hands against her slacks and turned to face him. "I prefer to get an early start, if you don't mind—"

The intensity of his gaze stopped her cold—and told her more about his frame of mind than she wanted to know. He was standing so close she could smell the subtle scent of his aftershave, feel the heat and energy pouring off him. A pleasant alarm trilled through her body. She didn't date much, but knew enough about men to recognize lust when she saw it. The realization shook her all the way down to her toes. Not just because she saw that disconcerting light in his eyes, but because she knew that same light was in her own eyes as well.

His flannel shirt hung open, revealing a well-muscled chest covered with thick black hair. His belly was flat and rippled with muscle. The hair thickened slightly below his navel before disappearing into the waistband of low-rise jeans. Fleetingly, she wondered what that hard flesh would feel like under her fingertips. Was he as dangerous as he looked? Or was he the kind of man who used that hard facade to hide a heart that was every bit as vulnerable as hers?

Disturbed by the thoughts rushing through her, Addison broke eye contact and stepped back. How could she be thinking of that muscular chest when she should be thinking about getting her life back?

His gun was lying on the coffee table looking out of place and menacing next to a crystal votive. She stared at it, wondering which was more dangerous at the moment, man or gun.

Only then did she realize she faced another kind of danger when it came to Randall Talbot. A danger that had nothing to do with masked men or guns—and everything to do with her heart.

"You should follow your instincts sometime, Ace," he said huskily. "Might be interesting for both of us."

"Animals follow their instincts." She met his gaze levelly despite the fact that her cheeks were on fire. "Human beings rely on intelligence."

One side of his mouth curved into an enigmatic smile. "I'll try to remember that next time you look at me that way."

Shaken by his words, by her own reaction to them, Addison turned away and headed for the safety of her bedroom.

chapter
10

THE SNOW-COVERED PEAKS OF THE ROCKIES ROSE UP out of the earth like ancient stone dinosaurs. Juniper, scrub, and bare-branched aspen jutted from the broken ridges, cradling patches of snow in their spindly boughs. The mountains had always been a place of escape for Randall. Even during that terrible last year with the NTSB, he'd made it a point to hike or camp in the mountains every chance he got. He liked to believe it was the tranquility of this endless expanse of rock and sky that had helped him hang on to his sanity as long as he had.

He felt stronger after nearly five months out of the field. Stronger, but not yet fully healed. He wasn't sure if he would ever recover fully. He wasn't sure a man ever came to terms with the kinds of horrors he'd seen.

Still, he knew he had to go back to D.C. And even as the thought sent a quiver of fear through his gut, he felt the pull of its seductive draw and knew it was something he had to do no matter what the cost to him personally. He'd been successful in D.C. A good investigator. Aggressive. Thorough. Tough. A man with integrity who commanded respect. He knew the wide-body jets inside and out. He knew the hydraulic systems, the Pratt and Whitney engines, the Rolls Royces. A pilot himself, he knew firsthand the stringent training programs commercial pilots went through.

But with all the invaluable knowledge and experience came the terrible, intimate knowledge of death that had pushed him so close to the edge. Death that knew no bounds and struck by the hundreds without regard to age or gender or status. He'd been arrogant enough to believe he was immune. But he'd only managed to fool himself. Death had left a permanent imprint on his heart and darkened his soul so that for months he'd felt its power pressing down on him, isolating him until he'd felt so alone he thought he would die. The nightmares had eased since he cut back on his drinking, but sometimes when he smelled smoke or heard an ambulance, the death and devastation came rushing back.

Refusing to think of the past or the shaky state of his future, Randall forced his attention back to the present—and to the young woman beside him. She looked fresh and wholesome and untainted, reminding him of everything he was not—and the countless reasons he ought to stay away from her. He let his eyes skim over her unfettered. Navy blue leggings hugged long, shapely legs. Her oversized sweatshirt sported a University of Colorado logo. The thick wool socks and lace-up hiking boots looked huge on her slender legs. He drank in the subtle outline of her breasts, her graceful neck, the delicate line of her jaw. Even in profile, she looked beautiful. But it was the sight of her full, wet mouth that turned him inside out every time he looked at her.

Lord have mercy, he'd forgotten what it was like to look at a woman and want to lose himself inside her.

He'd tried to talk her into spending the day at his office with Jack, but she refused. No surprise there—she wasn't the most agreeable creature he'd ever dealt with. He'd tried to convince her to meet with Van-Dyne then hole up the rest of the afternoon at Jack's cabin in Golden, but his efforts to sway her had failed. The woman could be downright exasperating when she put her mind to it.

But if he was honest with himself, he would be forced to admit he was glad for her company today. With his thoughts drifting back to D.C. with increasing frequency, he needed the diversion. He supposed she had no way of knowing she turned him into a walking hard-on.

Randall sighed, not happy about the situation. He couldn't remember the last time he'd been with a woman. Not since he'd been in Colorado. Maybe that was the problem; maybe he just needed some good old-fashioned mindless sex. A man's needs could only be shoved aside for so long. A bottle of Chivas Regal only went so far to stanch them. Maybe what he needed was a one-night stand, a moment of unfettered warmth and the release that went with it.

He wasn't buying it.

The last thing he needed in his screwed-up life was an attractive, complicated female in trouble up to her eyebrows. The problem was, he wanted her anyway.

It had taken every bit of self-discipline he could muster not to take her into his arms last night and get a taste of that heart-shaped mouth. Of course, she probably wouldn't have thought that was such a good idea. But he wasn't going to be able to keep his hands off her much longer, even though he knew where that would lead. The moment he touched her, he would not only lose the advantage of distance, but probably end up hurting her as well.

She didn't know about his diagnosis of post-traumatic stress disorder. Randall didn't plan on telling her. He didn't want her to know his life had been turned upside down. That he'd lost his integrity. His self-respect. Or that he'd been flirting with alcoholism for the better part of a year.

The smartest thing to do was to turn the case over to Jack, then haul ass back to Washington before he got tangled up with her. Before she found out what kind of man she was dealing with. When this was all over, she could go back to her coffee shop and find the kind of man she deserved. Someone who didn't have blackouts or spend most of his time thinking about the dead.

"Good thing I came along, Talbot. The way you're daydreaming, you probably wouldn't have been able to find the place without me."

Her voice jerked Randall from his thoughts. "I wasn't daydreaming," he growled.

"Were, too."

He glared at her, annoyed that she looked so damn good and that he couldn't seem to stop noticing. "I was thinking about the case—"

"Bull—"

"And what a pain in the ass you are."

Flipping on the radio, she tuned it to an alternative rock station and gave him a cool look. "Cranky this morning?"

He thought about telling her the real reason why he was feeling so surly, but decided the less she knew about his hormones the better off he'd be. "You'll know it when I feel cranky."

"I'll take that as a warning."

Studying her, he noticed the strain in her smile and realized the banter was a front. Damn. He should have realized this wasn't going to be easy for her. "You didn't have to put yourself through coming up here."

"Careful, Talbot, or you're going to say something nice."

"Don't get your hopes up."

They rode in silence for a moment. Then he asked, "Where did it happen?"

"Near Hoosier Pass, just off of Highway 9."

He looked away from his driving, noticed the pain in her eyes, and a jolt of affection shot through the center of him. "How much do you know about the accident?"

She made a show of brushing a piece of lint from her leggings. "I'd had Mom and Dad over for dinner that evening. I'd just moved into my apartment, and was having a sort of housewarming party. They left a little before midnight."

Her voice was carefully monotone. Randall steeled himself against it, knowing it was her way of hiding her pain. He'd done the same thing too many times himself not to recognize it. Funny how clear things became when they happened to someone else.

"They were almost home," she continued. "My father lost control on a curve. The car went off the road and rolled nearly two hundred feet." She stared straight ahead. Her hands twisted in her lap. "The sheriff's report said runoff from snow in the higher elevations earlier in the day froze after dark. My father hit a patch of ice. They didn't have a chance."

"Who investigated the accident?" he asked.

"The Summit County Sheriff's Department."

"We'll pay them a visit." Remembering his unpleasant encounter with Sheriff McEvoy back in Siloam Springs, he hoped the sheriff of Summit County would be a little more helpful. Damn, he hated small-town law enforcement.

ADDISON LIKED SHERIFF JEFFERSON WHITE THE moment she met him. He was a burly black man in his late forties with intelligent eyes and an undeniable air of competence. He wore a crisp khaki uniform with a chrome badge pinned neatly below his name tag.

"Sorry you had to wait." He extended his hand first to Addison, then to Randall.

"We appreciate your time, Sheriff." Randall removed his P.I. license from his wallet and flashed it at the sheriff. "We'd like to have a look at an accident report for a double fatality last February."

"The files are in my office." White turned and guided them down a narrow hall. "Want some hot coffee?" he asked.

"No."

"I'd love some."

The answers came simultaneously, inducing grins from all three. "It's stale, but hot." White handed a cup to Addison then motioned toward the end office. "Right this way."

The sheriff's workspace was overused and cramped. A large metal desk flanked by boxes faced the door. Addison seated herself in one of the two sled chairs opposite the desk. Randall sat beside her. The sheriff went to the file cabinet. "What were the names of the victims?" he asked.

Addison didn't like the word *victim*. She hated it that her parents, two vivacious, loving people, had been reduced to "the victims." "Patty and Larry Fox," she answered, forcing herself to relax her grip on her purse.

The sheriff flipped through several files. "Ah, here we go."

Addison's palms dampened as he pulled out a file folder with a case number typed in bold letters at the top. It was all that was left. Two lives condensed into a neat file with a typed label.

Settling behind the desk, the sheriff opened the file and gave it a cursory read before handing it to Randall. "Do you mind if I ask why you folks are up here looking at a file that's, what, ten months old?"

"They were my parents," Addison answered quickly.

Sheriff White touched the rim of his hat. "I'm sorry to hear that, ma'am. Tough to lose family."

"Thank you." She was anxious to get her hands on the file. The last time she looked at it, she'd been so overwhelmed with grief that she hadn't paid much attention to the details. She certainly hadn't been looking for evidence of murder.

"This is a beautiful country, but the weather's unpredictable as hell," the sheriff began. "Unfortunately, we have our share of accidents. I investigated this one myself." He pointed to the file. "There are a couple of photos of the vehicle in there. If my memory serves me, I believe the car skidded on a patch of ice. Happened sometime between midnight and two A.M. The driver lost control. Vehicle went off

the road and down a ravine. Rolled a ways before it came
to rest against a tree big enough to stop it."

Randall glanced at the sheriff. "Was there an explosion or
fire?"

"Small engine fire, but it was out by the time we got
there."

"What time was that?"

"Next morning. First light, a bicyclist called our office."

"Was the vehicle recovered?"

The sheriff shook his head. "No way. Two of my deputies
and I had to rappel down just to recover the bodies."

A shiver trembled through Addison at the mention of her
parents' bodies. She hated thinking of them in such ghastly
terms.

"What were the causes of death?" Randall asked.

"Trauma. Autopsy reports are there, too." The sheriff rose
from his desk and reached for the file. "Let me make you a
copy of this. You folks can take it with you." He lumbered
over to a desktop copier that groaned out two copies of each
report.

Randall sent a concerned look to Addison. "Are you all
right?"

"I just want to get this over with." She'd made it over the
first hurdle. She wondered how many more she would have
to leap before the day was over.

The sheriff handed the stapled copies to Randall. "If you
have any more questions or need any more information about
this accident, feel free to give me a call."

"We'll do that."

Ten minutes later, Addison and Randall were back in his
Bronco heading south on Highway 9 toward Hoosier Pass.
In the half hour they'd spent with Sheriff White, the afternoon sky had gone from a crisp, flawless blue to charcoal
gray. Ominous clouds billowed like smoke on the western
horizon.

Addison pored over the accident report, trying to make
sense of the handwriting and abbreviations. "This report lists

icy road conditions and excessive speed as the cause."

Randall glanced over at her.

"My father was a cautious driver," she said. "He didn't speed. Not on a mountain road at night, especially if the roads were icy."

"The roads weren't icy that night. The report says they hit an icy patch."

Frustrated, she looked down at the report. Her eyes skimmed down to the bottom of the page where the sheriff had written a short summary, including another theory that the driver may have fallen asleep at the wheel.

"This isn't right," she said. "There's no way my father fell asleep at the wheel."

"How do you know?"

"For one thing, my mother could talk a hundred miles an hour. She never stopped talking, especially if she had my father captive in the car." The memory made her smile. "Besides, I served coffee after dinner that night. Haitian Bleu, if my memory serves me. My father loved the dark grinds and drank it by the gallon. The man had enough caffeine in his system to keep the city of Denver awake for a week."

"The report says it was late, Addison. Well after midnight."

"My father was a night bird. He was retired and liked to stay up late and sleep late. I'm telling you he wasn't tired when he left my apartment."

"Are you sure he was driving?"

"My mother was blind as a bat at night. She never drove after dark."

For the first time since they'd left the sheriff's office, Randall gave her his full attention. "All the more reason to take a look at the vehicle."

Until now, she'd assumed he was only interested in seeing the scene of the accident, not the vehicle itself. "The car rolled over two hundred feet." She glanced through the passenger window, realizing how physically grueling a trek into a ravine would be. "How are we going to reach it?"

The look he gave her wasn't friendly. "Don't take this personally, Ace, but you're not going with me. You're going to keep that cute little butt of yours in the truck and make sure I make it back in one piece."

The reference to her backside annoyed her, but not nearly as much as him telling her she wasn't going with him into the ravine. "Don't take this personally, tough guy, but I'll damn well go into the ravine with you if I feel it's necessary and I just happen to feel it's necessary."

"Dammit, Addison, I'm not kidding around." He pointed toward the horizon. "There's a front coming in, and I don't want to be here when it dumps two feet of snow. It's great for skiers, but hell on drivers."

She'd been too preoccupied to notice the line of steel gray clouds building in the west. "I'm fully aware of the weather, but I don't see what it has to do with me taking a look at my parents' car."

"If that ravine's as rugged as I think it is, it's going to take me a while to rappel down. I don't need you slowing me down. I want to get in and out as quickly and as safely as possible. Then we've got to get down this mountain before heavy weather sets in. By the looks of those clouds, I'd say we have another couple of hours of decent driving left."

She hated it when he made more sense than she did. Granted, she was no rock climber, but it was going to be difficult to sit back and let him go into that ravine alone.

She was about to concede when he suddenly slowed the Bronco and pulled onto the narrow shoulder. To her right, Addison saw nothing but the tops of aspens and clear mountain air. She'd never been afraid of heights, but the sight of the drop sent a shiver through her.

"What mile marker does it say on the report?" he asked.

She paged through the report and found the mile marker number circled. "Forty feet south of mile marker thirty-five."

"This is it." Not giving her time to protest, he swung open the door and stepped out of the Bronco. "Stay put."

She shot him the best go-to-hell look she could muster.

He grinned and slammed the door.

Too restless to sit in the truck, Addison got out and walked to the rear of the Bronco. "I'm going with you."

Randall removed a nylon rappelling harness, a coil of rope, and a pair of worn leather gloves from the bed. A small disposable camera hung around his neck. But he didn't look like a tourist. He looked fit and determined and very, very capable.

"Shouldn't take me any longer than forty-five minutes to rappel down, take a few pictures, then climb back up." His eyes swept down to hers, looking as dark and dangerous as the approaching storm. "Wait in the truck."

The wind had kicked up to a cutting speed, whistling through the treetops, accentuating the quiet and the fact that they were totally alone. "I've every right to go—"

"Forget it, Ace. The terrain's too rough." He started for the ravine.

He looked like a seasoned rock climber in his faded Levi's, cleated hiking boots, and parka. Addison watched him loop the rope around the base of an aspen, clip it onto his safety harness, and test it with a yank. She couldn't help but notice his well-muscled thighs or the way the harness accentuated his male attributes. With a cavalier wave, he started into the ravine.

Addison waited until he was out of sight before venturing off the shoulder. While she stood shivering in the bitter wind, she noticed a path cut into the trees. Easing closer to the edge of the ravine, she saw the broken trunks and realized the sapling aspen and pine had been clipped close to the ground ten months earlier when her parents' Lincoln had plummeted over the edge.

She tried not to imagine the terror they must have felt in the seconds before their deaths. Had the roll into the ravine killed them? she wondered. Or had they suffered with broken bodies and the brutal elements? Had they died together? Or had one of them been forced to watch the other in the throes of death? They were excruciating questions. Questions that left her heart raw and a new bitterness in the pit of her stomach.

Suddenly Addison knew she couldn't sit in the truck and do nothing. As painful as the thought was, she wanted to see the car. She wanted to touch it. And she desperately needed to know if her parents had been murdered.

Shivering, she edged closer to the drop-off and looked into the ravine. "Fox, you're insane," she said, grasping the nylon rope. Mimicking Randall's form, she began an awkward descent down the steep incline.

She'd only traveled a dozen feet when she realized her mittens hadn't been designed to stand up against the rough surface of a braided nylon rope. By the time she'd traveled fifty feet, a hole had worn into the palm and the rope bit into her skin with the fervor of a hungry rat. By the time she'd traveled a hundred feet, she realized how foolish it had been for her to attempt the climb.

"Admit it, Fox," she said to herself through clenched teeth, "the Neanderthal was right." A branch from a sapling scraped against her face hard enough to open the skin and yank the muffs from her ears.

"Ouch!" She brought her only remaining mitten to her face, cursing when it came away red. Looking up, she spotted her earmuffs hanging from a branch like a cheap Christmas tree ornament. The Bronco was no longer in sight and, to her dismay, the climb back up looked worse than the climb down. "Oh, this is just peachy," she muttered.

Returning her attention to the ravine, she wondered how Randall had managed to get so far ahead of her so quickly. Simple, she thought. He does this all the time. Weekend warrior stuff. If he could do it, she certainly could.

Feeling like a fool, she resumed her descent. Early on, there had been no doubt in her mind that she could make it to the ravine floor. It was just a little hill, after all. But faced with the rugged terrain and rocks the size of Volkswagens, her confidence withered. Her mittens no longer protected her hands and, somehow, she'd lost the bow keeping her hair out of her face. Her arms were beginning to ache and, to her utter horror, her grip seemed to be waning. She considered retreating, but couldn't bring herself to admit defeat—not that she thought she could climb back up. But, dammit, the last thing she wanted was to give Randall the chance to say I told you so.

After fifteen minutes of struggling with the rope, she settled into a rhythm, easing down a couple of feet at a time, sliding her left foot, then her right. Despite the fact that her arms were aching and her legs felt like overcooked spaghetti, she thought she could make it.

With just over thirty feet to go, she took her right hand off the rope to shove the hair out of her eyes. When she reached for the rope, she missed. Adrenaline skittered through her when she felt her other mitten slip off. The last thing she saw was her hiking boots as they went over her head. Then she was tumbling backward.

Tree branches clawed at her face and hair while the heavier trunks punched her in all the wrong places. Something hard and sharp cut into her shoulder as she flipped end over end. She heard branches breaking, heard herself cry out as they bit through her sweatshirt. Then her body went still as suddenly as it had cartwheeled out of control.

The first thing she became aware of was the wind humming through the pines above her, the sound of footsteps, and pain.

"Addison!" Randall's voice pounded into her brain.

She moaned.

"What the bloody hell are you doing?"

She opened her eyes. He crouched over her, his expression as furious as it was concerned. Damp, dark hair fell across his forehead. A grimace tightened his jaw. "Are you hurt?"

"My mitten slipped off," she said, mentally tallying her injuries. It was the rock in the shoulder that had really done her in. Jesus, that hurt. She lifted her hand to her face where the branch had cut her.

"Lie still, dammit!"

"I feel like I hit a land mine."

"What the devil were you thinking?"

"I wasn't." An involuntary groan escaped her as she shifted her weight. "Am I dead?"

"Don't give me any ideas." He leaned close to her, his hands pressing her down. "Hell, I might just leave your ass here for the coyotes."

"Stop talking about my ass, Talbot. You're going to tick me off again." She tried to move, wincing when her knee protested.

"Hold still."

"God, you're a bully. Even when I'm hurt, you can't be nice to me."

"Can you move your toes?"

She closed her eyes against the pain, wiggled first her right and then her left toes. "Yeah."

"What about your fingers?"

"Check." Raising her hand, she looked at her once-perfect nails and groaned. "I broke three nails on just one hand. I don't even want to look at the other one."

"You're lucky you didn't break your neck," he growled.

"You didn't warn me that rappelling was so painful."

"Any pain in your back?"

"No. Just my shoulder. The right one. Jesus, I hate rocks. I should have dodged the rocks. I guess I just wasn't quick enough, huh, Talbot?"

"You have to be smarter than the rock."

"Kick a girl when she's down, why don't you?"

One side of his mouth quirked. Sliding his hands beneath her shoulders, he eased her to a sitting position. "Dizzy?"

"No. My shoulder hurts."

"Lucky you had that sweatshirt on."

"I don't feel very lucky."

"They always say God looks out for idiots and children."

"Stop yelling at me, I've been punished enough." She said the last word through her teeth as the pain in her shoulder clamped down on her like a vise. "Ouch. It hurts."

Without preamble, he lifted the sweatshirt up and over her shoulder. "Lean forward."

Addison obeyed without complaint, wincing only a little when the cold wind whispered over her bare back. Then she felt the warmth of his hand as he probed, and did her best to ignore the tingle of pleasure that followed. "It's getting a little breezy back there, Talbot. What's the prognosis?"

"Nice bra," he commented. "Front closure?"

Despite the pain, she smiled. "Let me know your size and I'll pick one up for you next time I'm at Victoria's Secret."

His laughter echoed through the trees. A rare, pleasant sound that made her stomach feel jittery. "Nothing's broken, but you're going to have one hell of a bruise."

"I'm going to have bruises over ninety percent of my body."

"It's such a shame to mar that lovely back of yours."

His mouth was so close to her ear she could feel the warmth of his breath. Trying to ignore the blood that had climbed into her face, she tugged the sweatshirt down. "I'm really glad I wore my good bra today, Talbot. Had I worn my sports bra you probably would have left me for the coyotes."

"I don't have anything against any form of lingerie, Ace." He rose and extended his hand to her. "But I've always been partial to pink lace."

"I can't see you in pink." Realizing she was still too shaky to rise of her own power, Addison accepted his hand, trying not to wince as he pulled her to her feet.

"That was an incredibly stupid thing to do." He glared down at her with an intensity that made her look away.

"I'm going to have to make time for a manicure now. Think we can squeeze one into our schedule between shootings this week?"

He didn't look amused. He was standing too close again, intimidating her with that nasty scowl and those dark, angry eyes. "I told you to stay in the damn truck. You could have gotten yourself killed."

Addison didn't want to think about death in a place where two people she loved dearly had perished. A powerful shiver went through her. "Think we could waive the lecture?"

He reached out and clamped his hand around her forearm, forcing her around to face him. "You're cut." He raised his hand and touched her cheek. "I've got a first aid kit in the truck."

"I don't think it's deep," she said, looking anywhere but into his eyes. She knew what resided in those murky depths. And it was much more than she wanted to deal with at the moment.

Giving herself a mental shake, she turned her face away from his hand. As if sensing her need for space, Randall released her and stepped away.

"Did you find the car?" she asked.

He pointed to a mass of skeletal vines and saplings. "There," he said with a grimace.

Addison looked past him. Then she was moving, on legs that no longer felt pain, on feet that were beyond cold. The mangled Lincoln was sitting at a sharp angle against an outcropping of rock. The car had once been silver, but ten months of mountain extremes had turned the crumpled metal to rust. As she drew nearer, she noticed the windshield was completely gone, perhaps in the crash, perhaps at the hands of the men who had come down the mountain to remove her parents' bodies.

Hesitantly, she peered through the windshield. The front seat was intact. The once plush leather was badly weathered and covered with dirt and moss. A bird had nested at some point on the dash, leaving a pile of dried grass and twigs atop the cracked vinyl.

Addison reached out and ran her hand over a small area of silver paint that was still as flawless as the day her father had bought the car. For an instant, she felt close to them. The way she felt when she went to the cemetery. When she held her favorite picture of them against her heart.

A vivid burst of memory flashed through her mind. Mom

and Dad at Christmas last year. They'd given her luggage, she remembered. A new espresso maker that matched her kitchen. That ugly-as-sin vase she now treasured. God, how she missed them.

"Addison."

The gentle utterance of her name startled her. She jerked her hand back as if the rusty metal surface had snapped at her. Randall stood next to her, looking at her much too intently.

Slowly, he turned her toward him and took both of her hands in his. "Christ, your hands are like ice. Where are your gloves?"

"I lost them. When I fell." Her voice was high and tight. Too many emotions crowding into her throat. She looked down at their hands. His were strong and warm and far too reassuring as they held hers. It wasn't something she wanted to get used to.

"Let's go, Ace. Your hands are nearly frostbitten."

Addison accepted his gloves without protest.

"Can you climb?"

The thought wasn't a pleasant one, but she couldn't bring herself to wimp out. Not after ignoring his warning to stay in the truck. "Unless someone installs a ski lift in the next five minutes, I don't think I have a choice."

They returned to where Randall had left the rope looped around a tree branch. Spreading her legs, she let him snap the safety harness into place and adjust it to fit her smaller frame. Slowly, mechanically, she began to climb, using the saplings and larger rocks for footholds when she could.

"Randall?" It amazed her how normal, how strong her voice sounded in the midst of such physical and emotional tumult.

From behind her, he answered with an irritated grunt.

"I was wondering . . . about my parents' car. Did you find what you were looking for?"

"Climb. We'll talk about it when we get out of this ravine."

Addison stopped climbing. "Tell me," she said.

He stared up at her, his eyes searching for weaknesses she hoped he wouldn't find. "I couldn't find anything useful," he said. "There was too much rust, too much damage."

"So we wasted our time?"

"Pretty much."

She considered the words for a moment, doing her best to fend off the dull wash of defeat. "I don't know if I'm disappointed or relieved."

"As long as you do it on level ground. Start climbing."

"But—"

"We'll talk more once we get out of this damn ditch."

Addison turned back to her rope. But as she began to climb, something niggled at her. Something about the way he'd looked at her, the way his gaze had skittered away when she'd pressed him. As she heaved her body slowly upward, she wondered if his reaction stemmed from what he'd seen in the ravine—or if that haunted look in his eyes was a result of his own troubled past.

chapter

11

HE ARRIVED AT THE CLIPPER TAVERN IN DENVER'S Brown Palace Hotel just before four P.M. Pushing his way through the tavern doors, he spotted his contact immediately, sitting alone in a booth set against a backdrop of well-dressed couples and businessmen gorging themselves on slow-roasted Colorado prime rib.

He made his way through the crowd, loosening the Hermes tie that had pinched his Adam's apple for the last eighteen hours, trying to ignore the pain that peeked out from behind his right temple.

"Mr. Fagan," he said when he reached the booth. It wasn't the other man's real name, but a pseudonym used for professional purposes. Neither man cared about such details.

Fagan stood. Looking like two businessmen about to negotiate a deal, they shook hands before sliding into opposite sides of the booth. Neither man spoke until the waitress had taken their orders and left their drinks on the table.

Finally, the man in the Hermes tie spoke softly, deceptively, masking the rancor behind the words. "Who the fuck is Jack Talbot?" The name stuck in his throat like a shard of glass, and he washed it down with a gulp of Tanqueray.

Fagan remained impassive, sipping his scotch and water, unaffected. "A private investigator. Mostly divorce cases. Cheating spouse surveillance. A few runaway teens. He's strictly small time. Nothing to worry about."

"I see." He reached into the pocket of his St. Laurent for his bottle of Percodan. Just behind his eyes, the headache lurked, as if waiting for exactly the right moment to clench his brain in a vice grip.

"Our girl hooked up with him after she returned from Ohio," Fagan said.

"This private investigator has become a problem."

"Do you want him eliminated?"

"Of course I do," the man in the Hermes tie snapped.

Fagan looked amused for a moment. "I must say I'm quite taken with this young woman."

The other man tossed back two of the pills and downed them with a gulp of gin. "Did you take care of the lawyer?"

"No longer a problem."

Two down. Two to go. Relief washed over him at the prospect of finishing this dreadful assignment. He only wished it wasn't so damned important—or the stakes so high. "When can you finish up?"

"That depends."

"Depends on what?"

"The private dick has a brother."

The man in the Hermes tie felt a swirl of panic at the thought of yet another person's involvement. Another loose end to deal with. Dammit, there were too many loose ends. The whole fucking mess was like a grass fire that had burned out of control and erupted into a forest fire. "Does he know anything?"

"Probably."

He cursed the man's calm demeanor, knowing the son of a bitch had nothing at stake but money. If life were only so simple. "Eliminate them. All of them. And I don't want any more questions raised."

The other man sipped his scotch. "I'll expect additional compensation."

"I anticipated that."

"Generously, I hope."

"You have three days."

THE SNOW WAS COMING DOWN SIDEWAYS WHEN RANDall clambered out of the ravine. It had started as an occasional flake halfway through the climb. Now, a rise of alarm slid through him at the sight of the thickening white blanket already covering the road.

Addison stood a few feet away, bent at the hip with her hands on her knees. Her breath puffed out in a white cloud with each exhalation. Her hair hung across her face in a brown, unruly mass. A small branch jutted out from behind her right ear like a crooked antenna.

"I knew there was a reason I never took up rock climbing," she panted.

"Stop complaining and I won't tell you I told you so." He still couldn't quite believe she'd followed him into the ravine without a thought as to her own safety. Talk about foolhardy. She could have dislocated her shoulder instead of merely bruising it.

But he had to admire her guts. She'd climbed back up the steep incline without so much as a single complaint. The problem was, it had taken them twice as long. Now they had the damn weather to contend with.

"Shit," he muttered, tramping through the driving snow toward the Bronco. "Let's get out of here."

Addison rushed up beside him, oblivious to the weather or the dangerous drive ahead. "This is why I live in Colorado."

"You recovered quickly." A fact that made him wonder about his own physical conditioning. He was going to have to get back into shape when he got back to D.C.

"I love snow. Isn't it beautiful?"

She looked wholesome and lovely as she lifted her arms skyward. Watching her, Randall felt a sudden, acute longing for something he couldn't put a name to. It stirred deep inside him, like the anticipation of coming home after a long, lonely trip.

"Just don't ask me to help you build a snowman," he growled.

"Don't worry, Talbot, I wouldn't want to send you into a state of panic. God forbid, you might have some fun."

"I hate to rain on your parade, Ace, but in case you haven't noticed, the weather's not getting any better." He glanced up at the treetops where the snow rushed between the branches like a white-water rapid.

A snowball hit him squarely in the back.

Surprised, and a little annoyed, he turned. Addison stood next to the truck with a silly grin on her face.

The logical side of him knew they should get going before the roads got hazardous. But the competitive little boy lurking inside him couldn't resist the opportunity to teach her a lesson.

"Ah, hell," he murmured and scooped up a handful of snow.

Another snowball whizzed by his left ear as he sprinted toward her. Realizing he was retaliating, Addison yelped and sprinted in the opposite direction. But she was no match for him. He caught up with her in a few yards. She spun at the last minute, threw up her hands, and shouted something ridiculous about her bruised shoulder.

Ignoring her protests, Randall threw caution aside and wrapped his arms around her. Their legs tangled. He spun in midair, then brought her down on top of him in an almost gentle tackle. She fell against him, uttering a very unladylike curse. Her laughter rose over the wind, filling the air around them with the sound of simple human joy. Her hair cascaded onto his face, tickling his nose and momentarily blinding him. She stared down at him and giggled.

"Didn't anybody ever tell you throwing snowballs is dangerous business?" he growled.

"You're just jealous because you got your butt kicked."

He was keenly aware of her body against his. His response was instinctive, spontaneous, and swift. Cupping the back of her head, he pulled her down to him and crushed her mouth to his.

Pleasure crashed through him at the initial taste of her. Soft. Sweet. Forbidden. Her scent surrounded him like a dizzying fog. Stark need pierced him, consuming him, blocking out the wind and the snow so that the only thing he was aware of was the woman he held in his arms.

She stiffened slightly, but he didn't stop. He couldn't stop. She was everything he'd imagined, only better. She smelled like heaven and tasted like a dream. Deepening the kiss, he parted her lips and explored with his tongue in an erotic dance that made his blood boil. Her hesitation stirred him. The sweetness of her kiss devastated him. He drank it in until his body was aching for more.

As quickly as the insanity descended, it lifted. Addison broke the kiss with a clever turn of her head. Disappointment speared through him. He blinked, stunned by the power of the sensations coursing through him.

Abruptly, she drew back so that she was sitting on top of him, and stared down at him as if suddenly realizing what had happened. "Pretty silly of us to be rolling around on the ground with a dangerous snowstorm moving in," she said breathlessly.

"That'll teach you to throw snowballs."

"Maybe you should duck next time." She tried to rise, but Randall stopped her.

"Is there going to be a next time?"

Her gaze skittered away, and he released her. Slowly, she got to her feet. "I don't know," she said. "You keep surprising me."

From her guarded expression, he couldn't tell where he stood with her. Christ, he wasn't even sure why he'd let that happen. All he did know was that in thirty-eight years, no other woman had ever moved him the way Addison did. The kiss had reached into him and touched something vital deep inside him. Something he'd thought was long dead. Something he wasn't sure he wanted resurrected.

Struggling to his feet, Randall brushed the snow from his parka, keenly aware that he was fully aroused. His pulse pounded, and he tasted frustration at the back of his throat. Out of the corner of his eye, he watched Addison shake the snow from her coat.

"I'm not sure why I let you kiss me," she said.

"I didn't exactly ask for permission."

Her cheeks were flushed with color when she looked at him. Her damp hair fell in wisps around her face. He'd never seen a woman look so beautiful—or seem so far out of reach.

"Maybe a snowball fight wasn't such a good idea," she said when they reached the truck.

"Fun, though."

"I don't want it to . . . change anything."

"We've got a more pressing issue to deal with." He nearly smiled when her eyes widened. Damn, she was refreshing. "The weather," he clarified.

"Oh. Right."

Snow covered the windshield. Randall felt a quiver of alarm go through him as he opened the driver's-side door and ushered her inside. "If the wind picks up, we may not have visibility at all in another hour."

Casting him a startled look over her shoulder, she slid across the seat to the passenger side. "We've got to get back to Denver."

"Unless you've got a set of tire chains in your purse, we may not make it."

"Very funny."

He started the engine. "That wasn't a joke."

"This is a four-wheel-drive, right? We'll take it slow—"

"There are a couple of motels off the interstate," he said.

She shot him a look that made him smile despite the circumstances. "Like we're going to find a vacancy this close to Christmas."

"You got a better idea?"

"I'm thinking."

"While you're thinking, we're getting snowed in."

"We're *not* getting snowed in. I can't get snowed in. Van-Dyne told me not to leave town."

He raised his hands in defense. "You're the one who insisted on coming down the side of the mountain like an extreme rock climber."

"You were shutting me out."

"I was using my common sense, which is more than I can say for you." He grimaced at the snow. "We'll have to find a motel. There are some truckers' motels—"

"Listen, Talbot, I don't know what kind of a testosterone-induced scheme you've concocted in that so-called mind of yours, but I'll be damned if I'm going to sit up here on this mountain with you for the rest of the night."

"You think I planned this?" he asked, incredulous.

Crossing her arms in front of her, she leaned against the seat. "After the way you kissed me a few minutes ago, I wouldn't put it past you."

He was starting to get annoyed. Not because she was wrong—but because she was right. "I'll let you know if and when I want to sleep with you."

She shot him a killing look, then turned her attention to the windshield where the wipers waged a losing war against the snow.

Even in profile, he saw the worry leak into her features, like a dark stain marring the flawless surface of a fine piece of porcelain. Reaching out, he plucked the branch from her hair. "We'll try to get back. If we can't make it, we'll find something along the interstate. There's got to be something off of Interstate 70. Maybe a truck stop."

"My parents lived just south of here, near Alma."

Randall contemplated her, realizing why she'd waited until now to mention it. "Are you up to spending the night there?"

The wind whistled around the truck with such force it trembled. The trees on either side of the road were barely visible through what was quickly becoming blizzard conditions.

Casting a dubious glance beyond the window, she nodded. "I don't think we have a choice."

THE HOME WHERE PATTY AND LARRY FOX HAD ONCE lived was a custom-built log cabin nestled in a pine forest at the end of a winding gravel drive. Randall rammed the transmission into four-wheel-drive and started up the steep incline, cursing Mother Nature when the vehicle slid too close to a stand of trees before the tires grabbed.

He chided himself for not telling Addison the truth about what he'd found in that ravine. But they'd had a grueling climb to make, and he hadn't been sure how she would react, so he'd put it off. He'd planned on breaking the news to her once they reached the summit. Then she'd gone and tossed that snowball at him like some kind of a kid. She'd looked incredibly beautiful and . . . undamaged, laughing and playing in the snow. Then, like the idiot he was, he'd gone off the deep end and kissed her.

"Shit," he muttered.

"What?"

He parked the truck in front of the garage and shut down the engine. Snow swirled crazily around them, pinging against the windshield.

Randall glanced over at Addison and felt a tinge of guilt. It had been wrong of him not to tell her; he couldn't put it off any longer. He wasn't going to enjoy hurting her, but she deserved to know the truth about what had happened to her parents regardless of how much it was going to hurt her, regardless of how much it was going to change this case.

She reached for the door handle, but he stopped her with a light touch on her arm. "Hold it," he said.

She shot him a wary look. "Okay, Talbot, you've got my attention. Why are you looking at me that way?"

"Your parents' car didn't spin out on ice, Addison."

"But you said—"

"Someone forced them off the road."

Her mouth opened, but she didn't make a sound. He watched a myriad of emotions scroll across her features. Disbelief. Denial. Profound sadness. Then a flash of anger. "I asked you back there. Dammit, why didn't you—"

"I didn't want to tell you while we were down in that ravine."

"Why the hell not?"

"I didn't want to take a chance on you falling apart on me."

She choked out a laugh. "Yes, the helpless female. Christ, you would think that, wouldn't you?"

"That's not what I thought. But with bad weather moving in, I didn't want to spend any more time down there than we had to. I know this is an emotional issue for you. I figured you might want to . . . talk about it."

"So you kissed me instead."

He ground his teeth. "I didn't plan for that to happen. It just . . . did." Oh, that was just brilliant, he thought sourly. When she remained silent, he added. "I made a judgment call."

"God." Turning away from him, she stared out the window at the snow piling up on the windshield. "Are you telling me someone killed them?"

"I don't know for sure, but it looks that way."

"Oh, God." She sighed. "How do you know?"

Randall scrubbed a hand over his face, refusing to acknowledge that he felt like a bastard for having to be the one to tell her that. "Let's get inside and we'll talk."

She didn't respond, didn't look at him.

"Addison?"

She cast him a cool look, her eyes contrasting darkly against her porcelain complexion.

"You got a key?" he prodded.

With a nod, she picked up her purse and began fumbling inside. Randall watched her, and he hated seeing her look so incredibly sad. On impulse, he reached out and touched her lightly on the arm. "We can try the interstate if you're not up to staying here."

"I'm up to it."

She wasn't happy with him and it showed. But even unhappy and angry, she was still utterly lovely. He resisted the sudden, overwhelming urge to touch her. To skim his fingers over her velvet cheek. Touch that lush mouth. First with his fingertips. Then with his lips.

Reining in his thoughts, he reminded himself that women like Addison Fox didn't fall for men like him. How would she react if she knew about his post-traumatic stress disorder? If she knew he'd botched a decent career because he hadn't been able to hack it and spent the last six months consoling himself with his bottle of bourbon? How would she react if she knew the thought of going back to his job in D.C. sent shivers of fear up his spine?

The last thing Addison needed in her life was a man like him. Hell, the last thing *he* needed was a woman in trouble. He had enough problems just taking care of himself these days. But Christ, she looked good sitting there, looking wild and inviting and vulnerable all at once.

"Let's go." Tearing himself away from her, away from thoughts that would do nothing but bring him grief, he opened the door.

The snow was driving hard, coming in from the west like a frozen tidal wave. Visibility was down to zero, and Randall knew they'd made the right decision by stopping. They wouldn't have made it to Interstate 70, just twenty miles to the north.

Keeping Addison in sight, he jogged toward the front door. She came up beside him a moment later, out of breath,

snow sticking to her hair and clothes like confetti. Without
speaking, she jabbed the key into the lock, twisted, and
swung open the door.

The cabin was small, yet designed with a flair that was
distinctly Colorado. The first thing Randall noticed was the
three-way stone fireplace that dominated the living room. It
was constructed of river rock and jutted from pine flooring
and ran all the way to the rough-hewn beams of the vaulted
ceiling.

"Colorado stonemasons don't mess around," he said in ad-
miration.

The living area was huge and largely bare. Most of the
furniture had been draped with sheets. A camelback sofa
faced the fireplace. Next to it, a heavy pine end table bore a
single, oversized lamp.

The place smelled of old pine and mothballs. But the most
pressing issue was the temperature. It was above freezing,
but barely. "Where's the furnace?" he asked, rubbing his
gloveless hands together in a futile attempt to warm them.

When Addison didn't answer, he turned to find her at the
double set of French doors overlooking the cedar deck. Beyond the wall of snow, he knew, were thousands of trees and
a spectacular view of Hoosier Pass. Concern inched through
him. Her hands were knotted in front of her, her shoulders
set and rigid. For the first time he realized just how difficult
coming here was for her.

"Are you all right?" he asked.

She nodded, but her eyes were wistful. "My mom always
loved snow. They loved this place. This house was their
dream, and they worked their entire lives for it. I hate it that
they're not here to enjoy it."

Awkwardness crept over him. He was a whiz at partaking
in an occasional argument, but light-years out of his element
when it came to dealing with emotions, particularly the female variety.

She continued to stare out into the blinding snow. "I've
only been here a couple of times since they died. I thought

it would be easier this time. I mean, it's been ten months."

He watched her from across the room, reading her as best he could, not knowing what to say or how to comfort. "Pain is a part of life, Addison. But so is healing. It takes time."

"I can't believe how quickly the months have passed. It seems like just yesterday when . . ."

Slowly, cautiously, Randall came up behind her and placed his hands on her shoulders. He felt the tremors rising up inside her. He wasn't sure if it was from the cold or the grief or, perhaps, a combination of both. "We didn't have to come here."

"Yes, we did." Shaking off his hands, she turned to face him. "I did."

"It's okay for you to grieve."

"I can deal with the grieving."

"Can you?"

"Yes." For the first time he noticed the anger smoldering in the depths of her eyes, crowding out the grief. "What I can't deal with is that they were taken from me. That somebody murdered them. My parents. They were good people. How could someone just wipe out their lives?"

For her sake, he wished he could dispute the truth. He wished he could tell her that Patty and Larry Fox hadn't been murdered. But he couldn't. He might be able to lie to himself, but he couldn't lie to Addison. He'd never been able to lie to someone he cared about, and he'd always been able to live with himself because of it.

Her tears came in a flood and with the same violence as the storm raging outside. Turning away from him, she slammed her open palm against the door. "Damn!" Her shoulders began to shake.

Something akin to panic swirled in his chest. He didn't know how to deal with tears. His instincts told him to walk away. But with Addison, he knew he couldn't. He wanted to comfort, to protect, though he wasn't quite sure how to approach this angry, hurting woman. The only thing he was certain of was that he wanted to wrap his arms around her and hold her and make her pain go away.

Cautiously, he reached for her, feeling her stiffen an instant before he turned her to him and pulled her close. His arms went around her. Her head fell against his shoulder. The clean, sweet scent of her filled his nostrils and titillated his senses.

When her arms went around his waist, he closed his eyes, rested his head against hers, and forgot about everything except the moment between them. She felt like heaven against him. Soft and small and . . . precious. He was acutely aware of her warmth, her scent, the way her body conformed to his with such utter perfection.

"Go ahead and cry if you need to," he said.

"I didn't want to lose it like this." She sniffed. "I hate crying."

"You're entitled."

"I didn't realize how hard this would be."

"You don't have to hold it in. Not for me. Not for yourself."

A sigh shuddered out of her. "Thank you."

"As long as you realize I'm a little out of my element here."

She choked out a laugh. "You're doing a good job. The hug is a nice touch."

Uncomfortable, he shrugged, wishing she'd stop looking so damn sad. "We need to talk about what we found today."

"And what we're going to do about it." She gazed up at him, tears glittering in her eyes.

He stared at her, willing himself not to want her when she was at her most vulnerable. Lust, he thought, shifting from one foot to the other to accommodate the ache in his groin. It's just lust.

Damn, lust had never done this to him before.

Giving himself a mental shake, Randall reminded himself

that she wasn't the only one who was vulnerable at the moment. His life wasn't exactly in order. He couldn't let himself get tangled up with a woman and spend the next year pining for her from D.C.

chapter
12

"I FOUND SOUP!" BENT OVER A LARGE CORRUGATED moving box, Addison snatched up the can and waved it.

"What kind?"

She looked up and spotted Randall stacking the last of the firewood next to the hearth. "No label." Twisting the manual can opener, she walked into the living room and sniffed the open can. "Chicken noodle, I think."

He grinned. "I was hoping for alphabet soup."

"Sorry." It wasn't easy rummaging through the boxes she'd packed at the height of her grief. Her heart clenched each time she ran across an item that stirred even the smallest of memories. The wicker napkin holder she and her mother had bought at a nearby antique shop. The electronic chess set that had kept her father entranced for hours while she and her mother had cried buckets over *Titanic*.

Shaking off the memories, she looked up to see Randall pull an old cast-iron skillet out of a box. He hit her with a devastating grin. "Will this do?"

Unable to keep herself from it, she grinned back. "Perfect."

Despite the mussed black hair and five o'clock shadow, he looked almost domesticated standing there in his jeans, T-shirt, and gray flannel shirt. He was too damn handsome for his own good, she decided. Granted, a little rough around the edges. Edges could be smoothed with just the right touch.

Knowing they were dangerous thoughts leaping through her mind, she carried the soup to the hearth, with its furiously burning fire, where Randall was digging through another box.

"Some spoons would be nice," he said, setting a toaster aside.

"Or we could just slurp."

They spotted the unopened bottle of cognac simultaneously. Randall froze, staring at it. His hands gripped the sides of the box so tightly his knuckles turned white. Several seconds passed before he moved. He reached for the toaster, set it back inside the box, and closed the flaps.

Addison's heart skipped a beat as the significance of his reaction dawned on her. He'd wanted a drink, she realized, wanted it badly. And a pang of concern for him tightened her chest.

"I think I saw a package of plastic spoons in the kitchen drawer," she said quickly.

His gaze swept to hers, and a silent understanding passed between them.

"You okay?" she asked.

"Yeah." He looked away. "I'm fine."

"I'm glad." She smiled, then went to get the spoons.

She returned to find the skillet full of steaming soup. He'd arranged napkins and two mismatched glasses on the coffee table. The setup couldn't have looked more appealing. They'd gone most of the day without food. After the grueling trek into the ravine, she was famished.

They sat on the floor with the coffee table between them.

Addison hadn't let herself think too much about what had happened to her parents. But now, having set her emotions aside, a hundred questions rushed at her like daggers. Questions about her parents' deaths and how that was going to change the case. Questions about the dark mystery she faced back in Denver. And questions about the troubled man sitting across from her.

"You're quiet."

She looked up to find him studying her intently. "I'm still grappling with what happened to Mom and Dad. I never would have imagined . . . murder." She didn't like the way the word felt on her tongue. The ugliness of it aggravated the slowly healing wound in her heart.

He stopped eating and watched her carefully from across the small table. "I'm sorry it worked out this way. And I'm sorry you have to go through this."

"It's okay. I needed to know the truth." She ate some of the soup, but her mind wasn't on eating. "What exactly did you see down in that ravine that makes you think someone forced their car off the road?"

"There was white paint on the bumper and on the left rear quarter panel," he said. "Had I not been looking specifically for that, I would have missed it, just as Sheriff White had."

"The paint was from another vehicle?"

He nodded. "I took some photos and scraped off a paint sample to take back to Van-Dyne for the lab. I'm going to try to get the Denver PD interested in this case."

"Isn't this out of Denver's jurisdiction?"

"Yeah, but you're not. Neither is Bernstein's case."

She bit her lip, struggling to put aside the uneasiness slicing through her. It still hadn't quite sunk in that someone had murdered her parents. That the same murderer had shot Jim Bernstein. Or that the same someone might be trying to kill her. The notion was so outrageous her mind just couldn't absorb it.

"I need to know why," she said. "I can't accept any of this until I know who's responsible and why."

"My guess is that someone doesn't want you to know your birth parents."

His words ricocheted around inside her head like a stray bullet, shattering the illusions of safety and security she'd held her entire life. Simultaneously, a new and infinitely terrible thought engulfed her. "Do you think they've also murdered my birth father?"

"It's possible—"

"He could be in danger."

"My priority right now is to keep you safe."

"My god, we have to find him. We have to warn him—"

"If anyone can find him, Jack can," Randall cut in. "Trust me. He's good at what he does."

Half-heartedly, Addison picked at the soup. "So, we're relatively certain whoever killed my parents is the same person who murdered Agnes Beckett and Jim Bernstein," she said, thinking out loud.

"And tried to kill you at your coffee shop," Randall reminded her.

"The common link is my adoption."

"That's the only connection I can see."

"Why now?" The next thought struck her like a blow. "Oh, my god."

Randall's eyes narrowed. "What is it?"

"I keep trying to think of an impetus. Why this happened now." She looked at him, felt the pain and guilt slinking through her like a fast-growing cancer. "My search. I'd just begun when my parents were killed. Oh, God. Oh, Randall, you don't think—"

"This isn't your fault."

"If I hadn't started searching for my birth parents, maybe none of this would have happened." The words were too ugly, too horrible to comprehend. It was bad enough losing her parents. But to know they had been murdered in cold blood because of something she may have done was infinitely worse.

"Don't go there," he said firmly.

"Four lives snuffed out in cold blood because of—"

"Goddammit, don't do this to yourself."

She stared at him, stricken.

"It's not your fault," he said fiercely.

Addison looked down at the soup, realized her appetite had vanished. "Why would somebody go to such lengths? What could they possibly have to gain? I don't understand."

"That's the ten-thousand-dollar question." Setting his spoon aside, he slid the skillet in her direction. "Eat. While it's still hot. Then I'm going to see to that cut on your face."

She ignored the soup. "My parents were decent, hardworking people. They never hurt anyone. They didn't have enemies."

"This wasn't personal, Addison." He spoke softly, as if expecting her to shatter if he said the words too harshly.

She wondered if he'd stick around to pick up the pieces if she did.

"I need to know why, Randall. I can't rest until I know why this happened. I can't accept it. I won't—"

"All right," he said. "Maybe your mom and dad knew who your birth parents were. Maybe someone didn't want that information getting out." He contemplated her from across the table. "After a baby is put up for adoption, sometimes the adoptive parents are allowed to meet the birth mother. It depends on the agency involved and, of course, mutual consent. But it happens."

She mulled over the possibility that her parents had met with Agnes Beckett all those years ago. She wondered what seeing a tiny, unwanted newborn had been like for them, if they'd loved her instantly, if they'd been anxious and afraid about taking her home.

She wondered if they'd been murdered for the knowledge they'd possessed.

"You've done your homework," she said.

"Crash course on the Internet." He paused. "Did your father know Jim Bernstein back then?"

"They went to college together." The connection tightened, solidified in her mind. "You think Jim handled the adoption?"

"I'll bet the farm he did."

"There's got to be a paper trail."

"If there is, we'll find it."

Addison stared at him, fear and outrage taking turns punching her. "I hate this. I hate not knowing who or why. I need to know who's behind this. And I need to know why. I want them to pay."

"Don't get impatient on me, Ace."

A sudden gust of wind hammered against the windows, driving the snow against the glass so hard it sounded like tiny stones. She started, looked uneasily over her shoulder.

"We're safe here," Randall said.

Embarrassed by her reaction, she turned back to him.

He held her gaze, his eyes dark with concern. "I won't let anything happen to you."

"I know," she said, trying to ignore the fear and frustration pumping through her. "What do we do next?"

"Our first priority is to keep you safe." He slid the first aid kit onto the table between them and opened it. "That means you're going to have to listen to me." When she started to protest, he raised a silencing hand. "You're going to have to trust me. If I tell you to pack your bags and check into a hotel for a few days, you're going to do it without question. If I tell you to stay with Jack or me for a few days, you're going to do it. No arguments. No questions."

"That's not going to help us find the person responsible."

"It'll keep you alive."

"You're hedging. You haven't told me our game plan. What we do next. How I can help."

His eyes hardened to cold steel, telling her in no uncertain terms that he was the one in charge. "Trust runs both ways, Addison. I have to be able to trust you. I have to know you're not going to do something stupid in an attempt to nail this guy."

"Oh, for Pete's sake, I'm not going to do anything to jeopardize—"

"You're letting your emotions do your thinking."

Frustrated and angry, she started to rise, but he reached out and stopped her. "Getting to the bottom of this is going to take some time. Don't get impatient on me."

She glared at him. "Don't hold out on me."

"That works both ways."

She sank back to the floor.

Randall withdrew a tube of antibiotic ointment from the kit and came around the coffee table to kneel in front of her. "Jack's working on gaining access to your adoption records." He squeezed a small amount onto his finger. "If we can get the file Bernstein was holding on you released without going through the courts, that might help. In the meantime, you're going to have to lie low."

"What about my shop?" she asked, a sudden, wrenching jolt of despair spearing through her.

"Hold still." Leaning close to her, he spread the ointment gently over the cut on her cheek. "That branch cut you pretty good. Does it hurt?"

She made a sound of frustration. "I need to be at the shop. It's my livelihood. It's not like I'm independently wealthy."

"Someone has declared open season on you," he snapped. "You're a sitting duck at the shop and you know it."

Dread lay heavy in the pit of her stomach at the thought of how drastically her life was going to change. The worst of it was that it was out of her control, and she was powerless to stop it.

Needing to move, to expel some of the negative energy winding up inside her, Addison rose and began to pace. Her shoulder was beginning to ache dully, its intensity matched only by the ointment stinging the side of her face. "Damn," she said as much from the pain as from the frustration billowing through her. "I can't stand not being in control of my own life. I can't stand it that somebody else is calling all the shots."

Randall rose and crossed to her. "The coming days aren't going to be easy. But if we play our cards smart, we'll win this. We'll finish it."

"How can you have so much faith?" she said angrily. "Someone could simply run us off the road tomorrow and no one would ever know it wasn't an accident. Just like my parents."

"That's not going to happen," he said fiercely.

"If someone wants me dead, how can you—"

"They're going to have to go through me to get to you."

In that instant, something shifted between them. No longer was he the indifferent private detective. No longer was she merely a paying client. In the span of a second, he'd transformed into a man and she into a woman with emotions and needs they had recognized and unwittingly acknowledged in each other's presence.

"I believe you," she whispered.

The flickering yellow light from the fire softened the hard angles of his face, easing the rigid set of the mouth that had kissed her so thoroughly just a few hours earlier. The harshness in his eyes had been replaced with something more elusive and much more unnerving. It was desire she saw flaring, as bright and hot as the fire, and she silently cursed herself for acknowledging it.

Randall moved toward her, reaching out. She jumped when his fingers encircled her upper arms. She wanted to stop what was about to happen. A tiny voice in the back of her mind urged her to put a stop to the insanity, to back away and try to forget that he was the only man she'd ever met with the power to make her heart pound.

But Addison held her ground, all the while her body vibrated with anticipation. She sighed when he pulled her against him. Her arms went around his neck. A shiver swept the length of her when her breasts brushed against the hard planes of his chest. The heat of his breath whispered against her cheek. The scent of his aftershave titillated her senses. Tilting her head, she searched out his gaze, found it locked on hers with an intensity that made her knees go weak.

She murmured his name, wondering in the back of her mind where all of this was going to lead. She wanted to close her eyes, to give herself over to this man who besieged her senses and shattered her resolve.

Before she could take a breath, his mouth swooped down and covered hers. One of his hands went to the back of her head and he deepened the kiss. His teeth clicked against hers. She opened to him, tasted male heat and desire, felt it intoxicate her like a drug. She accepted his tongue, offering her own. Arousal trembled through her. She closed her eyes, shaken by its fierce power, and kissed him back with an urgency that came from a place inside her she'd never dared to explore.

RANDALL COULD BARELY HEAR THE STORM OUTSIDE over the blood pounding in his ears. It pooled in his groin, making him ache with an urgency that verged on insanity. He wanted this woman with an intensity he'd never experienced.

He wasn't exactly sure when it had happened, but he definitely wasn't in control of the situation any longer. Perhaps he'd only been fooling himself to think he'd ever been.

He marveled at the way her body fit so perfectly against his. He was aware of her arms around his neck, her breasts against his chest, her ragged breaths in his ear. He wanted her closer, wanted her beneath him. He wanted to get inside her. The need drove into him like the sharply honed tip of a sword. And he knew he would sell his soul for the opportunity to lose himself inside that pretty body of hers.

But the timing couldn't have been worse. She was his responsibility now whether he wanted it or not. Until he figured out who was trying to kill her, he couldn't risk letting his guard down. Neither of them could afford to become personally involved at a time when they were both at their most vulnerable. That she had no idea just how screwed up his life was didn't help matters. He hadn't told her about his post-traumatic stress disorder. He hadn't told her he would be leaving for D.C. in a few weeks. Or that he was pretty sure he was an alcoholic.

The impossibility of the situation struck him hard. He told himself it didn't matter. They had tonight. A few hours. He wanted sex, not a vow of love. But something inside him didn't want to settle for that with Addison. With some surprise, he realized he respected her too much to use her.

Blowing out a sigh of frustration, Randall broke the kiss and held her at arm's length while his vision cleared. She stared at him, her dilated pupils and the color in her cheeks clearly revealing that the kiss had shaken her as thoroughly as it had him.

For a split second, he was tempted to scoop her into his arms and take her right there on the floor, his conscience be damned. Fleetingly, he imagined what she might feel like beneath him. Soft. Warm. He wondered how her nipples would feel against his palms. He wondered if the kiss had aroused her, if she was wet between her legs.

His body wanted sex, hungered for it. But his intellectual side knew he owed her more than just the release of an orgasm. He wasn't sure why he felt that way. His conscience had never bothered him before when it came to women. But he supposed he'd never met a woman like Addison Fox.

"We need to talk." His hands were shaking, and he couldn't seem to catch his breath.

"That's funny coming from you at a moment like this."

He tried to smile, but the need hammering through him wouldn't allow it. Unsettled, he raised his hands and cupped her face. "You don't know me, Addison. I'm not the man you think I am."

"You're not going to make some kind of a bizarre confession, are you, Talbot?"

"I'm trying to talk you out of making a mistake."

Her eyes grew cautious. "Define mistake."

"Sleeping with me." The words made him grimace. "I'll only end up hurting you."

"I'm a grown woman. I know what I'm doing."

"You're vulnerable."

"Maybe I'm not the only one who's vulnerable," she said gently.

He wanted to laugh it off, but her words had hit close to home. He didn't want to want her. But, God help him, he wasn't a good enough man to walk away.

Sliding his hands through her hair, he marveled at the silky feel of it against his palms. He wanted to kiss her. The need was like a wild animal trapped inside him, clawing him, tearing him up inside. But the cold reality of his situation refused to leave him alone.

Goddammit, he didn't want to be in this position.

Placing his hands on either side of her face, he rested his forehead against hers and closed his eyes. "I've got something to tell you."

Addison pulled back slightly and gazed steadily at him, her expression perplexed and very serious. "Okay. I'm a good listener."

Randall had known this moment would come. He should have been prepared, but he wasn't. He told himself it didn't matter what she thought of him—he would be gone in a few weeks. But he knew better. Her opinion of him mattered. Mattered a hell of a lot more than he wanted it to.

"Sit down," he said.

Watching him, she sank to a sitting position and leaned against the front of the sofa. Randall sat down beside her and draped his arm around her shoulders. He hadn't realized how difficult this was going to be. The old pain was like a rock in his chest.

"Jack told you I worked for the National Transportation Safety Board, didn't he?"

She nodded.

"For the last twelve years, I've been a crash site investigator. I worked my way through the ranks. I was good at it.

Damn good." He hesitated, uncertain, hating what he was about to say next, hating that the words made him feel so damn vulnerable. "Five months ago I was diagnosed with post-traumatic stress disorder."

She gazed at him, unfazed. "I know of the disorder. One of my regulars at the shop is a Vietnam vet. He's the vice president of an architecture firm two blocks over."

"It's a common affliction for soldiers who've seen action."

"I can't imagine the horror of a plane crash."

"I always thought I was immune." He let out a self-deprecating laugh. "That's why I was so good at what I did. I didn't get shaken up like most people. I didn't puke on my shoes, or have nightmares. I was too damn arrogant to even consider the possibility that I wasn't strong enough to handle the job."

"The disorder doesn't have anything to do with strength."

"Maybe. Maybe you're right. I don't know." He paused, grimaced. "For five years I denied the symptoms. I refused to see them, even though deep down inside I knew something was wrong. I told myself I was just burned out. Tired. I took some time off. Came here, to the mountains, and went camping with Jack. I started drinking. But it didn't help. Then last year, I got assigned the Allegiance Air crash in Minneapolis."

"My god. I remember it," she said. "Over two hundred—"

"Two hundred and fourteen men, women, and children." He gazed into the fire, remembering. God, how he hated remembering. It never ceased to amaze him how his mind could conjure up smells and sights and sounds and terrify him all over again.

"My team and I worked the first twenty-four hours around the clock. Not unusual for a crash like that, but I was tired. It was cold as hell. Rain coming down in sheets. I was hung over. I just stood there looking at what was left of that jet, of people's lives. Bodies. Toys. Jesus Christ." He broke off, felt the cold sweat on his neck, his heart racing in his chest. Clenching his jaw, he forced himself to continue. "After thirty-six hours, I fucking lost it. I broke down in front of my team. I sank down in the mud and cried like a goddamn baby."

"Oh, Randall—"

"That was the beginning of the end. After that, I merely went through the motions. I drank every day. I lost my integrity. My self-respect. My team lost respect for me. Eventually, I got reported." Humiliation burned like lava in his gut. "I got written up a dozen times before my superior did something about it.

"But I couldn't let go of that crash." Revulsion and nausea rushed over him as he remembered. "I started having flashbacks. I stopped sleeping to avoid the nightmares. I started hitting the bottle to forget. But the booze only led to blackouts. The blackouts led to lost days. I knew I was in trouble, but by then I didn't give a damn."

Raking an unsteady hand through his hair he faced her, looking for signs of pity, of disgust. To his surprise, he saw only compassion—and respect. The realization shook him so thoroughly that for a moment he didn't trust his voice to speak.

"When I stopped being effective in the field, my superiors sent me to the company shrink. Six weeks later, I was diagnosed and put on mandatory leave."

It had been the lack of control that bothered him most. Control over his career. Over the will of his own mind. It was that same lack of control that had eaten away at him every time he picked up a bottle and broke the seal.

"You came to Denver," she said.

"Jack and I grew up here."

"Has time away from the job helped?"

"I honestly don't know. The flashbacks have ceased. But I still have an occasional nightmare."

"It's not wrong or weak for someone to break under those kinds of conditions. There should be no shame in what happened to you."

"I'm probably an alcoholic." He watched her carefully as

he spoke, trying to gauge her reaction, and keep his own in check. "I don't know."

"You didn't open that bottle of cognac today."

"I wanted to. Goddammit, I wanted to open that bottle so badly I could taste it."

"But you didn't. That's what's important."

"Alcoholism doesn't go away, Addison. Not ever."

"Have you considered going to AA?" she asked.

"I've thought about it."

"What about counseling? I mean, for the post-traumatic stress disorder?"

"I see a guy, a psychiatrist, at the university in Boulder once a month. He's a Vietnam vet. He knows what it's like." He forced a smile that felt brittle on his face. "Didn't know you were hooking up with a nutcase, did you?"

Randall jolted when she reached out and brushed her fingertips along his cheek. "You may not believe in yourself," she said softly. "But I do."

He stared at her, wondering if she'd heard what he'd just told her, if the warning to stay away from him had registered in her brain. He wished she'd use her head and back off before his resistance caved.

"You've got some issues to deal with, Randall. But those issues do not change who you are. They don't change what kind of man you are. They don't change what's in your heart. And they certainly don't change the way I think of you."

Those were the last words he'd expected to hear. His chest tightened unexpectedly with the knowledge that she still believed in him. "I drink too much," he said hoarsely. "I stay up for days at a time. I have a nasty temper. I have nightmares, goddammit."

"You're dealing with it. You're working through it."

"When things get tough, I get drunk, Addison. I'm not a good person when I'm drunk. You've seen it firsthand, for God's sake. How can you say that's working through it?"

"When things got tough the other night, you ended up saving my life."

He stared at her, incredulous. "That doesn't make me a hero. It doesn't even make me a good man."

"Courage is a trait I happen to admire, even in mere mortals like you." A small smile brushed the corners of her mouth. "I don't expect perfection."

This wasn't exactly the way he'd had this scene mapped out in his head. He hadn't expected her to accept his shortcomings without question. He sure as hell hadn't expected her to look at him like he deserved anything even close to respect.

But in a small corner of his mind, he couldn't deny that he was secretly pleased. That it wouldn't have hurt if she'd turned away. "You don't want to get tangled up with me."

"You're so intent on trying to talk me out of being with you, I doubt you have the slightest idea what I want."

"We've been keeping close quarters," he said a little desperately. "I don't want things to get out of hand."

"Maybe they already have." Leaning close to him, she brushed her mouth against his.

The kiss hit him like the tail end of a tornado. The need, with all its reckless urgency, uncoiled inside him like a steel cable snapping under tension. Professional ethics went out the window along with every last shred of logic.

Without speaking, Randall rose, pulling her up with him. He saw shock in her eyes, but he didn't stop. Angling her face, he crushed his mouth to hers. He felt her breath on his face as it rushed out of her. He kissed her deeply, possessively, without the finesse she deserved. He parted her lips with his tongue and dug deep. A moan rose up inside him at the almost painful pleasure crashing through him.

Forgetting this was their first time together, knowing he was beyond the point of being gentle, he pulled her against him. He heard the quick intake of breath as he dropped his hands to her buttocks, squeezing the firm flesh, taking in the feel of her, amazed by the fact that he'd never wanted anyone so badly in his life.

Using the muscles in his arms, he held her tightly against

him and ground his throbbing erection against her cleft. "Goddammit, you make me want you," he growled.

"Stop fighting it."

His resolve to stay away from her shattered. He had to get inside her, or he would die of the need to feel her wrapped around him. Next to him, the fire popped and crackled, filling the air with the redolence of burning pine. Outside, the wind ripped around the cabin, tearing at the roof and driving the snow against the windows with the force of hailstones. In the midst of it all, Randall and Addison tended their own storm.

He moaned when her hands went to his chest to work at the buttons of his flannel shirt. Her fingers fumbled, teasing him and exciting him at once. He kissed her hungrily, but the taste of her only heightened his frustration. When his shirt opened Randall pulled away, worked it off his shoulders, and tossed it aside. Then her hands were on his bare chest, making him want her in a way that had him teetering on the thin edge between ecstasy and agony.

With shaking hands, he reached for her sweatshirt and dragged it over her head. Her hair fell in a thick blanket over her shoulders. The sight of her lacy pink bra against the velvety swell of her cleavage took his breath. "I've wanted you since the day you walked into my office," he murmured. "I want you now."

He felt shaken, off kilter. Christ, he felt out of control. Suddenly it was important to him to know that she wanted this as desperately as he did. He looked into her eyes. "Tell me you want this," he whispered. "Before we go any further. I need to know."

"I want this. I want you," she said simply.

Randall didn't miss the flicker of uncertainty. Nor did he miss that she was trembling. "You're nervous."

"This is . . . new for me."

Easing back, he looked down at her, relieved when he saw her smile. "It's been a long time for me, too."

He kissed her temple. Slowly, he reached between them

and released the clasp of her bra. She shivered in his arms. "Relax, honey." Never taking his eyes from her face, he slid the tiny piece of silk from her shoulders.

Her breasts were small, upswept, and exquisite. The tiny nipples were dark and fully erect. His hands trembled as he cupped them. Closing his eyes, he tumbled into a free fall and careened out of control.

THE FIRE WARMED HER BARE BACK AND CAST YELLOW light on the hard angles of his face. Her heart beat out a maniacal rhythm as his hands covered her breasts. She withheld a moan when he took a taut nipple between his thumb and forefinger.

White-hot desire cut through her midsection. She couldn't breathe as waves of passion splashed through her, shaking her and thrilling her at once. She'd never felt so wanton. She never thought she could so completely abandon the safe, responsible shell she'd been living in all her twenty-six years.

At some point, she'd started to tremble. Small shivers that grew quickly into knee-shaking quakes she could do nothing to control.

"Are you okay?" Randall's voice was hoarse. "You're not cold, are you?"

Addison shook her head, trying to still her knees, embarrassed by her powerful reaction to him. She tried to smile, afraid her inexperience would show, and silently cursed her lips for failing her. "Not cold," she managed.

"Still nervous?" He shot her a disarming smile. That crooked smile that gave his handsome face so much character. She was beginning to cherish that smile.

"No," she said.

"Good."

Heat blazed through her when he kissed her neck. His mouth lingered on the sensitive flesh and sent her senses humming. Addison felt as though she'd begun a tumble every bit as wild and tumultuous as the fall she'd taken down the side of the mountain. She was falling into unexplored and yet-uncharted territory. A new world that was as exciting as it was terrifying.

His hands were firm and controlled as they slid her leggings down her legs. Her knees felt like jelly as she kicked them aside. She resisted the shiver, but the tremor took her anyway, and she wrapped her arms more tightly about his neck to keep her legs from buckling. He slid her panties down, touching her in places that sent zingers of pleasure rocking through her brain.

Her world went into a slow spin when his hand found its way to the dark nest of curls at her vee. He kissed her deeply as his index finger found a place she'd never shared with another man. Addison closed her eyes against the waves of pleasure as he began to stroke her. She cried out, arching into him, telling herself this was just sex, knowing deep down inside she was a liar.

His mouth captured hers. He devoured her lips before sweeping her off her feet and lowering her gently to the rug in front of the fire. She was aware of his mouth on hers, taking her breath, stealing every last shred of rational thought. She was aware of her breasts aching to be caressed. The place between her legs pounding with each beat of her heart.

She moaned as he poised himself over her, resting his weight on his elbows on either side of her. For a fleeting second, she considered telling him that this was her first time, but she wasn't sure how he would react. Admittedly, she was afraid he would think it was strange that she hadn't experimented with sex during her college years or that she'd never been in love before.

"Look at me."

His voice drifted to her through the fog of passion. She looked into his eyes, seeing urgency and the same need that was rocketing through her. Only then did she realize the extent of her trust for him. She trusted him fully and without question. With a start, she realized she'd already lost her heart to him.

With his hands on either side of her face, Randall poised himself at the warm wetness of her opening. Murmuring her name, he closed his eyes and rested his forehead against hers. "I want to see your face when I'm inside you. I need that."

Whispering his name, Addison opened to him. With a small cry he thrust forward, breaking through the resistance of her hymen in a single, earth-shattering stroke.

The pain was intense for only an instant. She winced in a moment of surprise; felt him stiffen in response.

"Jesus, Addi—"

"Don't stop," she whispered and moved tentatively against him. The pain was forgotten as she was overcome with an intense new pleasure. Hard against soft. The sense of being stretched and filled. By Randall. She moved, awed and amazed by what was happening, relieved when she finally felt him relax. In response, she wrapped her legs around his hips and let him take her to a place she'd never been.

Randall took her to the top of a precipice she hadn't known existed. Together, they ventured higher and higher, oblivious to the dangers abounding, until they reached the crest and realized it was what they'd been searching for their entire lives.

chapter

13

"WHY DIDN'T YOU TELL ME?" RANDALL STARED AT the ceiling, his face profiled against the fire as they lay side by side on the rug.

Nestled against him, Addison pulled away just enough to see his face and tried to gauge his thoughts, telling herself it was only her imagination that he looked angry.

When she didn't answer, he propped himself on an elbow and turned to her. "Why didn't you tell me you'd never . . . done this before?"

There were a hundred different answers running through her mind but none of them seemed adequate. How could she explain that her virginity had made her feel as if she hadn't been attractive enough or outgoing enough or exciting enough to attract the amorous attention of the opposite sex? Was there something wrong with her because she'd never been in love before?

"I didn't want it to matter," she said finally.

He stared at her, his face set and slightly angry. It was obvious he didn't understand, but she didn't feel as if she could explain something so personal any better than she already had.

"It does matter, dammit. I could have hurt you. . . ." His words trailed. "I mean, I *did* hurt you."

"You didn't hurt me."

"I could have made it special for you."

The anger came quick and biting. "It *was* special. At least it was for me." Hurt, feeling like a fool, she started to rise.

He stopped her. "That isn't what I meant."

When she tried to turn away, he reached out and gently touched her bare shoulder. She glared at him, amazed at how quickly she could go from emblazoned with passion to feeling like a wounded soul. Good Lord, was it possible she was falling for him? Was he going to finish the job of turning her tidy life upside down?

"I'm not going to allow you to make me feel like some kind of . . . aberration just because I didn't screw around in college."

"Aberration?" He laughed outright. "Whoa."

When she started to protest, he put his finger against her lips. "You gave me a big part of yourself. I'm trying to tell you that had I known, I would have . . . taken things a bit more slowly."

She let him struggle through what he needed to say, mostly because she needed to hear it. Slowly, she relaxed against him and decided to give up on the idea of walking back to Denver tonight.

"Sex just never happened for me," she began. "My parents were in their midforties when they adopted me. My mother had unexplained infertility and, back then, she was simply told that she would never bear children." She paused for a moment, trying to imagine what it had been like for them to bring home a new baby after so many years of trying to conceive.

"Thanks to them, I grew up mature. I kept my nose to the grindstone throughout high school. During college, while the other kids were floating kegs and checking out Extasy and cocaine and marijuana, I was already focused on getting my own business. I didn't really even start dating until my fourth year in college." She laughed. "And then there was this stockbroker . . ."

His eyes narrowed. "Stockbroker?"

She laughed, enjoying the way he'd come to attention. "You know, Talbot, there may just be hope for you after all."

"I'd be happy to break his legs for you."

"I hate to spoil that damsel-in-distress image you have of me, but I really do know how to take care of myself."

Reaching out, Randall swept a stray hair away from her forehead. "I'm impressed."

"The fact of the matter is that I never met anyone I wanted to make love with." *Until I met you,* a little voice added. She looked at him, realizing with some embarrassment that he was staring at her with an odd combination of fascination and respect.

He moved his hand to the side of her face. "I hope this doesn't sound too corny for you, but I'm honored to be the first."

"I've always wondered why everyone makes such a big deal about . . . sex."

He arched a brow, but Addison didn't miss the quick flash of uncertainty in his eyes.

She chuckled, charmed and embarrassed and all too aware that her heart was bouncing around in her chest like a Ping-Pong ball. "Now I understand why," she said and kissed him.

RANDALL COULDN'T SLEEP. HANDS LACED BEHIND HIS head, he lay on his back and stared into the fire. Learning Addison had been a virgin completely unnerved him. He knew her first sexual experience was something she wouldn't take lightly. But he also knew that if she wanted something more, he was not the man for the job.

He cursed himself a dozen different ways for sleeping with

a young woman when he had absolutely no intention of sticking around. Christ, he couldn't believe she'd been a virgin!
He couldn't believe she'd given him such a precious gift at
a time in his life when he couldn't let it mean anything to
him. When he couldn't let it mean a goddamn thing to either
of them. She deserved better.

He felt like a son of a bitch for letting her settle for him.

The cold hard fact that he was going back to Washington,
D.C., in a few weeks loomed hugely. He knew he should
have told her by now. He should never have let things go
this far. But, sweet Christ, she'd caught him off guard. One
kiss and his willpower had shattered. He hadn't expected to
get sucked in over his head. He hadn't expected it to matter
so damn much. Not to her. Certainly not to him. But, as
usual, he'd fucked it up. The gravity of the situation floored
him. That he'd been her first awed him. The repercussions
sent the sharp scrape of panic up his spine.

This wasn't casual for her. She wasn't impulsive and she
sure as hell wasn't the kind of woman who did something
like this on a whim. Not Addison with her open heart and
naive view of the world. She might believe otherwise, but
she didn't know what kind of a man he was. She couldn't
understand the darkness in his mind, or the shadow that lay
over his heart. He damn well wasn't going to drag her down
with him just because he liked having sex with her.

Randall knew what he had to do, knew he was going to
have to look into her clear brown eyes and tell her this didn't
mean anything to him. That it couldn't mean anything to her.
It was going to kill him to hurt her. His only consolation
was knowing that in the long run it would be best for both
of them.

Shifting slightly, he turned his head and looked at her and
felt that odd sensation of free-falling that gripped him every
time he got close to her. She was lovely and kind and far
too smart to get mixed up with him. Too bad she was listening to that soft heart of hers instead of her head.

He gazed at her, drinking in her beauty, starkly aware of

her hair brushing against his shoulder. He breathed in the sweetness of her woman's scent, felt it go straight to his head until he was dizzy. The fire crackled, painting the delicate flesh of her face golden, like cream flecked with gold. He lowered his arm to nudge her awake, but she snuggled closer.

"Hey, Addison. You awake?"

Her eyes fluttered. "Hey to you, too."

When she stretched languidly and smiled up at him, his heart did a slow roll in his chest. He stared at her, unable to speak, unsettled, and a hell of a lot more troubled than he wanted to admit.

She'd gotten to him, he realized with a start. Somehow she'd managed to break through his barriers. And for his own peace of mind, he had to set the record straight before it was too late for both of them.

"Still snowing outside?" she asked, raising up on her elbows.

"The wind let up. That's a good sign."

"Oh." Tilting her head, she looked at him closely. "You look . . . troubled. Is everything all right?"

He wanted to smile, but he couldn't. He couldn't be with her like this and know he was going to hurt her. When she touched his arm, he turned away to stare into the fire. When his back was to her, he closed his eyes and spoke. "My leave is up in a few weeks," he said softly.

Next to him, he felt her stiffen. "What do you mean?"

He turned, saw the wariness flood her gaze. "I mean, I'm going back to D.C."

She blinked at him. He didn't miss the quick flash of hurt, had to steel himself against it. "When?"

"In a couple of weeks. I should have told you."

"Yes, you should have. I wouldn't have . . ." Her voice trailed.

"Slept with me?"

Tugging the afghan up to her chin, she tried to rise.

He stopped her. "Addison, don't—"

She shook off his hand. "Don't what? Feel . . . used?"

The anger came with surprising force. "That's not the way it was."

"It just feels that way."

"I didn't mean to complicate things."

"Well, you did a really good job of it."

Dammit, he hadn't wanted to hurt her. She didn't deserve to be hurt. She certainly didn't deserve to get emotionally entangled with a man who had every intention of walking out on her.

Needing her to understand why he had to go back, that his personal integrity and self-respect were on the line, that his entire life revolved around whether or not he had the courage to face his demons, Randall turned to her. "I have to know if I can do it. If I've got what it takes. If I've got the guts."

"What happened to you doesn't have anything to do with courage." She looked at him, an emotion he couldn't name flashing like quicksilver in her eyes. "What about the case?"

"What happened between us tonight or the fact that I'm leaving for D.C. in a couple of weeks doesn't change anything. I'm going to see this case through to the end."

"This can't happen again," she said.

"Not if you don't want it to."

"I don't." She sat up, pressing the afghan to her breasts.

Reaching out, he turned her to him. "I wanted you. I still want you. But I have to go back, Addison. I have to face what's waiting for me in D.C." *I didn't mean to hurt you,* a little voice added. But he knew the deed was done. He couldn't help but wonder how well his own heart would fare when the time came for him to walk away.

HE ENTERED HER APARTMENT THROUGH THE BEDROOM window. It was an act he'd committed countless times in a career that spanned two decades and three continents. An illustrious career that had engendered a mere two arrests, one trial—and never a conviction.

He was the best of the best in a high-stakes game where absolute discretion and definitive solutions were his trademarks. He flaunted those trademarks as proudly as a wartime medal. It was a reputation he'd earned through extraordinary talent, the complete lack of a conscience, and a ruthlessness that ran all the way to his soul.

Invariably, when the heavy-hitters needed a job done quickly and efficiently, they called on him. He was known by repute. There was never a personal visit made. The overpaid middlemen were the ones who inevitably did the contacting.

After all, anonymity was everything when it came to murder.

He'd killed for the first time when he was fourteen years old. He still remembered the kick of the cheap revolver in his hand. The shocking spurt of blood. The heady jolt of exhilaration that followed. He'd taken out dozens of faceless, nameless people since, but he'd never forgotten his first. He'd gotten his first taste of blood that day, and knew then that killing was what he was destined to do.

Now, at the age of forty-six, he could afford to be choosy about who he worked for, and he chose his contracts with the utmost of care. Two hundred thousand dollars per contract swept discreetly and expediently into the Swiss bank of his choice. He took three or four jobs a year and owned a house on the beach just north of Los Angeles and a penthouse on Fifth Avenue in New York City. He vacationed in the south of France and owned a villa in Monaco next to a small vineyard. Life didn't get much better, especially for a man who'd grown up in a one-bedroom tenement and gotten his education on the mean streets of Chicago.

Setting his feet soundlessly on the carpet, he scanned the room, letting his eyes adjust to the semidarkness. The ceiling fan hummed overhead. A clock ticked nearby. Satisfied that he was alone, he pulled a penlight from his jacket and shone it onto a frilly, unmade bed. The subtle scent of the Fox woman's perfume lingered from earlier in the day. Something sweet and earthy. Breathing in deeply, he savored her scent.

The perfume told him things about the woman who wore it.

Removing one of his gloves, he ran his bare palm over the inside sheet, wondering if she'd allowed the private detective into her bed. He smiled when he imagined how safe she must feel sleeping next to a man like Randall Talbot.

But he knew Talbot Investigations was nothing more than a low-budget sham. He'd done his homework and knew the two men passing themselves off as private detectives were nothing more than a crippled ex-biker and an alcoholic on the run from a failed career. As a professional, he knew incompetence didn't necessarily mean the two men were harmless. But their weaknesses would definitely make his job easier.

He walked to the night table and pulled open the top drawer. With a gloved hand, he quickly searched through the contents: a box of keys, a colorful array of nail polish bottles, a scented candle. He opened the lower drawer only to find it filled with paperback books. Methodically, he searched the entire room before moving on to the next.

Using the penlight, he quickly scanned the living room, taking note of the positions of the furniture, the telephone, and light switches before he spotted the manila folder on the dining room table. It was lying out in the open, as though it had been recently looked at. He approached the table and opened the folder.

Inside, he found a copy of her birth certificate. Beneath it, a sheet of paper with the Beckett woman's vital statistics typed neatly in the center of the page. There were handwritten notes. A letter from the lawyer. Smiling, he paged through each document, knowing Talbot had seen the file, perhaps even made copies of it.

He slipped the file into the waistband of his slacks. The way he saw it, both Fox and Talbot would be dead before they even missed it.

chapter
14

HE WAS GOING BACK TO D.C.

Addison told herself it didn't hurt. She'd known from the beginning what kind of man Randall Talbot was. Rough around the edges. Burned out. Cynical. Always looking out for number one. His actions on the day she'd met him should have told her all she needed to know to realize he was the kind of man to stay away from.

Of course, her heart hadn't been listening.

The storm had left a foot of pristine snow on the ground. At first light the snowplows were out in full force. By nine o'clock, she and Randall had climbed into the Bronco and were heading east toward Denver.

Addison called Gretchen from a service station in Evergreen, only to discover her daughter had gone into labor the night before. In light of such a wondrous event, she didn't have the heart to mention the terrible news about her parents. But she'd longed to talk to Gretchen. About everything that had happened in the last twenty-four hours. But mostly about what had happened between her and Randall last night.

She sent him a sidelong glance, taking in the brooding profile and strong cut of jaw. There was no trace of the tenderness he'd shown her the night before. No trace of the man who'd bared his soul, then apologized for it. This morning, he was all hard edges and hair-trigger temper. Conversation between them had been stilted at best. At the moment, she was feeling downright hostile.

Damn him.

What in God's name had she been thinking sleeping with him? How could she be stupid enough to lose her heart to a man who would do nothing but break it into little pieces? It frightened her to think she'd tumbled into this abyss of emotion with a man who was so wrong for her.

"After we stop by the office, I'm going to take you back to your apartment and you're going to pack a bag and stay with me for a few days." Randall's voice cut through her tumultuous thoughts with all the finesse of a chain saw.

The words set Addison's teeth on edge. She'd expected him to fall into the overprotective-male category. She could deal with that. What she hadn't expected was to feel so damn betrayed by his announcement that he would be returning to his job in D.C. How could she have been so naive? Just because she'd slept with him didn't mean he was going to change his mind and stay. He hadn't made her any promises. Dammit, she didn't want promises.

"You can drop me at my apartment," she said levelly. "I'll meet you at your office later."

His jaw tightened, but he didn't look at her. "Don't even think about arguing with me about this."

"Don't you have some sleazy divorce case to work on or something? I have some things to take care of," she said, pleased with the dark look her words elicited.

"Don't let what happened last night cloud your judgment," he said.

The logical side of her brain knew he was right. It would be dangerous for her to be alone, silly of her to think she could protect herself after everything that had happened.

Damn, she hated it that he was the one making sense. She hated the situation almost as much as the fact that she seemed to be so damn fallible as of late.

"I thought we had an understanding," he said reasonably.

"What we had was sex."

He glanced at her with narrowed, black eyes.

As much as she didn't want to admit it, she was angry. She told herself it wasn't because she wanted him to stay; she wasn't looking for a long-term relationship any more than he was. So why had she felt his words like a knife slipping between her ribs?

Raising her chin, she forced her gaze to his. "Just because we slept together last night doesn't mean you can step in and take control of my life."

"Is that what you think I'm trying to do? Take control of your life?"

She was really screwing this up. He was right, but she wasn't feeling particularly logical at the moment. He'd hurt her. Of course she couldn't *tell* him that. She didn't want to lay that much of herself on the line. She didn't want him to know he had that kind of power. "I don't need a fly-by-night protector."

The look he shot her had her questioning the wisdom of provoking him. "If you want to be stupid and get yourself killed you're going to do it on your time, not mine."

"Don't worry, I didn't expect you to stick around—"

Without warning, he mashed his foot down on the brake. The truck screeched to a halt, jerking her against her shoulder harness hard enough to jar her teeth.

Fury simmered behind his eyes when he turned to her. "You either do what the fuck I say or you fire me right now!"

Addison stared at him wide-eyed, her heart pulsing against her ribs as she took in the display of anger. His jaw was clamped tight, his eyes flashing like heat lightning. "I'm not going to fire you," she said.

"That's not good enough."

"What do you want from me?"

"I want you to be smart about this." His eyes cut into her brutally as he rammed the shifter into park. "We do this my way or we don't do it at all. It's your call. What's it going to be?"

She stared at him, hating it that he'd rendered her speechless. All she could think of was that she wanted her old life back. She wanted to be safe. She wanted her days to be predictable. Her nights . . .

Dammit, she didn't want him to go back to Washington.

"Addison, I'm trying to keep you alive. I know this isn't easy for you but you're going to have to cooperate."

"Then we're going to have to keep our relationship on a professional level," she managed after a moment. "I can't deal with you when . . ." Her voice trailed when she realized what she was about to say. "You're complicating things for me. This is hard enough without that."

He looked out the windshield at the snowy landscape beyond. "All right. We'll keep it professional from here on out."

"Promise me."

"You've got my word."

Not trusting her voice enough to speak, she looked out the window. The last thing she wanted to do was break down in front of him. The last thing she wanted him to know was that he'd hurt her.

Perceiving her silence as acquiescence, he glanced once in the rearview mirror and pulled back onto the highway.

THEY ARRIVED AT THE OFFICE OF TALBOT INVESTIGA-tions at noon. Jack sat behind the computer, looking bone-weary, but wired on technology, nicotine, and caffeine. Two days of stubble darkened his jaw. His ponytail hung loosely down the center of his back, flyaway strands of hair falling into eyes that were little more than red-rimmed slits.

"Morning, big brother," Randall said as he closed the alley door.

Addison walked into the office, taking in the odors of cigarette smoke and burned coffee. An opened quart of chocolate milk lay on its side next to the keyboard, a puddle of muddy ooze beneath its spout. The garbage can overflowed with paper, a half-eaten burger, and pages of handwritten notes. The surrounding floor was littered with paper, much of it creased by the thin tires of his wheelchair.

It was obvious Jack had been at it all night without respite. He looked dead tired. An uncomfortable pang of concern slid through her as she took in the dark circles beneath his eyes. At the same time, his tenacity touched her.

"Looks like you had a hell of a night," Randall said.

Grinning, Jack tamped out his cigarette. "You don't know the half of it."

"Any luck?" Addison asked.

"Some. Adoption files are tough."

Randall walked over to the desk and picked up the quart of chocolate milk. Absently, he smelled it, then tossed it into the trash. "Anything we can use?"

"Maybe." Jack dragged a stack of computer printouts across the desk.

Randall straddled a chair. Jack leaned close to him and said something just out of earshot. Curious, and more than a little annoyed that they were discussing something about her case without including her, Addison came up behind them and peered cautiously over their shoulders.

Jack pointed to the first printout, where he had concocted a haphazard flowchart. "I had five sources of information to work with that included the adoption agency, the hospital where Addison was born, the attorney who handled the adoption, the vital statistics office in Montgomery County, and the delivering physician. I knew from the start this wasn't going to be easy."

"I ran into problems with sealed records and confidentiality laws, as well," she interjected.

He nodded. "Exactly. So, I started with the easy stuff first. Namely the hospital where you were born."

Excitement zigzagged through her. Months ago, she had written to the very same hospital for copies of her records, only to have her request denied.

"I was able to hack into their historical accounts receivable records. I wrote some code and searched for the name Beckett. It came up with this." He handed a sheet of paper to Randall. "I thought it might be important."

Addison read over Randall's shoulder. Her heart kicked in her chest when she saw Agnes Beckett's name listed at the top of an emergency room invoice dated November of 1974.

Admittance time: 12:32 A.M.

Agnes Beckett
Age: 16   Female
Rt. 3 Box 72A Siloam Springs, Ohio

Sutures:	$19.98
Emergency Room charge:	$27.50
Attending physician:	$60.00
X rays (technician)	$46.50
Rape kit:	$22.19
Total Due:	$176.17

Trepidation built in her chest as she skimmed the invoice. She was wondering how the information was pertinent when two horrible words registered in her brain.

Rape kit.

Shaken, she stepped back. Blood pounded in her ears. Terrible knowledge ripped through her. Suddenly she couldn't breathe, couldn't speak.

She reached for the paper and ripped it from Randall's grasp, her eyes searching out the date. November 17, 1974. She'd been born in August the following year. Mentally, she tallied the months, her heart filling with dread.

She looked up to find both men staring at her, knowledge spread across their faces like dirt. *They know,* she thought.

Jack dropped his gaze to the computer screen in front of him. Randall held her gaze and gently worked the paper from her clenched fist.

"This doesn't mean anything, Addison," he said gently.

"The hell it doesn't." She wanted to scream in outrage. She wanted to shout that this was not how her life had begun. That she had not been conceived in an act of violence. "The timing is right."

"Don't jump to conclusions."

"Don't tell me how to feel."

Before she could turn away, Randall caught her arm. "Don't do this to yourself."

His voice cut through the sea of raging emotions. She tried to shake off his grip, but he held her securely. She raised a trembling hand to her face, rubbing the spot on her forehead where a headache had broken through.

"Don't do what? Say out loud what we're all thinking?" she snapped.

"You don't know anything for certain at this point."

"There's a very strong possibility that I was conceived through an act of rape, and we both know it."

He stared back at her, saying nothing. Addison knew him well enough to know he wouldn't lie to her. Not now. Not after everything they'd shared. She would have lost respect for him had he tried.

Randall shook the paper. "You may not like it, but this is exactly the kind of information we were looking for. We're going to use it to find the son of a bitch who tried to kill you. Don't lose sight of that, Addison, because you can't change the past. You can't change what's done."

She blinked at him, wondering for the first time if she really wanted to take this any further, if she really wanted to know her roots. "That paper doesn't tell us who the bastard was."

"If the police were notified, somebody made a report."

Jack pulled his chair closer to the computer and his fingers danced across the keyboard. "There's more information out there. I've got another search ready to go. I'll need a couple of hours or so to finish writing code. There are places I haven't even tried to access."

Shaking loose of Randall's grip, Addison turned to Jack. She felt as if she'd been forcefully knocked off balance by the news. "Was Jim Bernstein the attorney who handled the adoption?"

"His name came up a few times," Jack said.

She felt as if a giant piece of the puzzle had just fallen into place. "This ties everything together."

Jack nodded.

"And we're one step closer to finding the son of a bitch responsible," Randall reminded her.

Glancing up from the keyboard, Jack caught her gaze and winked. "And I'm just getting warmed up."

RANDALL WATCHED THE REARVIEW MIRROR AS HE SPED along the side streets of a residential neighborhood on the way to her apartment. Beside him, Addison gazed pensively through the window, her hands lying motionless in her lap. She hadn't spoken to him since leaving the office. He supposed she was trying to find a way to deal with the information Jack had thrown at her like a bucket of cold water.

He didn't like the way things were working out. Not with the case. Certainly not with Addison. While the case was progressing much too slowly, their relationship was barreling along at the speed of light. Christ, he hadn't intended for things to go this far. But he'd been too caught up in the moment to stop the magic that had happened between them the night before. He'd taken her virginity without so much as a thought to what the repercussions might be. Without considering her feelings. Never imagining that his own could get in the way, too. He hadn't stopped to think of how a single night might affect the way he felt about her. Or how it would affect the way he handled a case that was becoming increasingly dangerous.

The last thing he needed in his life was a relationship, especially with a complex woman who wielded the power to turn him inside out with nothing more than a look. The last thing she needed in her life was a man on the edge. He'd come to Denver to be alone, to recoup, to pull the broken pieces of his life back together. He hadn't bargained for Addison Fox getting inside his head. He sure as hell hadn't planned on her getting anywhere near his heart.

So much for best-laid plans.

What they'd shared in the cabin was an experience that would forever have its place in his heart. It had been his responsibility to draw boundaries, and make those boundaries clear to her. As usual, he'd ignored his responsibilities and taken the easy way out.

"You can park there."

Randall checked the rearview mirror, pulled the Bronco curbside, and cut the engine. Without speaking, he reached across her and pulled his Beretta from the glove box and shoved it into his shoulder holster.

"You've got five minutes to pack," he said.

Addison frowned at him as she slid out of the passenger door. "You're crazy if you think I'm going anywhere without a shower."

Randall blew out an oath as he stepped out of the truck. "One of these days I'll show you just how crazy I am."

Ignoring him, she strode to the front door of her building and shoved open the door. He trailed her, watching the street, checking the alcove near the mailboxes, not liking the uneasiness he felt in his gut. They rode the elevator in silence. At her apartment door, Addison removed her key and stepped inside. "Wipe your feet."

He checked his boots and entered behind her. Even after two days, the apartment smelled faintly of coffee, reminding him that he had yet to have a cup today. "I'd kill for a cup of coffee."

When she didn't answer, he turned, puzzled to find her stopped in the center of the living room, her face ashen. A rush of adrenaline sent his hand to his pistol. "What is it?" he whispered, scanning the room.

"The file." She darted to the dining room table, placed her hands on the surface, and looked up at him. "The file was right here when we left."

He remembered clearly sitting at the table, poring over the file as they'd consumed fried rice and egg rolls. "Are you sure you didn't move it?"

"I left it right here. I'm certain of it."

He slid the pistol from his shoulder holster. "Stay put."

In a few minutes, he'd searched the entire apartment, finishing in her bedroom. She met him there a moment later with a knife the size of a machete clutched in her right hand. "Did you find anything?" she whispered.

Had the situation not been so serious, he would have laughed at the sight of her. She looked like a waif poised for battle. "What the hell kind of a knife is that?" he asked.

"Chicago Cutlery."

"Looks like a damn machete." Crossing to her, he eased the knife from her hand and set it on the bed. "Whoever was here is gone."

She looked up at him with eyes that were large and frightened. "They took the file, Randall."

"I know." Something primal and dark stirred inside him at the thought of someone ransacking her apartment, touching her things. He tried not to think about what might have happened had she been here alone. "They came in through the window." He parted the drapes, exposing the broken glass and duct tape. "Whoever it was wasn't concerned with stealth. He knew you weren't here. He was watching the place."

She pressed her hand to her stomach. "That's a comfort."

Letting the drapes fall, Randall stepped closer to her and placed his hands on her shoulders. He squeezed to reassure, his mind fumbling as a fist of lust struck in the gut. Glancing down at the hollow of her throat, he wondered how she would taste if he pressed a kiss there, ran his tongue along the flesh. . . .

"What are we going to do without the file?" she asked. "I threw away my only other copy."

He chided himself for getting sidetracked. He'd agreed to keep their relationship professional. He owed it to her to keep his word. Dammit, he owed it to himself.

"Bernstein probably had copies." Randall hadn't made a copy for his own file and cursed himself for the blunder. "We'll see about getting them released."

Looking small and lost, she knelt and began picking up shards of glass, dropping the larger pieces into a wicker wastebasket. Randall studied her, taking in her pale face and shaking hands. Christ, she looked shell-shocked. She'd been through a lot in the last few weeks. First Agnes Beckett and Bernstein, then finding out about her parents, and now this.

The last thing she needs is a man like you, a little voice reminded him.

Gently, he put his hand on her shoulder and squeezed. "I'll get the manager to take care of that. We've got to go."

"I'm not leaving—"

"It's not safe here, Addison. We've got to go. Now."

She stopped picking up glass and glared at him. "I want my life back."

"I know. We're working on that."

Tossing the last piece of glass into the trash container, she rose. "What do we do now?"

"I'll fill you in on the way to the airport."

"Airport?"

Randall headed for the telephone to call Jack and Detective Van-Dyne to fill them in on the latest. "Pack something warm," he said. "Siloam Springs is cold as hell in December."

chapter
15

SHERIFF DELBERT MCEVOY'S CHAIR CREAKED AS HE leaned back and arranged his gut more comfortably over his belt buckle. Beneath the wide brim of his hat, his eyes darted from Randall to Addison.

"It's good to see you again, Miss Fox. Mr. Talbot." He motioned for them to take the chairs opposite his desk. "How can I be of service?"

Randall sat and looked around the small office. It was a different town, a different place, a different era of his life, but small-town law enforcement never changed, he mused. "We want to ask you some questions about Agnes Beckett."

McEvoy reached beneath his hat and scratched the top of his head. "I'm sorry to say that the status of the case hasn't changed in the last three days."

There was a hint of sarcasm behind the slow drawl that had Randall's teeth clamping together in irritation. He had no patience for smug public servants. "We may have some new information," he said.

McEvoy's eyes sharpened. "What new information?"

Randall almost smiled. "How long have you been sheriff here in Preble County?" he asked.

McEvoy pushed the wad of chewing tobacco from one side of his mouth to the other. "What new information you got on the Beckett case?"

"Who was sheriff in 1974?" Randall asked, intrigued by the sheriff's sudden interest in a case he'd shoved to the bottom of his priority list.

"I don't remember."

"I'll bet someone down at the town hall would remember." Rising, Randall looked at Addison. "Let's go."

The sheriff's chair came forward along with the two hundred and fifty pounds of lawman. McEvoy swung his gaze to Addison and then back to Randall. "Why in the hell don't you people just tell me what you want instead of beating around the bush all goddamn day?"

Putting his hands on the desk, Randall leaned forward. "We want to see a police report from November 17, 1974."

An emotion he couldn't put a name to flickered in the other man's eyes. "What police report?"

"We're looking for a police report from November 16 or 17, 1974, involving Agnes Beckett," Addison said.

"Doesn't ring a bell."

Randall's temper stirred. "Let me refresh your memory. She was sixteen years old. A minor, Sheriff, admitted to Good Samaritan Hospital in Dayton after being beaten and raped."

In his peripheral vision, he saw Addison stiffen.

The sheriff's face reddened. "I'm not sure where you're getting your information, Talbot, but I don't remember any such thing ever happening in my town."

"It happened right here in your tidy little town, Sheriff, and we'd like to see the report," Randall said icily.

McEvoy didn't flinch. "Siloam Springs is a small town. If something like that happened, I'd know about it. Nothing like that happened here. Not in 1974. Not ever."

Addison broke in. "Do you keep archive files? Would you

mind looking for us? Surely there's a file or a police report for something as serious as a rape."

"I don't think that's possible."

The initial burst of real anger cut through Randall. "Why not?" he asked.

McEvoy grinned. "For one thing, you can't rape a whore."

Raw fury speared through Randall. Without considering the repercussions, he reached across the desk. Addison gasped when he grabbed the sheriff's collar and hauled him out of his chair. "I'll have your badge for that, you son of a bitch!"

"Back off, city boy, or I'll give you a lesson in small-town law enforcement you'll never forget." McEvoy's voice was ominous and low, like the rumble of a storm in the minutes before it wreaked havoc on an unsuspecting town.

Their faces mere inches apart, the two men stared at each other in impasse, the only sound coming from their heavy breathing and the shuffle of boots against tile.

"I want to see that goddamn file," Randall said.

McEvoy shoved him. "Get your fucking hands off me!"

Randall stumbled back, catching his balance on the chair. McEvoy's hat tumbled to the floor. Tobacco juice dribbled down his chin.

"You're just aching to spend the night in my jail, aren't you, city boy?" He wiped his chin with the sleeve of his shirt, leaving a dark green smear.

"If you were going to arrest me, you would have done it by now," Randall said, praying his instincts were right.

Addison stepped between the two men. "We just want to see the report, Sheriff. Please. It's important. Agnes Beckett was my mother."

McEvoy rounded the desk, his eyes raking over her threateningly. "There is no report. That never happened. I suggest you forget about it and go home."

Randall's hackles rose. Stepping forward, he eased Addison aside, keeping himself squarely between her and the sheriff. "We have the resources to force you."

Taking his time, the sheriff adjusted his belly over his belt. "You can send a whole army of big-city lawyers, but they sure as hell ain't gonna find no police report from 1974."

"Why not?" Addison asked.

McEvoy's eyes glinted, as if he were a rodent who'd succeeded in stealing the cheese without getting crushed. "The records building burned to the ground in 1975. Everything inside, including one of the deputies, went with it."

Randall was aware of Addison sinking into the chair next to him. He struggled against the urge to comfort her. Instead, he watched McEvoy, hating the type, knowing he'd met too many men like him in his lifetime. "You can bet we'll check it out."

"Not here, you won't." The sheriff picked up his hat, swung anger-bright eyes to Randall. "Take your big-city attitude and get the hell out of my town before I arrest you both just for the fun of it."

"THAT SON OF A BITCH KNOWS SOMETHING." RANDALL started the engine and swung the rental car onto the street. "He would have arrested me if he didn't."

Even in profile, Addison could see the anger etched into his features, the tight clench of his jaw, the low, ominous brows. "I'm glad I didn't have to bail you out of jail, Talbot."

He shot her a dark look. "That fire is a little too convenient."

"You think McEvoy is involved?"

"I bet the farm he's in it up to his tobacco-stained teeth. The son of a bitch."

She raked her hands through her hair and turned in her seat to face him. "So where does this leave us?"

He breathed out a frustrated sigh. "The hospital might be a good place to start."

"I've tried getting records from Good Samaritan in the past with no luck."

"You've never seen my Magnum, P.I., impersonation. Works every time."

"Dirty Harry meets Magnum, P.I., maybe," she said.

She was thinking about small towns and gossip as they drove past the street leading to the mobile home park where Agnes Beckett had lived. Addison stared at the cluster of mailboxes. Her pulse jumped when she spotted the name Harshbarger.

"Stop the car," she said abruptly.

Shooting her a sideways glance, Randall pulled onto the shoulder. He put the car in park, then looked at her expectantly. "What?"

"I've got an idea."

"Since I'm fresh out, let's hear it."

Quickly, Addison told him about her visit with the elderly Jewel Harshbarger during her previous trip to Siloam Springs. "She's lived in this town her entire life."

"She might know something about the rape." He studied her for a moment. "You ever consider going into the private detective business?"

"Careful, Talbot, or you're going to give me a compliment."

"Yeah, I wouldn't want it to go to your head." Grinning, he put the car in gear and pulled onto the street. "Nothing worse than a P.I. with a big head."

She liked his smile, damn him. Even if he was going back to D.C.

"Turn the car around," she said. "The trailer park is right down the street."

BY THE LIGHT OF THE SODIUM-VAPOR STREET LAMP, Randall knocked for the third time, cursing when no one answered the door. Dusk had settled, bringing with it a wind-driven chill that invariably found its way to the bone.

"She's not home," Addison said.

"Doesn't look that way."

She'd made a valiant attempt to stay upbeat throughout the ordeal, but Randall didn't miss the fatigue and frustration etched into her features. He knew their lack of progress was wearing her down. If only they'd get a lucky break.

"She wasn't home last time I was here," he said.

He looked at Addison, only to find her eyes on the adjacent mobile home. Compassion stirred in his chest. For the first time he realized fully how long and grueling this search had been for her. Not only did she have to deal with the fact that someone was trying to kill her, but that the woman who'd given birth to her—and everyone else involved with her adoption—had ended up dead.

"I'm sorry this didn't work out," he said.

"It's okay. We'll think of something else."

"Aside from checking with the hospital, I'm fresh out of ideas, Ace."

"Then, let's go to the hospital."

"It's late. Let's check into the motel and see if we can—"

"Don't." Anger sparked like quicksilver in her eyes. "We had an agreement—"

"That wasn't what I was going to suggest." But he had to admit, the idea of getting her into bed appealed to him immensely. "I was going to suggest we try to come up with a game plan. Think this thing through."

She turned away, hugging herself against a gust of wind. "Right."

Randall knew his announcement that he would be returning to D.C. had upset her. Frankly, it was bothering him, too, particularly since they'd slept together. But what were his alternatives? Run from his demons indefinitely? Give up a career he'd invested twelve years of his life building? Drag her down with him?

He wasn't proud of the fact that in some twisted way, it pleased him knowing she cared, even if it was just a little bit. Not that he enjoyed hurting her. He didn't. Not by a long

shot. But it had been a long time since somebody cared about
him that way.

Needing to feel her close, he put his arm around her shoulders. "Let's get back to the car before we get frostbitten."

She didn't move, but continued to stare at the mobile home
where Agnes Beckett had lived and died. "When I think
about everything that's happened, sometimes I still can't believe it's real."

"You're shivering." He guided her down the front steps.
"Let's go."

Surprising him, she shrugged off his arm and stood facing
her birth mother's mobile home. "Just a few short weeks ago
she was alive and living right there. So close. If I'd found
her sooner maybe—"

"Don't even go there," he warned, knowing intimately the
crushing weight of guilt and the toll it could take on one's
sanity. "Don't second-guess yourself, Addison. It's counter-
productive as hell."

"I don't blame myself. Not really. I know I'm not responsible for her death. But I can't help but wonder what might
have been if I'd found her sooner." Turning, she looked up
at him. "I mean, for months now, I've wondered if she ever
thought about me. Is that silly?"

"No," he said gently.

"I want to take a look inside the trailer," she said.

A laugh escaped him, but it didn't hold any humor. He
should have seen this one coming. "Absolutely not."

"Why?"

"Because I'm not as insane as you think I am."

"I'll do it without you."

"No, you won't," he growled. Slipping his hand to the
crook of her arm, he forced her toward the car. It was the
only sane thing to do.

"I'm not suggesting we steal anything." She struggled to
free herself. "We wouldn't really be breaking the law. Just
taking a little look."

"Taking a little look in the state of Ohio will get you two to four in the state pen."

"We're here, dammit. I need to do this." Digging in her heels, she broke his grip, then stood staring angrily at him.

Uttering a curse, he faced her. The tattered remains of his professional ethics wouldn't allow him to say yes. But the way she was looking at him with those liquid brown eyes . . . so full of hope, of fear . . . Damn her, he'd probably jump through a flaming hoop if she asked.

"Do you have a key?" he heard himself ask.

"Do we need one? I figured you're probably a whiz at picking locks."

"I'm glad you have so much confidence in my criminal capabilities, but the answer is still no." But he knew if she persisted, he wouldn't be able to refuse her. So little had gone right with this case, he hated to deny her this one thing. Even if it was a hell of a risk and probably wouldn't accomplish a thing.

"You're bound and determined to get us arrested, aren't you?" he snapped.

"We won't get caught."

Randall laughed outright at the absurdity of his debating this with her. "Life's a bitch and then you die," he muttered.

"What?"

"I said, McEvoy will have an orgasm if he catches us in the midst of a B and E."

"There may be something important that the police have overlooked." She glanced over her shoulder at the trailer. "Besides, legally, it's my property anyway. If it ever went to court—"

"It's not going to court, because I'm not going to let you do it."

"This could be the break we need."

"No, goddammit." He started for the car.

"Please, Randall."

Her plea stopped him midstride. Turning, he looked into her eyes, realized with a start he was already in miles over his head. His resolve melted as her eyes reached into him and touched a place he'd carelessly left unguarded. For God's sake, the woman tied him up in little knots.

"I charge double for jail time," he grumbled.

She gave him a Mona Lisa smile. "We're not going to get caught."

"Yeah, well, if McEvoy shows up it's every man for himself."

After moving the car to a nearby side street, Randall walked back to the trailer, keeping to the shadows, hoping he wasn't about to make a mistake that would cost him his license.

"Let's get this nasty business over with," he said.

When Addison started for the front door, he hooked his fingers over the collar of her coat, pulling her back. "We go in through the back, Ace."

"Sorry. I guess I'm not used to this burglar stuff." Casting an uneasy glance over her shoulder, she fell in beside him.

Much to his relief, the rear of the trailer faced a plowed field, away from the prying eyes of well-meaning neighbors and bored deputies itching for some action. The wind slapped at their clothes as they headed toward the back door. A piece of the skirting flapped noisily in the wind, filling the night air with the tinny sound of metal against metal.

Randall tried the knob. Locked, as he had expected. "Of course," he murmured, wondering what the hell else could go wrong tonight. "You wouldn't happen to have a burglar's tool kit, would you?"

Behind him, huddled in her coat, Addison shook her head. "Left it in my other coat."

"Ha ha." He withdrew his Visa Gold card from his wallet and worked it into the seam. "If I can't get this door open, we're leaving. If you don't cooperate, I'll forcibly carry you back to the car."

"You'll get it open."

Cold bit through his gloves, numbing his fingers as he worked the card into the seam. An instant later the bolt slipped aside. He turned the knob. The door swung wide and clattered against the wall. "I'll be damned."

"You make breaking and entering look easy," she said.

"Yeah, I'm a real whiz." The smell of old wood and fuel oil rolled over him. Beyond, total darkness beckoned. "Come here."

Cautiously, she walked over to him and peered inside.

"You're not afraid of things that go bump in the night, are you, Ace?"

"Of course not."

"Good, because you're going in first."

She stared through the open door like a child about to face off with the bogeyman. "I'd rather you go in first."

"Oh, for chrissake, Addison." Heaving a sigh of exasperation, Randall turned away from her and hoisted himself through the door. Removing the flashlight from his coat pocket, he shone it behind him. "No one but us burglars," he said dryly and extended his hand to her.

ADDISON ACCEPTED HIS HAND AND LET HIM PULL HER up and through the door. The odors of musty carpet, old wood, and decay assaulted her nostrils. She hated to think of her birth mother living in such conditions. From all appearances, Agnes Beckett had lived a very hard life.

"Close the door."

She jumped at the sound of his voice. "It's too dark." The last thing she wanted to do was close herself up inside that trailer.

"Close it, dammit!"

She shut the door, enveloping them both in total darkness. For a moment, the only sound came from the wind, cutting around the trailer like an angry sea. She couldn't shake the thought that this was the place where Agnes Beckett had been so brutally murdered. Images from the crime scene photos played before her eyes, sending a chill up her spine.

"Turn on the flashlight," she whispered.

A tiny beam of light cut through the dark like a blade. "Better?" he asked, directing the beam to the floor between them.

Addison breathed out a sigh of relief. She could just make out his features in the dusky light, and she didn't miss the concern etched into them.

"Thank you," she said, berating herself for allowing her imagination to get the best of her. She couldn't fall apart now. Not when they were finally where they needed to be, and there was a very real possibility of finding some new piece of evidence.

"You okay?" Randall asked.

"I'm fine." To prove it, she threaded down the narrow hall, determined to do a thorough search of the premises. Ahead of her, murky light flowed in from the living room windows.

Her suede pumps were silent on the carpeted floor as she moved closer to the living room. She stopped when the trailer shuddered with a particularly hard gust of wind. "Can we turn on the lights?" she asked.

"No."

Behind her, she heard Randall trip over the small rug she'd barely managed to avoid. "How are we supposed to find clues without light?"

"If the neighbors see a light in here, they'll jam the phone lines calling the sheriff."

"Somehow I knew you were going to say that." Addison passed by a threadbare recliner and end table, spotting an ancient-looking TV on her left. She paused where the bar divided the kitchen from the rest of the trailer. There were canisters and dishes of different shapes and sizes on the counter. The cord of an old toaster dangled over the edge like a dead snake.

"We can start here." Randall propped the flashlight against the toaster so that it shone away from the front window.

"What are we looking for?" Addison opened the refrigerator, wrinkling her nose against the stench of rotting food.

"Anything and everything. Papers. Newspaper clippings. Just don't leave anything out of place."

"Like someone's going to notice."

He opened the first cabinet, sliding a container of salt and assorted spices aside. "And keep your gloves on."

Addison searched the top of the refrigerator, finding nothing more than a few outdated coupons and a month's worth of dust. As she searched, she tried to get a sense of the woman who had lived there. Everything she touched—the wooden spoon, the hot pad—she held for a moment, wishing in vain they could tell her something.

Methodically, she and Randall worked their way through the kitchen and living room, toward the rear of the trailer where the bedrooms were located.

"It looks like the police went over the place thoroughly," she said.

"She didn't have much."

Addison had known beforehand the search was a long shot. She should have been prepared for the disappointment. But she wasn't, and that she'd come up empty-handed again hit her hard.

"I didn't really think we'd find anything." She hated the resignation in her voice, and that she was lying to keep the disappointment at bay.

"Yes, you did."

Raising her gaze to his, she searched his face, surprised to see understanding. She wasn't sure why she let that affect her, but for a moment she had to blink away tears.

"Don't give up hope," he said gently. "We'll get to the bottom of this."

"I was hoping for a break."

Surprising her, he reached out and pressed his palm against her face. He was so close she could smell his aftershave. Memories of their lovemaking the night before played wickedly through her mind. She wasn't sorry she'd let it happen. The time had been right for her. He'd definitely been the right man. Too bad he had his sights set on another life in another state.

"I'll check the master bedroom." She turned away before she had the chance to do something stupid, like cry or let him kiss her.

"I'll take the other one."

She started for the larger of the two bedrooms, nearly bumping into the broken chair leaning against the wall.

"Careful." The beam of his flashlight played over the chair.

"You'd think the cops would be more vigilant about—" Her voice died in her throat when the flashlight beam illuminated a wide, dark stain on the paneled wall. At first, Addison thought it was rust from a leaky roof or hot water heater. But when she looked down and saw the stain spread out on the carpet, her blood ran cold.

She stared for what seemed like an eternity. The dark stain covered the wall and carpeting like an old wound that continued to seep in its injustice. Instinctively, she knew the smell pervading her nose was that of old blood. Of death. Of murder.

Randall averted the light. "Shit. I want you to wait outside."

His words cut through the shock, like light through fog. Before she could move, his hand gripped her wrist, turning her, pushing her toward the door.

Addison's feet felt anchored to the floor. A cold sweat broke out on the back of her neck. She felt seasick, chilled to the bone. The contents of her stomach climbed into her throat. To her horror her stomach clenched, and she realized she was going to be sick.

She staggered toward the door, choking back sickness. She wanted air, mouthfuls of cold, clean air.

Randall reached the door before she did, shoved it open, and guided her to it. At the threshold, Addison fell to her knees and threw up violently, her body shuddering convulsively with each retch.

Dizzy and humiliated, she gripped the jamb and let the icy wind wash over her heated face. For several minutes, she stayed that way, willing her stomach to calm. She refused to think about the crime scene photos. She refused to let her mind show her the splattered blood that streamed down the wall like a black waterfall.

Slowly, she became aware of Randall's hand on her shoulder, reassuring her with his touch. He stood over her, holding the door open, waiting patiently for her to finish. "Easy does it," he said gently.

"Just let me sit here for a moment."

"Take as much time as you need."

"Leave me alone. This is humiliating."

"Don't sweat it, Ace. I've been in your shoes before." He caressed her nape with the tips of his fingers. "I should have known better than to bring you here."

"It was my idea. I didn't leave you much choice."

"I hate to disappoint you, but I can hold my own when I put my mind to it."

When her stomach had settled to a manageable level, Addison raised her head, willing the dizziness away. "I want to finish searching the bedroom."

Randall helped her to her feet. "You're in no condition to do any more searching."

"I want to do this. Dammit, I need to do this." She leaned heavily against the jamb when dizziness threatened to send her back down.

He reached for her just in time to keep her knees from buckling. "You've had enough."

"We may not get another chance."

He raised the flashlight to her face, careful not to blind her. "Christ, you're pale as a sheet."

"I'm not leaving. Dammit, I feel better."

"Right." He touched her cheek with the back of his hand.

"I want to finish this."

"I'll search the goddamn bedrooms," he growled. "I want you to wait for me in the car."

Addison didn't have the energy to argue further. She turned to the door, then jumped to the ground. "I'll wait for you here."

"I'll be five minutes," he said.

"Be thorough. Don't hurry on my account." She turned her back to the wind, hoping the cold would take her mind off the stench of death that lingered like a dark cloud in the trailer.

By the time Randall jumped to the ground next to her, she was shaking uncontrollably. It had started with just her teeth chattering. After a few minutes the trembling had spread to her hands, her knees, until her entire body quaked with cold and the remnants of sickness.

"I told you to wait in the car." Grasping the sleeve of her coat, he forced her in the general direction of the car. "Your stubborn streak is beginning to annoy me."

"I could say the same thing about you."

"You catch pneumonia and I'm off the case. I don't do hospitals," he growled, but his voice was too soft for the words to sting.

Addison didn't miss the concern laced in between the nasty looks and harsh words. "Sorry I blew it, Talbot."

"Don't apologize for something you had no control over."

It was then, beneath the yellow light of the street lamp, that she realized he hadn't yet looked at her. Odd for a man who was a stickler for eye contact. "Why won't you look at me?" she asked.

Randall unlocked the passenger door. "Get inside."

Mechanically, Addison slid onto the passenger seat and removed her gloves, rubbing her hands together to warm them. He got in a moment later, started the car, and switched on the heater.

"Feeling better?" he asked.

Leaning back against the seat, she closed her eyes. "Peachy."

"We need to find a phone."

Her heart kicked hard against her ribs. She opened her

eyes and turned to him. "Did you find something?"

From the inside pocket of his parka, he handed her a small, black book. "This was on the top shelf in the closet."

"A bible?" She stared at the tattered cover, almost afraid to touch it. Mildew and the tang of dust tickled her nose as she took it from him.

Randall put the car in gear and pulled onto the street. "There's a newspaper clipping inside."

Feeling acutely the weight of his gaze, she switched on the overhead light and paged through the bible. The yellowed clipping lay within the tattered pages halfway into the book. She slid it from its ancient nest with two fingers, unfolded the delicate paper, and saw it was from the November 21, 1974, edition of a paper called the *County Crier*. She began to read.

LOCAL GIRL ALLEGES RAPE
Al Stukins, Reporter

A sixteen-year-old Siloam Springs girl reported on Tuesday that she was repeatedly raped and sodomized by an out-of-state student who had allegedly paid her for a night of sex. A spokesman for the local sheriff's department reported that they have been unable to substantiate the charges due to the lack of physical evidence and allegations that the woman was under the influence of LSD and possibly marijuana at the time of the incident. As of this afternoon, no charges have been filed.

chapter
16

JACK TALBOT LEANED BACK IN HIS WHEELCHAIR AND watched the computer screen roll by with each click of the mouse. He'd been writing code for so many hours he barely noticed the twitching in his eyes or the tight muscles at the base of his neck. He'd lost count of the hours. As far as he knew, it could have been days since he'd last eaten or showered or talked to another human being.

But he was so damned close.

"Come on, you sweet bitch." The screen continued a seemingly endless scroll. A blur of names and dates flew by. He slowed the flow of data when he saw the list of babies born on August 20, 1975, in Dayton's Good Samaritan Hospital. Delivering physician, Dr. Heimer Kourt.

"Yeah, baby, talk to me." He clicked the mouse. A dozen names scrolled by. Alpha order. He clicked the mouse. Halfway down the page, the name *Agnes Beckett* materialized.

It was the closest thing to an orgasm he'd had in five years. Victory, as sweet as a lover's kiss, made his chest swell. His breath jammed in his throat. With a trembling hand, he touched the monitor, leaving a greasy smear where the name Colleen Glass appeared. The name of her doctor. Heimer Kourt. He clicked the mouse and searched to see if the father had been named.

And he froze.

He stared in disbelief, knowing that somehow his high-tech lover had failed him. "This can't be." He punched the Print Screen key. The laser spit out the name in indisputable black and white. "Sweet Jesus."

The bell on the alley door jingled. Surprised, disoriented from so many hours of work, Jack spun his chair around, expecting to see Randall. Instead, a masked man dressed in black leveled a semiautomatic pistol at his chest.

Adrenaline danced through his midsection, but stopped at his hips. With an eerie calm, Jack noticed the silencer, realizing immediately he'd discovered the truth too late. His only thought was that he would never be able to tell his brother what he'd found. The injustice of it nearly sent him from the chair.

He cursed his legs.

Helpless to flee or to protect himself, knowing he could never reach the .22 revolver in the top drawer of his desk, Jack stared at the man as his heart pumped furiously. "The whole world knows," he said. "You're too late. You fucking bastard."

He watched powerlessly as the man's finger tightened on the trigger. Instinctively, he braced against the impending impact. A thousand thoughts rushed through his brain. The state of his life. The people he would leave behind. Cold, hard fear hammered at him as he imagined pain and blood.

An instant later, a nine-millimeter slug exploded in his chest.

ADDISON READ THE ARTICLE TWICE BEFORE SHE LET herself breathe, before she let herself feel. She told herself she'd already known what happened to Agnes Beckett, that this shouldn't be hitting her so hard. But to see the truth on paper shook her. One by one, the ugly words crept into a brain that didn't want to believe. The emotions swirled inside her like debris kicked up by a violent tornado.

She steeled herself against the pain, choking back the outrage, the injustice, and the bitterness that followed. Her only thought was that she had been conceived through a vile, incomprehensible act. An act of violence that made her feel dirty and sick to her stomach.

Forcing a breath into her lungs, she lowered the article, carefully folded it, and tucked it back into the bible. "That poor girl was Agnes Beckett."

"Probably."

She looked down at the article. "He raped her. My . . . birth father."

Randall's jaw flexed.

"They discredited her by mentioning drugs. My god."

"I think this town has a dirty little secret tucked away into its neat gutters," he said.

The thought jolted her. "What do we do now?"

"What's the byline on that story?"

She quickly scanned the article. "Al Stukins." She fought the hope rising in her chest. God, how she wanted to get off the emotional roller coaster.

"There's our witness."

"The story was written twenty-five years ago. He could be anywhere now."

"Or he could still be here in Siloam Springs."

Randall parked the car curbside across the street from McNinch's Bar. Its neon Beer on Tap sign glowed at the front window. "This is where your birth mother used to work," he said.

"This is where you spoke with the waitress."

"That's right."

Addison remembered vividly the night he'd told her about Agnes Beckett's sordid past. "The one who told you Agnes Beckett was a prostitute?"

He nodded. "There's a telephone inside. We can ask a few questions and have a sandwich if you're up to it."

"I'll settle for a soda and some information."

THE FAMILIAR AROMAS OF FRIED FOOD, SPILLED BEER, and cigarette smoke hit Randall in the face like a blast furnace the instant he walked through the door. In the last year, he'd spent more time than he wanted to admit in bars just like this one, drinking himself into oblivion, trying not to think about the state of his life.

He wanted a drink now. Wanted it so badly he could already feel the burn of whiskey at the back of his throat, that heady rush of alcohol to his brain. He wondered if the need would always be there to torment him. He wondered if he would have given in to that need yesterday if Addison hadn't been there.

Shaking off the cold, and thoughts he didn't want to deal with at the moment, he scanned the room. To his right, a scarred wooden bar ran the length of the room. Behind it, a burly-looking woman with a receding hairline watched them out of the corner of her eye. From the jukebox, Eric Clapton belted out an old rock and roll song about a woman waiting for another love. Except for the group of men playing pool at the back of the room, and a thin young man hovering at the bar, the place was nearly empty.

Randall was acutely aware of the male eyes sweeping to Addison. A knot of territoriality tightened in his gut with surprising force. Casually, he put his arm around her shoulders, telling himself it wasn't a possessive gesture. He guided her to a corner booth. "Good thing we had reservations," he said, sliding into the red vinyl seat across from her.

Dark smudges of fatigue marred the porcelain skin beneath her eyes. Her lack of color worried him. She'd put up a valiant front, but he knew the strain was beginning to wear her down both emotionally and physically. She wasn't prepared to deal with half of what was being thrown at her.

Dammit, she had enough to deal with without him complicating matters because he couldn't keep his hands off her.

As he stared into her fragile eyes, he almost wished he hadn't slept with her. Almost. She was beginning to mess with his head. More than just his head, if he wanted to be truthful about it. Crazy thoughts for a man who should be chomping at the bit to get back to his career. He hadn't intended for things to get so damn complicated. He hadn't intended for a lot of things to happen.

Across the table, she offered a wan smile. He had the sudden, overwhelming urge to reach out, pull her to him, and crush that lush mouth against his for just one more taste.

"Where were you just now, Talbot?"

He smiled, wondering how she'd react if he answered truthfully. "You don't want to know," he said easily.

The last thing either of them needed was another close encounter. If he went to bed with her again, his resolve to resurrect his failed career back in D.C. might not survive.

Reining in his libido, he let his gaze travel to the bar. "See the barmaid?" he asked.

Addison turned in the booth and glanced toward the woman behind the bar. "The one missing both eyeteeth?"

"Her name is Dixie. I spoke with her the last time I was here in Siloam Springs."

"She knew Agnes Beckett?"

"They worked together for a few months."

Craning her neck, Addison regarded the woman thoughtfully. "I want to talk to her."

Randall knew she wasn't going to like what the people in this town had to say about Beckett. He wished he could protect her from the truth, from getting hurt. But she deserved the truth. Even if it wasn't pretty.

"That waitress has lived in this little town for about ten years," he said.

Addison turned back to him, her eyes jumping with excitement. "Do you think she might be able to help us find Al Stukins?"

"It's worth a shot." He watched the barmaid approach the booth. "The burgers aren't bad."

She groaned.

The barmaid snapped down two menus and two glasses of ice water. Her movements were the short, decisive movements of a woman who'd spent too many years waiting tables and too many hours on her feet.

"Hi, there," she said with the slightest hint of a twang. "What can I get you to drink?"

Randall put on his most charming smile. "It's Dixie, right?"

She turned narrowed eyes on him before baring a hit-or-miss smile. "I never forget a face." She tapped her pencil against her temple. "You're that private detective feller. Randy."

"I was wondering if you'd mind answering a few questions."

"Are you kidding? This is the most excitement I've had all week." Pulling a green order pad from the pocket of her smock, Dixie propped a chubby hip onto the table. "What do you want to know?"

"Did you know Agnes Beckett?" Addison asked abruptly.

A host of emotions scrolled across the woman's face. Surprise. Suspicion. Curiosity. "Damn shame about what happened to her," she said cautiously.

Caught up in the moment, Addison didn't seem to notice the barmaid's reaction. Randall watched the exchange, knowing that if Addison didn't slow down, she could very well spook Dixie and blow the opportunity.

"What was she like?" Addison asked.

"Well . . ." Dixie's face pinched. "She was a damn good waitress. Hard worker. Fast, too. Kept up with the orders."

"What about personally?"

The waitress's eyes flicked from Addison to Randall and then back. "Darlin', she kept to herself mostly. Lived in that little trailer park at the edge of town."

"Did she ever mention . . . family?"

"Can't say she did. Lived with a guy for a while. A trucker, I think. From what I understand, she never had any kids."

Randall didn't miss the hurt that flashed across Addison's face. Something inside him winced at her pain.

"You kin?" Dixie asked.

"We're friends of the family," he cut in. Reaching across the table, he took Addison's hand, not surprised when he found it cold.

He looked at Dixie. "Do you know where we might be able to find a fellow by the name of Al Stukins?"

The waitress wrinkled her nose and put the pencil eraser against her temple. "Stukins," she repeated slowly. "An old guy?"

"That's right."

"There used to be a Stukins lived down on County Line Road just past the railroad trestle. Raised Appaloosa horses until just a few years ago."

Randall leaned forward. "So he's still around?"

"Last I heard, his son moved him into the old folks home over on Route 40. Shitty thing to do, considering the old man didn't want to go. Billy Cruz was tellin' me he put up a hell of a fight, but he has that old person's disease, Al Heimer's. Poor old guy. Gettin' old's a bitch, ya know?"

Randall groaned inwardly when he realized she was referring to Alzheimer's disease. He couldn't think of a worse affliction for a person he was going to question about an incident that took place more than twenty-five years ago. "Where's the old folks home?"

"The old schoolhouse. Small place. Red brick building half a mile west on Route 40. Can't miss it." She slid her rear from the table and poised her pencil on the pad. "Randy, what's it going to be? Cheeseburger, fries, and a double bourbon on the rocks?"

Pulling a twenty-dollar bill from his wallet, Randall pressed it into her palm. "We don't have time right now, Dixie. Thanks for the info."

Rising, he reached for Addison's hand. "Let's go. I think we just got our first break."

PARSON'S HOME FOR THE RETIRED WAS A TWO-STORY red brick building set back from the highway and nestled among the winter skeletons of fifty-year-old maples and oaks. Outside the double front doors, a stately blue spruce blazed with a colorful array of Christmas lights.

"How can you call this a break?" Addison asked, annoyed that he'd interrupted before she'd gotten the chance to thoroughly question Dixie about Agnes Beckett. If she didn't know better, she might have thought he'd done it on purpose.

"Stukins might remember something," Randall said.

"He's got Alzheimer's, for chrissake."

He pulled into a parking space and stopped the car. "Don't get cynical on me now, Ace."

"Of course not. That's your job."

Ignoring her, he swung open the car door and stepped into the cold. "Hopefully, we can get in without any trouble."

Addison met him on the sidewalk, wondering how a man with Alzheimer's disease was going to remember something that happened twenty-five years ago. She hated it, but things were beginning to look hopeless again.

"If anyone asks, you're his granddaughter," Randall said. "You're in for the holidays from Ohio State and you want to see dear old Grandpappy. Can you handle that?"

If she hadn't been so annoyed, she might have thought twice about what they were about to do. Admittedly, lying wasn't one of her strengths. But with so much at stake she felt she could pull it off. "I can handle it."

"Goddamn Alzheimer's," he hissed, practically dragging her down the sidewalk. "I just hope he's not in the advanced stages."

They ascended the steps and reached the double set of doors. Through the glass, Addison saw a small artificial Christmas tree blinking merrily. Randall opened the door.

She walked in, feeling her palms dampen with anxiety.

The first thing she noticed was the distinctly unpleasant smell. It was the medicinal smell of a hospital tinged with the dust and lemon wax redolence of a church. It reached into her, the smell of the old, of the neglected, saddening and offending everything inside her that was human.

Parson's Home for the Retired had looked different from the highway. Addison had expected to find caroling grand-children, gossiping parents, and the smiling faces of the el-derly. Instead, she had walked into an atmosphere that more resembled an ill-kept funeral home.

The lobby was deserted. Recessed lighting illuminated a large reception desk. On the wall behind it, a bland oil paint-ing depicted a huge tree covered with pink flowers. A spindly ficus in a plastic pot stood near the front door, soaking up more cold than light.

"Nice place," Randall said dryly, closing the door behind them. "Let's skip the front desk."

Even as he said the words, a skinny, black-haired man with a thin mustache appeared behind the desk and looked over at them.

Pasting a smile to her face, Addison squared her shoulders and approached him.

The man offered a plastic smile. "May I help you?"

"We're here to see Al Stukins," she said with her best college student inflection.

Smiling spuriously, the man opened a notebook and began paging through it while she held her breath. "Your name?"

"Addie Fox."

His brows went together as he flipped the page over and then back again. "You don't seem to be on the list to see Mr. Stukins."

"I don't get home very often." Addison forced another smile, hoping it didn't look as phony as it felt. She didn't like this little man, and she'd never been good at hiding her emotions. "I'm home for the holidays. He's my grandfather."

"Well, you're not on the list." He folded his arms across

his chest. "I'm sorry, but I can't let you in to see Mr. Stukins without permission from his family."

"I *am* his family." The lie came easily, and she let it fly with the fervor of truth.

"You can have his son give me a call tomorrow to put you on the list." He closed the book. "Until then, I'm afraid I can't let you in."

She was just beginning to think they'd met another dead end when Randall leaned forward and flipped open the notebook, ripping the list in question from inside.

"We didn't drive all the way from Columbus to be told we're not on the goddamn list," he growled.

Addison's heart began to pound.

The man's mouth opened, rivaling the width of his eyes. "Sir, you can't do that."

"When's the last time that man had a visitor?" Randall looked like an incensed bull about to maul a cowering matador.

"Uh, I don't—" The man stepped back, eyeing the notebook, not daring to reach for it. "I . . . I need my register back."

"What the hell's your name?" Without waiting for an answer, Randall plucked the man's name tag from his shirt, leaving a hole the size of a dime in the fabric. "I'll need this for my lawyer."

"Sir!"

"Who owns this dump?"

"You can't do this!"

"Watch me." Turning the tag over in his palm, Randall read it aloud with great distaste. "Adrian Grigsby." His eyes were black with anger when they swept to the terrified clerk. "When's the last time the health department inspected this dirty little hellhole of yours, Adrian?"

Addison stepped back, astonished.

Adrian's Adam's apple bobbed twice in quick succession.

"I bet they'd love to get their bureaucratic hands on you, wouldn't they? You'd probably be able to keep them busy for days, wouldn't you?" Randall smiled wickedly before turning to Addison. "Let's go."

She was so caught up in the drama, she had to clamp her mouth shut against a protest. If poor old Adrian didn't fall for it, they were sunk. Praying Randall knew what he was doing, she took his hand and they started toward the door.

"Wait a moment!"

Relief bubbled through her. Next to her, Randall stopped. Simultaneously, they swung around to face Adrian.

The man was panting, his slicked-back hair falling about his forehead as he came around the desk. "I can let you see him tonight and add you to the list tomorrow," he said.

Randall stared at the clerk as if he were trying to decide whether to punch him or strangle him. "Now, why didn't I think of that?"

A skinny hand clutched the fabric where his name tag had been stripped away. "After all, it *is* the holiday season."

"Yeah, no need to be unreasonable." Randall tossed the name tag and wrinkled list onto the desk. "Where's his room?"

Adrian led them down a wide, tiled hall trimmed with stainless steel handrails and wheelchair ramps.

"You drive a hard bargain, Talbot," Addison whispered as they made a right and started down another hall.

"No thanks to you." He grinned. "You're a terrible liar."

"Thanks, I think."

"When we get to the room, I'll deal with Stukins," he said. "You get rid of the skinny jerk."

"Shouldn't be too hard since you've got him warmed up for me."

The unpleasant smell of neglect seemed to emanate from beneath the doors they passed. Only then did she realize Randall had been dead serious about calling the health department. Parson's Home for the Retired was as inhumane as Adrian was irritating, and Addison promised herself that when all of this was over if Randall didn't call them, she would.

They reached the end of the hall and Adrian bent to unlock a door painted an institutional blue. "We keep the rooms locked after dark," he said in a conspiratorial voice. "To keep the folks from wandering off." He swung open the door and turned to them with the uneasy smile of a realtor about to show a filthy house. "Albert! You have company!"

The single-room efficiency was small, cold, and poorly lit. Addison held her breath as the stench of dirty linens and bathroom mildew permeated her nostrils. A single, grimy window faced the street. The sight of Christmas lights beyond made her feel like she'd just stepped into a prison.

A gaunt man with a day's growth of white stubble sat on a rumpled bed staring at a small black-and-white television. He raised his head when they entered, acknowledged their presence with a glazed scowl, then turned his attention back to the rerun of *M.A.S.H.*

"He hasn't had his shower yet today," Adrian said, ducking into the bathroom to scoop up a pile of towels littering the floor. "We've been short-handed because of the holidays."

"I'll bet," Randall grumbled.

Saddened and disgusted, Addison could only stare at the old man sitting on the bed, hoping this charade wouldn't harm him in any way.

Having collected the soiled towels, Adrian headed for the door. "Visiting hours are over at eight P.M.," he said over his shoulder. "But you can stay a few extra minutes if you like."

She forced a smile. "Thank you."

A few feet away, Randall took a chair and pulled it close to the bed. "Mr. Stukins?"

The old man raised his head and regarded Randall through cloudy blue eyes. "Are you the fella from the service station?"

"I'm Randall Talbot." He extended his hand. "I'd like to ask you a few questions if you don't mind."

Stukins stared at him blankly before accepting the handshake. "Questions," he repeated and turned his attention back to the television. "I don't have time for questions."

Needing to move, to be involved, Addison stepped forward and switched off the TV. "Mr. Stukins, we need to ask you some questions about a story you wrote for the *County Crier*."

"I was a reporter for thirty-two years. Worked my way up from the printing press." For a moment, he looked lucid. "The master cylinder went bad on my Chevy." He turned his gaze back to Randall. "Are you the fella from the gas station?"

Addison didn't miss the frustration on Randall's face, and she wondered if he had the patience for such a delicate interrogation.

"You were a reporter for the *County Crier*," he said.

The old man smiled, revealing a set of pearly white dentures. "Thirty-two years."

Addison slipped into the chair beside Randall.

"You did a story back in 1974 about a young woman who was raped," he said.

"I bought my Chevy in '68," Stukins said argumentatively.

Randall leaned forward, caught the older man's gaze, and held it. "You wrote a story for the *County Crier* in November of 1974 about a young woman by the name of Agnes Beckett. Do you remember Agnes Beckett? Do you remember what happened to her?"

Stukins's eyes widened. His mouth quivered. "They killed my dog."

To anyone else the statement might have seemed like an Alzheimer patient's rantings. To Addison, the old man's words made terrible sense.

"Who killed your dog?" Randall prodded.

"They were going to kill my family."

"Because of the story?"

The old man began to shake. Alarm skittered through Addison when his eyes rolled back. For a moment, she thought he would faint. He looked frail. Unable to keep herself from it, she rose and put her hand gently on his shoulder. "You're doing fine, Mr. Stukins."

His eyes focused on her. "Yale . . . ," he mumbled.

"Yale?" Randall repeated.

"He graduated the same year he hurt that girl."

"Who hurt her? Who are you talking about?"

"They were going to kill my family." Stukins looked over his shoulder as if he were expecting someone to come through the door. For the first time, Addison saw fear in his eyes. "I did what they told me to do," he said, his gaunt hands waving in agitation.

Randall cast her an uneasy look, then focused on the old man. "Who threatened your family?"

"That son of a bitch was guilty as sin."

"Who?"

"Tate beat the hell out of that girl. Did terrible things to her. Put her in the hospital."

The words went through Addison like a knife. She shivered, knowing he was talking about her birth mother. A sixteen-year-old girl. Beaten and raped. The thought sickened her. Was it possible she'd been conceived through such a vile act? Had someone threatened Stukins to keep the crime from coming to light? Had the people of Siloam Springs swept the entire ordeal under the rug?

"Tate? Is that his last name?" Randall asked urgently.

A string of drool stretched from the corner of Stukins's mouth to a stain on his pajama shirt. "Are you the fella from the garage?" he asked. "I'm stuck here until you fix my Chevy."

Frustration billowed through Addison. Rising, she went to the sink and dampened a paper towel and knelt before Stukins. "Who is Tate?" she asked, blotting the saliva from his chin.

He swatted her hand away. "If you're not from the garage, I don't want to talk to you. I want my master cylinder fixed." The old man's eyes turned toward the blank TV. "I don't like it here."

Grimacing, Randall rose and laid his hand lightly on Stukins's gaunt shoulder. "Thanks, old man." He looked at Addison. "I think that's it."

"But he remembered a name," she protested.

"At this point, we don't know if Tate is the first name or the last name," he pointed out.

Addison started to resist, but he stopped her. "What we did find out is that Tate may have graduated from Yale in 1974. That's something Jack can help us with." He cast a final look at the stooped old man sitting on the bed watching the blank TV. "Let's go."

RANDALL HAD JUST PULLED THE RENTAL CAR ONTO Route 40 when the pager clipped to his belt chirped twice. Shifting, he reached for it, expecting to see the office number. Instead, he found himself squinting at a Denver number he wasn't familiar with.

"Is it Jack?" Addison asked.

"No." An inexplicable jab of anxiety rushed through him. Recalling a telephone booth nearby, he made a U-turn and sped toward it.

Addison remained silent, but he felt her eyes on him as he stomped the car to a screeching halt at the curb next to the phone booth. Without speaking, he swung open the door and sprinted to the phone. Pulling his gloves off with his teeth, he snatched up the receiver and punched the phone and credit card numbers from memory.

"Van-Dyne."

Randall's heart pumped hard. "This is Talbot," he said, knowing instinctively something was wrong.

"Mr. Talbot, I had one of your business cards and thought I should let you know what happened."

"What the hell are you talking about?" He didn't want to think about who was vulnerable back in Denver.

"There was a fire at your office," the detective said.

"Where's Jack?"

"Paramedics took him to St. Joe's with burns."

Randall braced, his heart freezing in his chest. "How is he?"

"Critical."

The word echoed in his head, its meaning punching him like a giant billy club. The roar of blood through his veins deafened him.

"Mr. Talbot, your brother also suffered a gunshot wound."

Another punch, harder, more vicious, twisted his guts into knots. Randall closed his eyes, trying not to imagine how helpless Jack must have felt. "Did you catch the son of a bitch?" he hissed through clenched teeth as rage and fear took turns pounding him.

"We're investigating. So far we don't have a lot to go on." There was no urgency in the detective's voice. No drive behind the words. He was a cop doing his job. Nothing at stake except his reputation. His quota. His paycheck.

"Jesus Christ." A sickening realization plowed through him. "It's about the case."

"The case you're working on?"

"Addison Fox is involved." He wanted to explain but knew there wasn't time. He had to get to Denver. "It's complicated." He looked down at his watch, felt the panic slither more deeply into him. "I'll stop by your office when I get there."

He slammed the receiver down hard, jerked open the door of the booth, and stepped into the wind. He felt as if his entire world had just careened out of control. For a full minute he stood in the cold, trembling inside and out, trying to pull himself together.

By the time he reached the car, the shaking had eased enough for him to yank open the door and wedge himself behind the wheel. Battling the impotent emotions, the helplessness and rage, he started the engine and put the car in gear.

"What is it? What happened?" Addison's voice reached in

through the iciness surrounding him, offering him refuge from the cold.

"It's Jack," he choked. "Jesus Christ. They fucking got to Jack."

"Oh, my god." Her hand went to her mouth. "Please, tell me he's not—oh, *God*."

He couldn't look at her. Not when his control was slipping away. "I should have been there. I should have protected him."

"No—"

Randall slammed his fist into the dash. Plastic shattered. Pain zinged up his arm. "Why Jack, goddammit!"

"Stop it. Please."

He couldn't breathe. Couldn't swallow. Panic gripped his throat, like a hangman's noose. Terror sent tremors through his body. He felt trapped. Panicked.

He felt dead.

God, he needed a drink.

"Randall? Are you okay?"

He heard her voice as if through a fog. Addison. He sucked in a breath, felt the panic release its grip on his chest. "I'm okay."

He looked at her, found her staring at him as if he were a ghost. Maybe he was. "I'm okay, goddammit. Don't look at me like that."

She flinched but didn't look away. "How bad is he hurt?"

"He's critical."

"Oh, God, I'm sorry. Is he going to be all right?"

"I don't know." He punched the accelerator and sent the car screeching into the deserted street. "I should have seen this coming."

"It wasn't your fault."

Ignoring her, he drove like a madman through the silent streets of Siloam Springs.

"Your knuckles are bleeding. Jesus, you're shaking. Let me drive—"

The truck came out of nowhere. He mashed his foot down

on the brake. The car slid sideways, barely missing the truck, and screeched to a halt, jerking them hard against their safety belts.

Randall stared blindly through the windshield, taking short, shallow breaths. "They shot him. Then they fucking burned him."

"Oh, no. Randall . . . I'm sorry."

He couldn't look at her. Couldn't look into her clear, dark eyes and see her innocence marred by horror and ugliness. But closer to the truth, he didn't want her to see the blackness that lay in his own heart. The need for revenge. For murder. For blood.

chapter
17

AT FOUR A.M., THE USUALLY BUSTLING HALLS OF ST.
Joseph Hospital were hushed with a serenity too precarious
to acknowledge. Though she'd never been seriously ill, Addison harbored an irrational dislike of hospitals. It had been
in another hospital ten months earlier that she'd been informed of her parents' deaths.

She remembered with perfect clarity the mercurial silence,
the buzzing of the overhead fluorescent lights, the smell of
isopropyl alcohol and disinfectant, and other unfathomable
odors as the on-call physician had relayed the news. She
remembered the paging system blaring in the background,
the squeak of a nurse's rubber-soled shoes against tile, the
cool quiet of the room where she'd slowly lost control.

This was almost as bad.

She couldn't stop thinking about Jack. The terror he must
have felt. The helplessness. The pain. She found it incon-
ceivable that anyone could commit such a ruthless act, especially against a man in a wheelchair. She hated the dark
side of human nature she'd witnessed in the last week.

She worried about the way Randall was handling it. He'd barely spoken during the endless flights that had taken them from Dayton to Chicago to Denver. Though he tried to conceal it, Addison sensed the fear and the barely controlled rage seething just below the surface. She instinctively knew control was important to him—just as she knew he was clinging to its remnants by a thread. She supposed his need for control was why he'd had such a difficult time dealing with his diagnosis of post-traumatic stress disorder. It only frustrated her more that she couldn't seem to reach him.

Beyond exhaustion, she struggled to keep up as he strode into the surgical intensive care unit. Once through the set of double doors, he made straight for the brightly lit nurses' station in the center of the ward.

His face looked strained beneath the stark lights, the angles and planes of his features giving him a menacing appearance. A day's growth of black whiskers darkened his jaw. He looked like a man who'd been living on the edge for so long he'd forgotten how to find his way back.

There was a dangerous recklessness in his eyes she'd never seen before. A wildness in his manner that made her wonder just how close he was to snapping. Something frightening and powerful had been unleashed inside him, and she feared for anyone who crossed him.

Neither of the two nurses noticed when they reached the station. Randall put his hands on the counter. "I need to see Jack Talbot," he announced in a voice that dared either of the women to cross him.

A nurse with pretty eyes and short brown hair rose from her stool and smiled tiredly. Her name tag identified her as Susan Morris. A button pinned onto her uniform read: I CAN BE DIFFICULT.

"Are you family?" she asked, coming around the counter.

"He's my brother." Randall's voice was hoarse and hostile. A quick look told Addison he was quickly nearing the end of his endurance. She wished she could do something to comfort him, but so far her efforts had been rejected.

"How's he doing?" she asked.

The nurse grimaced. "They brought him up from surgery about three hours ago. He's awake and aware. Vitals are stable." She looked at Randall. "His condition is still critical, but you can see him if you want."

They followed her to a room down the hall. Outside the door, she picked up the chart, made a note, and then slipped into the room.

Randall turned to Addison. "Wait here," he said.

Before she could stop herself, she raised her hand and touched the side of his face. A jolt of emotion swept through her when he winced. Such a strong man, she thought. More vulnerable than she'd ever realized and in so much pain.

"Are you all right?" She knew he wouldn't tell her the truth. She knew he wasn't all right. That he wouldn't be all right until this nightmare was over. Looking deeply into his eyes, she wished there was a way she could ease his pain, take away the guilt, but there wasn't. All she could do was be there for him.

Surprising her, he closed his eyes and pressed his cheek into her palm. It was the first offer of comfort he'd accepted. A wan smile touched the corners of his mouth. "Better," he said and walked into the room.

RANDALL WAS SWEATING WHEN THE NURSE GUIDED him into the dimly lit room. His eyes were drawn immediately to the single bed, the indefinable heap beneath the white sheets that was his brother. Inwardly, he cursed, both fate and the bastard responsible.

Knowing he couldn't let his emotions get in the way of what lay ahead, he took a deep breath and kept moving. The room was high-tech, even for a hospital, and more closely resembled an operating room, equipped for emergencies, as if that sort of thing happened often in this ward.

Above the bed, two monitors beeped. Lower, an I.V. bag and two larger bags filled with bodily fluids and blood hung like grotesque ornaments. The hiss of the respirator filled the silence with horrible sound.

The sight of Jack hit him like a fist to the stomach. He held his breath, knowing his brother's eyes were on him, knowing he couldn't allow himself to react.

Jack was lying on his back with two small cylindrical pillows cradling his head. A quarter-inch-thick tube ran from the respirator into his mouth. A second, thinner tube protruded from his left nostril.

Feeling a drop of sweat trickle between his shoulder blades, Randall peeled off his parka and draped it over the back of the chair beside the bed. Then he met his brother's gaze. The two men stared at each other for a full minute, weighing reactions, reining in their emotions, giving the other time to do the same. *Only Jack would do that for me,* Randall thought, struggling to keep the fear and the rage at bay. This wasn't the place for it. He needed to be strong. For Jack. For the woman waiting for him in the hall.

"Hi, big brother." His voice sounded normal as he moved to the side of the bed. "Goddammit," he whispered as he drew near.

Jack managed a weak thumbs-up.

Randall's chest tightened. "Are you in any pain?"

Jack closed his eyes and shook his head. A thick section of gauze covered one side of his face from temple to chin. Another bandage ran the length of his arm, all the way to his fingers.

As the respirator pumped air into his brother's lungs, Randall watched, wondering how in the hell this could have happened, trying to convince himself it wasn't his fault.

"I should have been there for you," he said.

Jack tried to speak and ended up struggling with the respirator tube. Feeling awkward, knowing that, somehow, this was humiliating for him, Randall turned away as the nurse checked the respirator and murmured something about relaxation.

When he turned back, the nurse was gone and Jack's eyes

were closed. Randall crossed the room and pulled the ladder-back chair closer to the bed. "Jack?"

His brother's eyes opened and slowly focused on him.

"What the hell happened?"

Jack raised his hand, jiggling the I.V. tubes before letting it fall back to the bed at his side. Even through the pain-killing drugs and the remnants of anesthesia, his eyes took on an intensity that told Randall he had something to tell him.

Randall leaned closer until his face was inches from his brother's. He held his breath against the garlicky odor of anesthesia and the unmistakable stench of singed hair and flesh. "What are you trying to say?"

Jack made a sound that was closer to a groan than an intelligible word.

Suddenly crushed by guilt, overwhelmed by exhaustion and the jagged remnants of his own rage, Randall pulled back and lowered his face into his hands. For the first time in a long time, he felt like crying. Christ, he hadn't even spoken with the doctor, yet here he was questioning a man who was too weak to breathe on his own.

For a moment, the surreal hiss of the respirator was the only sound. But it was the unmistakable sound of frustration that snapped Randall's head up. Jack raised his hand, flexing his bandaged knuckles. Only when his index finger and thumb came together did Randall realize what he wanted.

Heart pounding, he jumped up and reached for his parka, withdrawing his checkbook and pen. Never taking his eyes from Jack, Randall tore a blank deposit ticket from the book and carried the pen and paper back to his brother.

"Is this what you want?" he asked.

Jack nodded.

Randall put the pen in Jack's right hand, closing his fingers around it. Then he held the back of his checkbook to the paper. "What are you trying to tell me?"

Raising his head slightly, Jack scrawled something on the paper.

Randall looked at the paper. The name scrawled in black ink cut through him like a shotgun blast. Stukins had been right, he thought with disbelief. He stared, his brain refusing to acknowledge the implications or venture to imagine what the repercussions might be.

When he was able, Randall tore his eyes away from the name and looked at Jack. "Addison's father?"

His brother nodded once before closing his eyes and drifting off to a place Randall never wanted to go.

He was gripping his brother's hand when the nurse came in to escort him out. "He needs to rest, Mr. Talbot," she said softly, placing a tray of syringes on a nearby tray.

Barely hearing her for the thoughts rampaging through his beleaguered mind, Randall slipped the deposit ticket into his pocket. "When will the doctor be here?"

"Dr. Gregory usually gets in around six." She slid a needle into one of the I.V. lines. "He should be here in about an hour."

Feeling as though he'd stepped into someone else's nightmare, one that was terrifying and dangerous, Randall left the room, wondering how in the hell he was going to break the news to Addison.

ADDISON KNEW THE MOMENT SHE SAW HIM THAT THE visit had shaken him badly. "How is he?" she asked.

"Sleeping." It was the only answer she got. "Let's go get some coffee. We need to talk."

A stark sense of uneasiness settled over her as they made their way to the hospital cafeteria. *He knows something,* she thought. Something important. Something terrible.

The cafeteria was a dreary basement room that smelled of vending machine coffee and yesterday's meat loaf. Randall bought two cups of coffee and ushered her to a corner table.

"What did you find out?" she asked when he was seated across from her.

"Jack told me who your birth father is."

The words struck her with physical force. She met his gaze. Cold wariness poured over her. There was something in his eyes she'd never seen before. Fear, she thought, only darker.

"Who?" She braced for the impending blow.

Randall withdrew the deposit ticket from his pocket and laid it on the table in front of them.

Heart pounding, she lowered her gaze.

Garrison Tate.

Shock spiraled through her. She stared, too stunned to feel anything but disbelief.

Garrison Tate. The name bespoke power and status. He was a political high roller. She'd seen him on television. Handsome. Charming.

A cold-blooded killer.

Her next thought was that Jack had made a mistake. His hacking programs had somehow failed him.

"Garrison Tate." Randall said the name aloud when she didn't speak. "He announced just last month that he would be running for a seat in the U.S. Senate."

"This can't be. There's got to be a mistake." She couldn't tear her eyes away from the scrawling letters. "This is insane. He's a respected politician, for chrissake."

Randall looked over his shoulder in a gesture that sent an icy finger gliding up her back. "Old man Stukins mentioned Yale. We can check to see if Tate went to Yale."

"A crazy old man's ranting doesn't prove anything," Addison snapped back. She refused to believe that such a powerful and respected man would go to such violent lengths to hide his past.

Randall slapped his palm against the table. "Dammit, think about it. Your parents. Agnes Beckett. Jim Bernstein. Jesus, Addison, it fits."

She could only stare at him as the horror seeped into her. Deep inside, she knew he was right. But the truth was so ugly, she couldn't bring herself to acknowledge it. "I can't believe a respected politician would resort to murder to hide the fact that he has an illegitimate daughter."

"You were conceived through an act of rape. Agnes Beckett was a minor. She was fucking brutalized. You saw the emergency room invoice. God only knows how badly she was hurt, or what else was done to her. That changes everything."

Her stomach clenched. Bile rose in her throat as the reality of his words struck her. She hugged herself against the sudden chill that enveloped her.

"He battered and raped a sixteen-year-old girl," he said harshly. "He bought and paid for McEvoy. He destroyed your birth mother's reputation and the entire, stinking crime was swept under the rug."

Outrage and sadness and an acute sense of injustice sent her heart hammering against her ribs. The pain was so intense, it hurt to draw a breath. Tears streamed down her cheeks as she thought of her birth mother. Sixteen years old. Poor. Uneducated. But with dreams as big as the sky was endless. She would have been dazzled by a handsome young student from Yale. She would have been vulnerable. She would have been without credibility because of her lack of social status. The perfect victim.

Garrison Tate had forever and irrevocably changed Agnes Beckett's life. In a single, violent act, he had ripped her dreams away and then systematically destroyed her.

Addison choked back a sob. Vaguely, she was aware of Randall reaching for her. Taking her hand. Squeezing.

"I'm sorry," he said.

She lowered her face into her hands. She felt sick inside. Sickened by the fact that she was the product of such a vile act. "God, Randall, it hurts."

"I know, honey. I'm sorry."

"Agnes Beckett didn't deserve that. My parents. Jim. Jack. None of them deserved what happened."

"Neither do you. That's why I'm going to nail that slimy son of a bitch."

She raised her eyes to his. "We need proof. We can't do anything without proof."

Randall scrubbed his hand over his face. "Maybe Bernstein has something in his office we can get our hands on. Whatever Jack was able to come up with was probably burned in the fire. I'll check it out, but it's probably gone."

"What about the newspaper clipping?"

"It's something. It will help. But Stukins will never hold up in court."

"Surely there was some kind of police report—"

"McEvoy said the police records were destroyed. As far as we know that son of a bitch is in Tate's hip pocket."

For the first time Addison felt the full force of the fury burning inside her. So many innocent people senselessly murdered. So many lives destroyed. All so one evil man could get away with his sins.

"We can't let him get away with this," she choked. "I want the bastard to pay."

Randall reached across the table and took her hands in his. "It's going to be a while before the doctor gets here. I need to talk to him. I've got to take care of Jack. In the interim, I'm going to get you checked into a hotel."

"I'm not leaving you. I'm not leaving Jack—"

"You need to sleep." He squeezed her hands. "Neither of us is going to be worth a damn if we don't get some sleep."

She didn't like the idea of separating, but she saw the logic behind it. She wouldn't last much longer without sleep. Neither would he. "You need sleep, too."

"I've got to talk to the doctor first. Then I'm going to check out the office and meet with Van-Dyne. I'll meet you at the hotel in a few hours."

"What are you going to tell Van-Dyne?"

"Everything except that we suspect Tate is involved. We need an ally, and I'll take whoever I can get at this point."

"What if he doesn't believe you?" she asked. "Let's face it. We're making some wild allegations. The only piece of hard evidence we've got is a twenty-six-year-old newspaper clipping that doesn't name names. Pretty flimsy, considering who we're going up against."

"True, but if I can convince him the attempt on your life and Bernstein's murder are related, I may be able to get him to begin an investigation."

THE DRIVE TO THE HOTEL WAS A TWISTING, HIGH-speed, single-car chase that had Addison clutching the dash and wishing she'd passed on coffee back at the hospital. Randall covered the entire city and half its suburbs at least twice before hauling the Bronco into the parking garage of the Loews Giorgio Hotel just southeast of downtown.

"I'm going back to the hospital with you," she said as he made a final check of the room. She barely noticed the Italian decor and European antiques strewn about like expensive beanbags. "I'll sit with Jack while you talk to Van-Dyne."

"No."

"I can't just sit around and do nothing." Her stomach clenched every time she envisioned him walking out that door without her. "I won't be able to sleep."

"Yes, you will." He slipped a small chrome pistol from his parka. "Take this."

Addison gaped at the gun. "You really know how to make a girl feel safe."

"It's a Colt Mustang semiautomatic. Take it into the shower with you. Take it to bed with you. Whatever you do, don't let anyone into the room unless it's me."

When she didn't move to take the gun, he reached for her right hand and placed the pistol in her palm. "Dammit, do as I say."

The gun felt like a chunk of ice in her hand. Surprisingly, the grip fit comfortably into her palm; her fingers reached the trigger easily. She listened half-heartedly as he explained how to use it. "The clip holds seven rounds. That ought to be enough to stop anyone if you get into trouble."

"How long are you going to be gone?"

"A few hours."

"Any longer and I'll come looking for you."

He looked haggard and tired and as dangerous as a cobra staring back at her.

She had the crazy urge to tell him she loved him. The idea shook her so violently she had to blink back tears. "Be careful," she said instead.

Raising his hand, he brushed his knuckles against her cheek. "Get some sleep." At that, he slipped away from her and left the room without looking back.

chapter
18

ADDISON SENSED HIS PRESENCE BEFORE SHE ACTUALLY awoke. She heard the muted sound of his shoes against the Aubusson carpet, felt the bed shift as he moved over her.

She jerked awake, terror at the back of her throat, a scream buried beneath it. The room was dark. Blindly, she flung herself across the bed, toward the gun.

Two strong arms gripped hers. "Whoa, Addison. Honey, it's me."

The gentle voice lapped at the fear, smoothing it down, and it drained away, like water discarded after a cleansing bath. She stopped struggling. Randall. Close to her, touching her. She reached for him.

"Tate was here." She shivered as the memory of the nightmare swooped down on her. Garrison Tate had stood by the window and smiled at her. He'd spoken to her, but she couldn't recall the words. His presence had been powerful, oppressive and terrifying. Worst of all, she'd sensed that he wanted to hurt her.

Randall stretched out on the bed beside her. "It was a

nightmare. Nobody knows we're here. We're safe."

A thin gray ribbon of light filtered in through the window. A glance at the crystal timepiece on the night table told her it was nearly eight A.M.

"How's Jack?" she asked.

"Critical, but stable. They removed the bullet earlier this morning. The doctor says he's going to make it, but he's got a long, hard road ahead of him."

Addison relaxed back into the pillows. "It just doesn't seem fair that he should have to go through this after everything he's already been through."

"Fairness just doesn't enter into it sometimes."

She thought about Agnes Beckett and her parents and silently agreed. "Did you find anything at the office?"

"The fire took everything. The computers. We didn't have fireproof files."

"I'm sorry, Randall. About the fire. About Jack. I'm sorry about everything."

"It's not your fault. You don't have control over any of this."

"How did it go with Van-Dyne?"

"He agreed to put two detectives on the case locally. If things pan out, he'll contact the feds in Washington."

"Just two men?"

"Says he's understaffed. He probably is. He's going to start with Jack's case, then delve more deeply into the Bernstein murder and the shooting at your shop. He agreed to contact Sheriff White up in Summit County about your parents."

She considered everything he'd said, but knew in her heart it wasn't enough. "What about Agnes Beckett?"

"We're going to have to play our ace."

"I didn't know we had one."

"The media. I called an acquaintance of mine who works for the *Wall Street Journal.* He's not a reporter, but he's got connections."

For the first time since this nightmare had started, she felt empowered. "They won't print anything that's not verified."

"No, but they damn sure have the resources to dig up the same information we did. I faxed him a copy of the newspaper article and told him everything. He's going to send someone to Siloam Springs."

"That's going to take some time."

"We need to lie low." He sighed. "Tate is a powerful, connected man. We'll come off as crackpots if we don't keep a low profile. We've got to be very careful. We know he won't hesitate to kill."

"Isn't there some way the police can protect us?"

"I asked Van-Dyne about putting you in a safe house. He hedged. They don't have enough proof to warrant the expense. We're on our own."

"What about Jack? He's vulnerable."

"I talked Van-Dyne into putting a twenty-four-hour guard on him. If he hadn't agreed, I would have hired private security." Randall regarded her through dark, somber eyes. "It's going to take indisputable proof before the authorities cross Tate."

"What can we do? There's got to be something. . . ."

"I know a retired private detective from D.C., Clint Holsapple. He used to work the political circle. He's from Texas. He's good and may be able to get me close enough to Tate so I can flush him out."

Her pulse kicked when she realized he hadn't mentioned her. "I'm the one Tate wants dead."

"This is no longer just about you."

"Don't try to shut me out. I'm involved, and I intend to stay involved until Tate is either behind bars or dead."

"I've already made reservations to fly to D.C. I'm not taking you with me. I'll put you up in a hotel in another city—"

"No! If you go to Washington, I'm going, too, damn you." Her voice shook with a sudden, wrenching burst of anger.

"It's too dangerous."

"I don't care about that. Don't you dare try to keep me out of this."

Cursing beneath his breath, he hit her with a look that would have sent a sane woman scrambling off the bed. Too bad he didn't know she'd traveled beyond the point of running away from him.

"This is dangerous, Addison. People have been killed—"

"I won't be shut out. If we're going after Tate, we do it together. Or I swear to God I'll do it on my own."

She started to rise, but he stopped her by grabbing her wrist. When she jerked away, he quickly rolled on top of her and pinned her to the bed. "He'll kill you, goddammit!"

"I won't let him."

"I can't work this case and look out for you, too. Dammit, I don't want that responsibility."

"That's not your decision to make, Randall. It's mine, and I've made my choice."

He stared down at her, breathing hard, his dark eyes flashing dangerously. Addison stared back, her heart raging. "I'm sorry," she said. "But I won't change my mind."

He scrubbed a hand over his face. "What the hell am I going to do with you?"

"Keep me by your side. Let me help you."

"It scares the hell out of me to think I can't keep you safe. If anything happened—"

"Nothing's going to happen," she said. "But there's no way you're going to prove he's a cold-blooded killer without my involvement."

"I didn't want it to work out this way."

Worry and exhaustion lined his face. She knew she was to blame because she wouldn't comply with his wishes, but there was no way she was going to let him ride into battle alone. This was her battle, too. They both had their reasons for fighting it.

"I've got a personal stake in this, Randall."

"So do I," he said harshly.

She kissed him, partly to quiet him, partly because she

needed to feel him close. "I want to win this. I want to finish it. And I want us to be alive when it's over."

Cupping her face with his hands, he kissed her gently. "I'm too tired to fight with you."

"Don't shut me out. Please, let me help. I don't want anything to happen to you because of me."

"I can look out for myself, lady." He kissed her jaw and nipped at her chin, trailing kisses down her neck. "I want you."

Despite the heat spiraling through her, she hesitated. "What about our agreement? About us getting too close."

"We're already too close." Never taking his eyes from hers, he began working on the buttons of his shirt. "I'm willing to consider that agreement null and void if you are."

"You're going back to D.C."

"I'm here now. You're here. We're together, Addison. That's pretty straightforward."

She wanted to tell him that wasn't enough, that it would never be enough, but the future was too uncertain, her need for him too great.

"We're going to end up hurting each other," she said.

"Never. I'll never hurt you." His jaw tightened. He gazed down at her soberly. "You're inside my head. I didn't want that to happen, but it has."

"We'll deal with it," she murmured, because a small part of her understood. He was inside her head, too.

"Come here." He pulled her against him.

A primal thrill barreled through her as he tossed his clothes to the floor and slid under the sheets. Her senses vibrated with tension and pleasure as he skimmed a hand along her side. She closed her eyes, amazed that in the midst of danger and ugliness, he could touch her and make everything seem so right.

She sucked in an involuntary breath as his stone-hard erection pressed against the tender flesh of her belly.

"This is what you do to me," he whispered, his mouth lingering at her earlobe. "I don't stand a chance against you."

She wore only her panties, having had nothing else to put on after her shower. His hands roamed over her body, making her ache with a craving she'd never known. Back at the cabin, she'd been excited and overwhelmed by the passion and newness of what had happened between them. There had been an instant of pain and then intense pleasure.

Now, she knew what to expect. From him. From herself. Her feelings for him had deepened, solidified into something profound and inevitable. She'd willingly made herself vulnerable. Her body. Her heart. Her soul.

She gasped when he cupped her breasts. Desire bucked through her, taking her breath. She arched into him, her nipples tightening in response. Murmuring his name, she closed her eyes and gave herself over to him.

He crushed his mouth to hers. She opened to him, accepted his tongue. The tip of his penis nudged her pelvis. His breaths came hard and fast against her ear.

She cried out when he took a taut nipple into his mouth. Caressing the tender bud with his tongue, he sucked it deeply into his mouth. The need ripped through her, overwhelming her senses.

God, she was in over her head, drowning in passion and desire. Even in her wildest dreams Addison had never imagined she could feel so much. Physically. Emotionally.

Exquisite sensation rushed through her when he touched the tender folds of flesh at the junction of her thighs. She opened to him, giving him full access to her most private place.

Her body was on fire, burning furiously out of control each time he touched her, like hot coals bursting into flame. He knew just where to touch her, how much pressure to use, when to back off. He stroked her, moving within her, sending lightning bolts of pleasure crashing through her.

Rational thought melted beneath the heat of his touch. Thunder roared in her ears as he took her to the precipice of her desire. "Come for me, Addison," he whispered between breaths. "Relax, honey." He kissed her breasts, one and then the other, crushing his lips against her flesh, stroking her, stroking. Driving her insane. Over the edge. Higher. "Come for me."

Addison couldn't speak. She'd traveled beyond self-control. Her body ruled her now. Her mind shut down as he drew her ever closer to the peak, and she went with it, trusting him fully to take her there.

Bright white light flashed before her eyes as the orgasm engulfed her. It crashed over her like a tidal wave, taking her breath, dissolving all thought. There was only sensation, his name on her lips, bursting forth with each crest, with each aftershock that shook her all the way to her soul.

RANDALL FELT HER SURRENDER AS THOUGH IT HAD been his own. He supposed that, in a way, it was. It frightened him to think he was falling hard and fast for Addison Fox.

The realization rushed over him like a violent flash flood, overriding his intellect and taking him against his will.

He hadn't believed it was possible for him—a veteran of life, of death—to have fate step in and show him a new trick. In his thirty-eight years, he'd learned to live without emotional attachments. He'd learned to believe love didn't exist. Then came Addison with her clean soul and faith in the human spirit. She still believed in right and wrong, good and evil. She'd proven to him that goodness was very much alive, more powerful and real than anything he'd ever known. He'd thought he was immune to her. He'd thought he was above it all. God, what an arrogant fool he'd been.

He watched her crest, then closed his eyes against the emotions churning inside him. He'd never felt so swept away, so driven by something as intangible as his heart.

For a moment, the only sound between them was the harsh sound of her labored breathing. He'd needed to see for himself that he could reach into her, affect her, touch her soul.

When she opened those dark, sweet eyes and smiled, he knew he was forever lost.

"I love you," she whispered on a breath.

The words jolted him, their meaning shaking him to his very core. "Those are dangerous words," he said.

"It's a dangerous world out there, Talbot."

She'd said the words carelessly, but he didn't miss the shadow of hurt. And he realized she'd expected him to respond in kind. The thought sent a ripple of panic slicing through his belly.

"I didn't mean to terrify you," she said.

"You didn't."

"Liar."

"Come here." Reaching for her, he pulled her close. He didn't trust himself to speak. He wasn't sure what he would say if he did. Something stupid, more than likely, that would suck him in even deeper than he already was. He cared for her, but for whatever reason, he couldn't bring himself to say the words. He didn't want to dig any deeper into his own soul. Nor did he want to dig any deeper into hers. One of them would be hurt if he did.

"Nothing this good lasts forever," he murmured.

She clucked her tongue. "Such a cynic."

How could he tell her he loved her when he wasn't even sure what the word meant? How could he let her get tangled up with him when he was leaving for D.C. in a few weeks? "You deserve better than what I can give you, Addison."

He didn't miss the quick flash of anger. "That sounds like a cop-out. You don't strike me as the kind of man who takes the easy way out."

"I care too much about you to hurt you," he said.

"Then stop talking about what I do or don't deserve and listen to what your heart is trying to tell you."

Closing his eyes against the rush of emotion, he moved over her and kissed her deeply. "It's not that simple," he said after a moment.

"Life's complicated sometimes."

He kissed her again, hungrily, wanting to lose himself in sensation. Lust hummed through his body. He concentrated on that. All he wanted to feel was need. Simple, fundamental, physical need. He wanted sex and release.

To hell with anything more complicated.

Cradling her face between his hands, he pulled back and looked into her eyes. "I want you," he whispered, suddenly afraid she was slipping away. "I want you more than my next breath, more than anything in the world. That's all I can say. That's got to be enough right now."

"That's enough," she murmured. "Make love to me."

He entered her slowly, watching her eyes glaze, her mouth tremble. He shook with sensation as her heat sheathed him. He closed his eyes as emotion exploded inside him. He cursed fate and thanked God in a single, ragged breath.

She moved against him, his name on her lips. Randall ground his teeth together as the pleasure ripped through him. *It's just sex,* a panicked little voice said in a last-ditch effort to convince him he wasn't in miles over his head.

But his heart was hopelessly lost, entwined with hers in a ritual as old as time. He'd allowed her to reach into him and touch the deepest part of him. She'd asked for his heart.

He'd given her his soul.

chapter
19

THE FLIGHT FROM DENVER INTERNATIONAL TO WASH-
ington National was as tumultuous as the emotions stumbling
around inside him. Randall had never felt so uncertain. He
doubted his competence as an investigator. Worse, he
doubted his ability to protect Addison. He'd been torn between hiding her in a hotel in another state and taking her
with him. But she'd insisted on coming along. The hell of it
was he didn't want the responsibility of her safety. Tate
played for keeps. Randall knew fully there were no second
chances. If he screwed up, Addison would die. It was as
simple and tortuous as that.

He gazed thoughtfully at her as she slept in the seat beside
him. Her skin was soft and pale in the gray light seeping in
through the jet's window. Her brown hair lay in unruly curls
at her shoulders. Her full lips were slightly parted, her jaw
relaxed. In sleep, she looked young and so vulnerable he
wanted to find a place to lock her away where he knew she
would be safe. It was that incredible innocence she possessed
that made his hackles rise at the thought of anyone harming

her. She had no idea how vulnerable she was. She couldn't imagine because she'd never been exposed to the blacker side of human nature.

He'd made love to her twice back at the hotel. His pulse kicked at the thought of everything they'd shared. She was the only woman in the world who could make his heart race. In the short time he'd known her, she'd become the center of his world. It was as though she was a life-sustaining nutrient he'd been deprived of his entire life. He couldn't get enough of her, knew he never would.

He thought about his plans to move back to D.C. and wondered how he could have let this happen. How could he have been so stupid, getting tangled up with a woman as decent and kind as Addison? But he supposed loving her had been inevitable from the very beginning. Just as leaving her was. He didn't want to hurt her, but he knew she'd be better off for it in the long run. He didn't even want to think about the shape he'd be in after he walked away.

The Boeing 767 dipped into a turn. Simultaneously, the uncertainty wrenched at his gut. They would be landing in twenty minutes. Right or wrong, he'd brought Addison with him. He winced inwardly as a little voice reminded him that it wasn't too late to turn back. There was still time to take her back to Colorado and check her into a hotel in Boulder or Colorado Springs.

But when he thought of the lengths Tate was willing to go to cover up his dirty little secret, Randall knew he'd made the only decision he could. He didn't want her out of his sight. Tate had already murdered four innocent people. He wouldn't hesitate to kill again. Randall knew as only a man of kind could that Tate's efforts were only going to get bolder—and that he and Addison both were his targets.

The thought sent a spike of fear through him.

Tate was a powerful man in the city of Washington. He was well connected, with a sterling reputation that wouldn't tarnish easily. He wouldn't go down without a fight. He was slick and smart with the cunning of an animal that killed for the sheer convenience of it.

They were on Tate's turf now, Randall thought darkly, two birds swept into the vortex of a tornado, their fate left to the eye of the storm.

Two hours later, after changing cabs twice, Randall and Addison checked into the Wyndham Bristol on Pennsylvania Avenue under the assumed names of Mr. and Mrs. Richard White. Using cash, he paid for two nights.

As Addison unpacked, Randall dialed Georgetown information, a little surprised, but glad, that there was still a listing for Holsapple Investigations. Not quite sure what he was going to say, he dialed the number and waited. A familiar voice answered on the second ring. An ally at last. Someone he could trust. Relief swept through him. "Taking on any new clients these days?" he asked.

There was an instant of surprised silence, then a guffaw of laughter. "Well, if it ain't the devil himself. What the hell you doin' back in D.C.? Thought you hightailed it to Denver to play Magnum, P.I., for a while."

"Clean air and mountains get to you after a while."

"Kind of like traffic and crime, huh?"

He watched as Addison carried their coats to the closet and hung them neatly. "Can you meet me? I need to get your opinion on a problem I encountered with a case."

"Well, it's just me and Jack Daniels these days. Where do you want to meet us?"

"I'm staying at the Wyndham Bristol. Can you meet me in the lobby?"

"If I'm not there in twenty minutes, start without me."

Clint Holsapple wasn't at all what Addison expected. She'd imagined him as a big and boisterous Texan donning a ten-gallon Stetson and ostrich-skin boots. Instead, he was a scholarly looking man, short of stature, with wire-rimmed glasses, blue jeans, and a red goatee. He looked more like a college professor than a cowboy turned private investigator.

Randall, having brought Clint up to the hotel room, introduced them.

Surprising her, Clint took her hand and pressed it to his lips. "Pretty lady, it's a pleasure," he drawled, his beard tickling the top of her hand. "You always could pick 'em, Talbot." He winked at Addison. "Lucky devil."

"You're going to get me into trouble, Clint." Randall checked the hall, then closed the door, turning the deadbolt behind him.

The older man smiled. "If I got this picture right, you already are."

Curious about the silver-tongued Texan, Addison eased her hand from Clint's and motioned to the sofa opposite the fireplace. "It sounds as though you two used to spend a good deal of time together," she said.

"Yeah, just me and Randall and our old friend J.D."

"J.D.?" Addison felt a sinking sensation in the pit of her stomach.

"Jack Daniels," Clint replied.

Randall strolled over to the bar and returned with a bottle and three glasses. Without meeting her gaze, he set the glasses on the coffee table and poured. "I thought you'd be back in Texas by now," he said.

Clint reached for his glass. "There's but one thing that can keep a Texan from Texas."

"Don't tell me you got married." Randall slid one of the glasses toward Addison.

She caught his gaze, hoping he recognized her concern that he'd poured himself a drink, but he looked away.

"Met a gal right here in Georgetown," Clint said. "We're not married yet, but I plan on asking her as soon as I get up the nerve. She owns a little bar and grill over on Wisconsin Ave. We've been together almost a year now."

Crossing an ankle over his knee, he studied the young man and woman before him. "You want to tell me what this is all about? You two look like a couple of rabbits holed up from a pack of coyotes."

Randall took a long pull of whiskey. "We're in trouble, Clint. I don't even know where to start because it's a wild story and you're not going to believe any of it."

The older man laughed easily, his hands coming down on his knees. "You're talking to someone who's been living in Disneyland for the last twenty years. I just about seen it all, *amigo*."

Trying to ignore her growing uneasiness over the glass of whiskey in Randall's hand, Addison listened intently. Randall explained in detail everything that had happened, beginning with her search for her biological parents and their deaths ten months ago, and ending with the attempt on Jack's life and the fire at his office.

For several tense minutes, the only sound came from the drumming of rain against the window and the hiss of the gas logs in the fireplace. The room had grown chilly and she steeled herself against a shiver that hovered at the base of her spine.

"Jesus H. Christ," Clint said when Randall finished. "I don't do much political work anymore, but I've known for years Tate was a slimy son of a bitch." He rubbed his face and beard with big hands, then looked at Randall over his fingertips. "Mostly women, a few shady investments. But damn if the TV cameras don't love that good-lookin' mug of his. Imagine him running his senatorial campaign on a family values ticket. Don't that beat all?"

Addison hated to think that the man they were talking about was her biological father. A man whose image filled her with hatred, shame, and stone-cold fear.

"Anything we can dig up on him and take to the media?" Randall asked.

Clint shook his head. "He's got a whole army of P.R. goons dedicated to keeping him squeaky-clean. Especially now since he's announced that he'll be a candidate for the Senate in November. I take it you've gone to the police?"

"The locals back in Denver," Randall said. "Unofficially, the *Wall Street Journal.* But they're going to be cautious."

Clint nodded, as if finally understanding why they had come to him. "They're not going to touch him without definitive proof."

"We don't have that kind of time."

"No, you don't." Clint's gaze slid to Addison, then back to Randall. "Tate's running a dangerous show. He's got a lot at stake. Everything, in fact. If he's running scared, you two don't stand a chance. I hate to tell you this, but you're probably still alive because you've merely been lucky."

"Here I was taking the credit," Randall said dryly.

Addison couldn't believe they could joke about something so serious. "That's hardly comforting," she said.

"Comforting's for mothers and whores." Surprising her, Clint leaned forward, put his hand over hers, and looked at her over the top rim of his spectacles. "But if you play your hand right, you can bluff him into making a mistake that'll cost him the game."

Her only thought was that it wasn't a game.

"I'm not willing to take a chance with her." Randall's eyes skittered to Addison, then back to Clint in a silent directive. "I don't want her involved."

"You know as well as I do that she's your ace in the hole."

Realizing she was gripping the armrest of the wingback so hard her knuckles hurt, Addison relaxed her hands and met Clint's gaze. "What do you have in mind?" she asked, forcing a toughness she didn't feel into her voice.

Randall shot her a nasty look.

"They always say the best defense is a good offense," Clint began. "Until now, you've been on the defensive. Tate's not going to expect you to come at him." He turned to Addison. "Call a meeting with him. Play him a little. Tell him you'll go to the media if he doesn't meet with you."

"We've already gone to the media," Randall cut in.

Addison knew Randall was only trying to protect her. If the situation had been different she would have been flattered by his staunch protectiveness. But the intensity of his argument, combined with the fact that he was allowing his emotions to impede his decision making, left her distinctly uneasy.

"He doesn't know that," Clint said without looking at him. "You need to think like a liar." His eyes latched on to Addison. "Make Tate think you want to blackmail him. That's a surefire way to get his attention. He'll come at you with both barrels."

"He won't touch it," Randall said. "There's no way he's going to meet with either of us."

Clint smiled. "The man's ego's bigger than Texas, man. He's gonna want to meet his resourceful young offspring. I imagine you've given him a run for his money so far." He reached for the bottle of whiskey and refilled his glass. "He'll want to get a good, long look at her before he kills her."

"Goddammit, Clint." Rising suddenly, Randall stalked to the fireplace, his back to them.

"But why the meeting?" she asked. "How will that help us prove anything?"

Randall turned toward them, his face dark with anger. "Clint wants to wire you for sound, Addison. That's his specialty. Bugs, wiretaps, goddamn human electronics. It'll be up to you to get Tate to fess up on tape."

Her throat constricted. She swallowed quickly to hide the lump of fear that had crept up it. "An unauthorized recording, even if he incriminates himself, can't be used against him."

"Not in court," Clint began, "but it'll damn sure be enough to speed up an investigation. The media'll love it."

Addison didn't even have to consider. She wanted her life back. All of it. Her peace of mind. Her freedom. She wanted to be safe again. She wanted to be able to walk into her coffee shop and not break out in a cold sweat every time the front door opened. She was tired of having to look over her shoulder every time she left her apartment or got out of her car.

"I'll do it." She had too much at stake not to speak up, not to fight back against a man who'd already taken so much away from her.

Randall spun on them, legs parted, eyes alight with anger. "I don't want her close to him." He jabbed a finger at Addison. "Dammit, you're not going to do it. I won't allow it. There's got to be another way. I'll meet with him."

Clint shrugged, unimpressed by the younger man's wrath. "He won't meet with you."

"He knows she hired me."

"He doesn't know you love her."

Randall just stood there breathing hard, glaring at Clint as if the words had rendered him speechless.

Addison's heart rapped in a steadily increasing rhythm against her breast. She looked at Randall and wondered fleetingly if it could possibly be true.

Without looking at her, he crossed to the coffee table, poured two fingers of whiskey into his glass, then tossed it back in a single gulp. "I don't want her alone with him and that's final. There's got to be another way."

Addison watched him, realizing for the first time that the only reason he was drinking was to drive her away. Damn him. Couldn't he see she wouldn't let him manipulate her like that?

Shaking his head, Clint studied his glass. "I've dealt with this kind of scum before. It may take some time, but he's going to come after you." He looked at Addison. "We can do it at my gal's restaurant."

Randall glared at him. "Out of the question."

Clint glared back, an equal, matching everything in the younger man's stare less the desperation. "That's why you came to me, son. You'd already thought of this. You were just hoping I'd have a better idea. Well, sorry to disappoint you, but I don't."

Randall sat on the sofa next to her. She could feel the

anger pouring off him, but there was nothing she could do to stop it. She'd made her decision, and she wasn't going to back down. Randall would just have to come to terms with it.

"What's the restaurant like?" he asked.

"Dark, jazzy, and just obscure enough for him to feel safe. Far enough down on Wisconsin to be considered quiet. The clientele are regulars, mostly happy hour. We're busy late on the weekend. A weeknight would be perfect."

"He'd spot me," Randall said.

"There's an adjoining banquet room we use for larger parties. We can rig up a camera and sound system. We can keep an eye on her from there."

Randall cursed. "I still don't like it."

Clint shrugged, turned to Addison. "Think you can do it?"

Refusing to let them see that her hands were shaking, she pressed them together and looked from one man to the other. "Tate murdered my parents. I'll do whatever it takes to put him away."

Randall's eyes burned into her, but she refused to look away. She couldn't. He was too angry. She was too afraid. Dammit, she wasn't going to back down. This wasn't his decision to make.

As if realizing they needed to discuss it further, Clint rose. "Let me know before I get any older," he said. He smiled at Addison. "It was indeed a pleasure meeting you, Miss Fox. I only wish it were under different circumstances."

She smiled back, charmed once again by his grandfatherly manners. "Likewise. We'll be in touch."

At the door, the two men spoke in low tones and then Clint passed a holstered pistol to Randall. They shook hands, then Clint was gone.

chapter
20

RANDALL DIDN'T LIKE BEING WRONG. WORSE, HE didn't like being wrong and fighting for it anyway. He'd lost all sense of objectivity the moment he'd touched Addison back at that cabin, and he hadn't even realized it—until now.

He'd lost his edge. Christ, she was thinking more rationally than he was. If he agreed to Clint's plan, he would be putting her right in the line of fire. How could he live with himself if he let Tate hurt her?

Turning away from the door, he dropped the holster onto the console table, then picked up the bottle of whiskey, taking it to the bar. Without looking at her, he pulled out a shot glass, filled it, and slammed it back, hoping the slow burn would stop the anger and fear from consuming him completely.

It didn't.

She was still there, looking at him expectantly as he refilled the glass a second time and downed it in a single gulp.

"That's not going to solve anything," she snapped.

"No, but it's sure as hell going to make me feel better."

He felt like getting roaring drunk. Anything to dull the ache splitting his chest.

"For an hour? For two? Until you come to your senses and realize that we don't have a choice but to do this?"

"We always have choices," he said. "I'm merely trying to save your life."

"Don't try to make my choices for me. I won't let you."

For the first time since Clint left, he looked at her, astounded that he could feel so damned taken aback by those eyes of hers. "You have absolutely no idea what this son of a bitch is capable of," he said angrily.

"Yes, I do."

"You can't imagine!"

"What do you suggest, Randall? Shall I just wait around for him to finish the job he started? Will it be a car accident, like my parents? Or will I get gunned down in the street? Or perhaps at my shop? Will they kill Gretchen, too?" She approached him, her cheeks flushed with anger. "I'm sorry, but I'm not willing to make that ultimate sacrifice."

She was standing so close he could smell the clean scent of her hair and the subtle, feminine perfume she wore. The alcohol was messing with his brain, making him want her.

Goddamn her.

He crossed to her. Without preamble, he cupped the back of her head and crushed his mouth against hers. Her body went rigid with shock. She tried to push him away, but he didn't relent. He kissed her long and hard, aware that she wasn't kissing him back, but he didn't care. He needed her. Physically. Emotionally.

Abruptly, he released her, watching dispassionately as she stumbled back. Her face was flushed, her breasts rising and falling with each breath. "You're an idiot when you're drunk," she said, backing away. "I hate it when you drink. I won't tolerate it."

He followed her, a predator cornering its prey. "If you get near him, he'll kill you. I won't have your death on my conscience, Addison."

"If we don't stop him now, it'll come when we least expect it. Sooner or later, he'll get us. I'd rather do it on my terms."

There was no right or wrong. Only danger and insurmountable risk. And ultimately safety, but it carried an exorbitant price. He looked into her eyes and wondered how much she knew about taking risks, if she realized she was putting her life on the line—and that she could lose.

He thought about the plan Clint had outlined and wondered if there was a chance it would work. Maybe Tate would refuse to meet her. Maybe he'd agree and then not show. Maybe he would—

Cursing, Randall hurled the shot glass into the sink, shattering it, splashing the last of his peace of mind over the counter. Frustration and helplessness reached their flash point. "Your life means nothing to him!" he raged.

Before he could stop himself he rushed to her, yanked her toward him, and shook her. "He doesn't care about you! He'll kill us both without forethought, without afterthought, and without missing his son's Little League game!"

"Stop it!"

"He'll kill you, Addison! I won't let that happen!"

"You're hurting me!"

"You're hurting me, too, goddammit!"

She stared at him, her eyes wide and startled.

Releasing her, he stepped back, cursing himself for touching her in anger. "Jesus."

"I'm . . . sorry," she said after a moment.

"Don't apologize to me after what I just did to you," he snapped.

"But I—"

He raised his hand. "Just . . . don't. Please."

For a moment the only sound came from his heavy breathing. Randall concentrated on calming himself so he could think rationally. He couldn't ever remember feeling so helpless, so powerless, and he hated it.

He knew she wasn't going to back down. She was going

to do this no matter what he said or did. Had the circumstances not been so bleak, her tenacity might have been admirable. It sickened him to think of what it might cost her. What it might cost him.

He knew she was only doing what she thought was right. Dammit, he didn't have a better idea. "I'll agree to this on two conditions," he said finally.

She eyed him warily. "What conditions?"

"We do it at Clint's bar. And you wear a vest."

"All right." Her voice didn't falter, and Randall wondered where the strength had come from. There was so much more to her than he'd ever imagined. So many twists and turns that made her the woman he'd fallen in love with.

The notion shook him to his foundation.

He crossed to her in two strides. Suddenly, the need to feel her against him, her heart beating against his, was so powerful, so urgent, that it struck a chord of panic inside him.

The fight went out of her the instant his arms wrapped around her. Her head dropped to his chest, and she leaned, vacillating, against him. She felt so small in his arms. So vulnerable.

"We need to do this, Randall."

"I know," he said, furious that she was right. He pulled her more tightly against him. "But I hate it. I fucking hate it." He tilted her head up and pressed his mouth against hers, reveling in the sweetness of her breath, the taste of her lips, the texture of her skin.

"Good still prevails over evil sometimes," she murmured.

He pulled away from her, looked deeply into her eyes, shaken by what he saw, overwhelmed by what he felt. "I love you," he said. A tremor passed through her, but he didn't stop. "I love you too much to let anything happen to you."

It was out. He'd said it. Christ, this was making him crazy.

"Jesus, Talbot, you never cease to amaze me."

"Yeah, sometimes I even amaze myself," he growled.

She touched his face with fingers that trembled. "Please, help me do this. Everything will work out. You'll see."

The need drove into him mercilessly, sending his mouth back down to hers, devouring. He pulled the sweater over her head, mussing her hair, making her look heavy-eyed and wild as she stared back at him.

Helpless to stop the urgency that rammed into him, Randall crushed her body to his, burying his face in her fragrant hair. He worked the tiny hook of her bra and bent to take a taut nipple in his mouth. "Did I tell you I love you?" he whispered.

"Yes," she panted.

"Good." Backing her against the wall, he pinned her arms above her head and suckled greedily on her breast. Throwing her head back in abandon, she moaned and arched against him.

"That drives me crazy when you do that." He released her hands.

She skimmed velvet fingers down his chest, over his nipples. A powerful shudder went through him. Her hands fumbled with his zipper. He was rock-hard and each time she brushed against him, he nearly exploded. But he didn't. That kind of control was too important to him. She was too important. This moment between them too precious.

He tugged her leggings down, and she kicked them aside. At the same time, she freed him from his jeans, touched him gently until an involuntary moan bubbled up from deep inside him. It was raw need she unleashed, primal, dark, and violent.

With a low growl, he swung her around, lifted her onto the bar by her hips, wedged himself between her knees, and drew them wide apart. Her head snapped up. There was surprise in her eyes when she looked at him, but he moved quickly. Cupping the soft flesh of her buttocks, he pulled her to the edge of the counter and thrust himself inside her.

He knew it was too rough for her, inexperienced as she was, but he wanted to possess her, if only for a moment, because he knew the moment was fleeting. No one would ever control her. As surely as he was hurtling himself to the edge of his own pleasure, she was slipping away.

Without the finesse she deserved, he pumped in and out of her, driving deep, gritting his teeth against the need exploding inside him. He wanted her. Had to have her. Like this. On his terms.

To his surprise, she began to move with him. Her fingers raked up and down his back. Her breaths came quickly until she was shouting his name. He ravaged her breasts with his mouth, with his hands, part of him wanting to hurt her the way he was hurting inside.

The orgasm was simultaneous and explosive. He held her so tightly he feared he might be bruising her, but he couldn't let go. He couldn't think, he couldn't see, he couldn't hear but for the ragged sound of his own breathing matched only by hers.

For several minutes, neither of them spoke. Instead, they held each other for everything they were worth, knowing that tomorrow or the next day or next week, it could all be gone.

CLINT WORKED BY THE LIGHT OF HIS BANKER'S LAMP, poring over last month's bank statement, wondering where in the hell he'd gone wrong. Beside the bank statement, a letter from the IRS outlined in ugly detail just how sorry his financial condition had become. It had taken him several years to reach this all-time low, and he knew there was little hope next month's financial statements would be any different.

Somewhere along the way, twenty years of work had been sucked down the proverbial drain like so much dirty water. The nest egg was gone, along with the money for the ranch he was going to build back in Texas. He had nothing left that would prove, even to himself, that at one time he'd run a decent, profitable, aboveboard business.

Tonight, that fleeting moment in time seemed like a lifetime ago.

At the corner of his desk, a tumbler of whiskey sat in its usual place, a ring of moisture permanently etched into the leather surface of the writing pad. He reached for the tumbler and drank deeply, trying to quench the hunger that never seemed to leave him these days.

He was merely an opportunist, he told himself as the liquor streamed down his throat. A businessman making the best of a bad situation. But the rationalization did little to quiet his conscience. And he was much too cynical to be bothered by that now.

He no longer believed in right and wrong, hadn't for years. Black and white no longer existed. He lived in a gray world where wrong could be stretched into right and iniquity transformed into something he could live with.

Finishing the whiskey, he poured another and brooded. He drank too much, he knew. And he spent too much time at the roulette tables in Atlantic City. But, Christ, that was life. A man who lived with his vices died with them. A man who denied himself life's little pleasures died unhappy.

Clint Holsapple just didn't want to die broke.

The climate had changed in D.C. since the days he and Talbot had run in the same circles. Clint had taken on jobs he would never admit to, wallowing in the muck with the rest of the men and women who'd sold their souls for the likes of money or power. He'd been introduced to people he wouldn't let pass through his front door. He'd been paid by nameless, faceless people for jobs he couldn't admit even to himself. He loved it and hated it with a passion that was insane, like a junkie waiting for that one big rush that never seemed to come.

Now, after all the personal sacrifices and professional compromises, he was broke. At sixty-one years of age the thought left a bitter taste at the back of his throat. His money-making days were over. Damn if he hadn't waited too long for the break that just wasn't going to come his way.

In today's world, it seemed like a man with a conscience was a man who held himself back. The men who lived and worked by the devil's rules prospered while the honest few paid the price. Ethics and money didn't seem to mix in this crazy town anymore. Why shouldn't he have a little piece of the pie for a change?

Talbot had come to him out of desperation, a fool in over his head, drowning in his own lust for a woman. In this case, a woman who knew too much about the wrong man. A man willing to pay megabucks for the right information, as long as it came from a discreet source.

A discreet source like Clint Holsapple.

Talbot had practically thrown this in his lap. How could Clint refuse an opportunity he'd been waiting for his entire life? As far as he was concerned, a man who didn't make his own luck was a man who didn't deserve it.

Grimacing at the irony, he drained his glass in a single, bitter gulp and reached for the telephone.

chapter
21

"To great expectations." Garrison Tate drank deeply from the crystal flute, blatantly admiring the striking redhead standing next to him.

"To favors granted," she said and drank, leaving a red lipstick stain on the rim.

"You're quite the negotiator, Mrs. DiRocco." Never taking his eyes from hers, he removed an eel-skin wallet from the inside pocket of his tuxedo and withdrew a never-folded one-hundred-dollar bill.

"One of my many talents." She accepted the bill, then expertly rolled it into a tight, seamless tube. "At least that's what my husband tells me." She handed the bill back to him.

Cradling the tube between his fingers, Tate watched as she slipped the thin straps of her dress from her shoulders. His heart strummed in anticipation. He wondered if it was from the sight of her ripe body or the drug he was about to consume.

As the rosy peaks of her nipples came into view, he bent slightly, put the bill to his nose, and snorted the line of fine white powder laid in neat rows on a beveled glass mirror. An instant later, the drug sent a brilliant burst of euphoria raging through his body. It sparked in his brain and traveled through his bloodstream like a lighted fuse, exploding in his groin with a sexual power that was stunning in its intensity.

"Your turn." He passed the bill to the eager young woman.

Brenda DiRocco was naked except for the thong-back panties that left little to the imagination. She was tall and large-boned with a wonderfully rounded body that was lush in all the right places. Her breasts were ample and hung like grapefruit before him as she leaned forward to suck in her share of the drug.

Tate reached out, sliding his finger into the front of her panties and pulling the tiny cover aside. "I've always wondered if the drapes matched the carpet." Starting with his jacket, he began to undress.

DiRocco laughed and danced out of reach. "Red is difficult to duplicate."

It was the first time he'd been with her and the anticipation between them was great. Her body and her appetites suited him. She was young, married, and excessively ambitious, key elements that made up the perfect lover in Washington, D.C.

A lobbyist by trade, Brenda DiRocco had come to him like a thousand others in need of a political favor. She'd been around long enough to know how the game was played. But, unlike Garrison Tate, she was far from understanding how to win.

She snorted delicately, then flashed him a dazzling smile. Her eyes were glazed from the barbiturate she'd consumed earlier.

Tate smiled, then reached out to cup her breasts. "Feel good?" he asked, rolling her nipples between his thumbs and forefingers.

"I always feel good when I get what I want." She closed her eyes and arched against him. "It turns me on knowing there are four hundred people downstairs who paid a thou-

sand dollars a plate to have dinner with you." She winced
when he squeezed particularly hard. "And you're up here
about to fuck me."

He guided her to the bed, pleased when she wobbled.
Nothing excited him more than vulnerability. Except, of
course, absolute power.

"Doesn't it turn you on even more knowing my wife is
two floors below us getting a manicure?"

"Is she really the bitch everyone says she is?"

He worked the panties down her thighs. She stared at him
through heavy-lidded eyes, her mane of wavy red hair splay-
ing out on the pillow beneath her like blood.

"She's a bitch, all right. But she'll make a terrific First
Lady."

"That's what counts, isn't it, Garrison?"

"That's the only thing that counts."

Sliding away from him, she crossed her arms over her
breasts and sighed. "I've been waiting for weeks for this
fund-raiser tonight. There are a lot of important people
downstairs. People I should be mingling with."

"More important than me?"

She smiled coyly. "Of course not."

"You've had one glass of champagne too many. Besides,
your professional reputation is much more precious than this
dinner. There will be more dinners. And there's an endless
supply of important people to go along with them. Next time,
you'll have a reserved seat at the table with all the important
people."

"You're teasing me." She looked at him through the drug-
induced haze and smiled, moving her hands away from her
breasts. "It's important to me, Garrison."

"I promise." He parted her knees. Slipping a finger between her legs, he found her wet and hot. His body stirred
in response. "I can do things for you." He stroked her. "In-
troduce you to people. Make you a powerful, successful
woman."

Moaning beneath his touch, she threw her head back into

the pillows. He reached for the prescription bottle on the night table and tapped one of the pills into his palm. "Take this. It'll make this even better for you."

"I don't need any more." She arched when he increased the tempo of his stroking. "Oh, God, don't stop."

He poised the pill at her lips. When she opened her mouth, he shoved it onto her tongue, then handed her a glass of champagne. "Down it, sweet. I'm going to give you a night you won't ever forget."

She swallowed the pill, closing her eyes against the impending orgasm. "Yes."

"That's a good girl." He set the flute on the night table, feeling secure in knowing that she would remember little in the morning. At least nothing she would want to discuss with anyone. "Turn over, sweet."

"Don't stop, Garrison. Get me off. I'm almost there."

Using his muscular arms, he flipped her onto her stomach. "We're going to make a great team, you and I."

She struggled weakly, the fleshy cheeks of her buttocks jiggling as she tried to turn herself over. "No."

Aware of his own heavy breathing, Tate grasped the ample globes and began to knead the flesh hard enough to make her wince. "I'm going to take you back here."

"No."

It was the sensation of utter and complete power over her that had his sex throbbing like a living, breathing thing. For now, it controlled him just as he controlled her. For Garrison Tate, it didn't get any better. Power was the definitive tool of seduction, the ultimate aphrodisiac. Better than any drug, more satisfying than any pleasure of the flesh.

Using her own moisture, he lubricated her there, enjoying the sight as she wriggled her buttocks from side to side. He toyed with her, feeling the power engulf him. She was his now, to do with as he pleased.

She cried out when he entered her. Brilliant streaks of excitement ripped through him at the sound of her pain, the sight of her nails bunching the sheets, the feel of her tight body as it spasmed around his. She bucked beneath him, but he continued his slow descent until he was buried to the hilt within her.

He rode her hard, doing his utmost to hurt, to control. When she cried out or shuddered with the pain of his brutal assault, he pounded harder, without mercy, driving himself closer to release.

By the time he withdrew from her, spent, she lay silent and still on the bed, her face buried in the pillows. An occasional sob emanated from within the mass of red hair. On the pillow next to her, a red fingernail lay broken on the sheets.

Tate walked into the bathroom and returned with a warm, wet towel. He spoke softly to her as he toweled the blood from the milky flesh of her buttocks, telling her how wonderful she had been and that she should come to him whenever she needed that special favor.

Though she would be sore in the morning, Brenda Di-Rocco would remember little of what had happened in this hotel room tonight. He would tell her that in the heat of celebration, she'd had too much to drink, and that he'd had one of his bodyguards drive her home. She would be embarrassed that the night had been a total blackout. But he would be reassuring, telling her it happened to the best of them from time to time.

When he got out of the shower, she still hadn't moved. Annoyed, he picked up the piece of broken fingernail and tossed it into the trash. Reminding himself that he had a speech to give in less than an hour, he dressed, then dialed his bodyguard's room number.

"Mrs. DiRocco is going to need an escort home," he said.

"I'll be right there."

Tate hung up and smiled. He had a crowd of supporters to dazzle, money to raise, babies to kiss. He called his own room two floors down, and informed his wife the meeting had ended and that he would meet her downstairs in ten minutes.

A knock at the door announced his bodyguard. Tate answered, motioning to the semiconscious woman on the bed. "Keep it discreet, Kyle. She's had too much to drink."

The burly man, wearing custom-made trousers and jacket, went to the bed and pulled the young woman to her feet. "I'll take good care of her, Mr. Tate."

"See that you do." Tate scribbled her home address onto a sheet of the hotel's paper and handed it to his bodyguard.

She moaned, her head lolling from side to side as the big man lifted her and slipped her coat over her shoulders. Her feet barely touched the floor as he guided her to the door.

"Use the freight elevator," Tate said in disgust.

Kyle nodded and closed the door behind them.

Tate looked at his watch, not quite sure why he felt so tense. Sex and the release that went with it usually relaxed him. Especially the kind of sex he'd had with Brenda DiRocco.

His personal cell phone chirped. Only two people had the number. That it was ringing now annoyed him. "What?"

"I just got a call from one of our constituents." The voice on the other end didn't bother with introductions or niceties.

Tate reached into the inside pocket of his tuxedo jacket and withdrew the monogrammed handkerchief, not liking it that his forehead was damp with sweat. "And?"

"There have been some changes in the Denver project."

He wiped the back of his neck, felt something inexplicable tighten in his chest. "What kind of changes?"

"We got an interesting call. Someone connected to her is willing to help us."

"By all means, let's take advantage. Discreetly, of course."

"Of course." The caller cleared his throat. "The two players are here in D.C."

"How did they get this close without my knowing it?"

"They moved quickly. Different hotel every night. The

woman wants to meet with you. She's been making some noise, sir, calling your office and campaign headquarters."

Tate forced a laugh as he adjusted a diamond cuff link. "Intriguing girl," he said, considering himself in the mirror. "So far the Denver project has been a dismal failure."

"How do you want to handle it?"

"I'd like her staff terminated. Then I'd like a personal meeting with her to discuss our options."

"A personal meeting?"

He ignored the surprise in the other man's voice. "Do it."

"Sir, I feel it's my duty to warn you that a meeting could be risky."

"A risk I'm willing to take," Tate snapped. "Set it up. I want to see her."

"When?"

"Let them sweat for a couple of days. Let them get anxious. Then set something up with the contact."

"Yes, sir."

"Make sure the contact is appropriately . . . compensated."

"Done."

His heart was pounding when he snapped the phone closed. An odd mix of apprehension and anticipation that had been building for days.

And the more he thought about a personal meeting with Addison Fox, the more the idea intrigued him.

"Mr. Garrison Tate, please."

"Are you calling regarding a political issue?" the voice on the other end of the line asked.

Addison identified herself. "I'm calling in regard to a personal matter."

"Let me put you through to one of his aides."

There was a series of clicks as the call was transferred. Addison took a deep breath, wondering why it didn't help the tightness in her chest.

"May I help you?" A male voice. Professional. Busy. They screened Tate's calls well.

"This is Addison Fox. I need to speak with Garrison Tate."

"I'm sorry, but Mr. Tate is in a meeting this morning. Are you inquiring about his campaign or a political matter?"

She chose her words carefully. "He's been trying to reach me. I'm sure he'll want to speak with me personally."

"I can take a message."

"This is the third message I've left."

"I'm sorry, but he's a very busy man."

"My name is Addison Fox. Tell him I'm in town." She recited the number of the cell phone Clint had given them. "I'd like to schedule a meeting with him. If he doesn't return my call, tell him I'll contact the *Wall Street Journal*." She disconnected.

It was the third such call in as many days and still Tate hadn't bothered to call her back. Discouraged, she blew a sigh and frowned at Randall. "He's not going to take the bait."

Sitting across the table from her, he gazed back at her, his dark eyes conveying that he understood her frustration, but he didn't share it. "We'll find another way to nail him."

His answer only heightened her agitation. Too restless to sit, she rose and walked to the window, barely noticing the traffic or the rain-soaked pedestrians moving along K Street below. "This is the last thing I expected to happen. He's been so aggressive until now."

"Maybe he's trying to wait us out." Coming up behind her, Randall wrapped his arms around her waist and rested his head against hers. "You're forgetting something."

The tension drained out of her body the moment his arms encircled her. It was a magic that was uniquely theirs, one she'd discovered quite by accident in the three days they'd been in Washington. Regardless of her frame of mind, whether she was angry or afraid or just feeling alone, whenever he touched her she knew that, somehow, everything would work out.

Beyond the window, the rain quickened its tempo. She closed her eyes, wishing the nightmare would end so she could concentrate on loving this man who held her like she'd never been held before.

"What am I forgetting?" she asked quietly.

"As we speak, there are two reporters from the *Wall Street Journal* up in Siloam Springs, U.S.A., harassing Sheriff Delbert McEvoy."

The image that came to mind made her smile, and she snuggled closer to him. "Interesting scenario."

"Downright amusing if you ask me." He nipped at her earlobe. "And Van-Dyne's investigating in Denver. Something will break soon."

She loved the feel of him against her. Solid. Reassuring. The need inside her stirred, its power never ceasing to take her breath. "Have you checked on Jack?"

"Earlier this morning," he murmured, nuzzling the tender flesh just below her left ear. "But I need to check in again." Groaning, he eased away from her.

"We're going to run out of hotels if Tate doesn't make his move soon," she said.

"D.C. is a big city—"

The telephone jangled as he reached for it. Their eyes met, hers startled, his sober and decisive. "If it's Tate, go ahead and set up a meeting," he said.

Heart pounding, Addison picked up the phone. Randall leaned close enough to hear the conversation. "Hello?" she said.

"It's Clint."

"Hi, Clint."

"No luck yet, huh?"

"Not yet."

"It ain't gonna do you any good to be impatient. That old dog's playing it safe. But, believe me, honey, he's feeling the heat."

"This waiting is making me crazy."

"Looks like I'm calling at just about the right time then.

You two have been cooped up for three days. I was wondering if I could drag you out for a drink and a bite to eat."

After three days of room service food, the idea appealed immensely to Addison. She cocked her head at Randall, knowing he would be more cautious. "We're still waiting for the call," she said.

"That's the whole idea behind cell phones. You can take 'em with you."

"Where do you want to meet us?"

RANDALL COMMANDEERED THE PHONE. "LEAVING THE hotel isn't a good idea," he said. "Tate knows we're in town."

Clint's slow drawl transcended over the static. "I'm not talking dinner, partner. That was for her benefit. I didn't want to scare her, but you and I need to talk. I got some news for you."

"What is it?"

"Not on the cell."

"Then meet me here," Randall said.

"Not at the hotel. There's an anonymous little Italian place on upper Wisconsin called Franco's. The food's decent. It's a quiet place. We can talk there."

Indecision hammered at him. Clint had information. From the sound of it, something important. But Randall hadn't wanted to leave the hotel.

As if sensing his reluctance, Clint added, "He's not going to make a move on you in his hometown."

Randall looked at Addison and cursed. "I don't know, Clint. I don't like the idea of being so visible." If it were just him, he wouldn't hesitate. He was armed and a decent marksman to boot. But he was responsible for Addison and didn't want to take any unnecessary chances with her safety.

"This won't wait," Clint said.

Randall knew the man was probably right. Tate couldn't

possibly know where they were staying or what they were driving. Randall had been too careful, checking them in to a different hotel each night under assumed names. He paid with cash, just as he had the rental car.

Turning away from Addison, he spoke quietly into the receiver. "Bring your piece. We'll meet you there in half an hour."

chapter
22

HALF AN HOUR LATER, RANDALL PULLED THE RENTAL car onto Wisconsin Avenue and headed north. He still didn't like the idea of leaving the hotel. Being on the street left them exposed. But there had been an urgency in Clint's voice Randall couldn't ignore.

Beside him, Addison chatted easily, taking in the sights of the city, filling the silence with a first-time visitor's observations, her voice subtly sexy and smooth as silk. He listened to her and watched the rearview mirror, trying in vain to rid himself of the uneasiness that had lodged in the pit of his stomach like a stone.

Casting her a sidelong glance, he felt the all-too-familiar protectiveness well up inside him. In the semidarkness, he watched covertly as she drank in the sights of Georgetown, the brownstone storefronts, the Christmas decorations and muted yellow lights of lower Wisconsin Avenue. It occurred to him that she'd never experienced D.C., and he suddenly wished he could share it with her. He wanted to wine and dine her at every restaurant he'd ever loved, take her to every museum, browse through every out-of-the-way antique shop he'd ever overspent in.

He found himself wondering if she'd be willing to leave her coffee shop behind for the lights of D.C., but quickly stanched the thought. It would be wrong of him to ask her to give up her career for his. His life was in turmoil. He had the post-traumatic stress disorder to deal with. Not to mention the drinking. The last thing he wanted to do was displace her. Her roots were in Denver. Hell, she'd probably turn him down cold anyway.

Christ, he was going to miss her.

Despite the resilience she'd displayed over the last several days, her bravado was wearing thin, just as his was. She was a woman of contrast, surprising strengths and carefully concealed weaknesses, all of which formed a unique, intriguing balance. She was strong without being tough, soft without being weak. Each human frailty was overshadowed by vitality, every flaw matched by sheer perfection.

God help him, because he'd fallen headlong in love with her. The realization shocked him, thrilled him, and scared the holy hell out of him.

She was the only woman he'd ever met who could move him with nothing more than a look or gesture or word. Against his better judgment he'd given up his heart, knowing full well he was going to pay dearly for it when the time came for him to walk away.

He stopped at a light, instinctively touching the butt of the pistol tucked into his shoulder holster. Around them, traffic was light. With a practiced eye, he watched the flow of traffic, singling out cars, looking for vehicles following too closely, trying to spot the same car twice, all to no avail.

He wondered what information Clint had uncovered. Though Randall understood the other man's reluctance to speak on the cellular, he couldn't help but wonder why the Texan hadn't agreed to meet them at the hotel. As Randall pondered the question, it was then that he realized Clint was at the root of his uneasiness.

*   *   *

AT THE ENTRANCE TO FRANCO'S, ADDISON PAUSED, taking in the smells of garlic, basil, and freshly baked bread. Her stomach growled. Colorful Tiffany lamps cast warm, amber light over a dozen or so mosaic-topped bistro tables. A massive wall menu boasted the best linguine in town.

She shook off the cold that had somehow crept through her coat. "Smells great," she murmured. "I'm starved."

Expecting a response, she turned to Randall and watched as he scanned the room, his eyes pausing on the family of four in the corner, the couple huddled together at a table for two, the man nursing a beer at the bar.

"What is it?" she asked, trying to ignore the uneasiness tightening in her chest.

"This doesn't feel right." He cast an uneasy look over his shoulder.

Adrenaline danced through her midsection. She'd spent enough time with him in the last few days to realize he was overprotective, but he wasn't paranoid. "We can go back to the hotel if you prefer," she said.

"We're here. Let's see what he's got, then we'll leave and get dinner later."

Out of the corner of her eye, she saw Clint at a table near the back of the room. "There's Clint."

Randall looked at her with an intensity that stopped her breath. "We won't stay long," he said, giving her a quick, hard kiss.

Addison clearly felt the anxiety pouring off him, and she was reacting to it. Uneasiness pressed down on her like a lead weight. By the time they reached the table, she was trembling.

Clint rose. "Any trouble finding the place?"

"No problems." Randall slid into the chair at the end of the table. Addison sat across from Clint with her back to the door.

"I took the liberty of ordering wine." Reaching for the

open bottle, Clint toppled his glass. Red wine soaked into the white tablecloth. His hand shook when he pressed his napkin over the spill. Addison looked at Randall and realized he'd noticed the shaking as well.

"Why are you shaking, Clint?" Randall asked. "What the fuck's going on?"

"Like I said, partner, I got news for you."

Addison held her breath, suddenly aware that something beyond her perceptivity was happening between the two men. The hairs on the back of her neck prickled. She resisted the urge to look over her shoulder.

"What are you talking about?" Randall took the bottle from him and lowered it to the table without pouring. His eyes were dark with anger and another emotion Addison couldn't put a name to.

Clint's eyes flicked toward the front door.

Inexplicably, her heart began to hammer.

"You son of a bitch." Randall rose, grasping Addison's arm. Roughly, he jerked her to her feet. His eyes were wild with knowledge and terror when they fell upon her. "Run out the back door and go to the bar next door. Call the police." Shoving the cell phone into her hands, he pushed her toward a set of swinging doors that opened to the kitchen.

Stunned, she stumbled away from the table.

"Go!" Randall shouted.

The look on his face sent a shock wave crashing through her. She moved toward the swinging doors. She sensed danger. It pressed into her with an almost physical force. She wanted to obey him. She trusted him. But a sudden, encompassing fear for his life made her stop and turn to him.

He'd taken Clint by the collar, his face contorted with rage.

He never saw the men come through the front door.

They were like phantoms out of her worst nightmare. Two men wearing long, dark coats, faces obscured by ski masks, hands covered with black leather, boots thudding heavily on the wood floor.

Terror pounded through her as the two men drew sleek, black weapons from beneath their coats.

"Randall!" Her scream pierced the air. Oblivious to the danger, she lunged toward him.

It was as though she were moving in slow motion. She watched as Randall swung around to face the two men. His right hand moved to his weapon. She saw fear on his face, realization in his eyes as the muzzles rose, leveled.

His eyes met hers. "Run!" he shouted.

The blast deafened her. She screamed his name, then watched in shock as the concussion sent him reeling back.

"No!" Denial ripped through her. Screaming his name, she lunged toward him, knowing what she'd just witnessed couldn't be happening. God wouldn't do that to her. He wouldn't take another loved one.

A second blast rocked her brain. She looked up to see Clint fall. Blood spattered the wall behind him.

Nausea crashed through her. Her legs buckled. She fell to her hands and knees, the cell phone clattering away. A few feet away Randall lay twisted and motionless. "Randall!" Panic sent her crawling toward his prone form. She had to see him. Had to touch him. Had to know he was alive.

Shoving a chair out of the way, she crawled toward him. The floor around her was slippery with blood. For all she knew it could have been her own. It was on her hands, like warm syrup, sticky between her fingers, soaking into her clothing.

An instant before she reached him, two strong hands clamped around her shoulders and pulled her to her feet. "No!"

Pain seared through her right shoulder. Enraged, she twisted and lashed out with her feet. An instant later, the realization that she'd been injected slammed into her. A minute to react, she thought. She had to reach Randall. God, she didn't want to die alone.

She struggled, but the hands dragged her toward the front door. She was aware of the stunning silence around her, punctuated by the sound of her boots scraping across the floor. In the darkness, someone sobbed. A telephone rang in another room. Sirens howled in the distance.

The police, she thought vaguely. She tried to free herself from the man's grip, but her body had gone numb. Her mind waned, thoughts floated in and out. By the time they dragged her outside, she was unable to feel the cold.

chapter

23

HE STRUGGLED TOWARD THE LIGHT. THE DARKNESS
terrified him. Darkness was death. He knew death intimately.
He'd seen it. Smelled it. Feared it. He didn't want to die.

The pain was blinding in its intensity. As if someone had
taken a shovel to his chest and shattered his sternum. He was
aware of noise around him. The keening of sirens. Unintelligible shouting. A man barking out commands. Someone
touched his chest. Something smooth and hard cupped his
face. Oxygen. He tried to draw a breath. Pain clenched his
chest like a steel trap.

The memory of what had happened rushed back. He remembered the gunmen. Shotguns. Blasts so close they'd left
him temporarily deaf.

His heart stopped when he thought of Addison.

He opened his eyes, struggled to sit up. Pain ripped
through him, sending him back down. He shoved the oxygen
cup aside. "Addison!"

"Easy, buddy. Take it easy."

Randall focused on the young woman kneeling over him.

She was wearing a navy jacket and rubber exam gloves. A paramedic, he realized. Firmly, she replaced the oxygen cup over his nose and mouth. "This will help you breathe," she said.

"Where is she?" He shoved the cup away from his face.

"Shhh, don't try to talk. I'm a paramedic. I'm going to stabilize you, then we're going to transport you to the hospital. Just try to relax, okay?" She gave him an everything's-peachy smile and slipped the cup over his face. "Now, take a few easy breaths for me, not too deep."

Fighting a rising tide of panic, Randall did as he was told, mentally tallying his injuries. At best, his ribs were broken. Maybe a collapsed lung. Christ, he was in bad shape. If it hadn't been for the vest...

The paramedic reached for his wrist and began taking his pulse.

With his free hand, he ripped the cup from his face. "Where the hell is she?" His voice sounded desperate and weak. "The woman who was with me—is she here? Is she hurt?"

Before she could answer, a man approached and gazed down at him. "How is he?" he asked the paramedic.

"No external trauma. Kevlar vest protected him from the bullet. He's probably got a few broken ribs. We'll need to take X rays."

The man's eyebrows rose. "Body armor, huh?" He shot a hard look at Randall. "Expecting a shoot-out, cowboy?"

"You a cop?"

"Detective Murphy, Georgetown PD. What happened here?"

Randall struggled to a sitting position, closing his eyes against the dizziness. Swallowing panic, feeling the seconds ticking away, he recounted the shooting, ending with a recommendation that Murphy contact Van-Dyne in Denver. He knew if the police detained him for questioning he could be tied up for hours. He couldn't let that happen. His only concern was for Addison.

"I'm a private detective," he said. "My I.D.'s in my wallet." Wincing with pain, he reached into the rear pocket of his jeans and passed the wallet to the detective. "There was a woman with me. Where is she?"

The detective studied his identification. "Bartender says the two men forced her into a car."

Randall felt the words like a physical blow. "I've got to find her. Jesus Christ."

"Easy, partner."

"They'll kill her."

"Who?"

"I don't know . . . hired thugs."

"Give me a description."

"Two men. Black face masks, long coats. They were packing sawed-off shotguns."

The detective's eyes sharpened. "You're making this sound like some kind of a professional job."

Randall knew better than to name names. No one would believe him, and he would risk turning the event into a media feeding frenzy. Van-Dyne could take care of the details. Right now, his single priority was to find Addison.

He wanted to trust the detective. He wanted to tell him everything; he desperately needed help. But there was no time. If he was detained for questioning, it would be hours before they released him. Addison didn't have that kind of time. "That's all I know."

"Your friend's in bad shape." Murphy frowned. "You're not helping matters by clamming up."

Randall watched two paramedics frantically working on Clint. Blood glistened on their gloves. *Don't die, you bastard,* he thought bitterly. Clint was his only link to Tate. As far as Randall was concerned, the man had been served his just reward. He only hoped the son of a bitch lived long enough to talk.

Grinding his teeth against the ice-pick jabs of pain, Randall struggled to his feet. The room tilted. Nausea roiled in his gut. He clutched the table and leaned heavily against it.

Spotting Clint's cell phone a few feet away, he bent and picked it up.

Two paramedics rolled a gurney into the restaurant and parked it beside Clint's form. A third bagged oxygen. They lifted Clint on a count of three and laid him on the gurney.

Randall watched, sweating, nauseous, and waited for his senses to return. "Any idea where they took her?"

"No."

"What about the vehicle?"

"We don't know yet." The detective gave Randall a sage look. "I'd like for you to come downtown with me, Mr. Talbot. I need a statement, and I'd like for you to answer a few more questions."

Panic swirled in his gut. "I'm in a lot of pain. I think I've got some broken ribs. Maybe a collapsed lung. I need to go to the hospital first, get myself checked out."

"I'd be happy to drive you over to Columbia afterward. A statement shouldn't hold you up but an hour or so."

As if on cue, the young paramedic strode up to them, clutching a medical case at her side. Despite her age, she managed to look official in her navy jacket and severe-fitting trousers. She looked at Randall. "I'm required to ask you if you'd like medical aid or if you're refusing."

"I'd like to be transported to the hospital," he said. "With my friend there." He looked at Clint.

"You family?" she asked.

"I'm all he's got." Randall felt the detective's eyes on him as he headed for the front door.

"We'll send someone over to the hospital for a statement, Talbot," Murphy shouted.

Randall had already forgotten Detective Murphy by the time he climbed into the ambulance.

SOUND DRIFTED IN AND OUT OF HER CONSCIOUSNESS like a lazy, meandering tide. The rhythmic thud of her heartbeat. The ticking of a clock somewhere nearby. An occasional creak.

She was lying on her side with her knees drawn up to her chest. Softness cradled her body. The air around her was too cool for comfort and held the distinct smell of dampness. Her mouth felt gritty and dry, as though someone had filled it with sand, then hastily emptied it. A gentle throbbing emanated from the base of her skull.

Her thoughts floated to Randall. Broken pieces of memory hovered just out of reach. She remembered the restaurant. Two shadows moving through the front door. Guns being raised. Deafening blasts.

The memory struck her like an electrical shock. Vivid images of the shooting flew at her like jagged shards. She bolted upright, a cry escaping her. Terror hammered through her. Nausea hit her like a fist to the stomach.

Randall.

She whispered his name. Involuntary. Instinctive. Clutching the bedpost, Addison sat up and blinked at her surroundings.

She was in an oddly shaped bedroom with unusually low ceilings. The lighting was muted, giving the wood paneling a rich, coffee brown patina. A vase of fresh-cut roses sat on the black marble surface of the built-in bureau. Opposite, a large-screen television was recessed into the wall. Full darkness had fallen beyond tiny round windows.

Despite the opulent furnishings, the room was as stark and austere as a funeral parlor. It was an oppressive room, filled with all the extravagances of a lush hotel, soured by the smell of her own fear. She felt claustrophobic, as though the intricately carved panels were closing in on her. Where in God's name was she?

It was the slight rocking motion that finally conveyed she was onboard some kind of boat or ship. A glance at her watch told her she'd been unconscious for just over an hour. Despair settled over her like a dark cloud. For the first time in her life, Addison felt utterly and completely vulnerable.

Helpless. For several minutes, she sat on the edge of the bed and trembled, trying to absorb what had happened, struggling valiantly to maintain control. To lose control now would mean to accept defeat. She vowed never to surrender, especially to Garrison Tate.

She knew firsthand what he was capable of. He'd murdered four innocent people. He'd almost killed Jack. She'd watched his thugs gun down Clint Holsapple.

Oh, dear God, she'd watched them gun down Randall.

She squeezed her eyes shut against the images, steeling herself against the sight of him jerking and crumbling. She raised her hands and looked at the dried blood caked around her fingernails and the creases of her palms. She wondered if it was his. A wave of hysteria bubbled inside her. Had his vest protected him? Or had the bullet struck his head or neck where an injury would mean instant death? Feeling her own vest press uncomfortably against her breasts, she felt only minutely reassured.

Holding her knuckles to her mouth, she told herself she hadn't lost him. He wasn't dead; he couldn't be. He was too strong. Their love was too strong. There was no way love could simply cease to exist. The world wasn't that cruel. God wasn't that cruel.

Refusing to give in to the doubts, she took a quick mental tally of her physical condition. Except for the throbbing in her head and badly skinned knees, she was uninjured. Her coat had been removed and draped across her, but she was shivering with cold. She glanced down at her clothes, appalled by the sight of bloodstains on her slacks.

"Oh, God." She pressed her hands against her cheeks. "Take it easy," she whispered, determined to stay in control. "Just . . . take it easy. Don't lose it."

Abruptly, the thought struck her that she'd been spared. Why hadn't he killed her when he'd had the chance? Why was she here? She knew he wouldn't let her live. Not now. Not when she could tell the world what she knew. What could Tate possibly have in mind for her?

The question made her shiver.

*   *   *

"Clint." Randall was so close he could smell blood. "Dammit, Clint, talk to me."

From the paramedic's seat next to the gurney, the young woman monitored Clint's vital signs. Outside, the siren blared like a banshee.

Randall watched as she inserted a needle into the I.V. line and depressed the plunger. "How's he doing?" he asked.

Shaking her head, she adjusted the amount of fluid dripping through the line. "He's pretty critical," she said with a grimace. "There's a trauma team on standby at the hospital."

When he turned back to Clint, he was surprised to see the other man's eyes open. "Jesus, Clint."

Clint's eyes were glassy and strangely unfocused.

"Where is she?" Randall asked.

The dying man opened his mouth. Flecks of blood splattered against the oxygen cup.

Randall leaned forward, lifted the cup from his mouth. "They double-crossed you, my man. Don't sell what's left of your soul for those bastards."

His eyes rolled back in their sockets.

"Where's Addison? Goddammit, they're going to kill her, Clint. I need to know where she is."

The bloody mouth formed a word, the voice came, a crude gurgling, unintelligible.

Randall cursed in frustration. "Damn you, Clint, don't you die on me. You owe me this. You owe it to yourself. Now, dammit, talk to me."

His tone drew the attention of the young paramedic. "You can talk to him, but don't agitate him," she warned.

Randall ignored her. "Where's Addison? Where the fuck is she?"

Clint turned his head. Blood trickled from his mouth, spreading onto the sheet like red paint. "Lousy ten grand. . . ."

He felt no sympathy for the dying man. Loss perhaps,

anger, the bitter taste of betrayal, but not sympathy. It was necessity that had him blotting the blood with gauze. "Where did they take her?"

"Glover . . . ark."

"Glover Park?" Hope flared inside him. "Where in Glover Park?"

Clint moved his head slightly. No. He closed his eyes, let out a breath. "Call Gavin. . . ." A fresh line of blood pumped from his nose.

Randall let it run. "How do I reach Gavin?"

". . . lover park. . . ." He coughed. Blood spewed onto the surrounding sheets.

The heart monitor began to wail. Even as the dying man's final breath slid from his lungs, Randall knew he didn't have enough information. He wouldn't get any more information from Clint.

The paramedic jumped from her seat and went to work.

Shaken, Randall moved back. He watched the young woman work, but he knew Clint was dead. He'd seen enough death to recognize it. Clint had merely been given the time in which to make his final confession.

Too bad it hadn't been enough to save his soul.

Fighting panic, he stood, starkly aware that time was slipping away. Indecision hammered at him. Dear God, he had no idea where to begin looking for Addison.

Clint had mentioned Glover Park. A year ago, Clint had lived in the upscale neighborhood north of Georgetown.

"Stop the ambulance," he said.

The paramedic looked at him uneasily. "This man is dying," she said. "We'll do no such thing."

"That's a fatal wound and you know it." Randall clutched the I.V. bar as the ambulance negotiated a turn.

"You don't know that," she argued.

He touched the young woman on the shoulder. "I'm a private detective. My client, a young woman, was kidnapped in that bloody fiasco back there." He searched her face, wondering if she saw him as just another crazy roaming the streets of D.C. He could only imagine how he must look, desperate, high on drugs . . . or insane.

Raking a trembling hand through his hair, Randall took a breath and lowered his voice. "I need to find her. Time is running out. If you don't stop this ambulance and let me out, I won't be able to get to her in time. They'll kill her."

Never taking her eyes from Randall, she turned to the driver. "He's a private dick, Dennis. Let him out."

The driver studied them through the rearview mirror. "Cops told me to make sure you went directly to the hospital."

Randall hadn't wanted to use violence, but he didn't have a choice. He reached for his pistol. Alarm skittered through him when he found his holster empty. He cursed, realizing the police must have taken it while he'd been unconscious. Knowing he was going to have to bluff his way through, he stuck his right hand in his coat pocket and pointed his finger at the driver.

"I've got a .38 in my coat and by God I'll use it if you don't stop this ambulance," he said.

The ambulance screeched to a halt. Hanging on to the I.V. bar, Randall managed to keep his balance. "It would have been a hell of a lot easier if you had just stopped when I asked." Reaching for the radio, he yanked the microphone from its base.

"Just get the hell out of here, you crazy son of a bitch!" the driver shouted.

Randall reached for the rear door latch and swung it open. The ambulance had stopped in the middle of a busy intersection. Horns bellowed as he eased himself onto the pavement. Behind him, the door of the ambulance slammed shut.

He lumbered through traffic to the sidewalk. Dizzy with pain, he spotted a Christian bookstore. Head down against the wind, he pulled the cell phone from his pocket and started for the store. Around him, the air was cold and held the threat of more than merely rain.

chapter
24

CLINT'S BROWNSTONE WAS LOCATED ON A QUIET
street on the outskirts of upper Georgetown. Randall had the
cab drop him at the corner, then waited until the taillights
were out of sight before ducking into the alley.

Ransacking Clint's house was a long shot, but it was the
only place he could think of to begin. He desperately needed
information, anything that might help him find Addison.
Clint had mentioned Glover Park. He'd referred to the name
Gavin. It was all Randall had to go on; it had to be enough.

He scrambled over a chain-link fence, trying in vain not
to jar his ribs. The pain came hard and fast, wrapping around
his chest like barbed wire. Head reeling, he went to his knees
in the grass and gasped for breath. He prayed his body held
out long enough for him to find Addison.

Cursing, he waited for his vision to clear and struggled to
his feet. He looked at the house. No lights. The street beyond
was quiet and dark. Satisfied, he lumbered toward the back
door.

Relief flitted through him when he found the screen door

unlocked. He let himself into the back porch and looked around for something with which to break the glass. Spotting a broom, he gripped it, drew back, and shattered the pane with a single stroke.

The sound of breaking glass seemed deafening in the quiet. Two houses down, a dog began to bark. Aware that he was about to cross the point of no return, Randall reached inside and unlocked the door.

The house was eerily still. The linoleum creaked under his feet as he made his way through the kitchen. The air smelled of dust and lemon oil, tinged with the faint redolence of the cheap cigars Clint had been so fond of.

"Damn you, Clint," he murmured, disbelieving his friend had betrayed him, hating it that Addison's fate dangled by little more than a thread because of it.

The image of her came at him out of nowhere. Her fragile eyes filled with horror as the guns were raised and leveled. Once again, the helplessness and outrage rose up inside him. He heard the blasts. He felt the tremendous force of the impact. He remembered the sight of her covered with Clint's blood. For a terrifying moment, he'd thought she'd been hit.

A drop of sweat slipped between his shoulder blades. He left the kitchen. His heart thrashed against his injured ribs like a wild animal trapped inside his chest. *Control,* he thought in a last-ditch effort to calm himself. *Lose it now and it's over, Talbot. For you. For Addison.*

Clenching his teeth against panic, Randall moved down the hall. He walked past the bathroom and strode directly to Clint's study. The smell of cigars was stronger here, mingling with the faint odors of whiskey and old paper. He risked turning on the banker's lamp.

Clint's desk was well used, but neat. A decanter of whiskey rested on the credenza behind it. Randall opened the top drawer, not surprised to find a nine-millimeter Beretta. He pulled it out, checked the clip, and stuffed it into the waistband of his jeans. Opening the next drawer, he rifled through a stack of past due bills, a few newspaper clippings, a *Play-*

boy magazine, and an old wallet stuffed with pictures.

Acutely aware of the passage of time, he yanked out the last drawer. He knew the police would show up eventually. Urgency pulled him in one direction while the need to be thorough pulled him in another. He tried not to think about Addison—or the terror she must be feeling. He tried not to think about what Tate might want from her. He couldn't bear to think that she could be hurting—or that she could already be dead.

He rifled through a drawer full of statements and bills. Beneath them was a legal pad. Randall pulled it out and spotted the address book. He dropped into the chair and paged through the book.

Most of the entries listed first names only, some with initials, some with no name at all. Under *G,* no Gavin. He cursed in frustration, slammed the book closed, and dropped his head into his hands. Somewhere in the house, a clock chimed. Time seemed to mock him.

He opened the address book again. Starting at the beginning, he went through it, page by page. Dr. Arnoff in Chicago. Brownie, obviously an alias or nickname. Dave at Foley's Bar. Martino. Desperation clawed at him. Closing the book, he glanced out the window. Beyond, the street was dark and quiet. Mist formed a yellow halo around the single street lamp.

"Come on, goddammit." Turning back to the desk, he scanned the writing pad. On the upper right corner, a scribbled name caught his attention.

Paul Gavin.

He opened the book. To his surprise, the name *Paul* appeared under *P.* Snatching up the receiver, he dialed the number.

"Yeah, it's Gav." Deep voice. Boston accent.

"I'm a friend of Clint's." Randall trusted his instincts and went in blind.

"Don't know any Clint, man."

"He said you'd meet with me."

A long silence ensued. "I don't know what the fuck you're talking about, man."

"This is about what happened at Franco's."

A quick intake of breath. Barely audible. And then silence. "Name the place and I'll meet you," Randall said, starkly aware of the desperation in his voice. "I've got money for you."

He heard the disconnect like a death knell. He felt defeated. Beaten. Lost. Slowly, he lowered the phone to its cradle and sagged into the chair.

"Jesus Christ, what now?" The pain in his ribs was wearing him down. Emotion cluttered his brain. Every time he thought of Addison, he felt his sanity slip a little more. "Where are you?" he whispered into the cold silence. "Where in the hell are you?"

Suddenly furious, with fate, with himself, Randall shoved the decanter of whiskey off the credenza. The glass shattered, the smell of whiskey rising to taunt him. Shaken, not knowing what to do next, he snatched up the receiver and dialed the hospital from memory. His voice was hoarse when he asked for his brother's condition.

"Mr. Talbot," the nurse began. "I've got good news. Jack's been taken off the respirator. The tube was removed this afternoon. Blood gases look good and he's doing fine. He's been asking for you."

Randall closed his eyes. "I need to speak with him."

"We're not supposed to—"

"It's an emergency, goddammit."

A moment later, Jack's weak voice filled the line. "Hey, little brother. What's going on? Where the hell are you?"

Randall swallowed the emotion welling inside him at the sound of his brother's voice. Four days ago, he hadn't thought he'd ever hear that voice again. "I'm in D.C., Jack. I'm in trouble. I need your help."

"You sound bad, Randy." Concern laced his brother's voice. "What the hell's going on?"

"Tate's got Addison."

"Jesus. How?"

"Clint. They bought and paid for him, Jack. Then they fucking killed him."

"What can I do?"

"I don't know where they're holding her. I know Tate's behind this, but I can't get to him." Randall's voice cracked on the last word. He took a moment, struggled for calm. Dammit, he needed to get inside Tate's head. He needed an angle. "When you were hacking, did you see anything about Tate owning any property? Someplace private where he may have taken her?"

"Not that I can remember. Damn drugs turned my brain to cornmeal." Jack coughed. "Christ, I wish I could get my hands on a computer."

"What about friends or bodyguards? Anyone he stays with regularly?"

"Wait a minute. I remember seeing something about a boat. His wife owns a boat. A big mother. Expensive as hell."

"Where does he keep it?" The telephone line hissed, reminding Randall of the miles between them.

"I think it was registered to the state of Maryland. He kept it in Boston . . . no, Baltimore."

"Get your laptop. I need help. Jack, I'm desperate. Call Van-Dyne. Ask him to contact the locals in D.C. and Baltimore. Tell him everything you know about the case. I'm going after Addison."

"How do you know she's there, Randy?"

"I don't."

chapter
25

THE DOOR WAS LOCKED. FOR TEN MINUTES ADDISON shoved, pulled, and beat, with her fists, her feet, her shoulders, all to no avail. Perspiring, she swung around and noticed the glimmer of light beyond the satin drapes above the bed.

Stepping up on the bed, she tore the satin aside. Disappointment plowed through her when she realized the windows were too small to accommodate her body. Furious, she snatched one of the brass candlestick lamps from the nightstand and yanked the cord from the wall. Aiming for the window, she swung the lamp like a baseball bat. Plexiglas exploded outward, sending shards clattering onto the deck beyond. Frigid air blasted through the opening.

Addison dropped the lamp, put her face to the window, and screamed as loud as she could. "Help me! Somebody help me! Please!"

The door behind her burst open.

She spun, dizzy with adrenaline, sick with fear. A man dressed in a black turtleneck and dark slacks came through

the door like an enraged bull. "Bitch, you just bought yourself a whole lotta trouble."

She turned to the window. "Help me, please!" Terror res-
onated in her voice. "Help me!"

Strong hands bit into her shoulders and yanked her back.
"Shut the hell up!"

A scream erupted in her throat as he pulled her away from
the window. A viselike arm went around her waist. Fisting
a section of her hair, he jerked her backward with brutal
force. When she tried to scream again, he let go of her hair
and slapped his hand over her nose and mouth, cutting off
her oxygen.

Addison struggled as she had never struggled in her life.
Forgetting about the window and her cries for help, she
clawed at the hand until panic had her writhing and twisting,
striking out with her legs, wanting only to take a breath.

Suddenly, they were falling. She felt his body tighten. He
released her to break his fall. They tumbled off the bed in a
tangle of arms and legs.

She landed on top of him, her face so close to his she felt
the warm rush of his breath against her ear. Instinctively, she
rolled away. Lurching to her feet, she scrambled toward the
door.

A talonlike hand clamped over her arm and spun her
around. The blow came out of nowhere with mind-numbing
force. A starburst of light exploded behind her eyes. Pain cut
through her cheek, jarring the side of her face all the way to
her sinuses.

She was aware of him releasing his grip on her arm. Her
knees buckled. She caught the doorknob barely in time to
keep herself from falling.

"Stupid bitch."

Every muscle in her body tensed at the sound of his voice.
Clinging to the knob, Addison shook her head, swallowing
the bile that had risen into her throat. She'd never been sub-
jected to violence, and it left her feeling sickened and helpless. She'd never thought of herself as physically weak, but

at the mercy of such a violent man, she felt utterly powerless.

Unable to move, she let the door support her, giving her senses a moment to regroup.

"Get up."

Using the knob for balance, she rose. Fear coiled inside her, but she forced herself to meet his gaze. "Who are you?"

He stared back at her, his face expressionless. "I'm going to have to put you in another room," he said. "Let's go."

She knew firsthand his strength and didn't want to cross him. But she couldn't bring herself to obey. "Let me go," she said. "I don't know who you are."

His smile sent a chill skating up her spine. "Move."

Her only thought was that this man wasn't human. There was no emotion behind the dull eyes, no compassion, nothing she could reach. When she didn't move, he grasped her biceps and forced her toward the door.

Addison balked only enough to slow him down. She needed time to think, to plan her next move. "At least tell me where I am," she said as he guided her down a narrow hall.

"You don't need to know." The hall opened to a small bedroom. "Get inside," he ordered.

When she merely stared, he shoved her roughly through the door. "If I hear so much as a peep out of you, I'll be back." A grin split his face. "Next time, I won't be so nice."

Addison started when the door slammed. She listened to his departure before turning and taking a quick inventory of the room. It was small, perhaps six feet square, with no windows. The furniture consisted of a bunk bed and a night table. A narrow pocket-door opened to a functional bathroom.

Absently, she touched the cut on her cheek. She'd never been so afraid, felt so threatened or so isolated from the rest of the world. Needing to move, to expel some of the adrenaline rushing through her, she began to pace. She tried to imagine what might transpire in the coming hours, realizing she couldn't fathom such insanity. She tried to come to terms with the possibility that her life may very well end on this horrible night. But the thought of dying with so many things unfinished, without ever seeing Randall again, nearly sent her over the edge.

She loved him. And she knew the power of that love would see her through this. If need be, her love for him would see her through to the end. In those black minutes as she contemplated her own death, she drew strength from him, knowing in her heart that, if he was able, he would come for her.

Clinging to that thought, she made her way to the bathroom and switched on the light. Her eyes scanned the room for something she might be able to use as a weapon, but there wasn't much. No plunger, no can of hairspray, not even a water glass. On impulse, she opened the medicine cabinet.

Her heart jumped when she spotted the black leather manicure kit. She reached for the case and unzipped the cover. A pair of gold manicure scissors gleamed up at her. Knowing they could mean the difference between life and death, she pulled them out. Checking the point with the tip of her index finger, she found it razor sharp. She was in the process of tucking the scissors into the waistband of her slacks when the bedroom door swung open.

RANDALL HIT THE INTERSTATE AT EIGHTY MILES PER hour. Clint's antiquated Toyota vibrated as the speedometer's needle slipped past ninety, but he kept his foot down, oblivious to the danger. He'd discovered the keys on the kitchen counter and found the small pickup parked in the alley garage. He hadn't needed any prodding to steal it.

Desperation drove him now, hurtling him along the outer fringes of control. He no longer considered the repercussions of his actions. He did what he had to, his only, single-minded goal to find Addison in time to save her life. Because he knew Tate was going to kill her.

If he hadn't already.

Randall knew he was skating a thin line. It was as if the same sinister resolve that drove men like Tate had been unleashed inside him. The need to kill. To enact the ultimate revenge.

At the crook of his neck, he cradled Clint's cell phone. A map of Baltimore lay spread out on the seat beside him. With one eye on the interstate, he dialed the hospital number and waited to be transferred to Jack's room.

"What do you have?" he asked when his older brother's voice rumbled through the line.

"The name of the boat is *Anastasia*. Eighty-three-foot President 830 motoryacht. D.C. registry."

"Where does he keep it?"

"He usually winters it in Fort Lauderdale. The Bahia Mar Hotel. But he didn't move it this year. It's at a country club in Baltimore."

"What's the name of the club?"

"Sparrows Point Yacht Club."

In the background, Randall heard Van-Dyne barking out orders that were ridiculous at this point. He wondered if he was going to get any help from the police. "Has Van-Dyne contacted the Baltimore PD?"

"He won't touch it."

Randall cursed in frustration. Dammit, he needed backup. He didn't have time for policy and procedure. He sure as hell didn't have time for departmental politics or political correctness. "Jack, see if you can get the Baltimore PD interested. Tell them anything. Just get a couple of black-and-whites out to Sparrows Point."

"I'll do it."

Randall disconnected and switched on the dome light. Folding the map, he squinted at the image of metropolitan Baltimore. If Addison was being held in Tate's yacht, that ruled out north and west Baltimore. He creased the map, catching the steering wheel just in time to jerk it off the shoulder of the highway.

He backed the speedometer down to eighty as his eyes

scanned the myriad inland waterways that made up the city's coastline. The Patapsco River to the south. The Back River to the east. Curtis Bay. Frustration clawed at him.

"Where the hell are you?" he asked in a voice so strange it frightened him.

Tossing the map aside, he snatched up the telephone, punched city information, and asked for the number to Sparrows Point Yacht Club. He dialed. A recorded voice told him the club's office hours were between eight A.M. and six P.M. Muttering an oath, he snapped open the map. "Come on, you—"

At the tip of his thumbnail lay Sparrows Point. Just past the Francis Scott Key toll bridge at Bear Creek. Silently, he began to pray. That he wasn't wrong. That he wasn't too late. That God would spare the only woman he'd ever loved.

He couldn't stop thinking of what she must be going through. They'd discussed Tate enough in the last week that she would know what she was up against. She knew what the odds were of her coming out of this alive.

The thought tore him up inside.

Knowing he was at least ten minutes from downtown, he pressed the accelerator to the floor.

chapter

26

THE SIGHT OF HIM STUNNED HER. ADDISON'S BREATH jammed in her throat. A surge of adrenaline jolted her. Terrified and somehow amazed, she stepped back, half expecting him to strike at her like an angry viper.

Garrison Tate stared at her through steel gray eyes. Her last living relative. Her birth father. The only human being in the world with the power to terrify her.

His stare touched her with an almost physical force, intruding into places she didn't want him to see, places that made her feel unprotected and powerless. In the last hours, her defenses had been shattered. As much as she hated the thought, she sensed he drew some sort of twisted satisfaction from her fear.

He appraised her without emotion, the way a prospective investor assesses a ten-thousand-dollar piece of horseflesh. He was taller than she'd imagined. Well over six feet. His European suit was tailored to a physique that bespoke of personal trainer finesse. But he had just enough softness around the middle to tell her he was a man accustomed to fine dining. His hair was dark with a hint of gray at each temple. His presence was commanding. His posture spoke of power and status and arrogance. But it was his eyes that unnerved her most.

Her only thought was that there was no resemblance between them. With that realization came a bizarre sense of relief that meant little in light of what she faced in the coming hours.

"You're quite a resourceful young woman." He motioned toward the narrow door that led into the hall. "Shall we go into the salon?"

The cold amusement in his expression chilled her. Had there been a route of escape, she would have used that moment to flee. But she knew there was no escape. Addison felt that acutely as she stared at his outstretched hand. She was trapped within this monster's lair. A murderer in disguise. A man who'd fooled a nation of millions.

She refused his handshake with the best go-to-hell look she could manage.

He smiled. "Ah, you impress me, Addison. I knew you would. I'm very, very pleased with you."

"You son of a bitch." Her voice shook, but she didn't care.

"This will be much easier for both of us if you stay calm and cooperate." Frowning, he reached out and touched the cut on her cheek. "I see you've met Kyle."

Addison endured his touch without reacting.

"I'll have a word with him about . . . his tendencies."

She wondered what he could possibly have in mind for her. What he could possibly have to gain. What sort of twisted game he was playing. The only thing she knew for certain was that her life was at stake—and she didn't intend to lose.

"Come with me. I'd like to talk with you for a few minutes." He motioned toward the door. "Please."

Hoping to stall for time, she obeyed.

The hall led to a wide salon that smelled of eucalyptus and heated air. The miniblinds had been drawn and closed

tightly. A curving double settee upholstered in white leather
lined the port side. Twin ebony coffee tables complemented
the settee. Opposite, an entertainment center replete with a
large-screen TV and stereo system dominated the entire starboard wall.

"Please, sit down."

Addison started at the sound of his voice. She'd been staring at the opulent surroundings, tormented by the thought
that it would be the last place she'd ever see.

Turning, she faced him, acutely aware that her knees were
shaking. "Why am I here?"

"I wanted to meet you, of course."

"You'll never get away with this," she said, swallowing
the fear that had lodged in her throat like a sharp bone.

"Get away with what, Miss Fox?"

"You brought me here against my will."

"I merely want to talk to you. Sit down."

She sank into the settee.

He walked to a small bar and poured two fingers of amber
liquid into a tumbler. "Would you like a cognac?"

"What I'd like, Tate, is for you to tell me what the hell
this is all about."

He poured a second drink and carried it over to her, setting it on the end table next to her when she refused to accept it. With the verve of a dramatic actor, he raised his
glass in a solitary toast. "Power, Miss Fox." Never taking
his eyes from her, he sipped. "It's all about power. More
valuable than gold. More sought after than money. The
greatest aphrodisiac in the world. Wars have been waged
over power. More men have been killed for power than for
all the jewels in the world." He set the cognac on the coffee table. "Frankly, I'm not willing to give it up for the
likes of you."

"You murdered my parents."

"Unfortunate, but necessary, I'm afraid. Your father knew
who your birth mother was. I couldn't risk exposure. I had
no choice but to silence them both."

"Agnes Beckett. Jim Bernstein. You murdered them in cold blood."

"How else is it that you kill someone? With warm thoughts? With regret?" He smiled. "I don't think so. A man does what he must to survive."

"This wasn't about your survival."

"I have no desire to see my life ruined by scandal."

He spoke of the people he'd murdered as though their lives had had no more significance than that of an insect. It took every ounce of her control not to launch herself at him, if only for a fleeting moment of primal satisfaction. For an instant, she imagined gouging those gray, emotionless eyes with the manicure scissors, slashing his face, drawing blood. Instead, she forced herself to relax and focus. It was time she needed now. Time was her only hope.

"Politicians have been forgiven for much worse than an illegitimate child," she said. "Ted Kennedy and Chappaquiddick."

"Ah, but there's so much *power* in a name. Look what happened to poor Mr. Hart back in the election of 1988. One indiscretion and he was ruined forever."

She pretended to consider his words; all the while her mind scrambled wildly. She needed time. To think. To plan. Questions would keep him talking. "What about Agnes Beckett?"

"The mistake of a, shall we say, irresponsible young man."

"Mistake? You beat and raped a sixteen-year-old girl. That's not a mistake. That's an atrocity committed by a monster." In the backwaters of her mind, she saw the tiny mobile home in the poor section of a town so small it barely made the map. She remembered the bloodstains on the cheap paneling, the ghastly pictures Sheriff McEvoy had left for her to see.

"Your mother was nothing more than a piece of white trash. An ignorant and uneducated whore who knew more about the carnal pleasures by the time she was sixteen than most women know in a lifetime. The only thing she had going for her and ever would was her body. I gave her exactly what she wanted that night. I drove her home. Things got hot and heavy. She didn't know her place." He shrugged. "I was just a kid. I had a bright future ahead of me. I couldn't let her ruin that."

"You're a monster."

His eyes glinted cruelly. "*Insatiable* is the word the men in town used to describe her. She liked it rough. And she knew what she was getting into. Let's just say she got paid to submit." He studied her, rubbing the cleft of his chin with his thumb. "The likeness is incredible."

"You son of a bitch!" She reached for the decanter and swung it with all her might. His face went from composed to utterly astonished. She aimed for the side of his head, but he deflected the blow with his forearm. The decanter slipped from her hand.

Out of nowhere, a pair of strong hands grasped her arms from behind. Cruel fingers sank into her biceps and jerked her back.

"You're a coward," she said between clenched teeth. "When this hits the media, you're finished."

Tate's face tightened with anger. "Let her go," he said to his bodyguard.

The man released her.

"Leave us," Tate said.

Over the pounding of her heart, Addison heard the other man leave the room. "Why now?" she asked. "After all these years?"

"You were getting too close."

"How did you know?"

A smile whispered across his features. "I kept tabs on you and your activities through our mutual friend, Mr. Bernstein. I employed him when I first learned he was delving into your mother's case."

Denial welled up and overflowed. "I don't believe you. Jim wouldn't . . ." The sense of betrayal sliced her. She couldn't finish the sentence. "He had no reason to—"

"The man had four sons." His eyes glinted like ice. "They all wanted to be lawyers like their esteemed father. Imagine the cost of sending four ambitious young men to law school. I simply offered to finance his children's education for his cooperation."

"Then you killed him."

"He'd served his purpose." He studied her intently. "If it's any consolation, Bernstein felt quite badly for what he did to you."

Addison stared at him, speechless and sick to her soul.

Tate continued. "Bernstein had been hoping Beckett's death would satisfy your curiosity about your birth parents and end your search. He was an idiot. I knew sooner or later you would cause problems for me."

"Now you're going to murder me, too. Is that it? Is that how you're going to solve this?"

"I never wanted it to come to this, Miss Fox. Murder is an unpleasant business to say the least."

"Especially when you get caught."

Cold amusement played behind his eyes. "You've got guts. I admire that greatly. This time, unfortunately, your bravery won't be rewarded."

Addison fought off nerves and struggled to keep the conversation moving, keep him talking. "I don't know why I'm here. What do you want from me?"

"I'm not sure what I had expected tonight. I was curious, I suppose."

"Curious about what?"

"You. My daughter."

The words sickened her. Without realizing it, she stepped away from him as if she'd suddenly realized that he was a carrier of a terrible disease. "You're insane."

"I assure you, I'm quite sane. You see, my wife has been told she'll never bear children. She's infertile. Therefore, you're probably the only offspring I'll ever have. I'm really quite sorry that our time together has been so short. It would have been interesting to know you better. Not many people intrigue me. You do, Addison. You're a very intriguing young woman."

He strode to the coffee table nearest her. Reaching into the breast pocket of his shirt, he removed a brown prescription bottle and tapped three blue pills into her drink. "This should make the coming hours easier for you."

Addison's heart banged against her ribs. *He's going to kill me,* she thought with an eerie calm.

He swirled the tumbler and handed it to her. "Drink it."

Terror thrashed inside her, like a bullwhip slapping at her nerves. "No."

"I can tell you now that your death won't be a pleasant one." Patiently, he set the tumbler on the coffee table. "In a few minutes, Kyle will return. On my orders, he will bind your hands behind your back. Then we're going to go for a little ride out to sea."

"There are enough people who know about this to put you away for the rest of your life."

"Like your private detective?" He chuckled. "Don't be naive. Surely you realize he's dead."

"He's not dead," she choked. "He's not."

For a moment, he looked almost sympathetic, but his eyes remained as cold and hard as granite. "I've hired Kyle to take the *Anastasia* to Fort Lauderdale for the winter. Once out at sea, he will weight your body with the auxiliary anchor he keeps onboard for such occasions. I don't need to tell you what will happen next, do I?"

A shudder ran the length of her.

He grimaced. "It's not my intent for you to suffer. I wish you'd reconsider and take a few sips of the cognac. The Valium will ease your panic. Death will be much easier if you're calm."

The thought of such a horrible death turned her insides to jelly. She choked on the bile that crept into her throat, and found herself wanting to reach for the tumbler.

After a moment, he shrugged. "We've got another hour or so. Let me know if you change your mind." His gray eyes sought hers and held them for perhaps a full minute before turning abruptly to depress an intercom button built into the wall. "Kyle, we're ready."

Addison thought she'd been prepared. A half dozen plans of escape and rescue played out in the back of her mind. Randall bursting through the door, backed up by a hundred of D.C.'s finest. An FBI helicopter hovering overhead, a federal agent speaking into a bullhorn for Tate to give himself up. She even envisioned herself making a break for freedom, reaching the upper deck just as a Coast Guard cutter happened by.

Instead, Tate's bodyguard descended the curving staircase. Terror paralyzed her when she spotted the nylon handcuffs that hung loosely from his right hand.

The bodyguard looked at Tate. Tate nodded brusquely.

Blood pounded in her ears, deafening her. Her throat constricted, smothering a scream. For an instant she imagined the freezing water of the Atlantic closing over her. She imagined the darkness, the helplessness of being bound, the horror of being thrown into the icy abyss.

The bodyguard started toward her.

Addison dropped her hand to the waistband of her slacks. She felt the pointed tip of the scissors beneath her sweating palm. Her hands were shaking so badly she wasn't sure she could grip them, let alone use them to protect herself. But she'd run out of options. These two men were going to kill her in the most horrible way. Her only chance was to fight back.

The bodyguard reached out and gripped her left forearm. "Turn around."

Heart pounding, Addison yanked the scissors from her waistband. Spinning, she drew back and slashed. She put every ounce of strength she had behind her arm. A scream tore from her throat as the scissors sank into his throat.

His hands flailed. She slashed again. The man shrieked as the blades cut the side of his face.

"You bitch!"

The sheer force of her attack knocked the scissors from her hand. As if in slow motion she watched them glide to the carpet. She looked up. The bodyguard's eyes found hers. A thin line of blood trickled from his cheek, making him look wild and dangerous. Knowing she had but a second to flee, she sprinted toward the staircase.

Two strides, and he tackled her. His arms wrapped around her hips. Addison went down hard. She writhed, lashing out with her legs. He bent, gripped her arm. She screamed as she was jerked to her feet.

"I'm going to enjoy hurting you," he sneered, forcing her back to the salon.

She wanted to defy him, but the fear numbed her so thoroughly she couldn't speak. In the salon, Tate stood in the center of the room, gripping the crystal tumbler with white-knuckled hands.

The bodyguard pushed her to her knees. "Get down."

Addison fought him. She cursed him. But she wasn't strong enough. Her hands were jerked behind her back. The nylon cuffs locked around her wrists and snapped into place. With his foot, he shoved her forward. Bound, helpless, Addison fell onto her stomach hard enough to take her breath.

For a moment, she couldn't breathe. She imagined the cold water closing in around her. The blackness. Panic dug into her. She struggled against the constraints. The nylon cut into her wrists, but she was numb to the pain. She tried to roll over, but a foot planted squarely at the small of her back pressed her down. She lay there breathing hard, unable to move, like a beaten animal about to face slaughter.

The two men were talking, but she couldn't understand their words or phrases. The voices were merely babel as her mind rebelled against what would happen next. In a few short hours she would be dead. Terror sparked and twisted inside her. She thought of Randall and her heart shattered. So much lost, she thought, and a sob rose from deep within her.

Aching with loss, Addison closed her eyes, wondering if she should have taken that sip of cognac.

chapter
27

RANDALL PARKED IN THE MARINA'S LOT, THREW THE
door open, and left the truck at a lurching run. He'd known
his tolerance for pain was high, but never imagined he could
keep going when the agony snapped through his body like
lightning and exploded like fire in his brain. He couldn't
function much longer. He was in no condition for a physical
confrontation. He doubted he'd be effective if he had to use
the Beretta. His only hope was that the police had arrived
before him.

But he knew the local PD would need indisputable proof
before making a move on a man of Tate's political stature.
Tate was a powerful man with ties to all levels of govern-
ment. He was certainly capable of ruining anyone who
crossed him.

Randall knew fully it could be morning before they sent
a squad car to check out the *Anastasia*. Days before they
picked up Tate for questioning. By then it would be too late
for Addison.

He wasn't willing to take the chance.

To hell with going by the book. To hell with bureaucracy. He was starkly aware that he was functioning on gut instinct. The fear that he could be wrong never left him. But if he'd learned anything in the last thirty-eight years, it was to trust his instincts.

Crossing the parking lot, he headed toward the docks. Tall, naked masts rose into the brisk night air, the rigging lines slapping hollowly in the wind. The smells of dead fish and diesel fuel hung in the air like a cloud.

Lights from the marina restaurant shone off to his left. Beneath the arched portico, a young valet huddled against the cold, waiting for his shift to end. An older couple, the woman clad in animal fur, the man sucking on a cigar, waited for their car.

Sticking to the shadows, Randall lumbered to the water's edge. The marina was well lit, with sodium-vapor lamps situated at intervals along each of the dozen or so floating concrete docks. Half the slips were without security. A few were empty. Most of the smaller vessels had been put into dry storage for the winter months.

Tate would have security. He wouldn't have brought Addison here without absolute privacy.

Randall headed toward the secure docks. A small, weathered structure the size of a walk-in closet served as the security guard's post. Inside, a young, uniformed man ate his dinner, his eyes glued to a small television. It would be impossible to climb over the six-foot chain-link gate without attracting the guard's attention. Randall walked to the window and knocked on the glass.

The security guard started, then slid open the window. "Can I help you?"

He was young, perhaps just out of college. Law enforcement type, Randall thought, hoping the kid was smart enough to know when to look the other way. He pulled his I.D. from his wallet and flashed it. "Where's the *Anastasia*?"

The kid's eyes narrowed at the identification. "You a private dick?"

"No, I'm just a dick. Now, where the fuck is the *Anastasia*?"

"Uh, dock four." He motioned in the general direction of the secured dock area. "You got a key?"

"I need you to let me in."

"That's a secure area, sir."

"Give me your key. I'll let myself in."

"I can't do that. Would you step away from the window, sir?"

Randall faced the wind, let it wash over his face to clear his head. Despite the chill, he was perspiring. The pain radiated through his torso, edging over to his spine, between his shoulder blades.

The kid was still spewing excuses when, in the distance, Randall heard the groan of a starter and the low rumble of a marine engine. He froze, cocking his head to listen.

"Who's scheduled to go out tonight?" he asked.

"Crew's taking the *Anastasia* down to Lauderdale."

"Dammit." Randall hadn't wanted to involve the kid. Knowing he had no choice, he drew the Beretta and leveled it at the young man's face.

The kid's mouth flew open, his tongue flailing for an instant before he found his voice. "What the hell—" Frightened blue eyes jerked to the telephone on his makeshift desk.

"Don't even think about it." Randall shifted the barrel six inches, squeezed off a shot. The telephone exploded on impact.

The kid's hands shot up in the air. "Do whatever the hell you want, man! We don't keep money out here!"

"Get your ass out here."

The security guard's hands trembled so violently, it took him several tries to open the door.

"What time is the *Anastasia* scheduled to leave?" Randall asked.

"M-midnight."

He glanced at his watch. Eleven-thirty. "Who's onboard?"

"I don't know. My shift started at eleven." The kid licked his lips. "Look mister, I got five bucks—"

"Shut up and give me the key to that goddamned gate!"

The kid unclipped the ring of keys from his belt and held them out with a quaking fist.

Snatching the keys from him, Randall removed his I.D. from his wallet along with Van-Dyne's card and pressed both into the kid's hand. "Now, listen carefully. I want you to run up to the restaurant and call the cops." In the distance, the engines rumbled ominously. "Give my I.D. to whoever's in charge. Tell them to contact Detective Adam Van-Dyne in Denver. It's a matter of life and death for a young woman onboard that boat. Go."

The kid backed away, then took off running. Randall ran to the gate and attacked the lock. Once through, he fell into a broken lope, checking the names painted onto the transoms of each vessel he passed.

He was halfway to the end of the dock when he heard the pitch of the engines change. The rpms revved. The boat was pulling out.

Panic struck him like a sledgehammer. At a dead run, he watched as an immense President 830 yacht pulled slowly away from the marina. From twenty yards away, he made out the Arabic lettering—*Anastasia.*

chapter

28

HE WAS TOO LATE.

Randall stood at the end of the dock, gasping for breath, and watched the boat pull away. "No!" he bellowed.

Tate was going to kill her.

Helplessly, he backtracked, staggering down the dock, uncertain of his next move. Around him, the night wind had picked up. The boats moved restlessly against their moorings. Nylon ropes groaned against steel cleats. Waves slapped against concrete piers.

A man was examining the gate Randall had left open, obviously perturbed. He straightened and watched Randall approach. "Are you the idiot who left the gate open? Anyone could have just walked in. I don't know about you, buddy, but I don't want some lowlife waltzing in here to take my boat."

Take my boat.

"Which one is yours?" Randall heard himself ask.

The man cocked his bald head. "Little Bertram up front.

I was just coming out to check on her. What the hell were you thinking, man?"

"Guess I wasn't." Randall smelled alcohol on the man's breath. He must have just come from the marina restaurant. His only thought was that this drunken man would be easy to overpower. "Do you leave your boat out here all winter?" he asked.

"Till Christmas. Then the wife and I take her down to Hilton Head. Damn Lauderdale's full of hop heads. Miami's full of Cubans. Just can't win, you know?"

"What's the world coming to?" Randall fell in beside him, eyeing the boats they passed, watching the man's hands. "So she's fueled and ready to go?"

"We're leaving this weekend so long as the weather holds up. She needs some minor engine work. Damn mechanic here at the marina's a real asshole. Rebuilt one of the engines—took him two months and then he tries to charge me three grand. I told him to stick it up his ass."

Anxious to get a look at the boat, Randall walked faster. "Thanks for the warning."

The bald man stopped in front of an old, sleek-looking Bertram. "There she is. All forty-four feet of her."

"Nice-looking boat. Got your keys with you?"

Alarm entered the man's eyes. "Look, buddy, I don't want no trouble."

Randall eyed the Bertram, spotting the flotation key chain dangling from the ignition. Heart hammering, he swung around and punched the man in the jaw.

The man's head snapped back. He raised his hands to protect himself. "What the hell! Hey!"

Gritting his teeth in pain, Randall shoved him into the water. He'd already reached the deck of *The Pulpit* when the sound of the splash reached him. He darted to the control console and turned the first of two ignition keys, silently thanking God when the starboard engine roared to life. The port engine grumbled, coughed like a sick cow, and then turned over. With the engines purring, he untied the moorings.

Randall didn't know much about the big vessels, but he'd been onboard plenty of smaller boats and was mechanically inclined enough to find the port and starboard throttles and clutches. Flipping on the lights, he checked the bilge and fuel alarms. Gripping the throttle with his right hand, he jammed it forward.

The boat quivered as the transmission jerked into gear. For an instant, the Bertram drifted. The engines whined. He checked the double tachometers. The stern bumped a nearby sailboat's taffrail. He spun the wheel. The big boat quivered, as if she'd been struck by a wave. With a recklessness he hadn't known existed inside him, he maneuvered the boat from its slip. Ignoring the No Wake sign, he pressed the throttle forward as far as it would go. The old Bertram jumped forward, its hull slicing through the black water with the grace of a racing boat.

The logical side of him knew better than to attempt to navigate the inland waters at such a high rate of speed. He didn't know depths or direction. He didn't have a nautical map. But the darker side of him scoffed at the notion of logic.

Finding the *Anastasia* would be nothing short of a miracle. The intracoastal waterway and the massive expanse of Chesapeake Bay were nearly as boundless as the ocean itself. The shores were chock full of undeveloped inlets, shipyards, marinas, and rivers. It was too much territory for one man to cover. He needed help, but there was no one left to help him.

He'd broken too many laws to count in the last several hours to expect any help from the local police. The detective investigating the shooting back at the restaurant had expected him at the hospital hours ago. He'd threatened a paramedic. He'd broken into Clint's apartment and tampered with evidence. Christ, he'd stolen a boat at gunpoint.

They're taking Addison out to sea, Talbot.

Terror twisted inside him. He should have known better

than to take her out of the hotel. He should have been able to protect her. Guilt pounded at him.

Determined to stay in control, Randall closed his eyes and let the cold, heavy air wash over his face. It wouldn't do her any good for him to lose it now. All he could do was keep up the search and hope for a lucky break.

He squinted into the darkness. Ahead, the lights of the Francis Scott Key Bridge spanned the Patapsco River. The boat shifted slightly as it entered the river's current. Turning the wheel sharply, he headed out into the bay.

On the horizon, two tiny specks of light shone like stars against the night sky. Too near to be land. Half expecting them to disappear like a mirage, Randall kept his eyes trained on the lights. As he drew closer, he realized they were the lights of a large vessel heading due south.

He adjusted the wheel and set a direct course for what he prayed was the *Anastasia*.

INSIDE THE PILOT HOUSE, GARRISON TATE MARVELED at the sheer beauty of the machinery his power afforded him. The breadth and width of the power he possessed touched him with an intensity that was almost sexual.

"How far are we from open ocean?" he asked, running his hand over the ergonomic instrument panel.

Kyle looked away from the darkened windshield and met his gaze. "Depending on the bridges and traffic, three or four hours."

"How's the surf?"

"Two to four feet. We picked a good night."

Tate nodded and let his gaze travel beyond the glass. "You'll need to drop me in Annapolis."

The other man nodded and continued to stare out into the abyss spread out before them.

Tate checked the Rolex strapped to his wrist and thought of the young woman belowdecks. Bringing her to the yacht had been a calculated risk. But he wasn't sorry for it. He'd enjoyed meeting her even more than he'd anticipated. A flicker of satisfaction settled over him. Yes, he thought, she was everything he'd expected. Beautiful. Intelligent. A compelling young woman with a lovely spirit and a sort of feminine cunning that shone bright behind the dark eyes she'd inherited from her mother.

But it was obvious Addison Fox was not the offspring of a dirt-poor high school dropout from Siloam Springs, Ohio. No, she'd definitely inherited his finer genes. She handled herself well in the face of adversity. Had the circumstances been different, he would have liked to know her better. As it was, he would be nothing but relieved once this nasty business was done.

He felt no real connection to her. The sight of her hadn't moved him or touched him in ways he'd imagined, in ways he'd feared. She was the only offspring he would ever produce. For reasons he wasn't quite sure he understood, or wanted to admit, he had become obsessed with meeting her in the last few days. Tonight, as he'd gazed into her eyes for the first time, he'd spent several desperate seconds searching for traces of himself.

A tiny, cruel part of him had wanted to see what he had spawned as a young man in the throes of a violent passion. Another, less familiar side of him had winced with regret. Not because of his plans to murder an innocent young woman, but because, after her demise, he would never father another child.

Needing a drink, Tate turned away and started for the salon. "Would you like a cognac, Kyle—"

The yacht lurched. The sound of splitting fiberglass and the screeching of metal against metal shattered the stillness. Tate fell sideways, the throttle housing ramming into his shoulder as he went down.

His first thought was that Kyle had run them aground. Rage poured through him at the thought. With an unwilling guest onboard, how could the man be so negligent?

The *Anastasia* shuddered. The engines coughed and died.

A startling silence resounded through the cabin, punctuated by the sound of waves slapping against the hull. Tate dragged himself to his feet. Glancing out the windshield, he felt his blood run cold.

A vessel, stark and white against the black water of the bay, rocked in the choppy water. He blinked at the surreal scene, disbelief and rage pumping through him.

Only then did he realize he'd underestimated Randall Talbot.

chapter
29

THE IMPACT SLAMMED RANDALL AGAINST THE WHEEL.
Pain ricocheted through his body. He groaned, felt his knees
give. A curse flittered through his brain, but he didn't speak.
Knowing he was dangerously close to blacking out, he clung
to the chrome support next to the wheel and hauled himself
to his feet.

Even in the darkness he spotted the other boat just off the
bow. The *Anastasia* sat low in the water, rolling in two-foot
swells. There were no lights, no engines, and no sign of a
crew.

The Pulpit listed sharply starboard. He knew instantly she
was taking on water. Pulling the Beretta from his waistband,
he checked the clip, wishing Clint had kept an extra on hand.
He opened the pilot house door. Cold night air and ocean
spray rushed over his face. He studied the position of the
Anastasia, realizing with alarm that the two yachts were
drifting apart. A kick of adrenaline had him ascending the
ladder. He had to board the other vessel before it drifted too
far away.

A bullet zinged past him as he reached the deck. The window behind him exploded, showering him with shards of Plexiglas. The flash had come from the other boat's pilot house. Blindly, he took aim, fired off six rounds.

Nine rounds left. Hoping he'd gotten lucky and hit his target, he clambered onto the gunwale and leaped.

THE IMPACT HAD THROWN ADDISON TO THE FLOOR. Hands bound, she hadn't been able to break the fall and tumbled amid the flying debris and broken glass, landing hard against the opposite wall. She was back on her feet in an instant, listening to the quiet rush of water and the sound of the waves pounding the hull. All the while Tate's words echoed in her ears.

Your death won't be an easy one.

The water terrified her. It was ice cold and ankle deep in the galley. Staving off panic, she waded toward the salon, clinging to the thought that Randall had come for her. That the Coast Guard had somehow stopped the boat.

Her gaze paused on the table where Tate had left the tumbler of cognac. The tumbler lay on the floor in pieces. She ran to it and dropped to her knees. Frigid water bit into her legs, but she ignored the discomfort, knowing she had only a few minutes to free herself. She turned her back to the broken glass and grappled for the largest piece. Using her right hand, she gripped the shard between two fingers and began sawing at the nylon handcuffs.

The sound of footsteps snapped her head up. The stairway door opened. Tate stepped into the room. He looked like an evil hologram, standing there with his black heart and malicious eyes. Though unable to tear her gaze away from his, she continued the back-and-forth motion with the glass.

"Put it down." He approached her. Without warning, he reached down, grasped a handful of her hair, and yanked her to her feet. "That son of a bitch killed Kyle."

The glass slipped from her hand. She strained against the

binds to no avail. Despair tore through her. The water was now nearly a foot deep in the galley, ankle deep where they stood.

"We're sinking, for God's sake!" she said.

A strange light entered his eyes. A bizarre combination of disbelief and rage. Addison watched as he strode across the room and lifted the cover of a rosewood hatch recessed into the wall.

He extracted a small pistol that gleamed like an evil diamond in the palm of his hand.

He turned to her, his eyes flat and dangerous. "Let's go."

"I'm not going anywhere with you."

Grasping her arm, he shoved her toward the staircase that led to the upper deck. "You'll do as you're told."

Reckless anger swirled dangerously inside her. She wanted to fight back. But with her hands bound there was little she could do.

The gun pressed between her shoulder blades. "Move."

She took a first tentative step, wondering if he was going to shoot her or use her as a shield.

"Your lover just made a fatal error," he said.

Her heart bumped hard against her ribs. Something akin to relief washed over her. Randall was alive. He'd come for her. She turned and looked at Tate. "Let me go," she said. "Please. You can still get away."

His smile frightened her even more than the pistol poised at her spine. It was a dead smile, devoid of emotion. Inhuman. Insane. "Walk up the steps," he commanded.

Numbly, Addison started up the staircase. She wondered if Randall knew Tate was armed. Not thinking of the repercussions or her own safety, she bolted, taking the steps two at a time. "Randall! He's got a gun!"

She heard Tate moving behind her. The sound of his wingtips against wet carpet. Ragged breathing. Her own sobs wrenching from somewhere deep inside her. She felt his hand on her hair. Pain flashed across her scalp when he jerked her back. She heard herself cry out. The sound of hair being torn from its roots.

Savagely, he twisted her hair. "You stupid bitch! Do as I say!"

"Let go of me!"

He spun her around to face him. The blow caught her left temple. Pain. An explosion of light. A scream of outrage tore from her throat. She cursed him through tears of rage.

"Don't try that again." He shoved her forward. "Now, get up those fucking stairs!"

Dizzy from the blow, shocked by the pain billowing through her, she stumbled up the stairs. When she reached the door, Tate stepped past her and swung it open.

Cold ocean air crashed over her as she stepped out onto the deck. Light rain fell from a black sky.

"Let's go find lover boy."

"I'm right here, Tate."

Addison choked back a cry at the sound of Randall's voice.

Boldly, he stepped into the open. Stance wide. Hands gripping an ominous-looking pistol. Even in the darkness she saw the glint of rage in his eyes.

The sight of him stopped her heart. "Randall." She heard his name, though she barely felt herself utter it. "He's armed."

"Are you all right?"

In spite of the gun poised at the base of her skull, it took every bit of self-control for her not to throw herself into his arms. "I'm okay."

He shifted his stance, aiming the pistol more squarely at Tate. "Let her go, Tate." Then his voice changed. Lowered to the sound of rapidly approaching thunder, the kind that struck unexpectedly and with deadly force. "Get your hands off her or I'll fucking blow you in half."

Tate touched the side of her face with the gun. "And risk my putting a bullet in this pretty face? I don't think so."

"Release her, and I'll let you walk away," Randall said. "If you hurt her, I'll kill you."

Tate made a sound of irritation. "Drop the gun, Talbot. Or I'll put a bullet in her head. Just above the hairline. Here, in the back. The medulla, I believe it's called."

Addison's nerves jumped as he ran the muzzle of the gun over her scalp. "Don't do it, Randall." Her voice barely carried over the sound of the wind. "He's insane. He'll kill us both."

"You're going to be front-page news tomorrow, Tate. Starting with the *Wall Street Journal*. They know everything." Randall's voice calmed her, told her that somehow he was going to get them out of this.

"Weak lies, Talbot. All of it. You and I both know there's no proof. Just as we know that no newspaper in the country will print such a ludicrous story without substantiation."

"The cops know about Agnes Beckett. They know about Bernstein. About Patty and Larry Fox. A Coast Guard cutter will be here any minute, Tate. Give it up." Randall edged closer, his voice smoothing out. "It's over. Give it up."

The macabre sound of Tate's laughter drowned out the last of his words. "Once the both of you are dead, this nasty little business will be finished forever. Now, get the hell back, you two-bit drunk."

The pistol shifted, digging into the tender spot just below her left ear. Addison shuddered uncontrollably as she imagined a bullet leaving the chamber and slamming into her skull.

"Let her go, Tate. You don't have to die over this. I'll let you walk. Just let her go." Randall edged closer. "You're a powerful man. You can run anywhere in the world. If they catch you, you can afford the best attorneys our legal system has to offer. Release her, and I'll let you go."

The pistol trembled against her scalp. Slightly at first, and then violently until the muzzle of the gun shook against the side of her head.

Randall moved closer, his pistol steady. "Let her go. You don't want to hurt her."

"She means nothing to me," Tate said. "I have no compunction about—"

The gun blast deafened her. Next to her, Tate grunted, his body jerking. He looked down in disbelief at the blood coming through his jacket. In the back of her mind, Addison knew Randall had shot him. Hope jumped through her. She waited for Tate to crumple.

Instead, he raised the gun and fired point-blank at Randall.

"No!" she screamed, watching in horror as the man she loved reeled backward and landed on the cold, wet deck. *"Randall!"*

Tate's arm snaked around her waist. "I warned him not to fuck with me!" he snarled.

Addison fought him with all her strength, but he was too strong and dragged her toward the rail. Twisting, she spotted Randall on the deck, crawling toward the gun he'd dropped. Relief exploded in her chest. He wasn't dead. The vest had saved his life a second time.

Tate shoved her violently against the rail. Her hip slammed hard against the wood. Rivulets of pain speared through her. Somewhere in the back of her mind she heard Tate shouting, but she couldn't make out the words. All she could think was that Randall was alive. And somehow he was going to get them out of this.

Suddenly, Tate's arms tightened around her. In the next instant, her feet left the deck. She was halfway over the rail by the time she realized what he was going to do. Horror raged through her. Oh, God. Oh, *God*! He was throwing her overboard.

"No!" she screamed.

"See you in hell," he said and shoved her over the side.

Addison flailed, the cold, thin air rushing around her. The ocean laughed as her own wrenching scream pierced the air.

She was falling.

Then the water rushed up and received her with sharp, icy

claws. It ripped into her, tore her open from end to end. Encompassed her like an arctic crypt. Her senses scattered as the shock incapacitated her, physically, mentally.

A rush of disbelief engulfed her. Her mind rebelled against the terror spiraling out of control inside her. *This can't be happening,* she thought with startling clarity. Not when Randall had been just a few feet away.

The water sucked her down. Her mind acknowledged the sensation of nothingness. A black void. An icy tomb. She struggled against her binds, not knowing up from down. A bolt of adrenaline surged through her muscles. She sucked in a mouthful of saltwater and choked. Panic swirled inside her like a tornado.

She opened her eyes to total blackness and felt the burn of saltwater against them. She kicked with all her might, cursing the boots that weighed her down.

An instant later she broke the surface. Sound and light and bitter cold assaulted her senses. She kicked, struggling to keep her mouth above the waves. The water tugged her down. Her face slipped below the waves.

And she was drowning.

chapter
30

RANDALL REACHED THE GUNWALE JUST AS TATE crumbled. An animal sound ripped from his throat as he leaned over the rail. Ten feet below, the unforgiving water churned angrily. "Addison!"

Desperate, he turned, spotting the cabinets set into the transom at the stern. Sprinting across the deck, he dropped to his knees. One by one, he ripped open the cabinets, finally locating a cache of life vests.

Jerking the vests from their nest, he rose. Ten feet away, the sight of Tate lying facedown in a pool of blood stunned him.

Randall shook himself and darted back to the rail. There, he secured one of the vests at his waist, lodging two more beneath his arms. Without a thought for his own safety, he climbed onto the rail. From atop the gunwale, he scanned the water and listened for cries that never came.

"Addison!"

It was December and the water in the bay couldn't be much over fifty degrees Fahrenheit. Randall knew how quickly hypothermia set in. Christ, how long could she tread water with her hands bound?

Panic hammered at him. Screaming her name, knowing there was no more time, he tightened his grip on the vests and hurled himself over the edge.

ADDISON WASN'T SURE HOW LONG SHE'D BEEN IN THE water. It seemed like hours, but it could have been minutes, even seconds. Cold numbed her body. She no longer felt her hands or feet. The muscles in her legs throbbed with the effort of keeping her head above water. Her clothes and boots felt like dead weight.

Oh, dear God, where was Randall?

Despair stabbed through her. She couldn't stay afloat much longer. The cold was zapping her strength with frightening speed. She couldn't see the boat; she couldn't remember which direction it was in.

A wave washed over her. Choking, she rolled onto her back and kicked. An eerie calm descended over her. She felt as if she'd been drugged. Detached. She closed her eyes. The darkness enticed with a warm embrace and a murky promise to end the pain. To end the struggle.

Her face slipped below the surface.

She sucked in water, felt it burn her lungs. Raw adrenaline speared through her. She surfaced again, coughing.

"Randall! Help me!" she choked. "Oh, God, help me, please!"

A wave crashed over her, pushing her down. She kicked violently, using the last of her strength to break the surface. One more time, she thought wildly, one more breath. One more minute of life. She took in a mouthful of acrid water. She coughed, shuddered with the effort, and felt herself slipping under.

She barely felt the hands lift her, forcing something solid beneath her arms. "Addison! Honey, it's me."

Randall. Beside her. Touching her.

"Talk to me, dammit!" Without finesse, he slapped her cheek with an open palm, shaking her gently. "Wake up! Honey, we've got to swim back to the boat."

She was aware of him struggling, the breath rushing between his teeth, the hardness of his body bumping against hers as he stroked through the turbulent water.

She tried to speak, but her mouth couldn't form the words. She felt warmer now. Slipping away to a place that wasn't so cold.

RANDALL COULDN'T BELIEVE HE'D FOUND HER. NOW that his arms were wrapped around her, he swore he'd never let her go. But she was cold. So cold it frightened him.

They were less than ten feet from the boat when he heard the low rumble of an engine. He stopped stroking and cocked his head to listen. The smell of exhaust reached him through the rain and wind. Terror ripped through him, shaking him to his very foundation as he watched the *Anastasia* pull away.

Tate was alive. And he was leaving them to drown.

Randall bellowed a curse. He slammed his fist against the water in outrage. Lying against him, barely conscious, Addison stirred.

Fighting panic, he shook her. "We're going to swim for the other boat. I need for you to kick your feet, Addison. Right now. Come on! Kick for me."

Even in the darkness, he saw the distance in her eyes. When she tried to speak, her words were slurred, unintelligible.

Christ, he was losing her to hypothermia.

Remembering his pocket knife, he fished it out of his pocket with numb fingers. Setting the blade against the nylon cord of the handcuffs, he sawed back and forth. "I want you to swim, honey." The cord gave, freeing her arms. Kicking furiously, he rubbed her arms briskly.

"Randall. Oh, God, Randall."

The sound of her voice crushed him. He closed his eyes, felt the weight of the world settle onto his shoulders. "That's right, honey. It's me. We're going to swim. I want you to kick your feet."

When she didn't respond, he shook her gently. Taking her hands between his he rubbed them vigorously. "Help me, dammit." Panic edged his voice. "I need your help. Kick your feet. You've got to swim."

She moved feebly beside him, but he knew it was useless. She didn't have the strength.

Randall rolled her onto her back and tied her vest to his, binding them together. He wasn't going to let her go. Dammit, he wasn't going to let her die. Not after everything they'd been through.

Determined to save the life of the woman he loved, he swam in the general direction of *The Pulpit.* He couldn't see the boat through the darkness and swells, but he trusted his sense of direction. With Addison in tow, he used the last of his strength stroking and kicking. He put everything he had into that swim, cursing every wave, every moment when that little voice inside his head told him they weren't going to make it.

When his arms and legs threatened to give out, he swam on adrenaline alone. When it became painful even to draw a breath, he thought of Addison, of everything that would be lost if he gave up now. When he thought he could go on no more, he used his own fury to fuel him.

Blinded by water, deafened by the wind, he drove himself mercilessly. His broken ribs took him beyond pain. Exhaustion hammered through him and the cold zapped his strength. The waves pummeled him. He cursed with one breath, prayed with the next.

Treading water, he tried to get his bearings. Next to him, Addison was silent and still. However much he longed to comfort her, to give her his warmth, he hadn't the strength left. He couldn't swim much farther. He couldn't take much more cold.

A bolt of adrenaline ripped through him when he saw the silhouette of the Bertram twenty yards to his right. A hologram against the horizon. Fading in and out of his vision like a mirage.

Hope burgeoned in his chest. Praying his mind wasn't playing tricks on him, he began to swim. "Hang on, Addison."

They approached *The Pulpit* from the stern. With weighted arms, he reached for the dive ladder and pulled himself out of the water.

The wind cut through his wet clothes, stunning him with cold. He murmured her name as he bent and lifted her out of the water. "Hold on, honey. We're safe. We made it."

A foot of water sloshed from side to side on the deck. Another hour and the boat would be at the bottom of the bay. Randall took her to the pilot house. Once inside, he closed the door, fell to his knees, and lowered her to the floor.

She spilled from his arms in a wet heap, cold, motionless, seemingly lifeless. There wasn't enough light for him to see her face so he couldn't tell how bad her coloring was. He checked her pulse at her throat, finding it weak and slow.

Acting on instinct, he quickly removed her boots and wet clothing, too frightened to notice the beauty of her flesh beneath. "Addison, honey, we made it." His voice was thick with emotion, uncertainty, and the remnants of his own physical strain. "You're going to be all right."

She coughed, her arms stirring.

Tearing himself away from her, Randall searched the small pilot house for something with which to cover her. She needed warmth. On a bench next to the door, he spotted a stack of neatly folded beach towels. He reached for them, snapped them open one by one, and placed them over her until she was covered from head to toe.

Brushing aside a shock of wet hair, he knelt and touched her face. "Addison. I need you to wake up, honey. Come on." His voice broke. He closed his eyes against the choking emotion. "Can you hear me? Can you move for me, honey?" He grasped one of her hands and held it between his, hoping to warm it, knowing his own were too cold to make a difference. "I've got to use the radio. I'm going to have to leave you for a moment. I don't want you to wake up and be afraid, because I'm right here."

"Randall . . . I thought you were dead."

"I'm right here. Everything's going to be fine."

"He was going to kill me."

"Shhh. It's over. You're safe."

"Where's Tate?"

He'd known she would ask. The last thing he wanted to tell her was that by some insane twist of fate, Garrison Tate was still alive. "I shot him, but he got away."

"Oh, God, no—"

"He won't get far. He's hurt. He's insane. The only thing that matters is that we're going to be all right."

Raising her hand, she touched his face. "You saved my life."

"You owe me big time, now."

Her smile devastated him. "Maybe we could work something out in trade."

"I bet we'll be able to come up with something," he said and pressed a kiss to her lips.

chapter
31

THE SNOW WAS COMING DOWN IN EARNEST AS ADDISON sank into the chair and put her elbows on the bistro table. She frowned at Gretchen and made a futile attempt to ignore the butterflies wreaking havoc in her stomach.

"He should have been here by now," she grumbled.

The older woman shoved a tall vanilla latte in front of her. "You're just nervous."

"Am not. I'm bitchy."

"Same thing." After wiping her hands on the ever-present apron at her waist, Gretchen gave the younger woman's shoulders a quick squeeze. "He'll be here. Trust me."

"How can you be so sure?"

"Call it wisdom. Call it age or whatever you like. But, honey, I know people. And just between you and me, I know men. Randall Talbot isn't going to let a little thing like a snowstorm get in the way of seeing you."

Addison watched her friend slip behind the bar and busy herself polishing the new espresso machine. How things

stayed the same, she thought. *How quickly things changed,*
a little voice chimed in.

Around her the Coffee Cup virtually hummed with customers. The sounds of muted conversation and cups clinking
against saucers combined with Sinatra's silky voice and
melded into the most comforting symphony she could imagine. Addison was delighted to be back, right in the center of
it all. The Coffee Cup was where she belonged, where she
felt at home.

Six weeks had passed since that fateful night onboard the
Anastasia. Christmas had come and gone. Jack had been released from the hospital and would soon begin physical therapy. The Coffee Cup had reopened in time for the new year.
Her insurance company had even supplied her with a new
espresso machine.

Just because she hadn't seen Randall in a month wasn't
any reason to fall to pieces. Was it?

He'd been tied up in D.C., the subject of a much-too-
thorough grand jury inquiry. He'd been distant when he'd
told her over the phone that he'd moved back into his old
town house. He'd been vague when she'd asked about his
next trip to Denver. She hated it that he'd been so upbeat
about his new desk job with the NTSB.

Addison knew a brush-off when she heard it.

The *Wall Street Journal* had done an exposé on the late
Garrison Tate, starting with the rape of Agnes Beckett
twenty-seven years ago and ending with the final, violent
hours he'd spent with Addison onboard the *Anastasia*. Sheriff Delbert McEvoy had been indicted on bribery charges. It
seemed Tate had sent the good sheriff and his wife to London
twice and paid for a Caribbean cruise and a trip to Ireland
in the last ten years. More serious charges ranging from arson
to murder were expected to be filed in the coming weeks.

From her hospital bed the morning after that terrible night,
Addison had found out that Tate had committed suicide onboard the *Anastasia*. Strangely, she'd felt nothing more than

a sense of closure. For herself. For her parents. For Agnes Beckett.

Her search had finally come to an end. She knew as much as she would ever know about her birth parents. As much as she ever wanted to know. She would ponder her roots no more.

Larry and Patty Fox were her parents. A childless couple who had given an unwanted baby a chance for a good life. They'd given her their love, instilled in her their morals, their sense of right and wrong, and built her into the person she was today. She could never ask for more, and she would forever cherish them as her only parents.

Addison glanced at her watch, wondering for the hundredth time how Randall would take the news. Aside from the time he'd spent with Jack, and the single weekend he'd come home, Addison hadn't seen him for four very long weeks.

It seemed like a lifetime.

She chastised herself for thinking that today would be any different from any other. She was at her shop. Customers were piling in to buy Sumatra coffee and Earl Grey tea. The china teapots were moving well. She should be overjoyed. To have her life back. To be alive.

Instead, she felt as though she was coming apart at the seams.

She'd heard the news just that morning, as shocking as a blast of frigid air on a hundred-degree day. During a follow-up visit to her doctor, she'd mentioned that her period hadn't come, believing it was due to the physical strain of the hypothermia she'd suffered six weeks earlier. Two hours later, the doctor had called her at the shop and reported that she was pregnant.

Since then, Addison had been riding the emotional roller coaster from end to end, up and down, over and over again. She went from elated to uncertain to frightened, then back again.

More than anything she wanted a family. A center to her

life. Someone to love. It was something she'd always imagined for herself. A child. A husband.

So why was the idea of having a baby terrifying her so?

Sternly, she reminded herself that she didn't need Randall Talbot to be happy. Nor did she need him to have the baby. They would get along fine without him. Telling him was merely a courtesy.

Not sure if her nausea was from nerves or the tiny life growing inside her, Addison shoved the latte away, dropped her head into her hands, and groaned.

"Headache?"

Her head whipped up at the sound of his voice. Her face heated with an unexpected blush. She wanted to be angry with him. For keeping her waiting. For making her feel so damned uncertain. For making her love him so much her chest ached with it.

"I hate it when you sneak up on me," she said nastily.

Thick dark eyebrows shot up. Innocently, he looked behind him as if to make certain the words had been directed at him.

"He came through the front door like all your other customers." Gretchen approached the table with a tray. "How was your flight, Randy?" she asked, her tone dripping with honey.

"Too long," he said, gazing steadily at Addison.

Randall pulled out one of the bistro chairs as Gretchen set a foamy latte and a plate of fresh-baked scones in front of him. "If you haven't already noticed"—she winked at Randall—"our queen for the day is in a bad mood." With a sly, grandmotherly smile, she turned on her heel and left them alone.

Randall reached for his latte.

Addison felt him watching her from across the table. Dropping her eyes to the plate of scones, she reached for one out of sheer determination not to be nervous.

"What seems to be the problem?" Bringing the coffee to

his lips, he slurped as only a male can slurp and get away with it. "Is everything all right?"

"Everything's just peachy." She sent him a disagreeable smile, took half the scone in a single bite, and let the crumbs fall into her lap.

"If the media's bothering you—"

"I've been media-free for almost two weeks now."

He studied her, looking too handsome and far too in control as he sat across from her. She tried to remember the exact moment when she'd fallen in love with him, realizing it had probably been that fateful day at his seedy little office two blocks away. She just hadn't realized it at the time.

God, she hated it when life just up and pulled out the rug.

"How's Jack?" she asked.

"He starts physical therapy on Monday."

"That's great."

"He doesn't think so."

"He will in time."

Silence pressed into the moment between them. Addison used it to retrieve her latte, despite the fact that she had no desire for coffee. "When are you going back?" She tried to make the question sound nonchalant, but both of them knew it wasn't.

"The investigation is over. I've been cleared of all charges."

She nearly dropped her cup. "You're cleared?"

He smiled crookedly. "Yeah."

"I'm glad for you."

He reached into an inside pocket of his parka and pulled out a sealed brown envelope. He placed it on the table between them. "I thought you'd want to see this."

Addison's heart began to hammer. She reached for the envelope, opened the clasp, and poured its contents onto the table. A heart-shaped locket, its faux gold chain tarnished with age, lay in a heap in front of her. She reached for it with trembling hands, touching the chain, her fingers finally resting on the locket itself.

"The clasp is broken," Randall said.

"Where did you get this?" she asked, unable to tear her eyes away from the tiny heart she held between her fingers.

"It was found in Agnes Beckett's mobile home."

Somehow, Addison had already known. She clicked open the locket and stared at the yellowed photo of a newborn infant with dark hair and a tiny, wrinkled face. "It's me."

"She loved you, Addison. That's why she gave you away. So you could have a life with all the chances she didn't have."

A dull, lingering ache wrenched at her heart. Tears filled her eyes, spilling down her cheeks unacknowledged. She raised her eyes to his. "It hurts to know she suffered so much for so many years. For me. I didn't even know it."

"It made her happy to know she gave you the opportunity for the kind of life she never had."

Addison closed the locket and gripped it tightly in her hand, struggling to control the flood of tears waiting at the gate. "Thank you." She slid the locket back into the envelope.

His gaze narrowed at a point across the room. "Why is Gretchen giving you hand signals from behind the espresso machine?"

"What?" Addison started, caught the puzzled look from him, and shifted in her chair to frown at Gretchen. Chagrined, the older woman resumed polishing the already gleaming brass of the espresso machine.

"Maybe this wasn't such a good idea." She started to rise.

He stopped her by touching her arm. "Whoa. What wasn't such a good idea?"

"This . . ." Exasperated with herself for acting so foolishly, she motioned dumbly at the table between them.

"You asked me to meet you here," he said. "I'm here. Now sit down and spill it."

She took a deep breath, reminding herself once again that she didn't need him to have the baby. Yes, he could hurt her. She'd relinquished that power to him long ago.

Knowing she couldn't put this off any longer, she sank into the chair. "I'm going to have a baby."

RANDALL'S WORLD SHIFTED. HIS CHEST SWELLED WITH love for the woman sitting across from him. He couldn't believe she didn't know how he felt about her. After everything they'd been through. For the second time since he'd known her, she'd surprised the hell out of him.

How could she possibly believe he wouldn't want their child? That he wouldn't be elated by the news? How could she not know that he was head-over-heels crazy in love with her?

She gazed into his eyes, searching for something that seemed to elude her. "You've been in D.C. for the last month."

"Not of my own free will."

"You haven't given me a clue as to how you feel."

"I love you, Addison. I've told you that."

"So you have."

"Those are big words for me."

"Like they're not for me?"

Indignant, he raised his voice. "Dammit, I follow through." When the two students sitting next to them turned to listen, Randall sent them a glare and lowered his voice. "How in the hell could you possibly believe I wouldn't want this baby?"

"You've never mentioned wanting a family. You've never even spoken of long-term commitment."

"That doesn't mean I don't want either of those things." He ran a hand through his hair, studying her from across the small expanse of table. "Until I met you . . ." His words trailed off. How could he explain his feelings to her when he barely understood them himself? How could he put into words feelings and emotions so strong they frightened him? Could that gut-wrenching kind of love even be described?

"I guess we're both going to need a little time," she said quickly.

All of five seconds, he thought as he pulled a tiny, velvet-covered box from the pocket of his parka. "It looks like we're both full of surprises today."

Satisfaction wafted over him as she stared dumbfounded at the box. "Like there's a rain check inside," he said with a hint of gentle sarcasm. "That would be really classy of me."

She reached for the box, holding it to her breast for a second before opening the lid. Her breath hitched as she took in the sight of the brilliant marquise-cut diamond set into a simple gold band. It gleamed beneath the muted lighting, a tiny star that burned brightly for both of them.

"I've been carrying this around with me for a month, agonizing over whether or not you wanted to keep me around."

"A whole month?"

"I've got a lot of bad habits, Addison. I've got some serious problems to work through." Randall reached for her hand and pulled her across the table until their faces were close. "But I realized that what we have, the love we share, is everything to me. To pursue our love. To have a family together. To be happy. It's our birthright."

"Birthright." She liked the sound of it, the way it felt on her tongue.

"I've permanently retired from the NTSB." He'd faced his demons, only to find they no longer existed. "Jack offered me a job right here in Denver as his partner. As long as I stay off the booze."

"You can do it."

"I went to my first AA meeting last night."

Her eyes filled. Simultaneously, a smile played at the corners of her mouth. "I'm proud of you."

A sense of rightness, of happiness settled over him. "I love you, Addison. I've never said those words to anyone but you."

He looked down at the stained tablecloth, gathering his

courage, his resolve, wondering why in the hell he'd waited until now to ask her. "Will you marry me?"

Through a haze of tears, she watched as he took the box from her and removed the ring. For the first time in her adult life, she felt true happiness. Stunning, she thought, and smiled when she saw the tears in his eyes.

"I'd love to, Talbot," she said, and he slipped the ring onto her finger.